LEVIATHAN

ALSO BY DAVID LYNN GOLEMON

Event
Legend
Ancients

LEVIATHAN

An Event Group Thriller

DAVID LYNN GOLEMON

THOMAS DUNNE BOOKS
ST. MARTIN'S PRESS 🜄 NEW YORK

This is a work of fiction. All of the characters, organizations, and events portrayed in this novel are either products of the author's imagination or are used fictitiously.

THOMAS DUNNE BOOKS.
An imprint of St. Martin's Press.

LEVIATHAN. Copyright © 2009 by David L. Golemon. All rights reserved. Printed in the United States of America. For information, address St. Martin's Press, 175 Fifth Avenue, New York, N.Y. 10010.

www.thomasdunnebooks.com
www.stmartins.com

Library of Congress Cataloging-in-Publication Data

Golemon, David Lynn.
   Leviathan / David Golemon. — 1st ed.
     p. cm.
   ISBN-13: 978-0-312-37663-5 (alk. paper)
   ISBN-10: 0-312-37663-4 (alk. paper)
  1. Event Group (Imaginary organization)—Fiction. 2. Imaginary wars and battles—Fiction. 3. Submarines (Ships)—Fiction. I. Title.
   PS3607.O4555L445 2009
   813'.6—dc22

2009010686

First Edition: August 2009

10 9 8 7 6 5 4 3 2 1

For Jules Verne and all of the other dreamers that followed.

For Brandon, Katie, Shaune, and Tram—
the children who supply my energy.

ACKNOWLEDGMENTS

To the United States Navy—the cooperation received from some name-less individuals was invaluable.

To the kind folks at General Dynamics—without their valuable insight into the future of submarines, this book could not have been written.

For Nicole Verdone and many, many others who keep this author grounded in reality.

The sea is everything. It covers seven-tenths of the terrestrial globe. Its breath is pure and healthy. It is an immense desert, where man is never lonely, for he feels life stirring on all sides.

—Jules Verne, *Twenty Thousand Leagues Under the Sea*

LEVIATHAN

PROLOGUE

CHÂTEAU D'IF, FRANCE
1802

Three years in darkness. Since Napoleon's coup in 1799, Roderick Deveroux had been imprisoned at Château d'If for refusing to reveal the secrets of his magical and mysterious designs for seagoing warfare. Without a trial—without so much as a word from his captors or his jailers—he was cast into the old castle's dungeons with the other supposed enemies of France. The fates of his young wife and father were as bleak to him as his own future.

Three years ago the new emperor himself had begged Deveroux for the designs, drawings, and mathematical calculations for his newest ships. The emperor had asked for them, then pleaded, and then finally threatened, but still Deveroux had refused to give the brutish little man what he desired: the design for an oil-fired ship that could drive the implacable British navy—the most powerful force in the world—from the surface of the seas.

As Deveroux lay against the cold wall of his cell, he could hear the sea far below crashing against the rocks of the small island. Roderick Deveroux knew his prison walls were coming very close to driving him insane.

The small door at the base of his cell opened, and his daily ration of meat and bread was pushed through atop a rusty plate. The meat was good, rich, and ripe, as Napoleon would not be pleased if his great prize died of malnutrition before he received the gift that would secure his place as master of the world.

The meal delivery was the same routine as always—he waited for the prison guard to close the trap before he allowed himself to move. This time however, the door remained open. Deveroux allowed his eyes to move toward the door and the still shadow beyond.

"Doctor, there is news from the outside. Perhaps after you hear it you will finally deliver to the emperor that which he desires."

Deveroux didn't move from the damp, moss-covered corner of the cell. He watched and waited.

"Your father has been executed for his monarchist leanings. It was done publicly in Paris."

Deveroux lowered his head and tried to bring to mind the face of his father, but found his memory failed him. His throat refused to work as he tried to swallow. His eyes filled with tears and he raised a hand to his bearded face and covered his mouth, biting his lip to keep the guards from hearing his anguish. The thought came suddenly to his mind and the question was out before he could stop it.

"My . . . my wife . . . is she—" He croaked the first words he had spoken in more than six months.

"Your wife? You fool, she committed suicide last year because she could not face the humiliation of your treason."

Deveroux wanted to scream but would not give them the satisfaction of seeing him break. Instead, he again bit his lower lip until blood oozed from his mouth, and then he buried his face in his hands. He remembered—*they told me she was dead with my unborn child in her womb.*

His decision was now an easy one. He would rather die than continue on in life without his family. As his tears dried, his eyes seemed to burn. He grunted to let the guard know he was there and listening. Then he rolled to one side, and slowly and cautiously slid the plate of beef toward him. He swatted the meat and bread from the plate and then harshly felt the edge of the thick tin in the darkness. He was afraid he wouldn't find what he was seeking, and then his trembling fingers found it—the outer lip of the plate had been worn to a sharp edge.

"The new emperor seeks my knowledge . . . still?" he asked.

"Seeks? He demands it, fool," the voice said from the far side of the cell door.

With shaking hands he slid his finger across the sharp edge of the plate once more, bringing the sensation he was looking for—the cutting of flesh.

Deveroux drew closer to the iron door, then he raised the plate and sliced the one area that would supply enough blood to be convincing to the captain of the guard—his head. He sliced deep and long through the ragged growth of hair, wincing as the plate's edge dug a deep furrow through his scalp. Soon he felt the satisfying flow of blood coursing down his forehead, and still he dug the sharpened edge deeper. There had to be enough blood to convince the keepers that Napoleon's prized prisoner was attempting to do the unthinkable.

As he lifted the plate from his head, Deveroux saw that blood was not only flowing but had begun to spurt, as he had dragged the tin plate through a small vein. He held on to the plate, moving the sharpened edge opposite his grip, and then lay down next to the food portal. He allowed his blood to splatter the iron of the door, and then he sighed and made gasping sounds. He reached up with his free hand and slapped at the growing puddle of blood, making sure it splashed into the corridor beyond.

"What—?"

"It is blood, Captain, the fool has slit his own throat."

The captain of the guard did exactly what Deveroux had hoped: He panicked at the thought of losing him to suicide. He could never explain that to the emperor. He heard the other man as he pulled keys in an attempt to get the door open. So, this was it, the moment of his death.

He never had any plans to escape, but neither did he have the courage for ending his own life, so he would force them to do it for him. A self-satisfied smile etched his wretched features.

"Hurry, you bumbling fool, he'll bleed to death!"

Finally, Deveroux heard the key slide home into the rusty lock. Then he heard the scraping sound as it turned, and then the hasp of the lock was thrown back, and then came the sound of a man straining to get the door open. He felt and smelled the first fresh air in over two years as it hit his face and he breathed it in, preparing himself, gathering what strength he could for the next few seconds—the last seconds of his life. He let his eyes flutter open and his eyes instantly felt the jab of pain from the candlelit corridor beyond.

He felt hands roll him roughly onto his back, and before the guard could react he swung the tin plate as hard as his atrophied muscles would allow. The sharpened edge came into contact with the man's neck.

The captain gasped as he watched the guard take a blow to his throat just as he turned the prisoner over. He straightened and started to shout for others, but Deveroux lashed out with his bare feet and caught the young captain in his left knee, bringing him down to the rough stone floor. Before the captain could fully react to the assault, the prisoner Deveroux had leaped blindly to his back and brought the tin plate solidly down onto the back of the man's head, imbedding the sharpened edge deeply into his skull.

Deveroux was crying as he rolled off the captain and lay still, listening for the footsteps that would signal his death. As he tried to bring his breathing under control, he opened his eyes to the glare of the candles. The pain in his eyes slowly subsided as he tried to focus on the darkened far wall. He swallowed and tried to stop his tears but found his control was lost. His hand tried to reach out and feel the chill stone beneath him for reassurance that the world was real; instead his hand hit the keys that had fallen from the guard, who was just at that moment taking his last, rattling breath.

He clutched the large set of keys with both hands and brought them to his chest. As his eyes looked about he saw the other cells neighboring his own. He wondered if each was filled with the cruelness and brutality he had endured the past three years. Was there a man behind each door who had been subjected to the same horrific treatment that he had endured? His mind refused to answer as he rolled onto his knees. The pool of blood from the captain had spread thickly on the blocks of stone that made up the floor of the corridor. He stumbled as he tried to rise, using the wall for leverage. He became light-headed, and then he felt his stomach lurch and he spewed bile as a geyser would let loose water. Still, he stumbled and fell, stood and slid down the wall until he found steps leading upward.

Deveroux made his way slowly up the stone steps, constantly aware that his dealings with the guards would soon be discovered from another, unknown direction he wasn't aware of. He kept climbing, still holding the keys to his chest as if they were his wife's crucifix.

He stopped when he heard sound. A door, iron by the sound, had opened. As he tried to see in the darkness forward of his position, he made out a dim hallway that curved off to the right on the next level. He heard the sound of men from what he believed were two levels above him. Not fearing death, Deveroux moved to the next level. Then he smelled it. The only thing that had kept him alive the past two years had been that smell. It was the sea. He could now hear the crashing of the breakers far better than he had ever heard them before. He moved forward once the landing of the next level was reached. Then he heard shouts as he had been spied from above.

"Stop!"

Deveroux heard the command and the running of more than one guard as he stumbled toward the sound and smell. He fell, cried, and found his legs would not work. Finally he spied the door through his flowing tears. This one was wooden, not iron. With the footfalls sounding louder, now on his level of the fortress, he stood and pulled down on the latch. As he did, the door swung open and he was blinded by bright sunlight from the setting orb that seemed to blaze just beyond the open window.

Several women gasped and one screamed as he fell blindly through the doorway and into the kitchen. The smells of cooking meat, fish, and garlic now rode roughshod over the smell of the sea. He erratically made his way toward the fresh air streaming through the open window. More screams, and then the sound of the door opening and men running inside.

With a burst of strength he didn't know he could muster, Deveroux ran for the open window. Through his hurting and failing eyes he saw the sea far below. The men would not stop him from sending himself down into that sea and its waiting embrace of death. As a hand grabbed a piece of his rotted shirt, Deveroux leaped.

The guard ran to the wide window as a woman screamed. He saw the thin man plunge a hundred and fifty feet to the rocks and the crashing sea far below.

Napoleon's prisoner was content to let the blue ocean take his body. The smashing caress of the water stunned him when he hit from such a dizzying height. He opened his eyes against the sting of salt and saw that breakers were pushing him toward the jagged rocks that made up the bulk of the island that Château d'If sat upon. To drown, or to be smashed upon the rocks? The equation didn't concern him; what did was the horrible thought of being pulled from his death by guards who were surely on their way down to recover his body.

With this thought in mind, Deveroux knew what he had to do. He opened his mouth to take in as much of the salt-laden sea as he could, so as to cheat Napoleon of his destiny. As his suicidal moment came, he felt a sharp nudge on the left side of his body and felt the skin of an animal, a shark possibly, push against him. Then another, and then still another. As he opened his eyes he saw he was in the middle of a family of dolphins that were playing with him, pushing him first one way and then the other. Suddenly he found himself being pushed toward the one place he didn't want to be, the surface. He kicked and kicked, trying to get the playful animals to let him die in peace, but they still nudged him toward daylight with their hard noses.

"Damn you," he whispered as water flooded his mouth. His imagination and hallucinations then brought his end into perspective—he felt small, soft, almost gelatinlike hands grab at his tattered clothing, keeping him afloat as the dolphins chattered around him.

Deveroux gasped for air as a breaker smashed over his head. He was then pushed back to the surface by the strange, dreamlike hands of angels, with fine hair and silken soft bodies. Were these mermaids of the old tales he had listened to as a boy?

When he managed to open his eyes he saw that he had been pushed almost a mile from the point where he had struck the sea around Château d'If. As he weakly treaded water he saw men at the base of the fortress searching the area where he had struck the sea. He laughed for the first time in two years, a hoarse, very desperate-sounding thing. The dolphins joined in with their strange chatter and swam about him as if they were a part of the warped and twisted joke. Of the soft-handed, strangely glowing mermaids, or angels, he saw none.

The tide was taking him farther from land; he could no longer see the coastline. Even the dreaded and cursed fortress was now but a small speck on the horizon.

Floating contentedly, awaiting his new fate, he felt a sharp pain as something hit him from the side once more. As he rolled his thin body over, expecting his playful saviors, he came face-to-face with a large tree trunk, detritus of the ocean. Several of the dolphins had pushed the tree toward him. He decided he would wait for the friendly creatures to leave and then he would allow the sea to do its best. For reasons he did not fathom, the smartest animals in the ocean wanted him to live.

As he floated for hours on end, Deveroux thought about why God was sparing him. He had sent his marvelous creatures, and what Deveroux thought of as angels, to delay the death of this poor man of science for a purpose. The thoughts and memories of his family swirled in his mind as darkness came. He was being swept farther out to sea as the moon rose and set, and then dawn was upon him once more.

The sound of breakers and the coldness of the waters awoke the delirious Deveroux from a nightmare-filled sleep. He had been dreaming not of the murders of his wife or father, but of the evil men who had taken them from him. The dream seethed with hate and a desire for vengeance upon these men and their master. The force of the nightmares had kept his heart beating throughout that cold night and into the hazy morning following. Two days and two nights he floated on the gentle currents of escape.

Now, the sound of normalcy returned to replace the cries of his unjust treatment. The cawing of seabirds strangely mimicked the cries of his dream wife and father as they swooped low to investigate the floating tree trunk. The chatter of his constant companions, the dolphins, made him turn toward their sound. There, a hundred meters away, was a small island. Scanty trees broke up the outline of its rock-strewn shore and made him think for a terrifying moment that he was floating right back into the arms of Château d'If.

A large breaker caught his floating tree and pushed him toward what he now knew would be his final moment; the jagged rocks lining the shore came at him at a breakneck pace. However, something strange was afoot; the dolphins were taking the wave with him, jumping and chattering as they rode the wave in. As the waters crested he lost his grip on the tree and found himself being sucked through the rocks and into a cave opening revealed at the low tide of the morning hours. He hadn't seen it from his position behind the breakwater, but as soon as he was swept inside, it was cold and dank, almost as lightless as his onetime prison cell. The dolphins pushed him to a small sandy beach, chattered, then swam away, as if content they had accomplished what they set out to do. Deveroux rolled over, feeling the blessed earth beneath his tattered clothing. He collapsed and allowed a dreamless sleep to overtake him.

When Deveroux awoke, he tried to sit up. The sun outside the cave opening was setting, but in its waning death it allowed light to be cast into the interior. The former prisoner of Napoleon stood on shaky feet but collapsed. Then, more slowly, he rose, braced himself, and looked around.

He tilted his head as he saw something recognizable to his salt-encrusted eyes. Lining the interior walls were torches. He stumbled, righted himself, and approached. They were old—very old. He removed one from the hole that had been carved into the wall and hefted it. He sniffed the burned, dead end and smelled the aroma of grease—old and dry, but grease nonetheless. As he turned to look back at the cave's opening, his bare foot struck something sharp. He reached down and felt the dry sand, running his fingers though it. He hit upon an object and brought it up into the diffused sunlight. It was flint, used at one time to ignite these very torches lining the wall. With flint in hand, he brushed up the cloth- and grease-covered tip of the torch, then he knelt and started striking the flint against the stone wall.

It took him more than thirty minutes and five bloody fingers, but in the end the torch finally smoldered, then caught and flared to life. As he averted his eyes from the brightness of the flame, he saw the skeletal leg in the sand. He stepped back, brought the flame closer, and followed the leg upward. There, lying against the wall, were the remains of a man. He was tied by rope and spike to the very wall where Deveroux had found the torch. The clothing on the skeleton was old and falling apart. The corpse had several gold teeth, and even more were missing. However, there was one feature that made Deveroux look around nervously. This was the fact that this man had been slashed through the head by a sword, shattering the front of the skull. As Deveroux held the torch closer, he could see that the sword had smashed everything from the skullcap through the nasal cavity.

He shook his head and stepped back nervously. The remains had to be more than a hundred years old, in his estimation. The bloused pants, tattered vest, and red shirt made the skeleton look as if he had been a Gypsy, like the flotsam he had seen in the streets of Paris in the past. The bony fingers had rings upon each, even the thumb.

Deveroux brought the torch around and looked farther into the cave. The body was sitting upon a small shelf that seemed to wrap around the large interior. The small cove that rose and fell with the tide was up at that time, so he moved cautiously along the wall, staying high above the water.

He had traveled for what he estimated was a half mile into the bowels of the cave when he came to a huge gate. As he brought the torch to bear on the makeshift wall, he screeched a hoarse bark and stepped back as he saw two more bodies. These were not like the first, which had been tied to the wall and executed. These two skeletons were lying beneath the sharpened points of the bottom of the wall, which was imbedded in the men's torsos, crushing their ribs and spines.

As Deveroux examined the trap, he could see that the wooden device at one time had been placed into a separation in the cave's natural ceiling. These men had somehow triggered the pitfall, and been impaled by the sharpened base of the wall as it crashed down upon them. Deveroux grimaced at the horrible specter before him. The men were dressed as the first man had been. Jewelry of every kind adorned the skeletons. The one major difference—these men had been armed. One still grasped the sword he had more than likely used against the defenseless man Deveroux had discovered tied to the cave wall.

Deveroux examined the wooden trap and surmised it would harm no other. He gently pushed on the gate. It creaked and bent, but held firm. With eyes wild, he knew he had to find out what was so important about the rear of the cave that men would be driven to create such horrible deaths for their fellows.

He looked around him, and using the torch for light he leaned down and pulled upon the sword entwined in the skeleton's bony grasp, then cringed when three of the dead man's fingers came off with his effort. He looked at the skeleton and watched its long dead and empty eye sockets for a brief moment. Then he raised the sword, and while still looking at the dead man, slashed at the wood with a weakened blow. The sword severed the rotten rope where it crossed another of the old wooden beams. The wood creaked, and then Deveroux fell to the sand as his muscles began to cramp with just one swing of the heavy sword. Deveroux cried out in pain as he went to his knees, trying to get the cramp to cease its hold, and then he suddenly stopped and looked around as if he were being watched. With his right arm throbbing, he swung the torch in his left hand to and fro, searching for the set of eyes that he knew to be there. He saw nothing but the darkness. He was the only witness to his transgression.

He switched the torch to his right hand, and with tears of pain he swung the sword once more, severing another rope, and then he yelled out in fear when the crossbeam fell from the gate and almost crushed him. He saw one beam fall, and then another, until a small avalanche fell free, the remaining ropes not able to withstand the weight. They fell, crushing the remains of the two lost souls trapped years before. When the dust cleared and Deveroux stopped shaking from fright, he saw the gate had succumbed to his minuscule efforts, thanks in most part to the rotted rope holding it together.

He rose from the damp earth, and on shaking legs stepped through the opening and easily swung the torch forward. He couldn't make anything out at first, but then he saw the stacked items along the wall. Three hundred large and small chests. Some made of wood, others of iron. Some were locked while others had come apart with age and water damage.

He approached one that had broken open and held the flame close to the spilled items. There, twinkling in the bright flame, were what he assumed were diamonds. A thousand pigeon-egg-sized pieces of glittering and sparkling stone that had been torn from the earth, possibly centuries before.

Deveroux swung the torch back and looked at the two skeletons. He examined their clothing again and thought, *pirates!* Buccaneers, free seamen. He had found what these men had hidden, and had obviously been murdered for.

He turned and examined more of the chests. Gold from Syria, Babylon, and Arabia, and diamonds from Africa. Arabic coins stamped with artisans' renderings of faces that were hundreds of years old. He held the torch against a lock that still sealed one of the large chests and saw the seal of England—the head of the lion and the three crowns of Richard I.

Deveroux fell to his knees, lowered the torch, and crossed himself. The rumors were true. He had found what was lost more than six hundred years before: the legendary lost treasure of the Crusades. Gold, diamonds, and other riches ripped and stolen from the Holy Land. King Richard was rumored to have invaded Jerusalem for the sole reason of pillaging, not its liberation. The king died soon after his return home and his treasure was lost, or hidden away from his own countrymen, later to be discovered by this marauding band of cutthroats.

Deveroux saw in the treasure the route and means to his revenge against Napoleon. By his quick estimation, and not figuring in monetary terms of pound, shekel, or carat, he calculated that he had found over fifteen tons of riches. Billions upon billions of francs' worth of diamonds and emeralds alone. The gold was incalculable.

He cried at seeing the redemption that lay before him. He would exact the revenge he had coming to his soul for the death of a wife and the murder of his father.

He would then use this wealth to continue the work he had started. He would make the world a better place and in the end he would challenge humankind not to need the very avarice that lay before him.

As he turned to look back toward the cave's opening, knowing the sun had set, he began planning. His brilliant mind was regaining its edge and complex thought was becoming easy once more. His thoughts were cutting through the detritus of a world that wanted what he had—command of the sea.

In the fading light of the dying torch, there was movement in the water. With wild and insane eyes Deveroux believed his horrid memories of the past years were returning in the form of men to reclaim his soul. As he slowly slid to the softened sand, he saw for the first time the true magic, the real treasures of the sea—and they were beautiful.

Deveroux stared at the magical creatures as they in turn watched him from below the crystal-clear waters of the cave. Gold, diamonds, and emeralds—they all paled in comparison to the miracle his eyes now beheld. Fantasy mixed with reality—biblical stories with that of fairy tales. It was there before him in the waters, legend, myth, and sea-tales. Reality and clarity of mind beckoned him. Then suddenly the clear-skinned, glowing, angellike mermaids were gone as if they had never been. The darkness, the sea breeze, and the sound of life slowly returned to his ears as a plan began to form for revenge and a reason to live once more.

Now he would claim the sea as his own.

UNIVERSITY OF OSLO, NORWAY, 1829

The old professor leaned closer to the makeshift gauge. The needle hovered at the 98 percent mark. He noted this fact in his journal and then looked up and tapped the gauge once more, making the needle jump minutely, only to settle back into the same position as before. He smiled. After twenty-seven hours, the electrical charge remained high.

He laid his pen inside the journal and closed it. He stretched and as he did, he saw his young son, twelve-year-old Octavian, lying peacefully on the makeshift bed in the far corner of the laboratory. Professor Heirthall, the man once known as Roderick Deveroux, pulled out his pocket watch and saw it was nearly two thirty in the morning. He shook his head and then decided to check his connections one last time.

Half of the large laboratory space was taken up with three hundred small, boxlike cubes. They were stacked on metal shelving that ran floor to ceiling. The mountain of material gave off deep shadows in the dim, gas-lantern-illuminated lab as the professor walked to the main cable connection and felt the insulation. He quickly removed his hand and then pulled out his journal. He checked the thermometer connected to the thick copper cable and then found the reading for his last entry. The cable's temperature was up sixteen degrees from the last mark two hours ago. It was now reading 120 degrees. This was a problem. The thick cable was not going to hold up for the duration of the electrical charge. Either his cables needed to be thicker, which was not beneficial to his end goals, or he would have to find a way to keep the metal cooler inside the leather insulation.

"Father, have you considered letting the sea cool your battery lines?"

The professor turned to see his son sitting up on his cot. He was propped on one elbow and yawned as he looked at his father.

"The sea? Do you mean run the cables outside of the enclosure?" he asked.

The boy placed his feet on the floor and pulled the blanket around his shoulders as he stood and slowly shuffled to where his father was standing.

"No, sir," he said through a yawn. "I am aware that seawater would invade the coiled copper wire inside the insulation, and corrupt it. However, would it not cool if cocooned in rubber, the same material as your batteries and inside a metal guard, inches from the cooling waters of the sea?"

"You mean as veins, like in a human arm, just under the surface?"

In answer, the twelve-year-old yawned once more, nodding his head.

"You must get your intelligence from your mother, for I am constantly overlooking the obvious," he said as he tousl°ed the boy's thick black hair. "You have a remarkable spark of intelligence bouncing around in that head of yours."

The admiration and love for his son was evident. The boy had been with him throughout the summer months, and was here with him now instead of enjoying his winter break for the Christmas holidays. Ever since the breakthrough in the spring, when his revolutionary electrical storage system began to show promise, the boy had been by his side, forsaking even the warmer company of his mother, Alexandria.

The boy had only been ten years old when he had completed the final assembly of the combustion motor. Converted from a steam piston drive, the motor was also revolutionary and very, very secret. Still, even at that young age, Octavian had figured out that the pump used to relay fuel into the combustion chamber was inefficient, just by studying its operation. He had tinkered with his father's design, and in three months, using only scrap parts, the boy had pieced together what he called a distilled kerosene-injection pump that utilized the motor itself for power. Kerosene derived from the recent discovery of crude oil from America. It had failed the first three times, and then when they had figured a way to filter the fine spray of kerosene, removing the impurities of the refined oil, it had not failed since.

Professor Heirthall smiled at his son and then pulled his pocket watch out of his white coat once more and examined it.

"Almost three A.M. Octavian; your mother is going to throw me into the fjord."

"Of all people, Mother knows you get lost in your work. She will be fine and fast asleep."

"Yes, I suspect so, but nevertheless I will call the carriage and have you taken home."

"Father, my time is wasted at home. Mother only talks of what a great man I will one day be."

The professor replaced his journal and smiled.

"The part of her that needs it will never feel the spray or touch of the sea again. This is a sad fact to her, son. Your mother, well—part of her is a very special woman, from very, very special people. And because they were special, and are still so, we have this," he said as he gestured around the laboratory. "All this is for them. We are dedicated to the sea, Octavian—it is in your blood, quite literally. Without that special part of her, your mother would have died a very long time ago."

The boy had ceased listening and was instead standing in front of the mountain of black rubber-encased batteries. He pulled the blanket around him tighter and was lost in his own world.

"Are you dreaming your underwater dreams again, Octavian?"

The boy turned toward his father and smiled, embarrassed.

"Is the story true—I mean, what people are saying about you?"

Heirthall was taken back by the sudden change in topic.

"You mean my magical escapades upon the sea, and of being a prisoner of Napoleon? Yes, it is all true. As for the treasure of King Richard—no, I'm afraid our wealth is derived from a long line of inheritance. Nothing as dashing and daring, I would think, as the rumors from France or other tall tales told in other countries."

Heirthall knew he wasn't fooling Octavian. The boy was just too smart for his own good. Not once did he ask about portraits of family heritage from either side—even though he knew other families of wealth had them. Yes, the boy knew the stories were true, but he had yet to guess the real secret of the Heirthall family. That would take a delicate touch.

Deveroux had met Alexandria after his escape and revenge upon Napoleon. She had been young, vital, and loving toward him at the first moment of meeting. Then, after the birth of Octavian, she had become weak and bedridden. Consumption, the doctors had told him. Only the intervention of the Deveroux angels had kept her alive all of these years. Now, even their grace from death was ending. The solution to her health was now her killer. He now feared Octavian—their precious offspring— might be cursed to the same fate as his mother. He was physically weak, and his blood held too much of his mother's.

The sound of loud footfalls, possibly that of several men, came through the thick double doors. The professor held his index finger to his lips to make sure Octavian quieted. Then he hurriedly took his son by the shoulders and pushed him toward the cot. He wrapped him tighter in the blanket, shoved him to the floor, and looked deeply into Octavian's deep and beautiful blue eyes.

"You stay under here and come out for no reason, am I clear, my son?"

"Father, who could these men be?"

"I don't know, but I have noticed strangers around the university, and several have been following me the past two months. Now, Octavian, answer me, do you understand?"

"Yes, Father." The boy looked up into Heirthall's tired features. "I can be of help."

"I know you could, but sometimes you must know when to use silence as an ally, not strength. Understand me, son, stay under the cot."

The boy nodded.

With his answer, Heirthall helped the boy slide under the cot until he could go no farther. Then he stood and faced the double doors. The hallway beyond the framed window was dark, but he could still see moving shadows there. A loud knock sounded.

"Professor Heirthall, this is Dr. Hansonn. May I come in?"

Heirthall walked to the door, started to reach for the handle, and then stopped short.

"Why would the dean of biology be here at this hour, Doctor?" he called through the thick wood. "And why is he accompanied by others?"

"I have a friend that wishes to speak to you."

"My work is not for examination by anyone, including you. Now please take your friends and go away, I wish to—"

"Professor Heirthall, I assure you, this is not about your fanciful dream of underwater vessels—it's about your fossil."

"The fossil has been lost since the last time you inquired about it. I see no reason—"

The doors split apart and crashed inward. Two very large men quickly entered, followed by three more. Dr. Hansonn was there, and standing beside him was a man that Heirthall recognized immediately.

"Why have you brought this profiteer of history to my laboratory?"

The rotund man removed his top hat and pushed by the Norwegian biology dean.

"I will be happy to answer that," the man said as he handed his hat to the larger of the two men. "Professor, we care not for your dreams of underwater fantasies, sir; we have come to buy the fossil from you. I am willing to pay handsomely for it, I assure you."

"You have already decried it a hoax. Why would you want it if no one believes it's real?"

The man turned and took a few steps away, deep in thought; he held his right hand to his lips. "I have to have it, Professor. Not for any public display, I have plenty of tomfoolery to enthrall the public. The unique specimen in your possession is for me alone—to amaze myself as to the wondrous nature of our world. I will not harm it or display it, only love it."

"Again, Mr. Barnum, I have lost the specimen. Now please take your men and get out."

Heirthall watched P. T. Barnum as the man deflated.

"I implore you, Professor, I am only a man who wishes to understand the world around me," he said as he noticed Dean Hansonn move to the far wall.

Hansonn walked toward one of the lanterns and blew out the flame. He then reached up, pulled the lantern from the wall, and smashed it to the floor, and the smell of lamp oil immediately permeated the lab.

"Now, we have but mere minutes, Professor, before the oil is ignited by my associates. So if you will, the fossil, please."

Heirthall looked at his Norwegian colleague. The man glared at him in return.

"How can you do this? This science is for the betterment of all, and you are willing to destroy that over a fairy tale?"

P. T. Barnum looked from Heirthall to the man he thought was helping him purchase the fossil.

"There is no need for threats of violence. Professor Heirthall is far too important to gamble," he said as he reached for a rag to clean up the spilled lamp oil.

The dean nodded to one of the large men, who stopped Barnum from going to his knees to clean the spill.

"Professor, we haven't the need for your amazing mechanical apparatus. Just the fossil, *please*," Hansonn said.

When Heirthall made no move to retrieve the fossil, Hansonn nodded for his men to take action. One held Heirthall and the others started tearing apart the lab as Dr. Hansonn stepped forward.

"Gentlemen, I implore you to stop this madness. The fossil is not worth losing this man's work!" Barnum cried out to Hansonn. "You will not receive one red cent, I assure you. This is not the way!"

Hansonn gestured to a large wooden vault on the opposite wall while holding a white handkerchief to his nose and mouth.

Heirthall was straining in the arms of the bigger man as he saw the men tear through the thick wood of the vault and pull the glass-encased, alcohol-protected specimen out. Barnum stood stock-still in the arms of Hansonn's hirelings and watched as the dean stepped up and placed a loving hand over the glass as he saw the remains inside.

"There truly is a God," Hansonn said. "Take it out of here and get it to the ship. We leave on the next tide." He turned to Barnum. "And I assure you, Mr. Barnum, you will pay me what is owed."

"If you harm the professor, you'll get spit from me. This was not the arrangement!"

"We will stop you. The world can never know about what that specimen represents," Heirthall said, straining against the man that held him.

"It's either this fossil or your wife, Professor. You looked shocked that I know about the medical procedure you performed on her several years ago. I know all about her illness, and how you arrested it. So it's either this fossil, or your wife. . . . Which is it?"

"You scum, you could never harm my wife!"

"Yes, yes, we know your estate is very well guarded, that is why we were forced to come here. We are not barbarians, Professor, the sea angel you have here is quite enough," Hansonn said as he nodded at the man holding Heirthall.

The knife went unseen to the professor's throat and sliced neatly through it.

"I am truly sorry, but I can't have the authorities chasing me forever. After all, I am going to be a very rich man from this day forward," Hansonn said, looking with dead eyes toward Barnum. "Now, spread more oil on the floor; the professor is about to have a horrible laboratory accident."

Barnum screamed in terror at what was happening.

"You bastard, nothing is worth this. I . . . will see you hang, sir!"

"Then you will hang right beside me, my American friend. After all, you will be in possession of the most remarkable fossil in the history of the world. So, Mr. P. T. Barnum, I would make sure there were two ropes hanging in the death gallery that day."

Barnum went down to his knees when the evil plan was made clear to him. The world would never believe that the verbose pitchman wasn't involved in this murder. He was doomed to go along.

As he slowly raised his head, he saw the boy hiding under the cot. Their eyes locked, and in that moment, Barnum learned more about himself than he ever thought he would. He shook his head, and with spittle coming from his mouth, said he was sorry so that only the boy could see.

Octavian's deep blue eyes went from Barnum to his father's body only inches from the cot. He tried to scream, cry, anything, but nothing came out. He heard the men leaving with their prize, and that was when he saw the dying eyes of his father. Roderick Deveroux, the man now known as Heirthall, was looking at his son, fully aware his death was imminent. The footsteps retreated to the nearby door, and a lighted match was tossed inside just before the doors closed.

The fire was starting to spread fast in the crowded lab and was working toward the highly explosive batteries. Heirthall managed to keep his eyes open even as his blood spread toward his cowering son. Then he tried to raise his hand. He extended his finger, but then his hand fell to the wooden floor and into his own blood. His eyes closed as Octavian reached out with a shaking hand and tried to touch his dying father. Heirthall's eyes opened one last time. Instead of raising his hand to indicate for the boy to run, he allowed his finger to do his talking. He only managed three letters: *HEN*.

Octavian was being told to get the assistance of Hendrickson, the family's American butler. However, the boy only reached out and grasped his father's still hand. Heirthall, eyes closing, tried to flick the boy's hand off his own, but failed. He tried to speak, but blood was the only thing to exit his mouth when he opened it.

Octavian could take no more. The fire was spreading and thickening, so he squeezed out from underneath the cot, sliding through the warm blood of his father. That was when the first and last tears ever shed by Octavian Heirthall appeared. As he stood, then slipped and fell, he screamed in anger as he felt his body was not responding. His hand fell upon his father's journal that had fallen from his coat pocket. Octavian retrieved it and started crawling toward the doors as the fire reached the batteries. Reaching up for the handle of the double doors, he managed to open them and start out on his hands and knees when his only world exploded around him.

SEPTEMBER 23, 1863
THE GULF OF MEXICO—
THIRTY-FOUR YEARS LATER

The day was hot and the seas were accommodating as the HMS *Warlord* plied the gulf waters 120 miles off the coast of Texas. Her destination was Galveston. A thousand yards to her starboard quarter was the HMS *Elizabeth*; at equal distance to her port side was the HMS *Port Royal*. The two smaller frigates had been sent by the Admiralty for the protection of HMS *Warlord*, a 175-foot battle cruiser of Her Majesty's Royal Navy.

On her teak deck stood two passengers dressed in civilian attire. The shorter of the two men was entrusted with the safety and well-being of the taller, far more intense person at his side. This gaunt man was one of utmost importance to Her Majesty's government because he and the young nation he represented were now the British Empire's newest ally. The man who calmly and silently watched the passing seas of the gulf was a diplomatic courier for the Confederate States of America.

The fledgling nation was close to the point of collapse. Abraham Lincoln's Union Army had recently taken the mystique of Southern invincibility away with a stunning move in Tennessee by a small bearded general named Grant, at a place the Union papers called Shiloh Meeting House. In addition, and almost simultaneously, General Robert E. Lee had been stunned while venturing northward from Virginia through Maryland and into Pennsylvania, where he had met a small band of dismounted cavalry that was the vanguard of the entire army of the Potomac. Robert E. Lee, the Army of Northern Virginia, history itself—none would ever forget the name of the small town where two of the greatest armies of men ever assembled on the face of the earth would clash: Gettysburg.

Special Assistant Thomas Engersoll, a close friend and advisor to Stephen R. Mallory, the Confederate Secretary of the Navy, was standing on the fantail of *Warlord* watching the gentle swell of the gulf and the gathering of seabirds which, he knew, signaled their closeness to the Texas coast, and the successful completion of his desperate and very secret mission. As he looked over the railing at the placid sea, he blinked his eyes as something resembling a jellyfish appeared. The animal didn't seem too alarmed by the thin man looking down upon it, and it kept pace with the wind-driven ship with very little effort. He was just getting ready to call over a seaman to ask about this exotic animal when his thoughts were interrupted.

"Well, Mr. Engersoll, you are close to setting your feet once more upon your home soil. Your thoughts, sir?"

The thin man turned and studied Her Majesty's envoy, Sir Lionel Gauss, for a moment as the Englishman smiled and reached up, placing his small hand upon Engersoll's shoulder. He thought about telling him about the strange blue-eyed creature, then changed his mind.

Thomas Engersoll did not return the short fat man's smile, but instead just nodded his greeting. He was tired and tried desperately to keep his lips from trembling.

"Home is a welcome sight for these eyes to be sure, but the thing that is of the utmost importance to my country is the signed letter and the accompanying documents locked up in the captain's safe. Those items, and those alone, sir, are what are desperately needed ashore, not myself," Engersoll stated without emotion.

The rotund courier representing Queen Victoria laughed and patted Engersoll on the arm.

"And with the might of the Royal Navy at your very disposal, I assure you, Thomas, the documents will be placed into the hands of your President Davis very soon. And the weapons, ammunition, medicinal supplies, and rations that are being carried in the holds of these vessels are just the start of our material friendship to your young nation."

Engersoll returned the smile with just a twitch of movement from his mouth, and even that sad attempt never reached his eyes. He knew he was as high a rank in the Confederate government as he would ever achieve. It was well known, in the South as well as in the North, that he had been against the war in the years leading up to this foolishness, and now it was *he* who carried the very machinations needed to carry on the bloodbath that maddened his countrymen on both sides of the Mason-Dixon line. He knew that hidden in the captain's safe was the answer to a Southern victory, and still this did not make him happy or proud.

The guarded gift was one of recognition—a political act that would finally drive the killing wedge between North and South forever. The words of men now but ghosts kept echoing in his mind: *divide and conquer.* One of two concessions that no American could ever tolerate, North or South, had been struck with his pen: the Royal Navy would forever have eight naval bases in the gulf of Mexico and South America, a deal with the Devil that would be a thorn in his young nation's side forever.

However, maybe, just maybe, this mission would answer his prayer and put a stop to the mass killing of his fellow citizens, North *and* South. With God's help, maybe then the split could at least be finished without the loss of more young men.

He turned away and watched as the seabirds cawed and swooped to the wave tops and then shot back skyward.

No more slavery—the single most important factor that had brought on the war was now a thing of the past. The one obstacle that stood between legitimacy and recognition by other nations, slavery, had been erased by a single swipe of his pen, bringing the South the most powerful ally in the world.

When the seas surrounding the three warships suddenly became silent, Engersoll looked up as the skies cleared of the diving and frolicking birds. He watched in amazement as they flocked away from the three warships.

"What's this?" Sir Lionel asked aloud.

A thousand yards away, Her Majesty's frigate *Port Royal* raised a line of signal flags. Then the sudden beating of a drum announced the crew of *Warlord* was going to battle stations. Eight royal marines quickly surrounded the two men as loud footsteps ran about them as the beating of the war drum became louder, as were the shouts of sailors as they took up their action stations.

"Is it a Union warship?" Engersoll asked.

"I don't know, but I must be informed of our circumstance!" The angry courier pushed past the armed guard. They had orders from the Admiralty that dictated they avoid contact with the blockading American warships at all costs. Gauss knew they must land the treaty and arms that day.

Captain Miles Peavey stood on the quarterdeck as he surveyed the situation farther out to sea. He watched as the frigates *Elizabeth* and *Port Royal* made sharp turns to come about.

"I need more sail! Put on more sail!" he ordered, his spyglass going from his view of southern waters to that of the *Warlord*'s smaller escorts as they maneuvered.

"I demand to know what is happening, Captain," Sir Lionel asked as he arrogantly stepped into Peavey's line of sight.

"Not now, sir!" Peavey shot back, not too gently shoving the man aside.

"I will report your boorish behavior, I assure—"

"Remove this man from my command deck!" the captain ordered, never taking his eye from the spyglass.

"Why, I never—"

"Now!" the captain shouted, turning away from the sight of his two escorts as they attempted to run interference for his larger ship.

The red-coated royal marine escort moved Sir Lionel forcefully away from the captain. Engersoll didn't need to be manhandled, so he avoided confrontation, silently and calmly joining the group of men. The *Warlord*'s first officer stepped up to the two men and whispered at close quarters.

"*Port Royal* has spotted a vessel five miles off. This . . . this ship has been spied several times in the last two days, and now appears to be making a move on our position."

"A single vessel?" Sir Lionel asked incredulously. "This is the Royal Navy, sir, no single vessel, not even one of their mighty ironclads could hope to stop us from our goal!"

The executive officer did not answer at first, but instead looked to where his captain stood ramrod straight, watching the seas of the open gulf to the south.

"The vessel that has been following us is unlike any we have ever seen. We're not even sure if it's a ship at all," he said feeling uncomfortable. "There is ridiculous talk that it's some kind of sea—"

"Mr. Rand, *Port Royal* is attacking at maximum range. Report ship's readiness!" the captain said loudly while still maintaining sight on the horizon.

Warlord's second in command just looked at the two politicos, half bowed, and then moved off to his master's side.

"All stations report battle ready, Captain!" he said, as he had been informed a moment before that all seventeen of the cruiser's thirty-two-pounder cannons were ready for action.

"Very good. Even though our sister ships of propeller, paddlewheel, and coal would be most welcome here, I figure we old sailing men can give the American Navy what for, hey, Mr. Rand?" The captain took his eye away from his glass for a short moment and winked.

"Yes, sir, we'll show them what the Royal Navy is capable of."

"Tell our gentleman guests they can stand at the stern railing and watch *Port Royal* and *Elizabeth* engage our new adversaries. They'll have quite a shock realizing that the Confederacy has a new friend on the high seas."

"Yes, sir," Rand answered without enthusiasm or further comment as he turned and made his way back to Sir Lionel and Engersoll.

Just as the three men stepped to the rail, they saw the flash of powder long before they heard the reports of the large guns of *Elizabeth* and *Port Royal*. Then, over the surface of the gulf, the loud popping came to

Engersoll's ears. It was unlike what he imagined naval gunfire to sound like, even at this extreme distance.

"Both frigates have opened up their port-side guns. That means they must have caught the enemy off guard and crossed the T, a formation allowing them to bring the guns of both ships to bear," Rand explained as he watched. "A fatal error by the American, if that's who he is."

"But why can't we see the American ship?" Sir Lionel asked.

"Well, they are more than likely over our horizon. We should be able to see them—"

A sudden, tremendous explosion lit up the blue southern sky as HMS *Elizabeth* vanished in a matter of a split second behind a solid wall of flame and smoke. All three men watched in astonishment as the sound finally reached them. *Warlord* shook beneath their feet as Rand started shouting orders. He spared a glance at Captain Peavey who stood stock-still, the spyglass slowly lowering to his side. Lieutenant Rand shouted to bring the ship about.

This order finally moved Peavey to action as he turned angrily toward his number one.

"Belay that order, make for the coast at all possible speed, we must—"

Without seeing the initial or even the second cataclysmic action, the sound wave of another explosion almost knocked Peavey from his feet. As he straightened and turned from his spot on the wooden deck, the mushroom-shaped cloud of red and black was rising from the spot where *Port Royal* had been just a moment before. In a matter of two stunning moments of elapsed time, two Royal Navy frigates had vanished without having the chance to reload their guns. As Peavey regained his feet and raised his glass, he could see no sign of either ship save for the debris and smoke still rising in the clear air.

"We have movement aft at five thousand yards and closing!" The call was shouted from high above in the rigging.

Engersoll tried desperately to spy the enemy vessel, but he failed at first. He gripped the handrail and then raised his right hand to his brow and strained to see.

Peavey shouted out orders and reversed his earlier command to run for the coast.

"My God!" Sir Lionel cried. "Look at that!"

Engersoll turned to the spot Sir Lionel was pointing to as *Warlord* turned hard to starboard to bring her main guns to bear on the suddenly visible target.

At a mile away from *Warlord*, Engersoll finally spied the enemy that had just cremated three hundred men in a matter of moments. It truly *was* a sea monster. The wave it created was spectacular as it charged the British warship. Three hundred feet into the air the wake rose, as water was pushed aside by a force no man aboard could have ever imagined.

"Come on, come on, turn, damn you, turn!" Captain Peavey pleaded with the slowly moving *Warlord* as she lethargically leaned over to bring her main armament to bear on the approaching juggernaut.

"God in heaven," Engersoll said as a massive gray tower rose from the sea, splitting the ocean like a sharp knife, sending foam and spray hundreds of feet into the air.

They all watched from the quarterdeck as the full view of the glistening tower came into sight. Engersoll's jaw clenched as two massive, semi-rounded bubbled windows appeared on either side of the great enclosure. Then he saw with dawning horror that rising from the streamlined tower's uppermost area and sloping to its monstrous round bow were large gleaming spikes, arrayed like the giant teeth of a great serpent in three long rows arching from bow to tower. As they watched, the beast accelerated to an incalculable speed.

The Royal Navy seamen watched slack-jawed as the strange apparition started to sink back beneath the sea.

Rand looked to his captain, who was standing in shock and not moving. His spyglass slipped from his hand and the lens shattered on the deck.

"Open fire as your guns come to bear!" Rand shouted, immediately taking command from the captain.

The massive thirty-two-pound rifled cannon started to open fire as they sighted on the strange monster. Rand was pleased to see the first three explosive rounds strike the beast before it went too deep. However, his joy was short-lived as this seagoing nightmare kept accelerating, shaking off the killing blows of the most powerful guns in the British fleet. Rand saw what was going to happen as clearly as if it were already history. He turned and grabbed for the ship's wheel, assisting the helmsman.

"Port, turn to port!" he cried.

It was an order that would never be carried out.

As the underwater creature approached, the swell of ocean rose around them, taking the great battle cruiser to a height that should have allowed the submerged giant to plow harmlessly beneath her. Instead, the 175-foot-long *Warlord* was rocked violently from beneath, struck so hard that her main mast splintered and came crashing onto the deck, trapping and killing Captain Peavey beneath the broken tonnage.

As Rand fell back he saw a great geyser of water knock free the four main hatch covers below the quarterdeck, as the force of the collision gutted the great vessel from below, smashing her thick keel as if it were made of nothing more than twigs. The heavy cruiser heeled to her port side as the ship's wheel was still turned in that direction. Lieutenant Rand fought his way to his feet as the great ship lost her battle for survival.

Engersoll watched in horror as the impact sent Sir Lionel to his death when the stern of *Warlord* was thrown into the air. Suddenly the ship rocked as the powder stores below erupted outward, splintering the oak ribs of the vessel out in a frenzy of destruction. Engersoll was thrown into the erupting sea.

Engersoll slipped under the water, trying to avoid one of the ship's spars as it crashed into the sea. All about him men struggled to stay afloat as *Warlord*, her back snapped like cordwood, broke in two with a death sound horrible to the ears of seamen. She quickly slipped under, dragging another fifty men to their deaths.

Engersoll felt a hand grab his long coat and pull him up from a death to which he had already resigned himself. As he spit out the warm water that flooded his mouth, he saw it was Lieutenant Rand pulling him free of the sea's grip.

As he turned away to grab for a piece of floating debris, Engersoll saw a sight that froze him into stillness. There, not two hundred feet away, rode the great metal monster. It surfaced with a loud hiss of escaping air and violent eruptions of water that rocketed skyward, creating a magical and terrifying rainbow effect.

As the metal ship centered itself in the middle of dead men and debris, Engersoll was shocked to see the giant tower sitting on the broad expanse of metal that made up the unimaginable sight of the iron hull. The great bubble window shaped like the eye of a demon was in front of him, and as he looked skyward, he saw a man standing in the spider-webbed framed glass. Engersoll saw a man with long black hair almost as wild as his blazing eyes as the seven-hundred-foot sea monster slowly gasped a great sigh of air, and enormous bubbles rose to the surface of the sea as the man and his metal monster vanished.

As Engersoll felt the suction of the vessel drag him down into the depths of the gulf, the last vision of the earthly world he would ever see were those eyes—those terrifying, hate-filled eyes.

APRIL 25, 1865
PENOBSCOT RIVER,
MAINE

The riverboat lay at anchor with the fog hiding her entire lower quarter, the gentle lapping of the river against her low-slung hull being the only sound. The many exterior and interior lights were ablaze in the thickening fog. The captain of the *Mary Lincoln* looked forward from the port bridge wing and saw nothing but the rising white veil of mist.

"Damn it all, sir, this is far too dangerous. What fool would be crazy enough to navigate the river in this kind of chowder?"

The heavyset man to his left did not respond. He knew exactly what kind of man would brave the Penobscot after dark and in heavy fog, but why say anything until he had to? After all, the captain was frightened enough.

The silent passenger pursed his lips and brushed at his gray beard. The upper lip was freshly shaven and his greatcoat recently cleaned and pressed. His top hat was placed upon his head, tilted forward so that most who spoke with him could not view his dark eyes. It was for the better, since most of the riverboat's crew did not know his identity.

The United States secretary of war, Edwin M. Stanton, watched deckhands pull taut the anchor ropes. They were in the grip of the deepest, widening section of river as it neared the sea.

As Stanton peered into the fog, he thought he heard a shout from across the way. He cringed and shook his head. Every man on this mission was under orders not to make any noise. He strained to hear left and then right, but there was no further disturbance. This damnable fog was acting like an amplifier, and that could doom them all.

"It seems we have caught a shift in current," the captain said as he ventured back inside the wheelhouse.

Stanton felt the large boat shift to the right, and his stomach fluttered as if the *Mary Lincoln* rose on a small wave.

"It's not a current, Captain; make no adjustment to your station. Our guest will make the appropriate course change in regard to your vessel," Stanton said as he took the situation in.

"What guest? The fog is not yet so thick I cannot see, sir. We have—"

The captain was cut short when the *Mary Lincoln* rose into the air along with the Penobscot River under her keel—ten, fifteen, and then twenty feet higher than just a moment before.

"My God—"

Edwin Stanton calmly reached out and took hold of the thick railing until the riverboat settled. "Calm yourself, Captain Smith; you are just feeling the displacement of water from the approach of the vessel."

"Displacement of water?" Smith inquired as he returned to the wing and looked out over the calming river. "The river is void of traffic—even in this fog I can see that! And what vessel would displace so much water as to almost capsize a boat of this tonnage?"

A small man approached from where he was standing just inside the pilothouse and cautiously made his way to the even smaller Stanton.

"Has the man arrived, Monsieur Stanton?" the small man asked in his heavily accented English.

The secretary of war turned angrily toward the Frenchman. "You are to observe only. You are not to speak; you are not to approach this man. I am acquiescing to a favor owed of your government. Otherwise, sir, I would not give you the time of day. Now stand to the far railing and disappear, and you may be lucky enough to witness one of mankind's greatest achievements."

The Frenchman placed his woolen cap on his head and backed away from the rotund secretary, knowing he was lucky just to be here on the Penobscot. However, lucky or not, he held information that would embarrass the U.S. government, and if he had not been allowed to board the *Mary Lincoln*, he would have taken his eyewitness accounts to the capitals of all Europe. Still, he had to play this cautiously. He wanted to know only if this amazing craft truly existed.

"Ahoy on deck, keep your eyes open. I hear movement on the river," the captain called out as he gained the bridge wing and stood next to the secretary.

Stanton nodded his head as giant water geysers shot into the air, causing the mist to eddy, swirl, and then finally part. Then as the two men
watched, the great ship rose from the depths. The giant tower parted the
river as if a mountain were being born right in the center of the Penobscot. The great glass eyes of the beast glowed green and red, easily piercing the fog.

"Holy Mary, mother of—"

"Such sentiments would not save you this man's wrath, Captain. He
is not one of God's children, but a devil born of man."

"What is that . . . that thing?"

Stanton walked closer to the edge of the bridge wing and watched as
the upper bulk of the great iron beast settled on the surface of the Penobscot. As it did, it sent surface water rushing toward the *Mary Lincoln*, making her rise once more on the swells and allowing the river to overflow her
gunnels. The water geysers ceased their roar and the river became still. It
seemed to Stanton he could hear the far off ringing of bells and the voices
of men giving commands. Then a bank of fog rolled in and covered the
great black submarine.

"The thing is called *Leviathan*, Captain Smith, and no matter what
happens here tonight, you are never to speak of this to anyone, not even to
your wife. I don't think I have to make any unnecessary threats, do I, sir?"

Stanton ignored the shocked look that covered Smith's face. He just
listened to the night and the sounds of water meeting iron. The night
had become deathly still, seeming also to await answers as to what this
strange object was. Stanton then turned toward a man that was standing
unseen inside the pilothouse stairwell. He nodded his head, and the man
slipped away unnoticed by all except the Frenchman, who was unceremoniously shoved out of the man's way.

Stanton's man gathered the five selected U.S. Navy seamen and gave
them each an oilcloth, which weighed in excess of thirty pounds apiece.
Then he watched as they gained the boat deck on the opposite side of the
Mary Lincoln and slipped over the side.

"Ahoy the riverboat!" Six deckhands ran to the starboard side, listened, and strained to pierce the fog. Then the call from the river repeated, "Ahoy *Mary Lincoln*, permission to tie up and board!" The voice
was deep, booming, and filled with command.

The first officer looked up at the riverboat's bridge for permission
from the captain to allow the unseen to board. Smith nodded his head.

"Permission granted! What is the number of your boarding party?"

"One," was the short answer as a long rope flew through the fog and struck the wet deck as if from nowhere. The deckhands tied off the rope as they heard the heavy footsteps on the gangplank lowered earlier.

Captain Smith watched his men on deck freeze as the unseen footsteps continued up the stairs at a leisurely pace. The fog swirled around the ship's railing as the footsteps stopped. Then the blanket of moisture parted, and there stood a man. He was a giant, standing at least six feet, five inches. His dark hair was long and wild. His blue seaman's jacket was plain and devoid of rank or insignia with the exception of four gold stripes at each cuff. The knee-high boots were as shiny as a polished deck.

"*Leviathan* requests permission to come aboard," the deep voice boomed.

"Permission granted. May I have your name, sir?" the *Mary Lincoln*'s first officer asked.

The man stood motionless at the top of the gangway. He was silent as his large eyes took in the riverboat's crew before him, an old and battered Bible clutched in his large hand.

"Express my greetings to Secretary Stanton, and convey to him that the man he wished to meet, Captain Octavian Heirthall, has arrived to end my relationship with the U.S. government, and to reclaim my family."

The first officer became confused as he looked from the dark form shrouded in fog at the top of the gangway to the captain and his guest looking down from the bridge. The crew heard footsteps as a lone figure made his way down to the main deck.

Edwin Stanton, using his cane, approached the ship's railing cautiously. His eyes never left the imposing figure standing over him; he felt as if he were a mouse watching an owl, and the owl was ravenous. The stranger's dark blue eyes burned through the fog and into his own. Stanton stopped ten feet in front of the man known to only a few—Captain Octavian Heirthall.

"Please, come aboard, Captain," Stanton said, looking up.

"My wife, my children—they are aboard?"

"Captain, please, join me on deck. Talking up to you, while not quite below my station, is, at the least, uncomfortable," Stanton said, acting as bravely as he could under the circumstances.

"My thoughts are, there is no station below yours, sir, save but one, and that is the hell you will be sent to upon your meaningless death. My wife, my son, and my five daughters, they must be here, or I swear to you, Mr. Secretary, you will fall so far and hard from grace that the mere mention of your name will be a loathsome experience for any soul saying it. I have already sent a dispatch to President Lincoln by ship's courier. If my family is not delivered here to me this night, the courier has instructions to deliver the letter, regardless of the consequences to my children and wife."

"Forgive me, Captain; you have been at sea, so of course you could not have heard the news. President Lincoln was murdered just eleven days ago in Washington, struck down by an assassin's bullet."

The large man seemed to deflate before Stanton's eyes. He reached for the rope railing to steady himself. He missed at the first attempt, and then grasped it with the weakened strength of a dying man.

"Horrible news, I know."

"He . . . he was—he was the only man of honor I have ever known," Heirthall said as he stepped down slowly from the gangway and onto the deck. "What of the president's promise to me for the protection of the gulf and . . . and its inhabitants?"

"You now know your courier will do you no good," Stanton said, ignoring the captain's question. "Your threat to me has fallen on deaf—or should I say *dead*—ears, my good captain."

Heirthall grasped his Bible with both hands, but he could find no solace in its touch. His blazing eyes turned to the river and his shoulders straightened. He then turned slowly to face Stanton.

"I am a prideful man, a God-fearing man. My words were harsh, so I ask you again, sir, please, my wife and my children, are they safe? —And the president's pledge to help me with—my discovery, this promise is still intact? I have done what you asked."

"May I remind you, Captain, you came to *us* for the protection of the gulf waters. It was just coincidental our spies in England learned of this foul treaty between England and the rebellious states. If they had consummated that despicable document, those bases would have been the death of your amazing discovery, would they not?"

"You had no right to remove my family from my island in the Pacific—I would have fulfilled my part of the bargain without you resorting to your obvious evil nature, Mr. Secretary."

Heirthall remembered the stories told to him by a father long dead. How Napoleon had done the same to his family, destroying them to gain access to the family science: a horrible history repeating itself.

Stanton lowered his head and turned away from those pleading blue eyes. He found himself unable to look the captain in his face as he said his next words. "Your son has died. Consumption, I was told. I am truly sorry."

The wail of the large man pierced the darkened night. River men who heard the cry would forever have it in their nightmares. A sound as such should never originate from a man of Heirthall's stature. He went to his knees and placed the Bible so that it covered his face.

The small Frenchman standing above on the bridge wing watched, his heart going out to this man he did not know. Such anguish chilled his blood. Suddenly, he knew he did not want to be here, even if it meant never confirming the sight he had seen two years prior while at sea, that of a great metal monster.

"It was never my intention for this sad thing to happen. Now you must understand my position, sir, you must continue your good work upon the seas. We cannot allow you to do any different. Your country needs you now more than ever. The foulness of the British try at power in this hemisphere will be attempted time and time again, and maybe your Gulf of Mexico will no longer be a safe haven for your find."

Captain Octavian Heirthall, with his long black hair covering the Bible he held to his face, slowly looked up at Stanton. He lowered the old book and gained his feet until he towered over the secretary. He reached down and straightened his jacket, pulling upon the hem.

Stanton never hesitated upon seeing his own fate embedded in those blazing blue eyes—he snapped his fingers and twenty marines came from the opposite side of the wheelhouse. They leveled rifles at the man standing before him. He became concerned when Heirthall did not react.

"Before you do something foolish, I will tell you that your family has been split up. Your wife and four of your daughters are close, but the fifth—the very, very special one, the one closest in nature to your mother—is being held at the armory in Washington. She will be the lamb that is sacrificed, so think well, Captain, before your next words come from your mouth."

Heirthall felt his chest clench as his destiny was presented to him. He had fallen into the same trap as had his father. Instead of Napoleon, it was Stanton pulling the strings of his naïveté. His mind snapped, but his features never betrayed that fact.

"Your magnificent science, sir, is all we seek, the details of which you will hand over to the department of the navy. Your vessel will be forfeit. It will be taken apart, piece by piece, analyzed and then rebuilt. Then you will offer up the knowledge of the seas, which is yours alone. Your cooperation is essential for the safety of your youngest daughter. After I am satisfied you have met my conditions, you and your family will be reunited, intact. Am I understood?"

"President Lincoln—he knew of this foul thing?"

Stanton shook his head and stepped behind the closest marines.

"Mr. Lincoln never understood anything beyond what was right in front of his face. As a country, we have entered a new world—a global society where the strong will dictate. This nation needs what you have— your friend Mr. Lincoln never understood that. He accepted your decision not to offer to us your science as a tool of war; I, sir, did not. Your mission for the president to stop the alliance of Britain and the traitors of the South was just the start. There will be many such tasks in the future, and you will perform them. If you fail in this, I will make public your discovery in the gulf, the Mediterranean, and Antarctica . . . needless to say, that will end your dream along with your family."

A moment of clarity struck Heirthall, as bright as a bolt of lightning. His eyes widened and he took a menacing step toward the secretary.

"Return my daughter to her mother and sisters, or there will be such retribution taken against you that you will believe Satan has risen to devour you and yours. I have known men such as you. Men—twins of you—murdered my father for the sake of owning the great secret of the seas. I once looked fondly upon my adopted country, until madness struck these shores as it had so many others." Heirthall took a menacing step forward and used his commanding, booming, deep voice: "My wife and children—produce them or reap a bitter harvest."

Stanton swallowed but held his position behind the marines.

"As I speak, your vessel, your great *Leviathan*, is being mined. Argue and fight and you will lose far more than just your oldest child."

Heirthall broke. Far too much had his mind and heart absorbed the past three years. The betrayal, the long separation from his children and his wife, the killing of innocent and guilty alike upon the seas, were too much for his once great mind. He threw his black Bible toward the cordon of marines and then turned for the riverboat's railing. As his hands touched the damp wood and rope, several shots rang out. Two minié balls pierced his back. One bullet hit his liver and one his upper back. He staggered, but managed to catch himself. He pulled with all of his strength until he could fall over the railing and into the river.

"You fools, what have you done?" Stanton cried out. "You men." He pointed at the four marines that had just missed taking Heirthall before he jumped. "Into the river. Bring the captain to me. He cannot have gone far!"

The marines dropped their rifles and started to climb the railing, but they never made it. Loud popping sounded through the thick fog and a hundred bullets cut the men down. A speed of fire no man had ever heard in the long history of firearms punctured holes in the large riverboat. Wood flew as even more bullets zinged through the fog. Stanton realized as he dove behind stacked barrels that he was witnessing something akin to the Gatling gun, but this was far faster, far deadlier. The remaining marines never had a chance to reload their weapons before large-caliber rounds sliced them to pieces.

They were facing another of Octavian Heirthall's miracle weapons.

The captain's wounds were mortal. He struggled to keep his head above water as he kicked with his legs. The fog and *Leviathan*'s automatic weapons were keeping the riverboat's marines at bay, but Heirthall knew the secretary would not have been satisfied with just the one surprise treachery.

Suddenly arms were pulling him up and out of the cold river. The captain felt the cold iron of *Leviathan* against his wet clothing as he was hauled aboard. The voices were jumbled and he sensed fear and anger in his crew. He fought to gain his feet and finally cleared his vision enough to see his first officer, Mr. Meriwether, standing at his side.

"Take her down, Thomas, we have been betrayed."

"Captain, your wounds, they are—"

"Down, take *Leviathan* down, set course upriver." He struggled to the giant tower where he collapsed against the thick iron hatch. He slowly but angrily stood, leaning against the frame, and then entered the vessel.

"All hands stand by to dive!" Meriwether called out as he saw the thick swath of blood that covered the deck and hatch combing. He then followed Heirthall inside.

"Two ships approaching from the far shore. Our echo-sound report says they are ironclads!" he heard as he half-stumbled down the ladder into the control center.

As the announcement came, an explosion rocked *Leviathan* from beneath the bow, and then in quick rapidity another rocked her from the stern.

"That was not shot from an ironclad, those were placed charges. Get me a damage report."

Meriwether then eased his captain into the large chair placed on a raised platform at the center of the control room. As he removed his hands, he saw they were covered in blood, thick and dark red.

"Report depth under the keel!" Meriwether called out while still looking at his hands.

"We have only thirty feet under the keel!" the helmsman called from the front of the control room.

"Come about, all ahead full!" Heirthall said in a pain-filled voice.

Meriwether turned to Heirthall. "Captain, we must make for the sea before we find our way blocked."

"My son is dead, my family hostages, and . . . and the president . . . is dead," Heirthall said as his eyes clenched closed in pain.

Meriwether saw his despair. His own anger could have been that of the man that he loved more than a father.

"What are your orders, sir?"

Heirthall struggled and used the chair to stand. He quickly waved Meriwether away when he lunged to assist him.

"Lieutenant Wallace—I need him."

A young man, no more than twenty, stepped from his post at the ship's ballast control.

"Diving Officer Wallace, here, sir!"

Heirthall waved him over without ever opening his eyes to see him. He reached out and felt for the young man, finally feeling him underneath his hand.

"I . . . have a mission . . . for you, boy," he said, trying to keep the pain out of his voice.

A solid shot rang off *Leviathan*'s hull. The echo was almost deafening.

It was the first time her crew had ever heard their vessel's hull struck solidly at point-blank range by another warship.

"Ironclads are opening fire, Captain."

Heirthall's eyes fluttered open and fixed on Wallace. The captain knew the boy had been sweet on his youngest daughter, Olivia. It was reported to him that the two spent never-ending hours together, talking and reading. Heirthall would not sacrifice this boy—instead he would use the young man's feelings for his daughter's sake.

"Mr. Wallace, when we . . . make our turn, our last run for the sea, you . . . will not be aboard."

"Captain?" Peter Wallace asked, looking from Heirthall to Meriwether.

"Take . . . some men—my . . . daughter is in Washington . . . the armory. Please find my Olivia, then . . . my wife and daughters. . . . Please, son." He grimaced again. "You're the youngest and the brightest—the best of us all. If need be, to secure my child, kill all in your path."

Wallace looked around the control room as every hand present was starting to understand the depth of their betrayal. The serious-featured young man straightened and saluted Heirthall. When he saw his captain was too weak to return his gesture of respect, he slowly lowered his hand.

"Take the deck watch, that's six armed men," Meriwether said, his eyes never leaving Heirthall's dying form. "I have more items to give you, with your permission, Captain?"

Heirthall could only nod his head once.

Meriwether disappeared and went aft of the control center. He returned two minutes later carrying a leather satchel and pouch. The pouch he handed to Wallace.

"There is enough gold inside to get you, your men, Olivia, and the rest of the family back home. Enough to buy a ship if need be."

The boy nodded, looking guiltily up and around at the rest of the control room crew. He felt he was betraying the men he had come to love by leaving them.

"Pay attention, Lieutenant." Meriwether then handed him the small satchel. As the boy held it, the first officer opened it and pulled out some old and much-worn pages. "When you have the child back home, you are to guard her with your life. You will be in command of the base, the only officer left. The men are loyal to the captain until their deaths; they will be the same for you, boy, and to the girl if her mother and sisters are not recovered."

Wallace swallowed and looked at the captain, but Meriwether slapped the boy lightly.

"This"—he grasped the yellowed pages—"is her family legacy; this is who she is, where she came from." Then he held up another book. "This is the logbook of *Leviathan*. It is also for her. You will have to make the last entry. The plans and specifications for *Leviathan* are on the island with all the captain's research. Olivia will one day know what to do with them. The last pages are of the life form—these are not to fall into the hands of our American brethren. Is this clear?"

Peter Wallace looked at the pages and then the logbook. His frown deepened when he realized his responsibility.

"You tell her the story of what happened here this night. Burn into her soul the betrayal that took place. She will eventually know what to do. Her father's and grandfather's designs are locked away. She is to learn—learn the science, and the sea is where she will discover who she really is and why the family is who they are. . . . Do you understand, boy?"

"I will not fail the captain, sir."

"I know you won't, lad." Meriwether looked around as explosions rocked *Leviathan*. "Godspeed, son, now be off. Jump over the side when we make our turn. Take care of Olivia, boy—love her as I already know you do."

Wallace turned and made for the tower hatch, stuffing the pages and logbook into the satchel as he did. The eighteen-year-old boy never looked back.

"We are at sixteen knots and three hundred yards, Mr. Meriwether," the helm called out.

"Captain, your orders, sir?"

"Take me to . . . the tower, Mr. Meriwether," Heirthall ordered, and then went to his knees. Several men left their posts as they saw their captain fall.

"Attend your stations!"

All eyes went to the bald-headed Mr. Meriwether, who stood like a rock beside Heirthall.

"We have one last mission to perform for our captain. We will do it right!" he yelled in his Boston accent just as more iron shot struck their hull.

Meriwether assisted Heirthall to his feet, and they made their way slowly up the spiral staircase and into the green-tinted tower. The first officer walked his captain to the auxiliary ship's wheel, staying long enough to make sure he was steady.

"Thank you, Mr. Meriwether," Heirthall said as he leaned heavily against the mahogany wheel. "Inform the crew that any who so choose can depart *Leviathan*." He closed his eyes in pain.

Meriwether saw the large pool of blood as it spread across the tiled decking. He was amazed that such an amount could be lost without death coming swiftly.

"Aye, Captain," he said as he turned and made his way back down into the control room.

Heirthall came close to losing his battle with consciousness as Meriwether's voice came across the sound-powered speakers overhead. When the dizziness passed, he looked around his familiar surroundings. He gently touched the handholds on the wheel, caressing them as he once had his beautiful wife. Sweat and tears of loss poured into his eyes, and he wiped them away with a swipe of his arm. Then he looked up and straightened as best he could as Meriwether returned. He saw his first officer cringe as a solid iron shot bounced off the exposed tower of *Leviathan*.

"The crew has been informed, Captain. The Union ironclads are drawing near, and the fog, I'm afraid, is lifting with the dawn."

"Do we have enough men to send *Leviathan* on her last mission?" Heirthall asked as he held Meriwether's gaze.

"Yes, Captain, we have the entire complement—minus the seven you sent over the side."

Heirthall listened to the words, but they could not be right.

"They—"

"—are following your last orders, Captain. They are *your* men."

Heirthall stood straighter and gripped the ship's wheel.

"Order flank speed, Mr. Meriwether. By the time we are a hundred yards off *Mary Lincoln*, I want *Leviathan*'s belly . . . rubbing the riverbed." Heirthall lowered his head. "I never wanted this. . . . They have . . . pushed me to it."

"The ironclads?"

"Target two of the new compressed air torpedoes on those fools," he said as a tear slowly rolled down his left cheek. "And Mr. Meriwether, will you thank the men for—"

"No sir, I will not. You do not thank those for doing their duty to a man who saved their lives repeatedly. One who gave those lives meaning."

Heirthall watched as Meriwether turned and shouted down the spiral staircase: "All ahead flank, stand by both forward-torpedo tubes, target the enemy ironclads with the new magnetic warheads!"

Belowdecks, men sprang into action just as the giant submarine lurched forward in the water. Her stern dug so low in the river that her main center propeller dug into the mud, sending a geyser of black muck a hundred feet into the air and announcing her intentions to all those on the river that fateful morning.

"My God, the madman is charging us!" the captain said from the bridge.

Stanton ran to the aft railing as the river erupted a thousand yards upstream. He held his hands to his ears as the two Union ironclads opened up a withering fire from their revolving turrets. They tried in vain to target the fast-moving submarine as it started its dive. The giant tower and triple rows of arched spikes were now the only visible sign above water that declared *Leviathan* was on her way. As they approached at more than fifty knots, the large bubble windows on the side of the tower were glowing an angry bluish-green, just as if they were the eyes of Heirthall himself.

Stanton backed away as the marines on deck started firing on the onrushing target. Then two explosions shook the *Mary Lincoln* on her keel. Stanton turned toward the tumult, staring in horror just as the two great ironclads blew up.

"What evil is afoot here!" he screamed, and then turned in anger. "Lieutenant, bring them out on deck and line them up against the stern railing. Make sure they are visible to this crazy fool!" he ordered.

The young marine ran below and disappeared. He soon returned with the four children and the wife of Captain Octavian Heirthall. The woman was calm, but Stanton could see the girls were frightened.

The small Frenchman was at Stanton's side. He pulled on the man's coat sleeve, ripping it.

"This is barbaric. You cannot do this—send the children over the side!"

Stanton pushed the Frenchman away.

"Quickly, allow the captain to see what he is to lose in this foolishness. Mr. Verne, you may run if you wish, but the *Mary Lincoln* will stand her ground!"

The marine reluctantly used his rifle to push the screaming girls and the silent woman to the rail. Then Elizabeth Heirthall slapped away the bayoneted rifle and gathered her children to her as they saw the great *Leviathan* run true to her course. The woman turned to look at Stanton, a knowing smile slowly spreading across her face. She shook her head as she hugged her daughters close to her.

"The ironclads are no longer a concern, Captain," Meriwether said as he used his binoculars, examining the spots where the two warships were sinking into the Penobscot mud. "The *Mary Lincoln* is getting her boilers going, but she cannot escape. She is at about two knots and—"

Meriwether's words cut off as he adjusted his glasses on the scene before him.

"No, no, no!" The words came out in more of a moan than a cry.

Heirthall, though barely conscious, heard the fear in his first officer's voice. His face was now ashen gray, the blood long since absent from skin and veins. He managed to raise his head but his vision was cloudy at best.

"The children—Captain, the barbarian has your wife and children on deck!"

Heirthall came fully awake and fell to his knees as he let go of the wheel. He tried to stand and was thankful when Meriwether once again lifted him to his feet. He left him, ran to the wheel, and tried to turn the giant ship. The rudder was nonresponsive as it was dragging in the thick mud of the bottom. He used all of his considerable strength to turn her, but the resistance was just too great. The mines Stanton had ordered placed against *Leviathan*'s hull, coupled with the weight of her ballast, were dragging the stern into the mud.

"She's not responding, Captain," Meriwether cried out.

Heirthall leaned heavily against the thick crystal of the viewing window. His eyes blank and his body dying, he still needed no binoculars to see his family lined up on the riverboat's stern.

"Elizabeth," he cried out weakly as his body slumped and blood seeped heavily from his mouth.

"Captain!" Meriwether cried out as Heirthall collapsed.

"What has thy vengeance wrought?" Heirthall said, the words coming out as a whisper.

Stanton ran to the railing and jumped over the side. His large body hit the cold water unnoticed by the riverboat's crew and complement of marines. The French news correspondent stood his ground as the great submarine rushed toward him. He suddenly tried to run and reach the woman and her children, but he slipped on the wet deck and went down hard just as the *Mary Lincoln* started a turn. The momentum of the large riverboat rolled the young Jules Verne into the river. Once the cold water closed over him, the Frenchman heard the scream of *Leviathan*'s three propellers as they pushed the huge mass of iron boat through the water. He kicked as hard as he could to fight his way toward the rocky shoreline of the Penobscot, crying as he did at the ruthless fate awaiting the woman and her children.

Leviathan's triple prow sliced the waters of the Penobscot cleanly, and her tower rose majestically over the doomed riverboat. It seemed as if Heirthall had aimed the killing apparatus directly at his wife and children, cleanly slicing into the *Mary Lincoln*'s stern. The tower of *Leviathan* followed the killing cut of the arched keel breaker. If any were alive inside the strange craft to see, they would have beheld a bizarre sight, as the first mate was covering his captain with his own body.

Leviathan was traveling in excess of fifty-eight knots when she made contact with the wood, iron, and brass riverboat. She sliced through her from stern to bow in less than three full seconds, with the impact only slowing her by six knots.

The *Mary Lincoln* simply folded over in two separate sections and sank as if she had never been, while *Leviathan* continued into the broad mouth of the Penobscot and the deeper waters of the ocean beyond.

Meriwether assisted Heirthall to his ship's wheel. The great submarine was dying. Water cascaded into the tower from the cracks in the nearly indestructible crystal of the viewing ports. He could hear the men below fight the flooding caused when her steel rivets popped upon impact with the steel and iron of the riverboat's power plant.

"I have killed that which I loved most, I—"

"It was not you, Captain, 'twas warmongers; it was the likes of Stanton. They are responsible for this."

Heirthall reached up and grabbed the wheel. She turned easily now that her rudder was clear of the river bottom. She had made it back to the sea—made it back to her home.

"Take her . . . to the continental . . . shelf, Mr. Meriwether; she'll die in deep waters," he ordered as his chin sank lower until it rested against the wheel's stanchion.

The lights flickered and then went out as *Leviathan* dove deep for the last time in her short life. As the red battery-driven emergency lights came on, Octavian Heirthall died.

As the crushing depths started to take a lover's hold on *Leviathan*, Meriwether and the crew were under no grand illusions about their fate.

Meriwether closed his eyes as the thick, meticulously machined crystal window cracked, the crack streaking across the surface like an invisible hand. Then the first inward bulge of the crushing effect popped loudly outside in the companionway.

"Down to the sea with heavy heart, we follow our captain. We are going home."

PART ONE

DOWN TO THE SEA IN SHIPS

The ship hangs hovering on the verge of death, / Hell yawns, rocks rise, and breakers roar beneath!

—William Falconer, "The Shipwreck"

1

The Event Group Center was as quiet as anyone stationed there had ever heard it. For the men and women of Department 5656, a dark and secret entity of the National Archives, the day was darker than even their mission for the United States government. They were saying good-bye to forty-six of their own people. One man in particular—Colonel Jack Collins, United States Army.

The assembled military, scientific, research, academic, and philosophical staffs were seated in the overcrowded main cafeteria of the complex, because the small chapel deep on level eight would have been too small for this massive turnout.

As the Dire Straits' haunting tune "Brothers in Arms" played, the mood was somber. Director Niles Compton had made the decision, and the new head of security agreed, that no eulogy for those lost would be given; the memorial would be a silent tribute to men and women lost in the Atlantis operation six weeks before.

The Event Group was the most secret section of the federal government outside of the National Security Agency. Their task was to uncover historical truths from the past, changes in the fabric of history that led to world-altering events. This helped identify them or their parallel in today's world, and advise the president of the consequences, good or bad, so he could make the decision whether to act or not act on a fluid situation that resembled an event from the past.

The agency was a ghostly rumor to almost everyone in government service. President of the United States Franklin Delano Roosevelt built the permanent Event Group Complex in 1943 under the strictest of secrecy. It served as a research and storage facility that protected the greatest secrets of the world's past. The concept was a child of Abraham Lincoln, thought of in the waning days of the Civil War, and finally brought into being as an official agency by Woodrow Wilson. The group's chartered mission was to uncover the civilization altering events that could change the course of history.

The Atlantis incident was the reason they were gathered today, to pay their respects to those lost. The scrolls of that once-mythical civilization, which described a weapon of immense power that could shatter cities by the manipulation of the earth's plate tectonics, were discovered thousands of years later by an unscrupulous society that attempted a financial takeover of the world. This group was responsible for the deaths of millions, including the men and women remembered today.

Captain Carl Everett stood hidden in the back of the cafeteria with eyes lowered. His best friend, the head of the security department, was why he was there. Now promoted into that friend's position within the Event Group, Everett was hesitant to start his new duties.

He failed to see a small man stand in the front of the room and move silently toward him. Director Niles Compton cleared his throat when he saw Everett was deep in thought.

"Sorry, I was someplace else," Everett said, adjusting the sleeves of his blue jumpsuit.

"You're not wearing your class-A naval uniform," Niles stated.

"I really didn't think I would find myself here."

"I see. Thinking about Jack?" Niles asked.

"Well, more Sarah than Jack."

"Captain, Lieutenant McIntire is where she needs to be. I ordered her home to spare her things like this. She doesn't need a complexwide gathering to remind her she lost Jack. She needs to heal up, and then return to the Group when she's ready, not before."

Everett only nodded his head.

Sarah McIntire had been in love with Jack Collins, and his loss had affected her far more than anyone. She was outwardly strong and wanted to stay, but Director Compton had ordered immediate convalescent leave at her mother's in Arkansas.

"Captain—" Niles caught himself being officious. "Carl, go back to your department. We have to get the Group restaffed. You have some flights to make to different bases for recruitment, to get the security department up and running again. The world moves on."

"Yes, sir," Everett said as the last refrains of "Brothers in Arms" echoed inside the large cafeteria.

The large assembly of Event Group personnel started moving out of their chairs, and passed by Everett silently. He locked eyes with two men, Lieutenant Jason Ryan, detached from the navy, and Lieutenant Will Mendenhall, a former staff sergeant in the army and recently promoted to second lieutenant. They nodded their greeting, and then walked past the captain.

Everett saw their strength. Saw that no matter what, they would move on, not forgetting about Jack Collins and the others, but keeping what they had with the man close inside themselves. Everett decided he would do the same.

They would all honor Jack by doing their duty.

THE WHITE HOUSE,
WASHINGTON, D.C.

The president was sitting in the Oval Office, looking over a speech he had written for his appearance at the United Nations the next day. His address would cover the humanitarian efforts currently being conducted by the free world to assist North Korea and the Russian Republic in rebuilding the areas of their countries ravaged by earthquakes during the Atlantis incident, about which the public knew nothing. The extremist cell behind the earthquakes had been dealt with in the harshest capital terms, and now the president was trying to put the pieces of a smashed world economy back into the black.

He was sipping coffee when the phone buzzed. "Yes," he said into the intercom.

"Mr. President, the director of the FBI is insisting upon seeing you."

"Send him in, please."

William Cummings and National Security Advisor Harford Lehman soon entered hurriedly.

The president looked at both men with his coffee cup raised halfway to his mouth.

"Billy, Harrison, it hasn't been a good couple of days, and you're not here to cheer me up, are you?" he said, placing his speech on the desk.

"We received this at ten this morning, addressed to me personally. I am instructed to forward it to you."

The president set his cup down, opened the red-bordered file, and read the first page.

"And you're taking this seriously?" he asked the director as he flipped to the next page.

"Yes, sir, the communication came in through a secure FBI covert channel used only for field operatives in foreign service. Someone knows an awful lot about our procedures to crack that little gem."

"You're thinking a terrorist threat?"

"That's our conclusion, but it really doesn't matter at this point."

"All it is asking is that we convince Venezuela to delay the opening of the oil production facilities in Caracas for seventy-two hours; then this faction, whoever they are, will address to the world the reasons why the plant cannot go online."

The president held up his hand when both men started to say something.

"President Chavez isn't exactly listening to us Americans lately; he won't want to delay opening that facility because of a threat passed to him through us. Remember, I signed the OAS petition to have him closed down. If he won't listen to his neighbors in the Organization of American States, he sure as hell won't listen to me, not with China and most of the European Union screaming for his product."

"Sir, some maniac is threatening him with a nuclear strike if that plant goes online," Harford Lehman said, pointing at the message.

"Of course we'll pass this on to the Venezuelan authorities with the highest alert possible, but they won't take this threat seriously. Are we chasing down any leads on this?"

"We have the obvious courses of action in the loop now, sir—Greenpeace, the Coalition for Green Solution, but they wouldn't issue such a threat; they know everyone would take it as a joke. A nuclear strike is somewhat beyond their power scope, and also a bit counterproductive to their goals."

The president looked from the director of the FBI to his security advisor. He then pressed his intercom.

"Marjorie, I need to speak with our ambassador in Venezuela. He has to get President Chavez to take a call from me; it's most imperative that he listen to what I have to say. If that fails, I need the ambassador of China to that country. I have to talk to someone down there. Also get the directors of CIA and NSA in here, ASAP."

"We wouldn't term this as plausible, but breaking into our secure computer system makes this more than just your average nut," the FBI director said, looking directly at the president. "They could have done God knows what to our system, but their only interest was to get our attention and to pass on this message."

The president closed the folder in front of him.

"Well, whoever they are did exactly that, didn't they?"

2

He was dreaming once again. As before in other dreams, he tried desperately for that one snatch of breath but found the effort far too great for the mere reward of air. He allowed the hot waters of the sea to claim his body even as his mind refused to submit. The past swirled about him as did the water, spinning him in all directions.

He saw in the dream the darkness close in, as did the feeling of loss, not for himself, but of something, or someone just out of sight of his dying consciousness. A womanly smile momentarily lingered at the edge of memory and then vanished. He felt the horrible pressure of the sea as it started to claim his physical body. He could stand it no longer; he opened his mouth and tried for the breath he so desperately needed. The hot waters of the exploding sea entered his parched mouth, and then the pain he had been feeling started to fade.

The sunlight from above dimmed, and his body grew limp. He was drowning, and while that was once a repugnant thought to him, it now became comforting. He knew he had succeeded in what he had started out to do, and so it was all right. His mind was at ease, except for that one thing his memory could not grasp.

The dream took a different turn, as it always did at this point. Hands were pulling him away, pulling him deeper. He always wanted to shout out that he was dying, so why not just let him get on with it. Regardless of his pleas, they would still pull him down until a false bright light filtered into his closed eyes. Then the pain started as it always did, but now for the first time, a new element was added to this most uncomfortable dream—voices from the dark.

"Our guest is coming around."

"Captain, you scared me. The last I heard you were sound asleep in your cabin."

"The last I heard, Doctor, I had the freedom of my own ship."

"Yes, ma'am, I was just—"

"This man is far more formidable than you are used to dealing with, Doctor. I do not want him to know where he is, and he is not to know who pulled him from the water. Can you keep him under?"

"I can place him into a coma if need be. If I may ask, why save him if he is a danger to you—to us?"

"I have my plans for him. With what I can learn from this man, the dangers are worth the risk of his being here, and we can avoid the risk of losing our asset inside his agency."

"Captain, why the sudden change of mind about placing the implant inside this man?"

"I believe your job onboard this vessel is as physician, mine as captain. That is all you need know."

The dream was fading and the man's mind seemed to be dimming with it. The voices in the dark had an echoing lilt to them as he fell deeper into the abyss of the mind, but the man managed to force his eyes open, if only for a bright, flashing moment. There was a figure standing in the dark. Then he heard a mechanical announcement: "Captain, we have come to the specified coordinates." *With that the figure turned and vanished.*

A moment passed, and then with blurry vision he saw another, very much smaller form step from the back of the room. Then a soft voice—

"Why did you allow the captain to cancel this man's surgery, Doctor?"

"You heard her, she's the captain and she—what are you doing with that? The captain said no implant!"

The man tried desperately to open his eyes. He saw the small figure holding a jar, or was it a glass? The figure handed the object to a man who was sitting down. Before his eyes fluttered closed, he saw the thing in the jar—a gelatinous, tentacled mass, clear, bluish in color, and about the size of an aspirin as it floated at the center of a clear solution. The man tried to frame a thought, but as he did the world went dark, and sleep started to overtake him once more.

Before going completely under, the man saw that someone was standing over him, looking at him for the longest time, as if examining him, seeking a truth of something he could not begin to understand. The smallish figure was but a shadow, but he could swear the eyes were bright blue and ringed in green, just as the deep and cold oceans.

"We need to keep a closer eye on our captain, Doctor."

SEVENTY-FIVE MILES OFF THE COAST OF VENEZUELA

The aged supertanker *Goliath* made her way slowly along the Venezuelan coast, her empty oil bunkers allowing the VLCC (Very Large Crude Carrier) to ride high, well above her loaded waterline. The newly constructed crude depot at Caracas waited to load her with its inaugural shipment of refined oil from the controversial facility. The many construction shortcuts and current unrest of union oil workers allowed a pall of contention and outright anger to hover over the plant's ceremonious opening.

The Panamanian-flagged *Goliath* was no stranger to controversy herself as she plied her way toward port. The old, decrepit tanker was a constant thorn in the side of most nations and oil companies, as her deteriorating double-hulled design was continually leaking her wares into the open sea. It was only the recently rogue nation of Venezuela that kept the supertanker viable and in business, as the other exporting nations shunned her almost to the scrapheap.

A mile to her stern was her ever-present Greenpeace escort, *Atlantic Avenger*, out of Perth, Australia. She shadowed *Goliath*, taking water samples and harassing the great vessel whenever she could. The Chinese diesel-powered attack submarine *Red Banner* shadowed both vessels at one kilometer away, far beneath the sea. The communist Chinese government was taking massive, and some would say illegal, steps to ensure *Goliath* made her delivery date in the next few weeks, as the oil-poor superpower sought desperately to feed her ever-expanding industrial might.

On the bridge of *Goliath*, Captain Lars Petersen scanned the waters just to the south. The telltale wake of a submarine periscope was cutting a wide, intentionally arrogant path through the Atlantic as the Chinese made their presence known to the activist ship shadowing them. Petersen smiled, and then walked out onto the bridge wing, scanning his binoculars to the south and west.

The *Atlantic Avenger* was starting to make her hourly run toward the stern of the giant ship. They would pass close to the supertanker, filming the leakage of her bunkers and holding up their protest banners stating his vessel was the scourge of the sea.

"We have surface contact bearing one-three-eight degrees. Contact is possible Venezuelan navy escort vessel."

Captain Petersen took one last look at the 100-foot Greenpeace ship, then turned to his first officer.

"Our friends are starting their harassment run. Watch them and make sure they keep the proper safety distance."

"Aye, Captain."

Petersen stepped into the giant bridge of the *Goliath* and scanned the horizon. He finally spied the vessel in question, and he could see by her silhouette it was their old friend, the *General Santiago*, a small missile frigate formerly belonging to the French navy and then sold to Venezuela five years before.

"I have visual contact. Send to *General Santiago* welcome and to please take up station to our starboard beam. Inform them we have a friendly submerged contact bearing one kilometer astern."

"Aye, sir."

Petersen was about to walk out onto the bridge wing and view the Greenpeace run on his ship when a sudden, piercingly loud alarm warning sounded.

"We have a submerged contact bearing zero-one-nine at two thousand yards. This is a hard contact, we wouldn't have heard it, but—oh, my God—someone is opening torpedo tubes to the sea!"

"What?" Petersen was taken back by the sudden, stunning announcement.

"We have high-speed noises, possible torpedoes in the water!"

The captain froze in abject horror. His first officer called out he had a visual on the spot of contact, but Petersen just stood frozen to the deck.

"Torpedoes?" was all he could get out of his frozen throat.

PRC (PEOPLE'S REPUBLIC OF CHINA) SUBMARINE *RED BANNER*

"What do you mean, torpedoes?" Captain Xian Jiang asked loudly as he picked up a set of headphones at the sonar station and listened.

The high-pitched sound was nothing like the turning propellers of any high-speed torpedo he had ever heard. His sonar man was saying something about the new quieter air-jet powered weapons the Americans had been working on instead of listening; he slammed his fist down on the operator's shoulder to quiet him. He heard the sound of the approaching weapons when a loud pop sounded in the headphones.

"More torpedoes in the water!" the operator called out. "They are actively seeking and are bearing right on *us*!"

"Distance?" Xian shouted.

"Three hundred yards—closing fast!"

"Impossible. Nothing could have gotten that close without being detected."

"Sir, nonetheless, we are under attack. The weapons went active as soon as they hit the water—torpedoes have acquired!"

"All-ahead flank, hard left rudder! Weapons Officer, match bearing on the attack line and fire! Countermeasures, launch a full spread!"

The Chinese Akula class attack boat swayed and dipped violently as she maneuvered her heavy bulk to the left of the attacking torpedoes. Arrayed along the aft quarter of the submarine, a line of canisters popped free and began to release a burst of sound cocooned in bubbles into the surrounding water that was a mimicked recording of her own electric power plant noises, including the cavitations print of her bronze propeller. As the massive vessel turned, the two strange missile-shaped torpedoes turned with her. The *Red Banner*'s propeller finally grasped the water and shot down and to the left, but she could not shake the oncoming weapons that had doubled the boat's speed—both weapons shot cleanly through the countermeasures without hesitation.

The captain froze as men started shouting orders. He knew they had but three seconds of life left to them.

The torpedoes struck almost simultaneously at the stern and under her keel amidships. The immense pressure wave cracked the Chinese hull like an eggshell and crushed all aboard in a microsecond.

Petersen finally caught sight of the two fast-approaching torpedoes that had suddenly popped toward the surface. In absolute horror he saw, in surreal slow motion, the Greenpeace vessel *Atlantic Avenger* innocently and unknowingly swing her razor-sharp bow into the oncoming path of the outside weapon. The torpedo struck, blowing her beautifully painted bow off in a violent explosion that shook the giant oil tanker.

Petersen now had a slim hope that the remaining weapon would not be enough to hurt his massive ship. As he grasped on to that lone shred of hope, a sudden explosion to the south sent water upward into a plume of white foam and violence that announced that two subsurface-to-surface missiles were launched, just as the errant torpedo had been sent into the wrong ship. First one, then the other missile arched into the blue sky. As one missile kept climbing, the other turned down, and to the north as it streaked far ahead of the waterbound torpedo. The missile slammed into *Goliath* at her stern, ripping free her rudder and sending men sprawling to her elongated deck.

"We're hit!" someone called from the bridge.

Petersen wanted to scream in frustration for the officer to tell him something he did not know. However, before he could he saw that the second missile had turned toward the advancing Venezuelan missile frigate. Just as he saw the naval vessel start a slow turn to the west, the first torpedo slammed violently into *Goliath*'s side, sending a giant mushroom cloud of steel and vaporized oil into the sky. Petersen tried to pick himself up off the deck as the ship was rocked again, this time from a distance as the second missile found its mark and slammed into the afterdeck of the guided missile frigate *General Santiago*, two miles away.

Who could be doing this? His mind raged as he reached for the sill lining the front windows of the bridge. *Could it be the Americans, the Russians?* They were the only two nations capable of such stealth and weaponry. The captain finally managed to gain his feet and look out onto the expanding horror that was *Goliath*'s foredeck. Fires were raging, and he could see the giant ship was starting to list severely to starboard.

"Mr. Jansen, counterflood! Goddamn it, counterflood the port bunkers!"

"More missiles in the air!" someone screamed.

As Petersen looked on in shock, six separate trails of fire exited the sea. Four streaked to the west, gaining altitude, and two came directly at them. He managed a quick glance down at *Atlantic Avenger* just as she started to slide bow first into the green sea, and crew and protesters were sliding and jumping from her decks. He closed his eyes in a silent prayer for them as the next two missiles found their mark, driving deep into the superstructure of the tanker.

The detonations shook the ocean for thirty-five miles in all directions as the old ship came apart and evaporated in her final, violent, split-second death. The expanding fireball that incinerated all who struggled to remain on the surface swallowed the surviving crew along with the remaining detritus of the *Atlantic Avenger.* Those who fought for survival beneath the water were torn to pieces by the pressure wave that slammed into them at over a thousand feet per second, sending their flesh into a billion microscopic additions to the raging sea, and also into the gathering mushroom cloud that was expanding like the rising sun over the green ocean.

CARACAS, VENEZUELA

The newly constructed crude-oil facility owned and operated by the Citgo Oil concern was a monstrosity that had displaced seventy-five thousand impoverished inhabitants in the suburbs of Caracas. Outside of her main gates, six hundred of these citizens stood side by side with five hundred union workers, protesting both their recent treatment by Venezuelan government and the nationalization of the oil industry, thus tossing the unions into oblivion.

Security was not only there for the protesters. Word had come down that there had been some sort of threat passed on by the American government concerning the opening of the world's most controversial oil facility.

Two miles inside the main gates, officials from China, Cuba, and Venezuela were on hand for the dedication ceremony. The concern was a joint financial venture between the three nations in an effort to thwart the United States and her allies—mainly Saudi Arabia—in what they considered unfair manipulation of the world's oil supplies.

The CEO of CITGO Petroleum and the interior minister of Venezuela shook hands, smiling broadly. The latter was there in place of president for life Hugo Chavez, a sworn enemy of the very democracies that had helped them in their national oil exploration treaties a decade before. Even after the threat that had been passed on by the president of the United States, Chavez still held firm that nothing and no one would stand in the way of his achieving an international power base and a strategic partner in China for his oil products. He even had announced plans for expanding into the Gulf of Mexico—an area that was quickly becoming a hot spot for environmentalists.

The interior minister was about to take the microphone to denounce the unpatriotic actions of the protesters outside the gates when air raid sirens began to blare loudly around the new facility. The Venezuelan minister looked around in confusion, the smile still stretched across his dark features, when three security men jumped upon the stage, took him by the arms, and moved him off the raised platform. The Chinese representative looked on in confusion, as did his Cuban counterpart. Then another set of military police appeared and harshly pulled the two diplomats to their feet.

"What is the meaning of this?" the Cuban minister cried out in Spanish as he was pulled unceremoniously from the dais.

"We have an air force warning of incoming cruise missiles. Please come with us, we have to—"

That was as far as the military security guard's explanation got, as the sound of four shrieking missiles froze everyone inside and outside the oil facility.

"Look!" the Chinese minister shouted as he pointed skyward.

As they turned, they saw the distinctive vapor trails of four missiles as they crossed over dry ground from their trek inland from the sea. The first missile dipped and came apart just over the crude-oil loading facility. A nuclear airburst set to detonate at three hundred feet vaporized both the docks and the pipeline that carried crude from the plant to the oceanside loading facility. The next three missiles traveled one, two, and three miles inland, then detonated over the two-mile-wide plant itself. The fireball created by the simultaneous detonations was in the yield range of 5.5 megatons each, a relatively light package by military standards, melting steel and flash-frying human flesh as the brand-new controversial facility, along with everyone present, ceased to exist in the blink of an eye. The weapons did not differentiate protester from government lackey, as all were instantly vaporized in a microsecond of heat and wind.

Twenty miles offshore the great monster rose from the sea to expose her conning tower and the large rudder fins at her stern—the tower so tall that if viewed it would have looked as if a mountain suddenly rose from the roiling sea. The great beast's interior electronics recorded wind conditions and temperature variants from the sea and outlying land coordinates, without a soul having to be exposed to the air. The gleaming black hull glistened in what remained of the morning sun and blue sky, which was quickly becoming cloud-laden and threatening rain. The darkening skies nearly matched the countenance of the giant vessel's captain, as the attack area was surveyed on monitors in the main control center and the conning tower overlooking the scene of devastation.

The captain stood, walked to the spiral staircase that wound its way upward through the skyscraper-sized conning tower, and then opened the hatch to the private observation suite. Once there the captain examined the waters outside the three-foot-thick, twenty-five-foot-diameter port viewing window sitting just above the waves that hit harmlessly against the vessel's sonar-absorbing hull.

As the captain scanned the now-calm sea, a body floated by, bobbing in the gentle swell. The captain's eyes closed as the body struck the hull and then continued, spinning and dipping in the sea. The dead had been a woman, dressed in civilian clothes, indicating she might have been one of the Greenpeace volunteers from the unintentionally destroyed *Atlantic Avenger*. The captain looked away just as orders were shouted below to get under way, and the burned and mangled body mercifully vanished from sight.

"Captain, we have a submerged contact at twenty kilometers and closing—possible submarine close-aboard. Computer says there is a ninety-three percent possibility it is a Los Angeles class attack boat. We will have her prop signature momentarily."

The captain continued to stare at the now-still waters where three ships and a submarine had once been. Then the deep blue eyes closed as three mushroom shaped clouds slowly rose from the west, indicating their attack there had concluded.

The war those fools sought had begun in the violent way all wars start, and the winner upon this new battlefront would be no nation that currently held power in the world. The winner would be *life* itself.

"Take her down to two thousand feet. As we clear the continental shelf, bring her up to seventy-five knots, on a heading to our next objective. It is neither the time nor the place to confront the U.S. Navy. They'll have other concerns very soon."

"Aye, Captain."

With that, the giant vessel slipped under the waves and silently departed the attack zone specifically chosen two years before this dark day, just after the announcement of the day that oil operations were to commence at the damnable facility.

The captain moved away from the thick acrylic window, using a control on the chair behind to close the clamshell titanium cover, and then slowly made for the control room. "Please send the surgeon to my cabin."

"Aye, Captain," the first officer said as he snapped his fingers at the bridge security officer and pointed aft, sending him to collect the doctor.

Around the fully holographic control center of the giant beast, the crew looked upon their captain with admiration and dedication.

The most amazing machine in the history of the world was brought up to her cruising speed, and then silently started making her way south.

On the surface above, only smoldering debris marked the spot where the giant vessel had been only moments before. The captain of this strange submarine knew that soon the sea would heal itself, and the sea life there would return to normal, never to be placed in danger by humankind again.

USS *COLUMBIA* (SSN 771)
125 KILOMETERS EAST OF VENEZUELAN
COASTAL WATERS

The United States fast-attack nuclear submarine USS *Columbia* was shallow as she attempted to gather readings from the air and water surrounding the boat. Then the large sub went back into deep water to evaluate their readings.

The Los Angeles class submarine had been on maneuvers with one of the newest Ohio-class missile boats, USS *Maine* (SSBN 741) while they conducted DSEM (Deep Submergence Evasive Maneuvering), a new drill thought up by COMSUBLANT (Commander, Submarine Force, U.S. Atlantic Fleet).

The *Columbia*, normally based in Hawaii, had recently finished a scheduled refit at Newport News, Virginia, at the general dynamics facility. From there she was ordered to conduct operations with *Maine* on her return trip back around the Horn of South America. The drill suddenly halted when the waters fifty kilometers to the south erupted in sound. While the *Maine* went deep and evacuated the area for security reasons, the *Columbia* went south at flank speed to investigate the war noises emanating somewhere off the coastline of Venezuela.

Captain John Lofgren watched the readings on the infrared detectors and frowned. He turned to his first officer, Lt. Commander Richard Green, and shook his head.

"Whatever happened up there, it was hot as hell. The water temperature is twenty degrees above normal. Moreover, what were those strange noises prior to all hell breaking loose? They weren't any torpedo sounds I've ever heard before. "

"We have confirmation, Captain," the chief of the boat called out. "We have elevated but still low radiation readings on the surface. Computers still say nuclear detonation, probably light in yield."

"We're also picking up elevated levels of airborne contaminate coming in from the west," a second tech called from his station.

"What in the hell is going on?" Lofgren asked as he returned to control. "Dick, we have to get this off to COMSUBLANT—let's get *Columbia* up to periscope depth."

TWO HOURS LATER

Captain Lofgren was holding the set of headphones to his ears as he listened inside of the BQQ-5E sonar suite.

"I still don't hear a thing," he said to his sonar team.

"It's there, Captain, five miles outside of the target area. Just as we were approaching station it passed right beneath us," Petty Officer John Cleary said as he adjusted the volume control to the captain's headset.

"Tell me again what in the hell it's supposed to be I'm listening for?"

The young petty officer seemed lost for words again as he looked from his captain to the first officer standing just inside the curtain of the sonar station.

"It's like . . . like . . . a pressure wave of some kind, and it's moving extremely fast. The only thing that can cause something like that is a large object moving through the sea. We hear the same thing with whales, only on a smaller scale."

"I just don't hear it."

"How fast did you say it was moving again?" the first officer asked.

This time the operator looked at his training partner, who had also failed to hear the strange noise. He swallowed, then looked at the two officers.

"About seventy-six knots. I measured the speed of the pressure wave against our static location."

Lofgren removed the headphones and looked at the operator, but Cleary kept his eyes straight ahead, not flinching away from his captain's questioning look.

"Captain, it went to almost eighty knots speed after I detected it, and at the moment it passed beneath us I felt the boat . . ." He stopped, knowing the explanation would sound too amazing to believe.

"Felt the boat what?"

"I have the computer and depth track on paper to back me on this, Captain."

Lofgren didn't say anything as he waited.

"*Columbia* actually rose in depth by eight feet as water under our keel was displaced by whatever it was that plowed beneath us when we came into the affected area." The sonar man pulled a graph and showed it to the two officers. "One minute we're at three hundred and three feet of depth, the next we went to two hundred and ninety-five—a difference of eight feet. Something monstrous passed beneath our keel at that exact time. What could move a Los Angeles class boat by that much depth from that far away?"

The first officer raised his eyebrows and looked at Lofgren.

"I guess it would have had to have been big to shove aside that much water. Are you sure the object was that deep?"

Again, the young man was hesitant to answer. "Captain, it was so deep that . . ." He saw the impatience showing on both officers' faces. "About fifteen hundred feet at first contact."

"Fifteen hundred feet of depth and then it suddenly sprang like a cheetah up to seventy-five knots? I can't buy that, Cleary. Not even the Russians have anything remotely close to half that," the first officer said.

"Write it up, Cleary, and get it to me. We'll bait the hook and send it out and see if anyone at COMSUBLANT bites."

As Captain Lofgren returned to the conn, he half-turned to his first officer.

"Before you say anything, Dick, we know the attack on the surface happened, and we know *Columbia* didn't do it. Therefore, someone else had to have done it. In addition, that someone did it in clear listening range of not only us, but also that Chinese sub they handled with ease. I'll bet my command that the attacker and Cleary's strange contact are one and the same."

The captain turned and saw the eyes of his crew looking at him. The unknowns being pondered frightened them, and he could see it.

Every man aboard knew they had something in the water that could outrun and outgun them, and nothing made an American submariner more concerned than an *unseen* and *unknown* enemy.

3

EVENT GROUP COMPLEX,
NELLIS AIR FORCE BASE, NEVADA

Director Niles Compton sat with the sixteen departmental heads of the Event Group, silently watching a briefing delivered to the President of the United States by his national security team from the White House. The council there did not know the Event Group was listening in.

"With our losses in the sea of Japan five weeks ago, our weakened status dictates that we have to redeploy our forces even more thinly than they are," the Chairman of the Joint Chiefs, General Kenneth Caulfield, said as he stood before the large situation board.

"Ken, we'll get back to that. What I want to know is what we have on the attacks in Venezuela."

Caulfield nodded toward Admiral Fuqua, the naval chief of staff, who opened a file folder and cleared his throat as if he were uncomfortable with what he was about to say.

"The detonations at sea against the oil tanker, the Greenpeace vessel, and the Chinese attack submarine were nuclear in nature. The yield of each weapon estimated at only five-point-six kilotons. As with the warheads detonated over Caracas, the radiation yield was almost nonexistent. These were the cleanest weapons we have ever come across. Dissipation occurred only hours after the attacks, and there are no lingering effects to air, ground, or sea."

"That's impossible," ventured the president's national security advisor. "No one has weapons that clean, we would have—"

"Andy, what have the boys across the river come up with on where this nuclear material originated?" the president asked CIA Director Andrew Cummings.

"Well, sir, the samples sent to us by courier from our naval asset in the area support no conclusions as to where this material was bred; they only raise more questions."

"Come on, Andy, I'm not going to hold you to it. Give me what your people are thinking."

"We have nothing on record as far as a nuclear fingerprint goes. This material may have been spawned by a breeder reactor that has not been identified."

"Again, that's impossible; the Nuclear Regulatory Commission has—"

"Damn it." The president slammed his palm down on the tabletop, cutting his security advisor short once more. "I think everyone in this room better have learned by now that there are people out there we know nothing about. The Atlantis incident should have taught you that. Assume we have someone out there that can toss clean nukes around. Let's concentrate on finding out who and why, not the impossibility of it," the president said angrily.

In Nevada, Niles Compton glanced at several of his key people, including Captain Carl Everett of the security department and Virginia Pollock, the assistant director of the Event Group. They both saw Niles nod toward them, indicating they would be assigned the task of efforting the problem of clean nukes on their end, at least historically speaking, to see if any research conducted in the past historical record could be uncovered. Without being ordered to do so, Niles hoped to help his old friend in the White House with something the Event Group might have in their database. The Event Group had vast archives on the discovery, engineering, and manufacture of fissionable materials for their study.

"We *may* have a break as to the *why* part of the equation, Mr. President," Cummings said in Washington as he opened another red-bordered file folder.

"Go ahead, Andy, something is better than nothing. I'm tired of finding things out at the last minute and playing catch-up; we've been bloodied the past six weeks by groups who have slipped by our intelligence services." He saw that his comment stung almost every man and woman in the room. Even his best friend in Nevada, Niles Compton, felt the rebuke.

"Sir, we do know that the supertanker that was hit was banned from every oil pumping station in the world, with the exception of Caracas, for environmental reasons. Venezuela had leased her, and China was the only nation that agreed to allow her to dock at their off-loading facilities in Shanghai."

"Okay, we have a starting point. Andy, get with the EPA and get me some exact numbers on the leakage. Knowing Chavez, he's going to start throwing around accusations, and we've been his popular target lately. I do not want another leader of a third world nation saying we did something we did not do. Steve, I want you to head up the relief for Caracas. Get as much food, medical, and other essential material down there as we can spare. Those people need help regardless of who their leader is."

Steve Haskins of Emergency Management nodded and made notes.

"Ken, Admiral Fuqua: best guess, who could have done this?"

"Ladies and gentlemen, with the exception of the Directors of CIA, FBI, NSA, the Secretary of Defense, and the National Security Advisor and the Joint Chiefs, would you please excuse us. Mr. President, I don't know who's on the other end of that camera, but I advise shutting it down," General Caulfield said, suspecting that the answer lay in the strange little man who had assisted in the Atlantis operation a few weeks before, part of the president's private think tank.

"I'll leave it on for now, Ken. With the exception of those named, please excuse us."

The rest of the cabinet and council filed quickly from the room.

When the room cleared, Caulfield nodded toward Admiral Fuqua, who stood and pulled down a viewing screen as the lights dimmed.

"Mr. President, we have information we received from the attack boat USS *Columbia*, one of our newest Los Angeles class subs. She is the asset I spoke of earlier. She may have picked up a glimmer of something else, maybe the attacking force, we're not sure. As you see, this is a tape of her sonar."

On the screen was the waterfall display from the BQQ passive sonar display on *Columbia*. It was a series of lines running downward on the screen, and these lines represented the water around the sub. As they watched, there was nothing out of the ordinary on the display screen. Then a shadow of darkness presented itself for a split second and vanished.

"This object was thought at first to be a glitch in the sonar, but we have learned the object was solid, and we caught it only because of the burst of speed it displayed when it started diving away from the attack area. It's three and a half miles off *Columbia*'s bow. The estimate of its size is close to a thousand feet in length, and it went from a static, or zero buoyancy, position to over seventy knots."

Several men started speaking at once while the president sat in his chair looking at the sonar display.

"This object was verified by a depth chart graph showing the keel of *Columbia* raised eight feet in depth as whatever this thing is passed beneath her—and that is substantiated. So with this strange blip on sonar, coupled with the massive water displacement, there's little doubt we have one hell of a problem out there," Fuqua added.

Far beneath Nellis Air Force Base, the conference room was silent. The events the department heads had been witness to while attached to the department would never allow for surprise at any one thing they were shown. Unlike the military and intelligence people at the White House, they were at least accustomed to holding their opinions until all the details could be brought out into the open. As Niles watched the Group, he saw Virginia Pollock was deep in thought, biting her lower lip.

"I don't believe anything can travel that fast," the president said from the White House.

"*Columbia* is due home this afternoon, sir. We have a team on standby ready to board her and take that sonar system apart. But as it stands right now, we may have something in the sea that will prevent us from securing the sea lanes," Fuqua answered, returning to his seat as the lights came up.

"Okay, thank you. Get me the information as soon as you can. I have a phone meeting with the president of China in fifteen minutes, so excuse me for now, gentlemen."

After everyone had left, the president picked up the phone and hit a small button.

"So, Bookworm, what do you think of that?"

Niles Compton looked around, embarrassed at the use of the president's nickname for him. There were smiles all around as the department heads started gathering their notes to leave. Niles quickly snapped his fingers and got Everett's attention, gesturing him back down into his seat.

"What I think is irrelevant at this point. If the navy is worried, it doesn't do much to spark confidence in myself, especially as weak as we are at the moment."

"You have people out there that can outthink *anyone* I have. Get someone on this and find out if history says we may have a problem here. Technology like this couldn't have sprung up overnight. The research for it may be somewhere in your vast files."

"Already on it," Niles answered.

"I hate using you as a crutch here, Niles, but—well, do your thing for me. Now, how's the Group doing?" the president asked with concern.

"Losing Jack and his people—well, we were never really geared for these kinds of losses, but we're moving on."

"Okay, Mr. Director, I have to go and speak with the Chinese about their destroyed sub."

"Yes, sir," Niles said as he terminated the call and turned toward Everett. "You seem to be someplace other than here, Captain."

"Is it that obvious?" he asked as he rubbed his tired eyes.

"Are you getting any sleep?" Alice Hamilton, the director's assistant since 1945, asked.

Virginia didn't say anything as she looked down at her notepad.

"Have you spoken with Sarah since she went home?" Alice asked.

Everett smiled at Alice's question. She always knew how to get directly to the point, and did it with a modicum of grandmotherly censure that didn't make you feel like a thief of her time.

"She'll heal. She is tougher than she thinks—hell, we all are."

Niles nodded his head, and then brought the team back to the business at hand.

"Virginia, get some expertise on naval functions from Captain Everett, and also start investigating these clean nukes. Somewhere in our files we have information on those who have come close to making such weapons. Not much, but that's where we'll start."

Niles saw Virginia nod her head once, but she remained silent as she took her notepad and left without acknowledging anyone.

LITTLE ROCK, ARKANSAS

Second Lieutenant Sarah McIntire sat in her darkened bedroom and stared at the wall. She absentmindedly reached up with her right hand and lightly rubbed her shoulder, which was still in a sling. The music she was listening to was as dark as her room, and her thoughts. The Moody Blues had been one of Jack's favorites, and Sarah now found that she couldn't get enough, particularly of the dark melody emanating from the small speakers in the corner. "Nights in White Satin," their most haunting song, sank deep into Sarah's soul and burned itself into her psyche.

A single tear built in her left eye and then slowly traveled down her cheek as she absently wiped it away. She was still weak from the bullet she had taken in the battle for the sunken city of Atlantis, and she knew that because of losing Jack, her recovery was lagging.

The door opened and her mother, not hesitating as she had done the past week, stepped inside, flipping on the light switch. Her next move made Sarah wake up as the stereo was turned off abruptly.

"From what you told me of this fella Jack, I don't think he would care for you sittin' here in the dark, moping around and feeling sorry for yourself. You need to get up and work some of this despair out of your system."

Sarah looked up at her mother. The woman was almost an older version of Sarah herself. Short at five feet, and with the same dark hair, only eight inches longer. She was thin and had none of the Arkansas homemaker demeanor about her. She faced her daughter with hands on hips and a frown on her pretty face.

"You tell me, is this any way for an officer in the army to act? I'm sure soldiers have lost friends before. Are you something special—the rules don't apply to you?"

Sarah looked from her mother to the far wall of her room, which hadn't changed one bit since she left home after joining the army six years before.

"Did it hurt you when Daddy left us?" Sarah asked, not able to look into her mother's eyes.

Becky McIntire half-smiled, sad attempt though it was, and then sat on the edge of Sarah's small bed.

"Oh, I hurt something fierce. Having you was what kept me from straying from the course of your upbringing. Without you, I doubt I would have been much good to myself. You were all I had." She smiled and touched her daughter's leg. "But you? Why, your letters to me tell of the people you work with, the way they all respect you, and the way you explained Jack in those letters, well, let's just say he didn't leave you like your daddy left me, honey. He was taken—and that is a world of difference. You know the folks you work with are hurtin' too. Maybe they need you back there at your base—just maybe they need help from you to make sense of this. You go on and hurt, but sooner or later you're going to get up out of that chair and do what your colonel expects of you."

"And what is that, Mother?" Sarah asked, knowing her mom's humor was about to be exposed for the first time in the week she had been home.

"To get your ass out into my garden and do some weeding, of course! Or get on a plane and go back to work. They need you more than I do."

For the first time since she awoke to find Jack Collins gone from her life, Sarah smiled, and then cried hard with her head in her mother's lap.

The next morning, Sarah boarded a plane bound for McCarran Airport in Las Vegas. She needed the men and women there because now she knew she could never heal without them. Second Lieutenant Sarah McIntire, with her arm still in a sling, was going home to heal among her friends at the Event Group.

TWO HUNDRED NAUTICAL MILES
OFF THE COAST OF WASHINGTON, D.C.

The room was dark and the man still slept his unnatural sleep. The doctor sat at his desk watching the comatose patient's breathing, and became worried at its shallowness. He heard the door to the infirmary open and then silently close with a pneumatic hiss. He knew who stood just inside the doorway, tucked into the shadows.

"We cannot keep him like this much longer. His breathing is shallow and his vitals, although stable for right now, are showing signs of deterioration."

"We will have need of him soon. He is vital for our assault; he will limit the possible response by their security for the second part of our response. You may start to bring him out of it if you wish."

"I read the file on this man that your spy sent us, Captain. You're right, he's a very dangerous individual," the doctor said as he finally turned his chair toward the darkness by the door.

"Yes," said the voice. "I will have security relieve you of him as soon as he is conscious. Is it possible to have him ready to travel within twenty-four hours, Doctor?"

"Possibly, with a shot of adrenalin and a vitamin B-12 booster after he's conscious, but I wouldn't recommend it." The doctor turned and saw the captain's eyes were heavily dilated. "Are you feeling all right, Captain? The prescription I gave you should have run out by now. . . . You . . . you are not abusing doctor's orders, are you?"

Silence was his only answer. The doctor looked at the clock on the wall and saw that it was only 0440. The combination of sleeplessness and her narcotic addiction worried him. In this condition she seemed docile and adverse to the harshness of her earlier orders. The captain stepped into the light, and he saw that she looked, at least for the moment, as if she were now more awake. Even the eye dilation was settling, allowing her pupils to shrink back to normal size. The heroin was wearing off.

"We are striking at the U.S. facility today—without a warning to the president being delivered beforehand." The dark shape of the captain's hand reached up and rubbed at the right temple area and then at the back of the head. "This will get the attention of the United Nations before we make our announcement to the world."

"Captain, let me at least give you something for sleep."

As he reached for the large bottle of pills he kept on his desktop, the door opened and allowed a momentary flash of light from the companionway outside the infirmary to enter. Then the door closed and the captain was gone.

The doctor looked at the bottle of sleep medication, then placed it back in its usual spot. He looked at his patient and watched his chest rise and fall.

After a few moments of thought, he opened the left-hand drawer of his desk and removed something that gleamed brightly in the dim light of his desk lamp. He stood, walked to the single occupied bed, and then snapped the handcuff to the man's wrist and looped the other end through the bedrail. As he did, he heard the first officer's voice on the speaker.

"Make all preparations for getting under way. Weapons Officer, prepare strike package Hotel-Bravo. Target: the Independence Oil refinery, Texas City."

The phone on the doctor's desk buzzed. The doctor swallowed and then picked up the receiver.

"Yes?"

"Why was the captain in sickbay?" asked the voice on the other end.

"Checking on her patient."

"You have failed to do what was asked of you?"

"I believe the captain has moments of clarity of what is truly happening. I cannot take the chance and kill this man. Right now, her only goal is consistent with your own—to find out what the outside world knows about us. She needs this man for that end."

"Have you any suspicions as to why she visits only in the early morning hours, or after she has been medicated?" the voice asked.

"No, and I will not make any assumptions. She is still the captain and I am still a part of her crew."

"Have you noticed any change in her aggressiveness during the times of her visit?"

"She seems . . . more thoughtful at those times."

"That can be worrisome. I want those drugs out of the captain's system; they cannot be good for decision making."

The line went dead.

4

Levels seventy-three and seventy-four consisted of 372 vaults. Each of these held an artifact gathered from the past. Security was electronic in nature, and was administered by the Europa computer system. Designed by the Cray Corporation, it was deemed impenetrable by an outside source. Security clearance was low for these two levels, as the artifacts housed in the chromed-steel vaults bore no historical significance for the national security of the United States. Still, the only people with access to the levels were monitored by key card and pupil eye-scan through Europa, and she in turn reported every few seconds to the security department.

On level eight, Lieutenant Will Mendenhall was on duty in the security center. He yawned and looked at the wall-mounted clock. He shook his head as the hour hand was a few minutes from hitting the number two. He was to be relieved by Jason Ryan at 2 A.M., but he could swear that the minute hand on the clock must have frozen in place.

Just as he turned in his chair to sign off on his computer terminal, the monitor lit up.

"Lieutenant Mendenhall, Europa has monitored a two hundred and fifty percent power surge on levels seventy-three and seventy-four—the security system on those levels is currently in failure mode as of oh-one-fifty-eight hours."

Mendenhall heard Europa's female voice and shook his head as Jason Ryan walked into the office, yawning and looking as if he hadn't gotten any sleep.

"What's up, Will?"

"Europa is reporting a power surge and security system failure on levels seventy-three and seventy-four. I was getting ready to—"

Ryan and Mendenhall felt a rumble pass through their feet just as warning bells started sounding throughout the facility.

"What in the hell was that?" Will asked.

"All damage-control personnel report to levels seventy-three and seventy-four immediately. This is no drill. It is recommended that all rescue and fire personnel utilize stairwells one-oh-one and two-oh-eight for access to the affected areas."

"Europa, continue broadcasting personnel direction and accept security override Mendenhall 001700. Let me know what's happened on affected levels!"

"Override accepted," Europa said. In the background Will heard her warnings still being broadcast through the complex communications system. *"All personnel—"*

Suddenly Europa went dead. The monitor was black and the sound system went down. The overhead lights flickered, went out, and then came back on. However, Europa was still nonfunctional.

"Damage report!" Will called through the intercom to the affected levels.

Jason Ryan pointed toward the door and Will nodded, knowing he was going to join the rest of security on levels seventy-three and seventy-four.

There was no reply from the lower levels. Will was getting frustrated because he couldn't direct the rescue and firefighting efforts. Then all of a sudden Europa sprang back into life, as if nothing had ever happened to her.

"Lieutenant, Europa has detected trace amounts of Composition Five explosive on levels seventy-three and seventy-four immediately after security shutdown. Total collapse of vault housings in one hundred two of three hundred seventy-two vaults. Preliminary examination of area is total loss of artifacts in seventy percent of vaults on level seventy-three and fifty percent on level seventy-four."

"Jesus Christ," Mendenhall said as he saw the video as Europa finally established a working camera on level seventy-three. The picture showed a total collapse of the rock ceiling, and somewhere fires were raging.

Captain Everett and Niles Compton surveyed the damage on level seventy-three. Temporary floodlights had been placed by the engineering department, and they cast eerie shadows on the granite boulders that had been blasted free of the excavated tunnel. Smashed and burned-out vaults had been crushed beneath the tremendous weight of the cave-in.

"Preliminary report?" Niles asked as he reached down and picked up a piece of pottery freed from one of the vaults by the rush of water from firefighting hoses. It looked Roman, but he couldn't be sure. Niles gently placed the shard on a small outcropping of rock.

"We estimate only ten pounds of C-five were used. The engineers said you don't need much to bring down the ceiling in any of our corridors except for the reinforced residence and lab levels. As for the fire, Europa is working on what accelerant was used, but it looks like something new and not on the books." Everett held up his hand and a gleaming, silvery substance shimmered. "At least, I've never seen an accelerant like this. Storage level seventy-four only sustained cave-in damage, and only three vaults were a total loss. My thinking is the target was level seventy-three, not both."

"So, we're looking at an intentional act of sabotage."

Everett walked over to the computer terminal that was dark and without power since Pete Golding had the system momentarily shut down. He reached up and touched its face.

"Europa reported a power failure on these levels moments before the explosion and fire. I checked her records; the electrical conduit was severed by a small charge, but only after our saboteur gained access to the level," Everett said as he turned and eyed the director. "The question, Dr. Compton, is why wasn't the identity of that person noted by Europa with her eye-scan procedure? This level is low security, but you still have to gain entry by key card and eye scan."

"I see where you're going with your line of thinking, but to get to your target area, Captain, you would have to assume someone deleted Europa's clearance history for these levels—that's why the temporary failure of Europa."

Everett didn't avert his eyes, because he knew that the only logical conclusion was upsetting to say the least, enough so that he didn't want to voice it.

"Then it had to be someone with a level one-A security clearance."

"A department head." Everett finally voiced the unthinkable.

"Damn," Niles said, kicking at a small stone statue.

Niles Compton was at his desk on level seven with Alice. She had been alerted at home in Las Vegas after the sabotage at the complex. Niles placed his glasses back on and then stared at the nineteen folders sitting on his desk. Every department head in the Group was accounted for including himself, Alice, and Virginia. To the right of that pile, Carl Everett had delivered his own, Ryan's, and Mendenhall's, the hierarchy of the security department. Located in one of those personnel files was something that might tell them who the traitor in their midst was.

"What has me baffled is, why level seventy-three? Are we moving on that question?" Alice asked.

Niles took a deep breath of air and then let it out slowly.

"I have Captain Everett and Virginia on that now. They're compiling a list with Europa of the contents of every vault on both levels. I just find it hard to believe that one of our people could be responsible for this—"

The double doors to his office were suddenly pulled open, and Virginia Pollock entered and went right to the desk.

"Did you find something?"

"You haven't heard?" she asked as she hit a button on Niles's control panel. The large center-screen monitor came to life as Virginia placed the channel on the twenty-four-hour Pentagon news service. "Someone just attacked the Independence Oil facility in Texas City."

The view was of a massive refinery fire. The image came from a helicopter circling the plant ten miles distant. Far below, you could see hundreds of firefighters fighting the blaze among the rubble and ruin of buildings and machinery.

Niles pulled his top right-hand drawer open and pulled out his direct phone line to the president. His hand hesitated over the handset, and then he slid the phone away from him.

"He may be a little busy at the moment. Have they stated any casualty reports, Virginia?"

"It's a miracle. Unlike the fatalities inside the Venezuelan attack, they think there's only one death thus far, thanks to the warning that was sent and this time heeded before the missiles struck. They do know for a fact they were sea-launched weapons."

"They are reporting that the plant was warned ahead of time?" Alice asked.

Virginia nodded as the scene on the monitor switched to show the three hundred employees of the refinery standing outside of the gates, watching their livelihoods vanish before their eyes.

Niles looked from the monitor to the two women. Virginia, for her part, averted her eyes.

"What in the hell is happening?"

At twelve midnight, Niles walked into the complex cafeteria and took a tray from a stack. He looked around the eating area and saw only a few technicians sitting and drinking coffee. He slid his tray down the cold line, eyed the egg salad sandwiches in their see-through wrapping, and decided he would settle for a cup of coffee and piece of pie.

He had just placed his tray on the table, sat and removed his glasses as Captain Everett walked over with Pete Golding in tow. Everett dropped a computer printout on the table and then sat in an empty chair, Pete following suit. Neither man looked happy.

Niles didn't bother putting his glasses back on as he raised a piece of pie to his mouth. Halfway there he thought better of it and put it back down.

"Europa says she admitted no one to the lower levels before the detonations," Everett said.

"Europa doesn't lie, Captain, although she can be fooled. We have a saboteur here, and as soon as you grasp the fact that it's someone with the clearance and someone who knows the Cray system, the sooner you can start your hunt in earnest," Pete said, pulling the piece of pie over to his side of the table and starting to eat.

"We also found this mysterious accelerant on level seventy-four. It just failed to ignite. So that means the target could have been any one of six hundred vaults—if they were targeted at all."

Niles rubbed his tired and itching eyes and looked at Everett.

"It has to be someone with intimate knowledge of Europa and her subroutines, wouldn't you say, Pete?"

"Absolutely. Not all department heads even know they can bypass her security. I would say less than six people have that knowledge."

"What about an outside influence?" Niles asked with hope.

"You mean to break into Europa and flush her security protocol?" Pete asked indignantly.

"Why not? Her main job is to backdoor other systems; maybe she was done the same way," Niles persisted.

"I uh . . . why . . . no! That just can't happen, not to Europa!" the computer genius said with a mouthful of pie.

"Take it easy, Doctor. That would still leave a physical presence here inside the complex to lay the explosives and accelerant. Europa can do a lot of things, but that isn't one of them," Everett said, watching as Pete finally swallowed the piece of pie he had in his mouth.

"Okay, what I want you to do, Pete, once an inventory list of every vault on both floors is compiled, is to go through them with a fine-tooth comb. By looking at that, we may be able to find something to give us the why of it. Captain, until further notice, all department heads are locked out of Europa and confined to the complex."

"Yes, sir."

"I reported to the president, but he hasn't returned my call. With the Texas City and Venezuelan incidents on the front burner, we may be on our own for a while."

THE UNITED NATIONS, NEW YORK, NEW YORK

The UN general assembly was in short session, as many of the delegates wanted to be close to their consulates while the world figured out who initiated the three attacks. Accusations were tossed around as freely as the insults that preceded them.

As Venezuela took the floor, accusing the United States of dragging its feet on letting the world know the evidence they had in their possession, the lights dimmed and sixteen large viewing screens lowered from the ceiling. A blue field appeared and steadied.

The General Secretary of the UN, Sir John Statterling of Great Britain, stood and slammed his gavel hard on the main dais, then held his hand above his eyes to shade them from the sixteen bright xenon lights of the projectors at the rear of the building. He quickly ordered security to find out what the malfunction was. The general assembly became raucous, making some in attendance feel as if they were back in grade school, acting up when lights suddenly went out.

The screens flashed brightly, and then a sentence appeared. Every screen was utilized, and every language of the UN was spelled out, correctly and precisely, in clear block letters.

ATTENTION: THE FOLLOWING MESSAGE HAS BEEN COURIERED TO EVERY MAJOR NEWSPAPER AND NEWS ORGANIZATION IN THE WORLD.

Several UN security personnel were banging on the door of the audiovisual room, six floors up. The door had been locked from the inside and spot-welded shut. The video slides had been programmed two hours before by a technician with impeccable UN credentials.

The general assembly floor was silent but uneasy. There were shouts of indignation from individuals, but most felt that this had a very ominous ring to it.

The picture changed and more words appeared in white against a blue field, and still in every language represented by the assembly.

THE NATIONS OF THE WORLD HAVE LOST THE RIGHT TO USE THE SEAS FOR COMMERCIAL PETROLEUM AND CHEMICAL TRANSPORT. ALL DELIVERIES OF PETROLEUM PRODUCTS AND CHEMICALS ARE HEREBY BANNED FROM THE SURFACE OF THE EARTH'S OCEANS.

THE WHITE HOUSE, WASHINGTON, D.C.

The president was eating a late breakfast due to an earlier-than-usual national security briefing that morning when a Secret Service agent entered the private dining room. He went straight to the president and whispered into his ear, then handed him a fax just received from the Department of the Navy and the FBI.

"They received these simultaneously?"

"Yes, sir, also the State Department, the Interior Department, the United States Coast Guard, the NSA, and the CIA, plus every news organization with a typewriter or a video camera. All the copies say the same thing."

The president read the first of the faxes. His wife and daughter watched him as his jaw muscles clenched, and the blood slowly drained from his face.

THE UNITED NATIONS, NEW YORK, NEW YORK

Several of the members were standing in shock. Others were yelling at the top of their voices at anyone within earshot.

The screens flickered again and a new message appeared.

THE OCEANS OF THE WORLD ARE NOW AT 61 PERCENT LOSS OF SPECIES DUE TO CRIMINAL NEGLIGENCE BY THE OUTLAW NATIONS GOVERNING THE SEAS. THE SEAGOING PRODUCTION OF ALL OIL AND NATURAL GAS WILL CEASE IN THIRTY DAYS, OR THEIR CORRESPONDING PLATFORMS OR PUMPING STATIONS WILL BE DESTROYED. ALL REFINERIES LOCATED WITHIN A ONE-KILOMETER DISTANCE OF SHORELINES WILL CEASE OPERATIONS WITHIN ONE YEAR. WHERE THEY ARE RELOCATED IS AT THE DISCRETION OF PETROLEUM-PRODUCING AND -CONSUMING NATIONS. YOU ARE HEREBY WARNED—THEY WILL REMAIN INLAND OR BE DESTROYED.

AS OF THIS DATE, FORCES INVULNERABLE TO MILITARY ACTION, AS DEMONSTRATED OFF THE COAST OF VENEZUELA AND THE UNITED STATES, HAVE RECLAIMED THE SEA. NO MILITARY VESSEL WILL BE ALLOWED PAST THE THOUSAND-METER DEPTH IN ANY OCEAN OF THE WORLD, UPON PENALTY OF IMMEDIATE AND RUTHLESS REPRISAL. YOUR WARS REMAIN YOUR OWN; YOUR LANDS REMAIN YOUR OWN. HOWEVER, THE SEAS HAVE BEEN FORFEITED THROUGH YOUR NEGLIGENCE, ARROGANCE, AND AVARICE. AS A GESTURE OF GOOD FAITH, CIVILIAN TRAVEL UPON THE SURFACE OF THE SEAS WILL BE PERMITTED.

HEED THIS WARNING. THE NORTH AMERICAN GULF COAST AND A THREE-HUNDRED-MILE EXCLUSION ZONE OFF THE COAST OF VENEZUELA ARE CLOSED TO ALL COMMERCIAL SEA TRAFFIC. A PROPOSAL TO AFFECTED NATIONS WILL BE FORTHCOMING. END COMMUNICATION.

THE WHITE HOUSE SITUATION ROOM, WASHINGTON, D. C.

The director of the FBI stood from his chair. The room was dim with the exception of the four walls where map projections of the world's oceans dominated. Three large red stars were placed in the sea near Venezuela, the capital itself, and in the Gulf of Mexico, at Texas City, Texas.

"The New York police department was the first law-enforcement entity to arrive at the UN. They secured the audiovisual department until our people could get there. Interpol is claiming jurisdiction in the matter, due to it being international property. Nevertheless, we had time to do a hurried forensic search of the area. No fingerprints other than those of authorized personnel were found. The UN A/V department's ten technicians were all accounted for during the incident."

"CIA?" the president asked.

"Sir, we just don't have enough to go on. The slides could have been done commercially or on any one of three hundred million home computers with Photoshop. The systems are just that prevalent. We just don't have enough."

"Well, we obviously have to maintain freedom of the seas, so from that aspect, even though I am taking this threat seriously—" He looked at the faces around the room. "—we have no choice but to continue oil and gas shipments. Admiral Fuqua, do we even have half the resources to guarantee the safety of these vessels?"

"Sir, we're spread so thin at this moment that we can't even guarantee the safety of our own warships, much less that of commercial shipping. It will be a good three months until we have our battle-group strength up to our normal peacetime standard, much less being placed on a wartime footing."

"Thank you for your candor. Does analysis have anything on the wording of the document? And how in the hell are all of our supposedly secure computer systems being compromised?"

The question was not directed at any one individual in the room. However, National Security Advisor Harford Lehman stood and directed another question to General Kenneth Caulfield. The general had become somewhat grayer in the last six months, and was beginning to show his wear.

"Ken, have we advanced any theories on the weapons or entity used in the attacks on Venezuela and Texas City?"

"Nothing from the intelligence end of things, and the nuclear fingerprint is a dead end. That material is from an entirely unknown breeder reactor. As for the vessel, or vessels, all we have is the sonar tape that shows something that everyone, even the General Dynamics Electric Boat Division, says cannot exist."

The National Security Agency assistant director cleared his throat.

"Go ahead," said the president.

"The wording of the document has indications of American or British leanings, but nothing at this point is verifiable. The words our analysts call 'old school' have them leaning toward not just an ecoterrorist, but a religious one at that."

The president spoke up. "For right now, let's just say we have a threat from someone with a lot of punch backing their words. Ecological terrorism, no matter how noble a cause, is still terrorism. I want facts delivered to me on the claim noted in the text about how damaged sea life has become. This will be something I have to address in the press, although I doubt this entity is out to garner public sympathy with the point they are making."

The men around the table became silent as the president turned away and looked out of the large window. Then he spoke without turning back.

"Admiral Fuqua, order this threat tracked down and destroyed by any means necessary."

EVENT GROUP CENTER, NELLIS AIR FORCE BASE, NEVADA

Niles sat at one of the desks in the upper tier of the amphitheaterlike computer center. He watched as Pete Golding on the floor far below instructed his department on how he wanted Europa's every transaction of the day before tracked. He called it bleeding her system. He likened it to the old ways of physicians bleeding a person to assist in healing. They were about to break down the most powerful computing system in the world and siphon her information out, one program and one line of code at a time.

Niles placed his glasses back on, gathered the latest communiqué from the president that listed the threat to the nation and the world, and was about to rise when suddenly every light in the computer center flickered, went out, came back on, flickered again, and then steadied.

"What in the hell is going on around here?" Pete asked as bells started to chime.

"*Dr. Golding, my internal messaging system has been compromised,*" Europa said electronically and in print on the main screen.

Pete glanced up at Niles, who was now standing and peering at the glowing green type on the thirty-foot-wide and twenty-foot-high main viewing screen at the front of the center. He then walked over to his desk situated at the center of the technician stations lining the floor. He leaned into his microphone. Before he could say anything, Carl Everett walked in; he had been in the hallway outside when the computer alarm sounded. He exchanged a look with Niles, who shrugged his shoulders.

"Europa, query; compromised by whom?"

"*Unknown source, Dr. Golding. I have instructions.*"

"Europa, initiate your security protocols," Pete ordered as if he were scolding a child.

"*I am unable to comply at this time, Dr. Golding. Security override Alpha-Tango-Seven is in effect.*"

"I have not authorized an AT-seven override. Shut down outside access."

"What in the hell is an AT-seven security override?" Carl asked Niles, who was now looking very concerned.

"Alpha-Tango-Seven is an override that can be initiated from a terminal other than Europa. Even our Group cell phones, laptops, and home PCs are Europa secured. This message is not from an internal source—someone from an unauthorized computer has used one of Pete's most secure overrides to get a message to us," Niles explained.

The double doors of the center opened and Alice joined Carl and Niles.

"What in the hell is happening?" Alice asked. "Every computer terminal in the complex went offline!"

Niles didn't answer her; he was looking at the main screen.

"Jack Collins used this security override last month during the Atlantis operation, when he accessed Europa from an unsecured location."

Everett remembered that indeed they had, from a cybercafe.

"*Shut down complete—*"

"Thank you, Europa, now begin a trace as to—"

"*Alpha-Tango override reestablished. Incoming message being received,*" Europa said, cutting Pete off.

"Goddamn it, shut down the outside source. Authorization, Golding—"

"Pete, allow the message through," Niles called from his elevated position.

"Niles, this could be a virus!"

"Allow it through; we may be getting something from our mysterious saboteur. Besides, if they wanted only to send Europa a virus, they could have done it without us knowing, since they seem to know our systems as well as we do. Let the message through."

Pete shook his head in exasperation, but leaned over the microphone to comply with his orders.

"Europa, content of message?" Pete asked.

The main viewing screen went dark as Europa complied. As they watched, bright red letters started appearing, and scrolled with incredible speed.

DEPARTMENT 5656, DR. NILES COMPTON, GREETINGS FROM A FRIEND. UNDOUBTEDLY, BEING AN AGENT FOR THE UNITED STATES FEDERAL GOVERNMENT, YOU ARE IN POSSESSION OF THE DOCUMENT DELIVERED TO THE UNITED NATIONS AND TO YOUR PRESIDENT.

Niles passed the message he had received earlier from the president over to Alice and Everett. He noticed Virginia's absence for the first time.

AS A SCIENTIFIC AND HISTORICAL BODY, YOU MUST APPRECIATE THE GRAVE SITUATION PRESENTED BY THE LOSS OF SEA LIFE IN THE WORLD'S OCEANS DUE TO THE CORRUPT MEASURES TAKEN BY GOVERNMENTS AND INDIVIDUALS AROUND THE WORLD. THE DEFENSELESS NOW HAVE A DEFENDER. THE THREAT OF FORCE ISSUED IN THE UNITED NATIONS COMMUNIQUÉ IS GENUINE, AND ITS PARAMETERS CAN AND WILL BE ENFORCED. THEREFORE, WE CALL UPON YOU, DR. COMPTON, AND YOUR DEPARTMENT TO ASSIST ME IN MAKING YOUR GOVERNMENT, AND THUS THE WORLD, UNDERSTAND THEIR DIRE POSITION IN REGARD TO THIS MATTER. FAILURE WILL RESULT IN THE TOTAL DESTRUCTION OF EVERY MAJOR SEAPORT IN THE WORLD BY A NUCLEAR RESPONSE.

IN A SHOW OF GOOD FAITH, I WILL TURN OVER TO YOUR GROUP AN ITEM THAT WAS LOST TO YOU SOME TIME AGO, ONE THAT YOU WOULD WISH TO RECOVER. I ASK FOR A TRADE, DR. COMPTON: YOU FOR THIS ARTICLE. THIS DEMAND MUST BE MET BEFORE THE DEADLINE MENTIONED IN THE COMMUNIQUÉ. THERE WILL BE ONE ATTEMPT MADE, AND ONE ATTEMPT ONLY. UPON FAILURE IN THIS ENDEAVOR, THE MANIFESTO DELIVERED TO ALL GOVERNMENTS WILL TAKE EFFECT IMMEDIATELY WITH EXTREME FORCE, AND THE ATTACKS MENTIONED IN THIS COMMUNICATION WILL BE IMPLEMENTED IN A WEEK'S TIME. DR. COMPTON, THIS IS THE ONLY WAY YOUR PRESIDENT CAN VALIDATE THE SERIOUSNESS OF THIS MATTER.

LATITUDE 41.071 N, LONGITUDE -71.85706 W 0230 HOURS.

END COMMUNICATION.

Movement on the computer center main floor started immediately as technicians ran to their stations. They didn't have to receive orders from Pete to move.

"Connection terminated at oh-nine-twelve and thirty-two seconds—origin has been traced by Europa to the Eastern seaboard, location unknown," one of the white-coated technicians called out.

"Microwave relay station Greenland is the closest we can get to a trace. It dead-ends there," another said aloud.

"Get me the location of those coordinates!" Pete ordered.

Europa used the main viewing screen as she pushed the pirated communiqué aside, then brought up a satellite map of the United States. The view adjusted to the eastern half of the U.S. and then centered on Long Island, New York. It kept magnifying on a large object by the sea.

"Europa computes latitude 41.071 north, longitude -71.85706 west is Montauk Point, New York—specifically, the lighthouse," Pete's assistant said as he straightened from his console.

"Okay, let's start digging deeper on that trace; they had to have left more of a footprint than just the Greenland microwave relay." Pete looked up at Niles and the others. "Boss, I have a feeling that whoever they are, they have codes for some or all of the U.S. communication satellites."

Niles listened to Pete's orders and comment, then looked at the three people around him. "Alice, get all department heads into the conference room immediately. Captain, make travel arrangements for New York, fastest possible route. Plan defensively; we're dealing with a very shrewd criminal at the very least."

"Yes, sir. May I ask your thoughts?" Everett said.

"Captain, this is no coincidence. This is the same person who destroyed two levels of our complex, and obviously the one responsible for the UN message. Therefore, our priority is to damn well find out what it was they didn't want us to know on levels seventy-three and seventy-four. Let's move. We don't have a lot of time."

"That's not what I mean. You're not going to trade yourself for whatever it is they have, are you?" Everett asked, knowing that Jack would never allow the director to place himself in harm's way for something that had not been substantiated.

"I have every intention of meeting their demands." He looked at Everett and the others one at a time. "We need to know who and what we're dealing with, so unless we can find out something before tonight, yes, I'm going."

As Carl Everett met with Jason Ryan to decide how to proceed to this mysterious meeting, Pete Golding and Alice Hamilton asked for a meeting with Director Compton to deliver extremely bad news. They were shown into Compton's large office, where Niles was meeting on a video monitor with the president of the United States.

"I'm sorry, Niles, I would like to have the luxury of time, but I don't. I have ordered the navy to provide escort for all oil shipments heading to U.S. shores. The Russians, Chinese, and British are joining the effort. Not all vessels will be covered, at least in this first phase, because there are just so many already at sea. Starting tomorrow, though, no ship leaves Middle Eastern waters without guns surrounding them. As for regular commercial traffic, we are quarantining all ships in port and ordering those at sea to come home. The coast guard will try and get them in, but again, we can't protect everyone."

"We still believe that whoever was responsible for the sabotage here at the complex is responsible for the world threat. They want to meet, and will provide a good faith measure to attain that meeting—they want to trade whatever they have for me. They insist upon me being a go-between. I need your permission to proceed," Niles said as he rubbed his right temple.

The president sat silent for the longest time. Then he picked up a piece of paper from his desk.

"My analysts believe we're dealing with a terrorist element that is only using ecological concerns to mask their real intensions. The U.S. Department of Agriculture says their claims of sixty-one percent loss of seagoing species are hogwash. This may be a move to throw our economy—which, I might add, is more dependent than ever on foreign oil—into utter chaos. Thus far, I'm leaning to that suggestion, because in all honesty, Niles, no matter how bad we think things are with the ecology and global warming, economically we can do nothing about it. We need oil and that is that. I'm not here to debate the right or the wrong of it."

"I'm not defending these people, Mr. President; I'm a realist, and I know we can't just choke ourselves to death because of our thirst for oil. However, my people are telling me that this communiqué is telling more of a truth than what your people are saying. The sea has at the very least lost fifty percent of all life that it once supported, and that is a direct re-sult of overfishing and water contamination."

"I'm not about to sit here and argue with you, Niles; you tell me what to do. Do I just toss seventy million Americans out of work because an outside nutcase says that his group is shutting down the sea lanes? Am I supposed to look at the people of the northeast and say, sorry, no heating oil this year? We don't have the strategic reserves to see us through one damn winter."

Niles took a deep breath and shook his head.

"However, since this is the only lead we have on these people, I want your security chief to liaise with the director of the FBI—you are to stay in place in Nevada. Any attempt by you to go to the meeting, I'll have you placed under house arrest." The president held up his hand when he saw Niles start to protest. "The FBI is in charge."

"My people are leaving within the hour, and will be in New York at the U.S. Air Force facility at Kennedy by six tonight."

"Who's leading the Group?"

Niles looked into the monitor. "Captain Everett will handle our end of things."

"I'm sorry, Niles; you're too valuable to swap for anything they may have at the moment."

The monitor went dark and Niles slammed his glasses down on the desk.

"What have you two got?" he asked rubbing his eyes.

Alice moved toward the credenza and poured Niles his fifth cup of coffee in the past hour and a half.

"Niles, our culprit erased the inventory and forensics files on all arti-facts stored on the two affected levels," Pete announced as Alice sat down in her usual chair in front of the large desk.

Compton looked up and saw Pete was angry and tired.

"I really don't know why we expected any different. There would have been no sense in destroying the articles physically if you left a com-puter record of those finds available." Alice didn't say this to anyone in particular. She also looked tired, far more than Niles had ever seen her.

"I hate to ask this, Alice, but no one knows those vaults any better than you and the senator. Do you think—?"

"Yes, but it will take time. Garrison and I will go through the paper files. Maybe we can see what was in them to help you. Since this faction hit even the old Cray system at the old facility, we lost those records also. They were goddamned thorough. However, we're flying in the hard copies from Arlington. I've already asked security to pick the senator up at home and bring him in."

"Well, at least the senator had the foresight to have the hard copies of the files stored in Arlington; otherwise our saboteur might have gotten to those also," Pete said, perching his glasses on his forehead so he could rub his eyes.

"Okay, have them all faxed out here."

"Is Carl ready to go out East?" Pete asked.

"Yes, he's taking Ryan and Mendenhall. I'll tell him the bad news about the FBI; he's not going to be happy," Niles answered, replacing his own glasses. "I suspect the FBI will set up an ambush to retrieve our item, and try for at least one or two arrests."

"Is that advisable?" Pete asked.

"I didn't have much of a choice. Look, one thing we better get used to here, threats have been made by an unknown source to make the nation do something that would send us back to the Stone Age. We, as a country, for better or worse, have set ourselves up for this through our arrogance. Now someone is trying to pull the plug on our neon society, and we can't let that happen, not yet, not until we can get alternatives online and people accept them. The president wants other eyes out there and is desperate for information. I can't really say I blame him, Pete."

The door opened and Virginia Pollock walked in. She looked tired, and her eyes refused to meet those of her friends.

Niles looked at Virginia, wondering where she had been. Then he looked at everyone around his desk.

"Every American knew this day would come, and now it has. If they didn't stop whoever this was, a hundred years of ignoring the earth was about to come back and haunt them. Now pay attention. Pete, we're calling an event for in-house personnel only, and from this moment on, I want you to order Europa to close the complex. No external communication is to be allowed. I want cell frequencies jammed, and all passes revoked. Captain Everett and his team are the only exceptions, and I hate to say this, but I even want his phone monitored while off base. Shut down the gates; turn off communications for the pawnshop. Keep it open, but seal the elevator into the tunnel." He looked at Alice. "All senior department members are to be escorted by security and will be quarantined in the main conference room for the duration of the FBI's and our department's operation. Pete, use my terminal and order Europa to seal the complex."

Golding did as he was ordered.

Alice and Virginia exchanged looks. Never had the Event Group gone to such a total lockdown over security.

"Now, let's find out who attacked us, shall we?" Niles said with a nod.

"And find out who our traitor is," Pete added.

THE GOLD CITY PAWNSHOP, LAS VEGAS, NEVADA

The old man went unnoticed at the city bus stop for the hour he had been sitting. His aluminum walker was perched in front of him—just an old man resting his aged body.

His keen eyes were watching the shop across the street. He had thus far not recognized one employee at the Gold City Pawnshop. The heat was almost intolerable, but the man sat and acted as though the sun were a blessing.

Suddenly his eyes picked up something inside the shop that made him move his head so his vision could pass across the plate-glass window in the front of the store. He coughed as he finally recognized a familiar face. He had run into this man on more than one occasion in the past, and knew him to be a favorite of his superior officers. His computerlike memory flashed back to two years before in the Arizona desert, and then again last year in the heat of the Amazon. He became satisfied as the black man's name came to mind: Mendenhall—Staff Sergeant Mendenhall. It was comforting knowing that certain things had not changed in the year he had been . . . away.

The old man rose clumsily to his feet and used the aluminum walker, leaning heavily upon it as he slowly crossed the busy street. A car honked and swerved to the other lane, but the old man was intent on the pawnshop in front of him. The black man inside looked up at the sound of the horn, and he quickly moved to open the door.

Second Lieutenant Will Mendenhall held the door for the man, who nodded his head in thanks. The old man had not known the former sergeant had received his second lieutenant's bar after the Amazon mission.

"Car almost got ya there," Will said as he quickly let the door close behind the man and looked at his watch. He could see the deeply etched wrinkles and figured the old gentleman was at least eighty years old. His white moustache was well trimmed, and for someone his age he had expressive blue eyes.

"I wanted to throw my walker at the smart-ass bastard, but then what would I have done?"

"Yeah, wouldn't have blamed you, people around here are in a hurry to get to nowhere," Will commented. "Well, what can I help you with?"

The old man raised his right liver-spotted hand off the walker in a mock surrender.

"Son, you have me. I . . . I just wanted to feel this air-conditioning for a moment before I head back out to that damn bus stop. Missed the last one—hell, I fell right to sleep."

Mendenhall smiled and nodded his head, "You bet. If you want there's a seat up by the counter." He looked at his watch again, knowing that Captain Everett had called him five minutes ago and ordered him off gate 2 duties. "Right now I have to clock out and get out of here."

"I thank you, but right here's fine with me. The air is cool and I can see that damn bus comin' through the window, but thanks anyway, son."

Will was just turning away when the old man's other hand slipped from the walker and he started to fall. Will reached out quickly and caught the man, who was far heavier than he looked.

"Whoa, you okay?" he asked, stabilizing the man.

The old man reached out, grabbed Mendenhall's forearm, and expertly placed the tracking device, which was no larger than a microbe and was injected by what seemed to be just a jagged piece of the old man's ring. Mendenhall felt the jab and reacted with a hiss.

"Oh, my . . . oh . . . I'm sorry. This old wedding band's seen better days." The man finally grabbed hold of the handles to his walker as Will rubbed the underside of his forearm. "Wife's been dead for the better part of eleven years now; just been too lazy to take the ragged thing off." He reached into his pant pocket and drew out a handkerchief. "Got a little scratch there, better wipe it clean."

Mendenhall held up his hand. "Nah, it's all right, I'll put a Band-Aid on it when I go in the back. You take it easy now. If you need a hand getting back across the street, you ask the clerk at the counter, and he'll get you there."

"I'm much obliged, son, much obliged, but look here, there's that damn bus now." He smiled and made for the door. Will shook his head and held it open for him again. He waved as the old man slowly made his way to the street, then, looking both ways, went across.

Mendenhall rubbed the scratch and watched as the old man waved, wobbled once more, and then smiled as the bus doors opened. Will turned away and went through the back, or gate 2 as it was known, and into the underground maze that led to the top-secret Event Group.

The old man sat at the rear of the bus where there were no riders, leaning the walker in the aisle as he sat heavily into the large backseat. He chanced a last look out of the tinted bus window and watched the Gold City Pawnshop slide past. His eyes narrowed as he thought of the black man, knowing that standing that close to him would have made his death that much more unexpected and pleasurable. However, the man wanted Mendenhall together with the other members of the Event Group, so they would meet their fate at the same time. They would meet his wrath, his vengeance.

The man reached up and peeled the gray moustache from his upper lip and pulled the grey wig from his head, and then pulled out a bottle of aloe lotion and squeezed in into his hand. He slowly rubbed it into the skin of his face, loosening the glue he had used to create the realistic-looking wrinkles and removing the makeup-induced liver spots.

When he felt his face was clean, he watched the casinos on the strip slide by, and as he did, Colonel Henri Farbeaux, an archenemy of the Event Group, missing for the past year, caught sight of his own reflection in the window, a face that now held little humanity. Like everything else, that had been lost in the Amazon Basin well over a year before.

Farbeaux had lost his wife Danielle while he himself, against every natural instinct he had, helped the Event Group save the lives of young students on an expedition to the gold mine El Dorado. He lived because of a moment of weakness brought on by Colonel Jack Collins and his heroics in saving the group. He had assisted Collins, and paid for this weakness with the loss of his wife.

Yes, Colonel Henri Farbeaux needed to seek what he longed for in the last year—vengeance against the men and women who had cost him everything, Danielle and his faith in himself. Jack Collins and the rest of his people would learn that Henri Farbeaux was here, and those responsible for his thinking he was human would die.

He spread his hand out on the window and totally blotted out his image.

The room was cast in total darkness. The man sitting upon the bed rubbed the area around his wrist where the handcuff chafed his skin. His thoughts were on removing that handcuff chained to the railing of the bed and ending on his right wrist. He couldn't swear to it, but he thought he knew how to get the restraint off of his wrist. How he would know this was beyond him. The elderly man, his doctor he assumed, had said that his memory would be shaky for a day or so after waking, but to think he had a memory of how to escape handcuffs was worrisome and problematic. Was he a criminal? Was that why he would know? In addition, he had seen several people, men and women, enter his darkened room to check on him and bring him meals. Upon study, he had decided that he could handle them physically as well.

The man leaned back against the headboard of the steel bed. He was thinking about what he could remember. Only his death came to mind. A strange thought to say the least, only because the answer was right in front of him, as he was obviously not dead.

Through the wall and steel at his back, he was feeling movement. He knew this because he had a keen sense in his stomach that said he was moving. Every now and then, he had noticed the pitcher of water on his nightstand sway, indicating that whatever transport he was on was turning. Therefore, what little memory he had said he was on a ship.

The door opened. He shielded his eyes with his free hand as someone, or was it two people, stepped into the room. They quickly closed the door, shutting out the lights from a hallway beyond. The man heard shuffling, and as the dim light of a desk lamp came on, he saw the old man, the doctor, but he felt a presence in the back of the room. This person stood by the door and was watching him. He knew it, felt it.

"Well, my friend, it's time for you to leave us," the doctor said with a half-smile.

"Who are you?" the man asked, making no move to sit up.

The doctor laughed. It was a mournful little chuckle that wasn't mirth, but a sad sound.

"I apologize, but aren't you more concerned on just who it is *you* are?"

"I know that will come soon enough, but if I'm leaving you, I would like to know who you are."

"We're friends. Will that satisfy you for the moment?" the voice said from the darkness. "The doctor informs me that as soon as he triggers your memory with your name, it will all come back to you."

The man tried to peer into the inky blackness beyond the foot of his bed. He could barely see the darker shape as it stood against the far wall. Then the voice emerged again from the darkness.

"You are going home. I just wanted to tell you before your departure that I am a great admirer of yours, and of the men and women for whom you work." The female voice hesitated, then continued. "When you get home, tell your people you were treated well and that you were dealt with respectfully. In a few months, my wish is that I may still be able to call you *friend*. The doctor will now explain where you are, and who you are."

The door opened. The bright light flared once more, and the woman left the room. The man could see she was tall, at the very least six feet; she was dressed in dark green and her hair was jet-black, but that was all he saw before the door closed.

"It's not often that she would grace someone she doesn't know by speaking to them. But then again, I should have thought she would. I'll tell you this much, she visited you at least three times a day. It was quite unsettling to my sleep cycle having her pop in at ungodly hours," the doctor said in an English accent.

"Who is she?" the man asked, finally sitting up on the edge of the bed.

The doctor laughed again; this time the humor came through his hardy sound.

"Who she is, at the very least, is a loaded question. Suffice it to say she springs from a family of geniuses and is, by leaps and bounds, the most brilliant human being the world has ever known. Just leave it at that." The doctor shook his head but kept the smile on his face. "When all is said and done, go away with the knowledge that she respects you. That is something you will be able to tell your grandchildren. She spoke to you and she liked you; not many can say that."

"Am I supposed to be honored?" the man asked, clinking the chain that held the handcuff in place.

"Oh, that. It was for your own protection, until your memory cleared up. We didn't exactly know how you would react when you awoke. Your . . . how should I put this? Ah, your preeminence in the art of death precedes you, sir."

A spark of memory flared in the man's mind. He tilted his head and looked at the doctor.

"That's right; it's teasing you right now, isn't it?" The doctor stood, went to a closet, and pulled open a door. He reached in and removed an item from inside, then closed the door and turned. He held up a small silver key, obviously one that would unlock the handcuff. As the man examined the doctor, he saw that the white lab coat had a patch on the left-hand breast pocket. It was an *L*, with what looked to be two dolphins on either side, making it look like ~ *L*~. Beneath that was the symbol for a medical doctor, the twin-snake motif.

"Now, would you like to be filled in on who you are and what is expected of you? If you behave, I think we can dispense with the security measures." He went to the bed and tapped the handcuff.

5

MONTAUK POINT, LONG ISLAND, NEW YORK

Carl Everett stood just inside of the parking area of one of the most famous lighthouses in the United States. Jason Ryan and Will Mendenhall stood on either side of him, waiting for the mysterious rendezvous to take place. Behind them sat a stretch limousine with its motor off and headlights on. They had been at the point for thirty minutes watching as the fog became thicker each passing moment they waited. The only sound that was audible through the thickening mist was the seaboard dinghies with their forlorn toll.

"Goddamn FBI, how can they plan for an entity they know absolutely nothing about?" Everett mumbled, his eyes never leaving the shore-line.

"Director Compton should have acted without presidential knowl-edge," Ryan said, looking to his right at the closest FBI HRT member laying low underneath the cover of a large bush. Hostage Rescue out of Quantico had been called in for the ambush, and several of them were half-buried in the rough and rocky sands of the point.

Everett turned, chanced a look at the naval lieutenant, and sniffed.

"Some people like to go by the book, Mr. Ryan, even if you don't."

"I've known Compton to toss that book away from time to time," Ryan countered.

Everett didn't respond to the challenge. He just pursed his lips and then turned up his coat collar.

Mendenhall looked at his watch, then turned around and looked at the limousine that was minus one important element inside its interior: Director Compton. He also tried his best to peer through the swirling fog beyond, feeling uncomfortable. Absentmindedly he rubbed the scratch on his arm, wondering if he was going to get some sort of infection from that old man's ring this afternoon.

"Okay, what's on your mind, Will?" Carl asked, noticing it was the tenth time Mendenhall had turned to look to the rear.

"I can't shake this feeling that someone is out there, behind us. I've had it ever since we got here."

"There *are* people behind us; it's the FBI, and they have one hell of a lot of guns," Ryan said.

"I'm beginning to think Jack taught you something after all, Lieu-tenant. I'll let you in on a little secret. I have the same feeling." Carl turned and looked at Jason Ryan. "And it's not the FBI. Whoever it is, is far better at hiding than they are."

Ryan turned and looked at Mendenhall, who raised his brows as if to say *I told you.*

"Well," Ryan said, also looking at his watch, "our ecoterrorists are officially late—it's now oh-two-hundred and—"

Suddenly a larger-than-normal breaker crashed onto the beach and rocks, hard enough that seawater washed over into the parking lot and covered their feet. The sea retreated, and the breakers went back to their normal surge.

"You guys are navy boys. Is that normal? Like, was it a tidal surge, or maybe a rogue wave or something?" Mendenhall asked as he shook water off his shoes.

"You've been watching far too much Discovery Channel, Will," Everett said as he watched the fog in front of him, knowing they were no longer waiting for their company.

Everett reached behind him and placed both hands underneath the back of his nylon coat. He felt the nine-millimeter automatic, chambered a round, clicked off the safety, then brought his hands free of his coat. Ryan and Mendenhall mimicked his action.

Carl switched on the voice-activated microphone attached to his wristwatch.

"All units and positions, we have movement out at sea. Stand by. We don't know anything definite with this fog, so hold station."

The fog eddied and swirled around them. Carl chanced a glance at the limousine parked fifteen feet away. The fog should have been sufficient to cover the fact that Niles Compton was over two thousand miles away in Nevada.

"Ahoy the beach!"

The voice came from a loudspeaker. Everett couldn't track it because of the denseness of the fog.

"All units, we have voice contact only. Remain in place," Everett said. He took three steps toward the water, puting one hand behind him to stay Ryan and Mendenhall. "Ahoy the boat. I am Captain Everett, United States Navy. Identify yourself."

"Advance to the water's edge with Dr. Niles Compton, please."

Everett turned and looked back at Jason and Will for a moment, then turned back toward the fog-shrouded sea.

"That's not the way this game is going to be played. Dr. Compton keeps his station behind me until such a time as I'm satisfied with the situation and his safety."

"I assure you, Captain, we do not play games. Nonetheless, upon your word as a United States naval officer, we will approach the beach."

Everett hoped the FBI special agent in charge heard the response from their guests. Carl could feel the fifteen weapons of the hidden agents ready to open up.

The sound of water being pushed aside came to his ears as he finally caught sight of the boat that had lain offshore. It was like a Zodiac rubber craft, but far larger. As it approached, he could see only two figures inside. It grounded almost noiselessly onto the rocks, narrowly missing two large boulders that jutted out from the shore. Everett heard no engine sounds, so that meant they were using a form of propulsion that was silenced to a large degree. A large man quickly stepped easily over the gunnels of the Zodiac and stood looking at the three men.

"Captain, I am here to exchange one of your people for Dr. Compton. Would you present him, please?"

The captain saw the man was wearing a coverall, not unlike those worn by military personnel in the Event Group complex. There were patches arrayed on the long sleeve and shoulder and some sort of rank was evident on his collar, but that was as far as his vision would allow.

"The name of your vessel, sir," Everett called out.

The man lowered his head and then shook it. "That is not for me to answer, Captain, but suffice it to say you will learn all there is to learn upon Dr. Compton's return to your complex under the desert."

"I guess they're well informed," Ryan whispered to Mendenhall.

"Now, Dr. Compton, please, Captain."

Everett knew he had to make his play. The sniper in the lighthouse would take the man standing next to the boat, hopefully wounding him, and a two-man team in the water would take the hostage. There was only one man, so taking a prisoner was no longer an option. He felt as if he were betraying a trust, but a presidential order had been given, and no matter the distaste, it was now his duty. He raised his wrist to his mouth.

"Team one, execute." He closed his eyes, expecting the lone shot that would signal the rescue attempt.

The man in front of him laughed. He reached into the boat, pulled the seated man to his feet, and helped him over the gunnels of the boat.

Everett pulled his weapon and pointed it at the man. Will and Ryan followed suit. The effect of having three guns on him seemed lost on the large man, who looked at the three Event Group security men but continued to assist the second man to shore.

"Perhaps you better signal the HRT unit again, Captain."

Everett knew that although the man stated his faction didn't play games, he was being toyed with nonetheless. He lowered his weapon.

A whistle sounded in the fog from behind them. Then, from high above them, something whistled down from the top of the lighthouse. It smacked into the sand at Everett's feet. He stepped back when he saw it was upper torso body armor. He knew it to be the style he had seen the HRT suiting up with earlier.

Ryan turned around when a noise sounded behind him. Immediately, several red dots sprinkled his bulletproof vest. As he looked up, he saw black shapes coming through the swirling fog, and each carried a laser-sighted weapon. Some were aimed at Ryan, but the bulk were centered on Mendenhall and Everett's backs.

"Captain, we have company."

Without turning around, Everett placed his nine-millimeter into his waistband and pulled the coat over it, knowing they themselves had been ambushed instead of the other way around. He heard the sound of the fourteen ground members of the HRT unit as fifty men in black wetsuits pushed them roughly from the fog.

"Disappointing, but expected, Captain." The man looked around as the fog started to lift around them. "The FBI unit are all intact. A little embarrassed, maybe, but that will pass eventually."

"You didn't really expect us to treat whoever you are as honorable people, did you? Your actions against helpless vessels and shore installations don't speak well for you."

"We understand you were under orders from your president, Captain. We knew he wouldn't chance losing Dr. Compton. As for the attacks, those were acts of war, sir; you of all people should know the difference. Now, you have played out a losing hand with your deceptive actions regarding the FBI."

"The president was acting in the best interest of the country, and would—"

"However," the man said, cutting Everett's point off. "We will still keep our end of the bargain and release your Group member, to once again show good faith. Do not disappoint my captain again, or the American people will suffer beyond measure. Please, I implore you; have Dr. Compton, and any member of his department he wishes to accompany him, at McCarran airport in Las Vegas in three days. His transport will be at charter gate five at ten A.M. Heed this warning, Captain."

Suddenly the man released the hostage and returned to his boat. He and it backed away silently into the fog until once more the mist enveloped them.

The hooded man collapsed to his knees into the water; the small breakers started lapping at his thighs. Carl turned quickly and saw the wetsuited assault team had also vanished. The HRT unit was still there, still tied, and kneeling in the sand.

Everett turned and ran to the water to help the unknown person to his feet. Carl could feel the bulk under the black coverall and knew it to be a man. The hostage had a black hood on his head, and seemed weak as he struggled to stay upright. Everett hustled the man to the black limousine, removed the hood, and without looking any further, shoved him quickly into the backseat, telling the driver, Staff Sergeant Rodriguez, to watch him. He then turned and ran to assist the agents.

As Everett was cutting the plastic wire-tie off one of them, he turned and looked back at the fog-shrouded sea. With the exception of the breakers, all was quiet.

As he turned back to the task of releasing the agents, Everett heard a loud explosion of water. When he turned toward the sound, his eyes widened. He saw the topmost section of a submarine's stern fins sinking beneath the waves through the swirling remnants of fog. He straightened as he saw the three-story-high, sharklike rudders vanish, and then watched in awe as the amazing craft displaced several thousand tons of water on its way back out to sea.

"That son of bitch must have been in place long before we arrived." Ryan didn't look up as he freed the last of the agents, and didn't see the nightmare vision Everett had seen even as another giant surge of water pushed up on shore.

Everett stood and started for the car when he saw a small man in an FBI windbreaker come toward him. At his side was the sniper from the lighthouse. He recognized the agent in charge.

"I wasn't briefed on just who you people are, but your little meeting was compromised, and it had to come from your end. These people knew we would be here. Can you explain that?" The agent made the mistake of grabbing Carl's arm.

Ryan and Mendenhall reacted immediately, pulling the agent away before the captain had a chance to react. They had seen Carl confronted before, and knew that sometimes he acted first and then thought about a situation later.

"Get your hands off of me. I want an answer," the agent said, looking from Will to Ryan.

"Look, we don't know if the meet was compromised; they may have just had the game rigged from the beginning. They set this spot up, not us," Ryan said as he held the agent back.

"Fucking amateurs," the man said as he shook off Ryan's hands and then turned toward his men.

"He's right; someone told them that the FBI would be here." Everett tried to calm himself. He knew the agent in charge was only mad because his hostage rescue team had been placed in harm's way and left out to dry, just because someone on the Group's end couldn't keep their mouth shut.

"Whoever it is that's screwing with us almost cost the lives of a lot of people tonight," Mendenhall said as he watched the angry FBI unit start to assemble and make their way off the beach.

"Let's get the hell out of here," Everett said as he looked one last time back out into the Atlantic, where the vision of what couldn't have been cornered his thoughts.

The three men walked to the limousine and saw that Sergeant Rodriguez was kneeling on the backseat with the door open.

"How's our guest, Sergeant?" Mendenhall asked as they approached.

Rodriguez stepped back out of the car and looked at the three men, shaking his head.

"You're not going to fucking believe this," he said, looking from face to face as he moved out of their way.

Inside the limo, the dome lights were on. A big man sat reposed in the backseat with his head back and his face turned away from them. As Everett stepped up to the open door, he leaned down and touched the man on the leg.

"How are you doing?"

The man slowly turned his head. Everett, who was standing on the balls of his feet, lost his balance as he recognized the face immediately. He had a six-week growth of beard and looked pale in the false light of the car, and his eyes were heavily bloodshot, but Everett would have known this man anywhere, in any condition.

"I'll be damned, you tough-to-kill son of a bitch!"

Ryan and Mendenhall exchanged a look as Everett straightened and then pulled the man from the car and hugged him.

"Jack!"

Carl pushed Colonel Jack Collins at arm's length as Ryan and Mendenhall joined him in a dreamlike sequence that none of them could possibly have ever imagined.

Jack blinked his eyes and tried to focus on the faces in front of him. His hair, although combed straight back, was longer than Collins had ever worn it, but the eyes—those were still the same as they bore first into Everett's and then roamed to Ryan and Will. His lips moved, but no words came.

"Jack!" Carl said, giving Collins's shoulders a small shake until his eyes refocused on the captain's.

"The sea," Jack mumbled as his eyes locked with Carl's, and then the gaze changed and his head looked around him. "They said I was dead." He suddenly looked back at Everett.

"How in the hell is he here?" Will asked, swallowing.

"Goddamn, those people must have been there." Everett turned and looked at Mendenhall. "They must have saved him, pulled him from the water," Everett answered, laughing for the first time in weeks. "Oh no, you're not dead, Jack, you're going home." He tried to turn the colonel toward the open door when Jack pulled his arm free and stared at Everett.

"The sea," he said again, closing his eyes and swaying as Carl reached out and steadied him. Jack opened his eyes when his dizziness passed and focused on the three men once more. His eyes darted back to Everett and narrowed. "Mr. . . . . Everett."

"That's right, Jack. Will and Jason are here, too."

Jack's eyes went to the two men standing beside the captain.

"Will, Ryan . . . I tried to hold on . . . and I did . . ."

"Hold on to what, Colonel?" Mendenhall asked, feeling creepy about this whole thing. It was like conversing with a ghost at the very least.

Jack took a step back until he fell into the limo's rear seat and hung his head. It looked as though he was trying hard to remember something. He slowly looked up at the expectant faces.

"Sarah." That single name coming from his mouth explained all. The three officers exchanged a look. "She's dead, someone shot her?" he asked, looking like his world was gone, as if he had failed her.

Everett knelt by the open door and placed a hand on Collins's leg. He tried to smile but failed.

"Let's go home, buddy. We need to explain a few things to you."

THE ATLANTIC OCEAN, 100 MILES
OFF THE NEW JERSEY COAST

The control room was dark, and the men and women were silent in deference to the somber mood of the great vessel. On the surface, the radar mast and antennas broke the clean lines of the calm sea, slicing through the water as a sharpened scythe through wheat, their stealthy design broken by sharp angles.

"No airborne or surface contacts at this time, Captain. Sonar reports the signatures of three Los Angeles and one Virginia class submarine close-aboard, but are not deemed threats. They cannot pick us up. Stealth has been achieved."

On the darkened, raised platform at the center of the control room, the captain nodded and gestured toward the weapons station.

The first officer approached the raised pedestal and leaned in close to his captain. He looked around him, then lowered his voice.

"Captain, you know I have never once questioned your orders."

The captain smiled and looked down on a man she had known since her childhood. "I suspect that precedent is about to be broken."

"Ma'am, you had planned on delivering ultimatums to all countries before any attacks began." He looked around him once more, making sure all hands were attending their stations. "Now we've sunk four vessels and attacked two nations. Why have we stepped up offensive operations before these countries find out why we're doing it? This isn't like you at all, and—"

She looked down, and her bright blue eyes, dilated as they were, stayed the first officer's words.

"Apologies, Captain, I—"

"You have other concerns, James?"

"Why are you insisting on bringing strangers aboard? The attack on the complex achieved your goal."

"We have to know exactly what knowledge these people have on us."

"Captain, our asset inside their Group confirms they know nothing. Sergeant Tyler and his security department have been screaming about the unnecessary risk of what you are—"

The captain's piercing eyes settled on the first officer, and he could only nod his head.

"James, the ploy to lure their top security men from their posts worked." She looked around the control center and saw that her seamen were doing their jobs. Only Yeoman Alvera had turned from her station to watch the captain. "Now we can better coerce the people I need to come onboard with minimum bloodshed; isn't that what you wanted?"

"Yes, ma'am, I just—"

"Vertical tubes six through twelve are flooded, birds are warm," the weapons officer called out.

"Captain, the boat reports all stations ready for launch," the first officer said after being cut off by the announcement. He turned away from the raised platform and examined the holographic board in front of him.

The captain nodded her approval, then closed her eyes.

"All hands stand by for vertical launch. Tubes six through twelve, Operation Cover Four has been ordered to commence. Navigation, once tubes have been emptied, take the boat to four thousand feet at flank speed, then steer a course south at seventy-five knots. We will take up station in the gulf before dawn."

"Aye, sir," both navigation and weapons called out from their stations.

"Permission for weapons release, Captain?" the first officer asked, watching the still figure in her chair. Her not talking was a bad sign—he knew migraine headaches had begun to plague her the last few weeks.

Once more, there was just a simple nod of her head from the raised platform.

"Weapons officer, launch vertical tubes six through twelve in numerical order," the first officer ordered, looking at the captain with worry.

A hundred feet aft of the great streamlined conning tower, six of the forty-six vertical launch tubes opened to the sea. Suddenly large, explosive water slugs ejected six sixteen-foot-long, black, streamlined missiles with no telltale maneuvering fins. Now airborne and clear of the water, their solid booster rocket fired and sent the six missiles skyward. Once they reached an altitude of twenty thousand feet, they started a slow turn to the west and then picked up speed, still climbing. They would soon reach three times the speed of sound as they headed for the interior of the United States.

Far below the sea, the giant vessel dove at an amazing rate of speed, slowly ramping up to more than seventy knots. Then she dipped her nose and dove even deeper, where no American warship could ever hope to follow.

The great vessel set her course due south for the Gulf of Mexico, and part two of Operation Cover Four.

Twenty-two radar stations, warships, National Space Command, and U.S. early-warning satellites warned of a massive missile strike over the United States, and all started tracking the assault. Soon more than a hundred warplanes on the eastern seaboard and the Midwest lifted free of the earth, in pursuit of what were deemed cruise missiles, as they plowed their way through the stratosphere, heading west.

PART TWO
THE SEA CHASE

I have strived to meet my kind with open arms of shared brotherhood, but alas, the distance to cover is too great, the wounds too deep, and the memory of brutality too sharp and clear. So all I will ask my former brethren is to leave me to my sea.

—**Roderick Deveroux,**
former condemned prisoner,
Château d'If, France

6

The four VTOL (vertical takeoff and landing) aircraft suddenly went low to the ground. Their unique design was far stealthier than anything the Americans or Russians had on their drafting boards. Instead of being propeller driven, like the Marine Corps V-22 Osprey, these craft utilized a twin-engine turbojet.

When the four tilt-jet aircraft came within ten feet of the ground, their ground radar computers took over the flying, avoiding the many bumps and telephone wires crisscrossing the desert around the air force base. From the underbellies of each of the assaulting planes a small dish popped free and sent out a stream of microwaves that went invisibly toward the control center of one of the most advanced air force bases in the world.

The control tower sitting high above the airstrip suddenly went dark. All radar screens died within a microsecond of one another. Down below in the command and control area, the phone lines went out and their screens ceased to function. Traffic control was dead, as well as any response the base could muster. It seemed an eternity until the emergency generators kicked in, but in the three seconds it took for the circuit to be made, the attacking aircraft were already past them and down on ground level, beyond their radar search.

The four strange-looking craft overshot the darkened runways at Nellis and turned north toward the old firing range that hadn't been used since 1945—their target: the hidden underground complex of the Event Group.

EVENT GROUP COMPLEX,
NELLIS AIR FORCE BASE, NEVADA

Pete Golding had been working eighteen straight hours. He had been back and forth with Europa since the security lockdown was initiated. Several technicians were still inside the darkened computer center, but three of the six were dozing; the soft drone of Pete's voice trying to be as patient as possible with the supercomputer had lulled them to sleep. Once more, he went at Europa.

"Okay, let's try this again. Let us assume that a security breach from outside the complex occurred at the same moment the breach message was initiated. Is it possible you missed a back door in your programming, perhaps designed by your original program team at Cray?"

"Not possible, Dr. Golding. The internal algorithm ciphering my security program would have been disturbed, thus setting off my shutdown protocols."

Pete rubbed a hand over his balding head. "So, what you're saying is that it would have been impossible to have received the message without a door being left open from inside the complex, with the validation of a departmental manager?"

"Correct."

With the recent call in from Captain Everett, Niles knew the people who had sent the message had been tipped off that the FBI was lying in wait for them. That meant that someone here had to have communicated with the terrorists at some point after the security shutdown. Europa had indeed shut down all systems of communication. No one used any of the phones, and it would be impossible to get a cell phone call out of the complex. Europa closed all e-mail access, so that was eliminated. The director even cut Everett short when he wanted to explain who they had recovered from the meeting. Security at the moment was just so porous, he didn't chance anything.

"Shutdown was ordered at oh-nine-fifty-five this A.M. Was there any computer access just before I ordered you to close all internal loops?"

"*One.*"

Pete shook his head in exasperation. "Well, do you want to share that with me?"

"*Terminal is located in office forty-five-seventy-six, sublevel seven, and logged at oh-nine-fifty-three from the office of Assistant Director Virginia Pollock.*"

The blood in Pete's face drained. "No, Virginia doesn't have it in her." Still, Golding was scared.

Pete moved to his desk on the main floor, picked up the phone, and started punching numbers. He didn't hear anything. He flicked the disconnect a few times and then listened.

"Europa, did you shut down communication for the comp center?"

When he didn't get a response, Pete turned and looked at the large center screen monitor he was using for Europa's typed-out responses. It, too, was blank.

"Europa, respond."

Golding slapped the shoulder of one of the dozing men and woke him.

"Europa's down. See if you can make keyboard contact," he said as he started for the risers that led to the doors two stories above the main floor.

The other technicians awoke and looked around as the main lights flickered, steadied, and then went out. Pete reached the top and pulled the door handle. The door had locked, automatically he assumed, when Europa went down.

"What in the hell is going on here?"

Sarah McIntire had arrived two hours earlier from Arkansas. She was sitting alone in the cafeteria drinking a cup of coffee after she found she had no desire for sleep. Her aching arm held firmly to her chest with a sling, she realized it wasn't just the plane ride back, but the fact that Carl, Jason, and Will were all off base, making her feel her homecoming was put on hold.

She spied Alice Hamilton off in the far corner of the room, and was shocked to see former director and retired senator Garrison Lee sitting with her. They had files stacked to right, left, and center of their table. She thought about saying hi, but they looked engrossed in what they were doing—reading, arguing, nodding, and then arguing some more.

Sarah decided to try sleep again. As she stood to leave, she saw Virginia Pollock walking past the double doors of the cafeteria. She called out, but the assistant director kept walking. Strange, because Sarah knew she had heard her call out.

"This place isn't right somehow," she said as she left for her room, just as the overhead lights started to flicker.

THE GOLD CITY PAWNSHOP, LAS VEGAS, GATE 2

Lance Corporal Frank Mendez sat behind the counter reading his favorite book, *Watership Down*, a book he had read three times already, finding the story about rabbits more realistic than a lot of books calling themselves literature these days. He stopped reading as the front door chimed and two men walked inside. Mendez looked down at the computer screen under the counter to get a security clearance for the two men through a thumbprint match taken from the ornate door handle. He was surprised when he saw the screen was dark. He hit the power switch three times: on, off, on—nothing.

Mendez placed the book on the counter and stood. He checked the two men who were looking at stereo systems on display at the front of the shop. They looked harmless enough, so he turned and stuck his head through the curtain in the back.

"Hey, man, my monitor's down, and I've got customers out here."

Army Staff Sergeant Wayne Newland was on duty behind the desk. He looked at his monitor and saw it was dark also.

"Hmm, Europa's down all right. You better get back to your customers and I'll check the back room."

"Right," Mendez said and went back to the counter.

Newland stood and opened the door behind him. Inside was a desk with a computer monitor on it and a man behind it. The man looked up as the sergeant looked in.

"Europa's down. I think we better close the gate until she comes back up."

The desk sergeant safed the weapon under the desk and disarmed the tranquilizing darts embedded in the false front of the wooden desk and computer while Newland was in front of it. Then he picked up his phone and hit a button. The lone number connected him to the duty officer in the complex. Newland saw a funny look cross his features.

"What is it?"

The sergeant hung up the phone and looked up. "Phone's down, too."

"Shit, this isn't right," Newland said, and turned back for the back room and the store beyond. "Hit the alarm, let someone know we're down."

The desk sergeant hit a large black switch under the lip of the desk, but nothing happened. There should have been a steady blinking from a small LED placed in the button. The sergeant then rearmed the dart defense, but there was nothing there, either.

"Goddamn it!" he said as he removed the Ingram submachine gun from its clip under the desk, then he reached out to a small calculator-sized control board and hit the elevator emergency cutoff. Again, there was nothing. "Damn it, now anyone can just waltz into the shop and get into the complex." He started for the front of the store.

Mendez had just come around from behind the desk when he saw the two patrons. He smiled, knowing the nine-millimeter Beretta was tucked comfortably into his waistband. He was just about to greet the two men when Newland, followed by the desk sergeant, broke from the back room. He gave them a look that asked, *What in the hell is wrong?*

As Mendez turned back to the customers, he saw that the exact same nine-millimeter weapon as the one he had was staring him right in the face. The only difference was that this one had a foot-long silencer attached.

"Buddy, this is one place you don't want to rob," were the only words he could think of to say.

"Mendez, we're closing down. Case Blue . . . you hear me? Case Blue—"

The tranquilizer dart caught Newland in the throat. Unlike in the movies, the drug wasn't instantaneous, and the impact of the dart hurt the sergeant like a kick in the neck.

"Hey, what the—"

Mendez was shot and drugged next. The man with the nine-millimeter covered the second man while he placed another dart into the breech of his handgun.

The desk sergeant came around the corner near the display of CDs and caught sight of Mendez's feet as he lay sprawled in the next aisle over. He quickly aimed the Ingram at the man with the silenced weapon. He started to pull the trigger when a fired dart bounced off the machine gun, almost knocking it from his hands. He adjusted his aim quickly and tried to fire at the man who had shot at him.

The man with the silencer had no choice; he cursed his bad luck and fired one round into the desk sergeant's head, blowing his brains all over a rack of sunglasses.

The second man quickly ran over to the front door and opened it. As he waited, twenty men quickly moved in from an abandoned store to the right, and another ten from the alley next to the pawnshop. They entered the store with purpose, following the first two men into the back.

The taking of the Event Group Complex had begun.

Sitting across the way in a rented van, Colonel Henri Farbeaux watched in stunned disbelief at the taking of gate 2. He raised his field glasses and watched as thirty-two heavily armed and hooded men entered the store and disappeared into the back. He was confused and amazed that he was witnessing a breach of Group security such as what was happening at that moment.

Farbeaux saw an opportunity. He wouldn't need the tracking device on the seat beside him, nor the tracer he had infected the black sergeant with.

He removed his own weapon and clicked the safety off. He opened the van's rear doors and slowly walked across the street, fully intending to follow the assault element inside. Even if this was a drill of some sort, he would take advantage.

For the colonel—in case this was a real assault—having someone else kill Collins was not going to do. For the loss of his beloved wife and his own esteem, no one but he had the right to kill Jack Collins and his men.

No, the security personnel of the Group were his.

Farbeaux slowly removed the hidden gun and held it at his side as he calmly moved inside the pawnshop, following the assault element.

EVENT GROUP COMPLEX,
NELLIS AIR FORCE BASE, NEVADA

There were only six logistics men and women working the underground loading dock on level 3 at that early hour of the morning. They had little to do since the security alert had been called, shutting down all shipping to the complex. Now all six were inventorying material that was to be shipped in the next few days after being released to the National Archives and the Smithsonian. When they heard the sound of the monorail heading their way, they paid it no mind, as they thought it was gate-2 security coming home after their shift.

The loadmaster, an air force sergeant, looked at his watch and took a double take.

"This isn't right," he said, looking up from his watch at the approaching tram. It was now on its last two hundred feet of centerline rail as it straightened out from its dive into the earth from Las Vegas, ten miles away. "There's no scheduled security change, and there's no one allowed to arrive through gate two during the lockdown."

"So, maybe one of the guys is sick or something. You worry way too much, Sarge," said one of the men as he checked off the weight of a large crate.

"Then why didn't Europa notify us?" he asked as he gestured for a female specialist to check the computer for a missed command.

"She's down, Sergeant," the woman said as she exited the small booth on the massive loading dock. She tossed an M-16 to the sergeant and another to the man next to him, who dropped his clipboard in his effort to catch the weapon. She herself drew a nine-millimeter from a holster at her side.

The sergeant took station next to the large crate, and the others followed suit as the sound of the approaching tram slowed, then picked up speed again. They saw the glow of the monorail's glassed-in interior as it sped to a stop at the loading dock. It was empty. All seven cars and their plastic seating were void of any passengers. Still, the air force sergeant approached cautiously with his weapon at the ready. He chanced a look into the darkened tunnel beyond, but could only see the fluorescent blue and green track lighting fading away in the distance.

"Specialist, illuminate the tunnel, now!"

The female specialist ran to the controller's shack and hit the switch that would turn on the overheads lining the massive tunnel's ceiling. Nothing happened.

"We have a problem here, Sarge. Europa may have killed this panel when she went down."

"Damn!" he said, just as a dart slammed into his chest and then another into his cheek.

Small sounds echoed off the concrete walls of the monorail tunnel as twenty darts streaked toward their targets, embedding themselves in the five remaining personnel on the dock. The female specialist had the fortitude to remain on her feet and slam her hand into the intruder alarm as she fell forward. Again, there was nothing.

Soon, thirty-two men stood in the dark, illuminated only by the blue and green running lights of the tunnel. For now, the dart guns were holstered and submachine guns took their place. The men started forward, chambering rounds as they did. They knew from this point on, the Event Group personnel would not be so easy to subdue.

The fall of the Event Group complex was now more than just a plan; it was close to a fact.

Three hundred feet above the loading dock, the four VTOL aircraft popped into the air a hundred feet short of the dilapidated hangar that was the cover for gate 1. As each aircraft peeled off, two to the right and two to the left, the gunners in the open doorway brought their night-vision goggles down to cover their eyes. They chambered the larger dart rounds into a large pneumatic six-barreled cannon. Soon, the gunner in the lead aircraft had several targets.

Event Group security kept a small squad on duty outside of the massive hangar where large loads were brought into the complex. The first of these soldiers, a marine, saw the strange craft slow. He took aim at the unauthorized intruders and was about to open fire with his M249 machine gun when the sound of a hundred bees surrounded him. Several of these angry insects struck him in the chest and the torso. As he fell forward with the darts protruding from his body, he saw several of his team succumb to the same quick fate.

Soon, the entire eight-man squad of Event Group security was eliminated as a threat to the assault units now landing outside the old hangar. Soon forty more heavily armed men stormed inside the hangar and lined the giant elevator. Within thirty seconds the dark-clad men were headed down into the heart of the Event Group.

Niles Compton rubbed his eyes and then picked up his phone. He punched in the three-digit code for the computer center. The line was dead. He then swiveled in his chair and turned on his Europa monitor, but all that appeared was a blue screen. Concerned, Niles replaced his glasses and stood from his desk. Just as he was about to move toward the oaken double doors, they opened and several hooded men dressed in navy-blue body armor and BDUs came through. Niles froze as three submachine guns, the likes of which he had never seen before, were leveled at his chest. The man in the center of the five intruders gestured quickly for his team to lower their weapons.

Niles saw through the open doorway that his assistants were being rounded up, and plastic wire-ties were being used to bind their wrists.

"Dr. Compton, you have our sincerest apologies for this sudden intrusion," the tall man in the center of the group said as he moved quickly to the bank of monitors lining the wall. He flipped a switch marked GATE 1 and watched as the security camera sent its signal from the mock dilapidated hangar. Satisfied when he saw several of his own men in command of the gate, he turned to Compton. "You'll pardon our haste, but I understand your Captain Everett is due to return shortly with his men, and I am led to believe that he would not take too kindly to our visit."

One of his men stepped forward and whispered something. He was holding a small radio in his hand.

"Doctor, I assure you, your people are being well treated. There have only been five casualties thus far, four of them from your interior security department, and I am informed two of those will live. We do not wish any more loss of life."

"You knew from the start the meeting in New York would be compromised," Niles said, standing straight and looking directly at the man as he removed his hood. Niles risked a quick glance at the closed-circuit camera that was independent of Europa, and saw the small red light was still on. The same system that was installed at gate 1, they had intentionally not shut it down because they needed eyes on that gate.

"Yes, but the ruse was useful to get Captain Everett and the more experienced members of his team out of the complex. He and his men would have made the taking of the most secure location inside the United States, well, to say the least, a challenge."

"And now your plans are?" Niles asked.

The tall man moved to Compton's desk and looked it over. The man was average looking, his hair was somewhat longer than a military-style cut, and he had a decidedly menacing quality about him. His English had an Irish lean to it. Compton knew that if the closed-circuit camera was working, their conversation was being recorded along with this man's face.

"Your presence is required by my superiors for two reasons. One is information; two is so you can bear witness to what the world is up against."

"And if I refuse to come along?"

"You won't. I don't need to make threats against your people, that's the stuff of television. We are under orders to act accordingly. So if you will follow us"—he pulled up his sleeve and looked at his wristwatch—"we will depart."

Sarah was riding the elevator down to the personal quarter's area on level eight when the elevator lurched, and then continued on to her selected floor. She didn't like it when there was anything out of the ordinary about the elevators. She knew they rode in a tube and were raised and lowered on a cushion of air.

Finally, the indicator said she had arrived on level eight and the doors slowly slid open. Then the power failed. The elevator again lurched. Sarah wondered why Europa didn't compensate for the loss of pumped air; she decided not to take a chance and dove from the car just as it hissed and then was sent crashing down into the complex. Sarah rolled over her sling, crying out as she hurt her damaged shoulder. That was when she hit someone standing in the hallway. The dark figure looked down, quite surprised when he saw a woman at his feet. He maneuvered his weapon just as it crossed Sarah's mind as to what kind of screwed-up security drill Carl was running, but she was in too much pain to think, only react. Then she saw the weapon in the man's hands point down toward her prone body.

Taken with the default of the elevator, she realized instantly that this was no security drill. She pivoted on her hip and kicked out with her right leg, hitting the man right at both ankles. His legs were knocked out from under him and his weapon discharged, creating bright flashes in the darkened hallway. The bullets thumped into the plastic wall as the man struck the carpeting. Sarah, still on her back, quickly raised her left foot and brought it down into the man's face, her heel striking precisely where she had aimed it: the nose. The man grunted in pain, then lay still.

She heard a shuffling coming down the hallway and knew immediately the downed man hadn't been alone. Sarah was blind and on her back. She quickly felt around for the man's fallen weapon and finally hit upon it as ten silenced rounds thumped into the wall and carpeting around her, with one actually striking the cast on her arm, breaking it apart in large chunks.

"Bastard!" she mumbled as she quickly raised the strange weapon. She prayed it wasn't on *safe* because in the dark she would never find the selector switch on a weapon she knew nothing about. She squeezed the trigger. The weapon erupted with fire and a loud clacking noise as the silencer did its job. Bullets struck the wall, floor, and ceiling, and then in the flare of the muzzle, she saw bullets stitch a crooked pattern on a man no more than six feet from her, with a bullet finally striking him in an unprotected spot just above his body armor.

Sarah was shaking badly as she tore the night-vision scope from the face of the man under her. That was when she noticed his companion's bullets had struck him several times in the side. She quickly held the scope to her eyes and looked around frantically. She tried desperately to control her breathing, thinking that anyone in a hundred-foot radius could hear her terror.

"What kind of screwed-up homecoming is this?" she whispered to herself, hoping her sour humor would allow her to inject more bravery into a terrifying situation.

Sarah picked herself up and then quickly felt her arm. She realized she hadn't hurt it any more than it had been; it was sore, but at least she could move it. She hefted the heavy weapon and made for the stairwell beside her, knowing she had to get to either level seven or at the very least the computer center where she knew Pete Golding and his techs were always working.

For the first time in over a month, Sarah wasn't thinking about the loss of Jack Collins.

Senator Garrison Lee was in his element. He sat with his longtime live-in companion in the cafeteria and went through each file that he himself had okayed in the years leading up to deprioritizing the items in the vaults on levels seventy-three and seventy-four.

"That's it, Garrison, we've covered all six hundred and seventy-two vaults. What do you think?"

"I think I want some of that coffee, old girl, if you would be so kind."

Alice shook her head and stood, tired herself. She decided she would have tea just to offset the mood that the caffeine would put the senator in.

Garrison looked at one file he had placed on the left side of the table, separating it from the others.

"Why that one?" Alice asked. She placed the cup of coffee on the table and sipped her own tea just as the lights in the cafeteria failed. The bright emergency lights came on, and Lee continued.

"Because, woman," Lee said, also looking around him at the emergency lighting, "it's the only vault that would make any sense. I'm surprised you didn't pull this file immediately after learning the facts of the attacks at sea. I think you're slowing down some."

Alice raised her eyebrow but said nothing as she sat down.

"Okay, Mr. Lee, how about explaining?" Alice asked while she looked around in the now-shadowy cafeteria. Then the lights came back on at full strength.

"Point number one: This report from the USS *Columbia* states that the vessel that launched the attacks on Venezuela was like nothing ever encountered before. I quote, 'a submarine of extraordinary capabilities,' end quote. We've had a partial answer to why the complex was attacked from the very beginning. Someone was afraid of what we had stored in vault number 298907. A vault that was classified as cold and relegated to the storage level, all testing and analysis completed." He slid the single folder over to Alice, who looked at the name and number on its outer jacket.

"*Leviathan*," she said to herself.

"That's right, *Leviathan*. Recovered in nineteen sixty-seven by the Woods Hole Oceanographic Institution off the coast of Newfoundland, with parts of her discovered as far south as Maine."

Alice slid the file back to Garrison.

"The advanced submarine was estimated at more than one hundred years old, conservatively speaking, and"—Alice quoted from memory—"'with a kerosene-and-diesel-mix electric power system that rivaled the diesel submarines of today.' At the time you believed this vessel was what Jules Verne based his fictional *Nautilus* upon. Is my memory serving correctly?" she asked.

"Like a computer, young lady," Garrison said as he slid a liver-spotted hand over hers. "Not bad at all for a woman approaching the century mark."

"That's you, my dear, not I." She smiled and patted his hand. "Now, if I do remember correctly, carbon dating and other tests placed her destruction in a ten-year time frame between eighteen sixty and eighteen seventy-one. What does that have to do with today?"

"I don't believe in coincidence, never have. Advanced submarine in the past, advanced submarine in the present, explosion that takes out what material we do have on level seventy-three, one-plus-one-plus-one equals someone wanted us not to reference that boat in our vault. Now we know why, and we know what attacked us—all we need is the who? Is it something in that vault that will give away this vessel's technology, or on the other hand, maybe her metallurgy? Her home port or waters, or was something left aboard the relic that will assist in identifying the man behind such an advanced craft?"

"We better report to Niles and—"

That was as far as Alice got before several men broke through the double doors of the cafeteria and started rounding up the few people inside. In the next moment, a submachine gun was pointing right in Garrison Lee's face.

Alice placed her hand on Garrison's, letting him know that he was not to try anything foolish.

"Young man, please aim that weapon in another direction, unless of course you plan to murder us. If not, you little bastard, point it somewhere else."

The masked gunman smiled inside his black nylon hood at the woman who continued to confront him with her eyes, even after he moved the weapon and aimed it at the floor. He then pulled a list out of his armored vest and looked at the typed names and their pictures. He looked from Alice to Garrison.

"Mrs. Hamilton, your reputation precedes you, ma'am. Would you and the senator please follow me to the main conference room?"

As the man spoke, the power grid flickered as it had before, and then the overhead lights went completely out.

"Don't worry, ma'am, we have just sealed this level from the others, and that means we have successfully taken control of the most secure facility in the American government."

Alice looked at Garrison Lee in the emergency lighting shining from the corners of the cafeteria. His one eye was glaring at the man standing over them. Once more, she took his hand and started to stand.

"Very well, young man, it seems you have the advantage," Alice said as she assisted Lee to his feet.

"At least for the moment, you little prick," Garrison Lee said directly into the man's masked face, and as he did, he used his hand to slide the file they had been examining onto his vacated chair.

The man's laugh sounded muffled, but it traveled through the entire cafeteria as he reached down and gathered up the folders on the table to take with him.

"I'd hate to run into you two in a dark alley," he said as he gestured for them to head for the cafeteria doors.

Sarah cautiously opened the stairwell door one level up. She looked down the dark and curving hallway using the night scope, being careful not to look at the dim emergency lighting at the far end.

She held the door ajar by the barrel of the weapon, allowing her to see the comp center directly across from her. There were figures moving inside, but she couldn't make out who they were. Then she smiled as she saw the form of Pete Golding throw a chair against the bulletproof glass as hard as he could, but all it did was bounce back and almost strike him. In the green haze of the scope, she saw Pete as he screamed in frustration. The sound didn't penetrate the glass, but the gesture was almost comical. Pete just wasn't the herculean type.

With the weapon opening the door farther, Sarah stepped into the hallway, allowing the door to close gently behind her. She slowly made her way to the center and tapped on the glass doors with the gun barrel until Pete looked up. He twisted his head because he couldn't see who was out there in the dark. Sarah waved him over, and the relief in Pete's face was apparent. She mouthed something he couldn't understand. Then, with her sore arm she reached into her jumpsuit pocket, brought out a Sharpie felt pen, and hastily scrawled, *Attacked*.

Pete nodded, and then he suddenly started pointing frantically behind Sarah as if the Devil himself were there.

Sarah turned and there were two men standing directly behind her. One grabbed the barrel of the weapon and pulled it from her grasp while the other grabbed her by the throat and shoved her against the glass. Pete and his comp team were frantic. They was gesturing wildly and banging on the glass, screaming threats that went unheard. The man who had grabbed the gun saw Sarah's cutoff sleeve, the sling, and the remains of the cast on her forearm. He reached out and hit her in the upper arm above the elbow, and Sarah immediately collapsed in agony.

Pete Golding and the other techs saw this and started throwing their bodies against the glass doorway. They were desperate to keep any harm from befalling the little geologist.

The masked man moved his weapon aside on its strap, then reached down and grabbed Sarah by the collar and pulled her to her feet.

"This is our little hero from level eight."

The other man stepped back. "No casualties—remember the orders."

"Unless in self-defense," the smaller of the two said as he brought his weapon back around.

Sarah grimaced in pain, and then suddenly struck out with her right foot, trying desperately to kick at the two men, but her tennis shoes were striking nothing but empty air.

"These people just don't know when to quit," the larger assailant said, laughing at the violent way Sarah struggled.

Suddenly, the hooded face jerked violently forward and Sarah felt the splash of warm blood hit her in the face. There was a crack of a bullet, but only because it had penetrated the man's skull and passed through, hitting the glass of the comp center. The other man tried to turn, but two bullets struck him in the side of the head and neck. As he fell, he pulled the stunned Sarah down with him.

Pete and the comp center technicians stopped banging on the glass as the blood from the first man obscured it. Pete straightened in shock as he prayed Sarah wasn't hit. He looked from her form to the darkened hallway beyond. He couldn't see anything.

Sarah kicked at the man who had fallen on her legs and at the same time struggled to get ahold of one of the fallen weapons. As her hand found one, there was a calm voice echoing from the bend in the long dark corridor.

"Little Sarah, always a fighter."

The voice was familiar. Sarah searched the darkness, raising the automatic weapon toward the darkness.

"Not advisable, at least for the moment," the voice said, as if reprimanding a child. "Tell me, dear Sarah, is Jack with you?"

Her recognition of the voice came flooding into her memory. Pictures of the man it belonged to hit her like ice water. Colonel Henri Farbeaux.

"Come now, you owe me your life. Surely worth the price of an answer."

"This isn't your style, Henri, extravagant though it is." Sarah still twisted the weapon until its muzzle pointed into the dark.

"I'm what you would call a stowaway. As well as these people planned, it was far too messy. But then again, I don't know the motivation behind it. Nor, dear Sarah, do I care. I'm here for the man that cost me the life of my wife."

"What in the hell are you talking about, Colonel?"

"She never returned from our little Amazonian excursion. Our Major Jack was the cause of that."

Sarah made a face as she tried to sit up. "And you're blaming the colonel?"

"Colonel? Colonel Collins? Ah, the rewards for having my wife meet her fate in a godforsaken lagoon. This is getting rich, little Sarah."

"Henri . . . Jack is—" Sarah lost her voice for a moment. "Jack's dead."

There was silence from the hallway.

"He didn't kill Danielle; we didn't even know she was lost. Jack Collins never would have wanted that. He wanted everyone to make it out— even you, Henri." Sarah twisted and tried to rise to her feet.

She tried to peer into the darkness, but she saw no movement. She thought about reaching down for the goggles, but decided she wouldn't make the effort. Finally, she heard movement.

"A shame. I will not ask about the possibility of a lie, I can see the truth of it in your face. It hurts, does it not?"

Sarah saw the darker outline of the man as he stepped from the wall.

His weapon was still held at belt level and it was aimed right at her. She looked at the heavy weapon in her hands, then slowly tossed it away.

"A part of me died that day." Sarah looked into the face of the Frenchman and didn't flinch.

"Yes, loss will do that to one," he said. He looked into her eyes as his silenced pistol finally wavered and then lowered. "You have been injured, I see."

Sarah remained quiet as she looked at their old enemy. He had lost a large amount of weight, and his eyes were dark below and above the lids. There was a sense about him that he no longer held himself on a pedestal above others. Sarah could see that he was broken, mentally and physically. In addition, she was seeing something drain from the man like a tipping water glass. His hatred and willingness to strike out at something familiar, in this case Jack, were gone, as if hearing of his death completed the trade for Danielle.

"Stand aside, Sarah McIntire, and I will assist you in freeing your friends before one of them seriously injures themselves. Then I will leave you."

Sarah finally turned and saw Pete Golding, forehead bleeding and holding his shoulder, furiously gesturing for his technicians to ram the door again. Sarah shook her head. Pete was magnificent with a computer keyboard, but in rescue attempts, he left a lot to be desired.

Farbeaux walked up to Sarah and looked at her for the longest time. His eyes bore into her own as if he were looking at someone he remembered from his past with fondness. Then he reached down, picked up the fallen goggles, raised them to his eyes, and at the same moment raised the pistol and aimed at the locks in the glass door.

Sarah was just relaxing when Farbeaux suddenly jerked and then tried to turn around. The silenced automatic fell from his hand as he gasped for breath. His other hand pulled the large dart from the back of his shoulder. He looked at Sarah as if she had been responsible; then his legs gave out. Sarah reached out for him as he collapsed.

As she looked up, twenty men approached. Several flashlights illuminated the stricken Farbeaux. Men spread out and covered the glass fronting of the computer center where Pete stared in shock at the four people standing at the center of the group—Director Compton, Virginia Pollock, Alice Hamilton, and Senator Garrison Lee. They were not bound, but each had an armed escort. A man stepped forward, separating himself from the group. He wore no hood, and he had loosened his upper body armor, undoubtedly for comfort.

Sarah watched the man examine the scene before him. His eyes went from his two dead commandos to the unconscious Henri Farbeaux.

"Lieutenant, are you all right?" Niles asked.

The man quickly held a hand up as his head turned and looked at Sarah. "Silence please, Doctor."

"If you harm any more of my people, you may as well shoot us all right now," Niles said, shaking a guard's hand off his arm and stepping forward.

The man continued to look at Sarah with cold and very dark eyes.

"This one comes with us," he said as he gestured one of his men forward.

"Sarah, are you hurt?" Alice asked as she held on to the senator.

"Just my pride," she answered, as she was roughly turned and her hands wire-tied behind her back. Her eyes met Pete Golding's, who stared through the glass in frustration.

"Is that . . . is that Colonel Farbeaux?" Compton asked.

Sarah was turned roughly about so she could face the group. Her anger was apparent as her eyes went from the man in front of her to the man who had tied her. With her arm and shoulder screaming in agony, she shook the man's hands from her.

"Yes."

"Is he . . . a part of this?"

Sarah thought about saying something about the colonel's intentions, but she knew there was no point. She looked at Niles and shook her head.

"You know Henri was always an opportunist. What better way to get into the complex and steal than during a murder raid?" She said the last words looking right into the tall man's eyes.

"We must go. We have several flights of stairs to traverse to get to the hangar," the man said as he pulled Sarah roughly forward toward the others.

The tall man looked down at the Frenchman and then to the two bodies on the floor beside him. Then he pulled a nine-millimeter handgun from a shoulder holster, approached the prone Farbeaux, and placed the gun to his head.

"The same rules apply to him. You kill him, kill us," Niles said, desperately trying to keep Farbeaux from dying. He despised the man, but he didn't want him murdered in cold blood, either.

The leader of the assault closed his eyes in thought. After a moment, he straightened and holstered his weapon. He ordered two men to take the still form of Colonel Farbeaux, then turned to face Compton.

"You're quickly running out of favors, Mr. Director. I will bring this man with us, only to ask for his execution for killing my men."

"I thought violence and murder were not part of your orders," Niles persisted in his antagonizing tone.

"I have been known to adapt, Doctor, to react to a flowing situation. Do not push me."

Alice pulled Niles back and made him assist in supporting the senator. On their way past the leader of the assault, Assistant Director Virginia Pollock shot him a look that had murder etched in it. The man just smiled as the others were herded toward the stairs.

The Event Group Complex had fallen in less than twenty-five minutes.

NORTHERN FIRING RANGE (INACTIVE), NELLIS AIR FORCE BASE

The UH-60 Black Hawk had met Everett, Mendenhall, Ryan, the limo driver Rodriguez, and the improving Jack Collins on the military tarmac at McCarran airport in Las Vegas. Everett was on the headphones talking with the chief warrant officer flying the large helicopter. The others watched as Everett shook his head negatively and shouted something into his microphone. Ryan and Mendenhall exchanged looks. The captain angrily removed his headphone and then went into the rear compartment.

"It seems Nellis just went on alert. They wanted us to vector back to McCarran, but we're still trying to get the okay to proceed to gate one."

"What's up?" Ryan shouted.

"They have missiles heading this way, target unknown. They've been tracking them for the past two hours; they were zigzagging all over the place, and then started this way. The launch area was off the Jersey coast—which means our new friends may have been responsible. At least they are the more viable candidate at the moment. In addition, all search radar and communications are down with the exception of hard lines. Emergency systems at Nellis are just coming back online."

Everett looked at Jack, who was looking back at him and trying to understand what it was that was happening. Everett patted him on the leg.

"Don't worry, buddy. Sarah's going to have the surprise of her life when she gets back from her mama's."

Collins forced a smile and nodded. His head was filled with cotton, but ever since Carl and the others had started talking to him on the flight back from the East Coast, his memory was now returning in waves instead of dribbles. The most important memory that came first was Sarah's death as he held her in the waters of the Med, and then his closed-eyed prayer of thanks when Carl smiled and told him she was alive. Everything else was placed in the back of his mind as his body immediately relaxed with the knowledge he would see Sarah again.

The Black Hawk banked sharply and headed for the deck. Carl held on to the seat as he turned and saw the copilot give the thumbs-up from the right seat.

"Okay, we just got permission to get to the house."

As the Black Hawk screamed low over the desert, the pilot was shocked when his radar detected a missile lock on them. He figured his bird had picked up a stray beam from the circling F-22 Raptors flying combat air cap over the prized air base. He became worried when the tone in his headphones became louder and steady. He pulled his stick back into his belly, slammed it over to the right, and the large helicopter fought for altitude while rolling to the right. Chaff, small explosions of aluminum foil, started popping out of the tail boom, and flares bright as the sun flew from the Black Hawk's underbelly, all in an effort to thwart the missile lock that had them zeroed in.

"Hang on," the crew chief called out.

As Everett sat and strapped in, a sudden bright explosion rent the side of the Black Hawk, throwing shrapnel into the large right-side T700/CT7 engine. Large chunks of hot metal severed the fuel lines, and the rest shot up and into the composite rotors, removing huge chunks from the aerodynamic edges. The big chopper keeled over to the right far farther than its pilot intended. The copilot was on the radio screaming mayday and that they were under attack.

"Jesus Christ," Ryan screamed as he braced himself against the aluminum bulkhead.

"If this is for my benefit, I admit, you got me," Jack said loudly.

With the rotors vibrating, the Black Hawk shuddered and started to fall from the sky. Then one of the four blades flew from the hub and the rest of the rotors sheared away because of the massive torque placed upon the unbalanced rotor assembly.

"Oh, shit," Everett said as he saw the ground rushing up to meet the falling aircraft. "Hang on, this is going to be sudden!"

The Black Hawk luckily slammed into the false dilapidated roof of the hangar building of gate 1. It careened back into the air and actually slid through the air, finally landing on its belly, minus its rotors. The Black Hawk slid about a hundred feet through the Nevada scrub, and then the airframe hit a large rise of sand and flew back into the air and onto her left side, tearing free the landing gear assembly. She finally came to rest, her right-side engine burning.

"Get the hell out!" Everett yelled as they all unfastened their seat belts, holding on to each other because of the awkward position with the Black Hawk lying on its side.

As Everett first reached the doorway, a hand shot through and pulled him up. He saw that it was one of the gate 1 security men dressed in his desert camouflage. As Everett turned to assist the others, several loud thumps slammed into the bottom of the chopper.

"Hey, someone's taking potshots at us!" Mendenhall called from the interior.

Everett turned to the lone security man.

"Where in the hell is the rest of the security element?"

"Out. We were hit twenty minutes ago; all hell is breaking loose down in the complex."

Finally, Ryan was the last man lifted from the downed Black Hawk. Everett, Rodriguez, and Mendenhall had already drawn their nine-millimeters and were firing into the hangar.

"In case you didn't know it, Captain, we're outgunned here," Jack said as he took cover next to Carl.

"You haven't missed a beat—same old song and dance, outnumbered and outgunned," Carl said as he fired two rounds into the dark, then risked a look back at the colonel. "Welcome home, Jack," he said with a smirk.

The air suddenly filled with a loud buzzing. The sound was almost recognizable as a V-22 Osprey, but the engine noise was different; it had more of a whine to it.

"Are the marines landing here at Nellis?" Mendenhall asked as he fired, emptying his weapon.

"I hope it's them," Ryan said just as his gun jammed.

Without warning, the hangar's interior lights were turned on and alarms started sounding. They could see close to fifty men inside as they suddenly tossed off goggles and held their hands to their eyes in the brightness of the floodlights.

"Well, someone back in the complex finally woke the hell up," Will said, pushing in another clip of ammunition.

Collins reached out, took a set of binoculars from the case of the camouflaged security man, brought them to his eyes, and rose up above the protection of the helicopter.

"Damn, I count over forty, no, fifty-plus bad guys . . . and . . . no, wait . . . cease-fire. . . . cease-fire, damn it!" Jack called out. "They have hostages! What in the hell is happening here? Damn, they have the director."

Everett pulled the glasses from Jack and looked inside.

"Alice, the senator, Niles, Virginia—" he called out, and then he became silent, turned, and slid down the fuselage to a sitting position after seeing one other person who was being carried by two men in dark Nomex.

The sky above them screamed as a large aircraft, a kind they had never seen before, shot overhead and then flared at the last moment before flying headlong into the façade of the old hangar. It was an unrecognizable tilt-rotor craft. Then another and another, until the fourth set down outside the hangar. Large and fierce looking, the aircraft had two loud and piercing jet engines in the place of the turbofan propellers of the American V-22 Osprey. As they landed, the engines pivoted, and were positioned to pull the aircraft instead of providing it with lift.

As the security men of the Event Group watched helplessly, the hostile element was seen running with their captives to a lowering rear ramp. The tilt-engine craft was large enough to accommodate all of them easily. In two minutes, the black-painted aircraft revved its engines, pushed out of the hangar, and was airborne in five seconds. It shot low over the desert and was soon climbing. The other men ran to their assigned craft and loaded. Everett was impressed with the time it took to load their assault element. The egress from the landing zone was all done in less than thirty seconds.

Mendenhall tugged at Everett's sleeve and pointed into the dark sky. Two F-22 Raptors, America's newest top-of-the-line fighters, shot through the air in pursuit of the attacking craft.

"Inform Nellis combat ops to observe only, not to engage. American hostages are onboard," Carl said to Ryan as he commenced broadcasting with the handheld radio.

The sound of more fighters were heard as they went to afterburner to get airborne from the airstrip at the main base. Mendenhall counted ten in all, including the two already in pursuit of the attackers.

Finally, Collins sat hard into the sand and looked at Everett. "How in the hell could they have gotten in and kidnapped the four highest ranking people we have?"

Carl didn't answer right away. Instead he looked at his friend and hoped Jack was going to accept what he had to say.

"Jack, they're not the only people they took." He looked from Collins to Ryan, who was still talking with combat operations at Nellis. "I swear, I thought she was at home recovering," he finally said.

Jack didn't ask who. He just waited.

"They took Sarah."

Collins looked from Carl to the ground, and then slowly stood and stared out to the east, in the direction the strange aircraft had taken.

Ryan lowered the radio and Will Mendenhall looked from the sky to the colonel. Everett rose and watched as Jack Collins started walking determinedly toward the now-empty hangar. All three noticed he walked without the slightest bit of fatigue showing in his step.

The assault on the Event Group home had awakened a man who was not in the frame of mind to allow this attack to go unanswered.

As the F-22 Raptors took up station behind the four stubby winged aircraft, they saw their airspeed had vaulted just past the speed of sound, impossible for a tilt-jet airframe. Still, there it was, their instruments confirming that they were indeed creeping toward mach 1.4.

Every threat detector on all ten fighters suddenly illuminated and started screaming their warnings into the headphones of every pilot in the flight.

Overhead, the missiles that had been launched off the coast of New Jersey two hours before had been on glide mode until a signal was received by the strange lead craft the fighters were pursuing. Then the six cruise missiles dipped their rounded noses and streaked for the fighters far below. Suddenly the outer casings of reinforced composite material ripped free, sending three separate parts flying into the air, and releasing ten separate radar-guided missiles. Now instead of six missiles to contend with, the Raptors were faced with sixty. The odds failed to register with the air force pilots as they broke formation and started to scatter, trying to avoid the sixty projectiles heading right for them. Threat detectors warbled, and chaff and flares started to fly from each of the Raptors in the hopes of confusing the incoming threats. Each of the ten Americans couldn't believe their stealthy craft were being picked up so easily.

By twos the fighters screamed high overhead. Vacationers visiting Las Vegas turned their heads skyward as each jet slammed their throttles to their stops, going to afterburner in their attempted escape of the planned ambush. The guests of Las Vegas's fabulous hotels oohed and ahhed as even more bright flares of exhaust converged on the Raptors, which each had seven missiles targeted upon it.

The crowds gathered on the strip were suddenly startled when the smaller flares of fire merged with the larger exhausts of the F-22s, and bright flashes of explosions lit up the already bright Las Vegas night. They watched as two of the American fighters dove and then jinked, outmaneuvering their attackers. The Raptors flew so low that one of the composite wings smashed through the great light above the pyramid of the Luxor Casino, sending glass and debris raining down upon the running crowd.

Another Raptor was struck as it tried the same maneuver as the first two, but it wasn't as lucky. The radar-seeking missile exploded just as it pulled up from its dive. Shrapnel pierced the canopy, killing the pilot immediately, and then the plane careened off the roof of the old Flamingo Hotel and crashed into a parking garage across the street.

All told, the ambush that was ordered and launched two full hours before the attack on the Event Group complex to cover the escape of the terrorists had claimed five lives at the base and eight lives in the air.

The four large aircraft continued on their way without any further hostile actions by the United States. Their course: the Gulf of Mexico.

7

At the late hour, the president insisted the national security briefing take place in the less dramatic Oval Office instead of the war room below the White House. He was tired and he was angry. He listened to the briefing by the navy secretary without comment.

"Sir, we have the escort plan for the four supertankers we're attaching to the Nimitz battle group. The *Nimitz* is currently steaming to their appointed rendezvous and will join with the Royal Navy, who is escorting the four tankers. They plan to make the Atlantic run from Devonport, England, and convoyed by the frigates HMS *Monmouth*, HMS *Somerset*, and the Royal Navy submarine HMS *Trafalgar*. At the same time, we are coordinating a simultaneous convoy with the Chinese—they have a group leaving Venezuelan waters tomorrow with a Chinese battle group surrounding the two tankers. Our mysterious enemy cannot be in two places at once."

At that moment the president's secretary entered the office and gave him a message. He read it and then passed it around the room.

"Nellis?" he asked the secretary of defense.

"Damn it, the missile launch from the Atlantic made contact with ten F-22 Raptors out of Nellis," General Caulfield explained to the fifteen men in the room. "Eight were destroyed by a cruise missile system undocumented by any intelligence service."

"Do we have anything happening at Nellis that would warrant an attack?" Fuqua asked, looking to the secretary of the air force.

"Nothing. Red Flag is there—war games, that's it at the moment," the secretary answered.

The president lowered his head for the briefest of moments when he realized what else was at Nellis Air Force Base.

"Gentlemen, proceed with your plans, and keep me informed. For now, please excuse me."

The secretary escorted the security council from the office as the president turned, opened his top left drawer, brought out a small laptop computer, and opened the lid. He tapped in a command and then waited. A simple line appeared: DEPARTMENT 5656. The president waited, but no one came online.

"Jesus," he mumbled as he picked up the phone and dialed a ten-digit number. He pulled the phone away from his ear when there was a loud screech and then a recorded voice.

"The federal agency you are trying to reach is currently experiencing an emergency shutdown. This is a temporary situation. Please try this department at a later time."

The president lowered the phone into its cradle and leaned back in his chair. The feeling that he was nothing more than an amateur started to creep into his thoughts. Nellis being the target of a missile attack and the Event Group being offline was not just a coincidence, but because of the Group's secrecy from Congress and the law-enforcement community, there wasn't much he could do at the moment. For now he would have to wait for Niles to let him know just what in the hell was going on out there.

It would be a long night for the president of the United States.

THE EVENT GROUP COMPLEX, NELLIS AIR FORCE BASE, NEVADA

Jack, Everett, Ryan, and Mendenhall assisted the injured pilots, crew members and the field security team into the complex using the giant elevator inside the hangar. As the grated floor cleared the first level, they could hear alarms sounding from below.

"Whatever happened here, happened on my watch. Jack, I don't know . . ."

"Stow it for now, Captain. Someone opened the door for these people. Our men can't be expected to secure the complex if someone's passing out keys to the damn locks."

Everett slowly nodded, not at all appeased he had failed the Group.

The elevator hit level 3 and the men were met by security, who at first stared in shock as Jack Collins stepped from the large platform. Men and women gathered at the loading dock and stared at the man who had returned from the dead. A sergeant wearing the insignia of an army soldier stepped up and saluted the colonel, then turned and looked at Captain Everett, his immediate commander.

"Sir, we have five dead and seventeen wounded. Thirty-two tranquilized Group members, one of whom is in shock. We have damage to gate two and gate one. We have five missing personnel that we assume have left the complex with the hostile assault element."

"Thank you, Sergeant. Has all power been restored?"

"Yes, sir, Dr. Golding has all systems back online."

Jack didn't wait to hear anymore as he started for the elevator across from the loading dock.

"Carry on, Sergeant. Lockdown is to be strictly enforced. Get every available security man and shut this place down tighter than a drum."

"Yes, Captain."

As the elevator doors opened on level seven, Jack stood in the doorway for a brief moment. The hallway facing them was a tangle of wires, broken plastic, and personnel. They all turned and saw who it was standing just outside the elevator doors looking at them. All were shocked to see the colonel, and one by one, they broke their paralysis and made their way to greet him as he stepped into the hallway. He was patted on the back and heard whispers of welcome home. Then he saw a familiar face parting the crowd in an attempt to reach the elevator.

"Colonel?" Pete Golding was shocked beyond words as he stared at Jack.

"Doc, I take it we had a problem?" Collins said as he took Golding's hand in his own and shook.

"They hit hard and fast, Colonel," Pete said sadly. He escorted the four men past the Group personnel and finally entered the computer center, where Pete sat on the edge of one of the desks.

Jack saw the damage to the bulletproof glass and the blood that still streamed down the wall nearest the door.

"It was my fault. I assumed the virus planted in Europa had run its course after having delivered the message. I never considered that the virus would mutate at a chosen time and shut down all security systems and . . . and . . . well, everything, just everything."

Collins looked at Everett and shook his head. Everett had given a

complete report on what was happening in the world since his trip to
Valhalla, but Carl just didn't know how much of the information Jack
had retained.

"Doc, is Europa online?"

"Well, her peripheral systems, such as lights and phones, yes. But
until I can tear down her advanced programs and find that bug, she won't
be of help to us for at least twelve hours."

Jack patted him on the back. "Get whatever help you need, even if
you have to bring in the Cray people, but get her up. We need her." Jack
shook Pete's shoulder until he finally looked up. "Is there anything else,
Pete?"

Golding looked away and then down at the floor.

"We tried to help her, Colonel. She was right there in front of us, but
we couldn't get to her."

"Who?" Everett asked,

"Sarah. She was fighting back . . . hell . . . she was the only one fighting after security was taken out. When we thought they were going to
kill her, a man came out of nowhere and stopped them. They took him
also." He looked into Jack's eyes. "I'm sorry, Jack."

With a pat on Golding's back, Collins looked around the computer
center at the many technicians that were already tearing into Europa's
peripheral systems. He knew Pete would have to head for the clean room
to get into her deep-seated programming. He decided to leave Golding
to his daunting task.

"By the way, Doc," Jack said, turning around and facing Pete before
he reached the door. "You're in temporary command of the department—
acting director. We'll meet again in a few hours, so get a replacement
lined up in the comp center." Jack looked at his watch. "Until then, I'll
report to the president—he'll want to speak with you, so don't get lost."

Pete watched Jack as he turned for the door. He was in shock that the
chain of ascension had never once occurred to him during this entire
god-awful mess. Then he remembered something.

"Colonel Collins?"

Jack stopped but didn't turn around, but Everett, Ryan, and Mendenhall did.

"I have to meet with you and the captain in private. I may have discovered who the mole and traitor is. However, I need Europa to assist me

in confirming it. Also, the man that saved Lieutenant McIntire's life—" Pete bit his lower lip and acted nervous, but continued after a moment's pause. "It was the Frenchman—Henri Farbeaux."

Collins closed his eyes as his jaw muscles clenched. Then he took a deep breath and left the center.

"Jesus, this is getting better and better," Mendenhall said as he kicked at a large chunk of still smoldering wiring on the floor.

An hour later, Pete was on his back inside the Europa XP-7 clean room, where the brain of the system was housed. Pete had several clear programming rods in his mouth as he battled with a series of fiberoptic lines. Jack was watching him after showering, shaving, and getting a shortened checkup at the infirmary, only after promising he would be back for a more thorough exam.

His memory was retuning nicely, but the days leading up to his release were still fogged with more questions than answers. The doctor had the opinion that this memory loss may have been intentional because she found a substance in his blood that corresponded with induced coma. She suspected Jack was intentionally kept in a comatose state.

Everett joined him inside the clean room, which was anything but at that moment. None of the ten technicians present were dressed in electrostatic clothing or face masks.

"Jack, I placed Ryan and Mendenhall in charge of gathering everything we have on the attack. As soon as Pete hands off his duties to a replacement, I would suggest he continue on his mole hunt—that alone could answer a lot of questions for us."

"Agreed," Collins said as he watched Pete finally replace the crystal programming parts back inside the giant mainframe. Jack leaned over and turned on the microphone that would feed his voice into the programming chamber. "Doc, we have an appointment to keep in five minutes, and I don't think he likes to be kept waiting."

"We also have this, Jack." Everett held out a plastic-covered sample pack. Inside was a silvery substance. "There is no record of an accelerant such as this—highly flammable, very stable."

Jack looked it over and gave it back with no comment.

Pete was still sitting on the floor as he looked up through the thick glass. He pushed his glasses back up his sweating nose and saw it was the colonel, and instead of protesting about his time being usurped, he just nodded his understanding at the same moment another man entered.

"Excuse me, gentlemen, but you have to leave now. When I reboot Europa's systems, fun time is over and everyone goes back to playing by the clean room rules."

Everett stepped out of the way of the small man. He closed his eyes and shook his head. Jack had to smile because he knew that Carl and Dr. Gene Robbins did not ever see eye to eye about anything.

"Well, the little dictator of the clean level has arrived," Everett said.

Robbins ignored Everett and turned to Jack.

"Colonel, it *is* nice to see *you* again. Believe me when I say that your return was most welcome, and it made us in the computing division very happy. Welcome home," he said, turning to look at Everett. "I assume, Captain, you have some bad guys to shoot and torture or something else heroic, so, if you'll excuse me." He reached over and informed Pete they were ready for the restart.

Jack raised his eyebrows and crossed his arms, and then quickly stepped back out of Robbins's way while nodding for Everett to join him in the corner of the clean room.

"God, what an ass," Everett whispered.

"Yeah, but he's good at what he does."

"That's one of the things that's so infuriating about him."

"I'm glad you two get along so well," Pete said as he joined the two men, rolling his sleeves down. "Because you just met my replacement, the man who'll be assisting you, Captain, in your quest to find the mole."

Jack smiled as he clapped Everett on the back.

Everett didn't notice Jack and Pete leave the room. He was busy thinking about the time he would have to spend with the most irritating and infuriating man in all creation.

Pete Golding sat down behind the desk of the director, never feeling more out of place in his life. Collins nodded that the link had been made, and the president was in and up at five thirty in the morning. The large monitor that was sided by fifty others came to life with the seal of the president. Then the picture switched to the man himself sitting at his desk in the Oval Office. A questioning look crossed the president's features as he quickly saw that it wasn't Niles on the Nellis end.

"Dr. Golding, isn't it?"

"Uh, yes, Mr. President. As you may have heard, we've had some trouble here, both at the complex and Nellis itself."

"I've been briefed on the air force losses, but nothing from your end." The president looked uncomfortable, but continued, "Doctor, why aren't I being briefed by Dr. Compton?" he asked worriedly.

"Sir, Niles, Dr. Pollock, Alice Hamilton, Senator Lee, and one of our officers, Sarah McIntire, were taken by the terrorist element that attacked the complex."

The president grew quiet for a moment. Hearing about the loss of his friend hit him hard, but he knew he couldn't allow that to hinder his thinking.

"So, it all falls to you, Dr. Golding. Let's start with the how. How in the hell did they get into my most secure reservation and kidnap my people?"

"We believe the Long Island meeting was a ruse to get our top security element away from the Group. They were not only one step ahead of us with the nonlethal ambush of the FBI, but actually two steps ahead with their assault here in Nevada. In both cases, none of these events could have been accomplished without inside assistance from our end."

"Jesus!" The president forced himself to calm down and then looked into his camera. "Doctor, do you need a team of air police or marines to cover your complex and assist Captain Everett while you put the pieces back together out there?"

"Actually, I have a man here that would like to speak to you; he's back home and has assumed his duties."

Jack Collins sat at the small conference table and pulled one of the camera-equipped monitors toward him.

The face of the president did not register a reaction at first, but stared into his monitor with a quizzical look.

"I'm getting that reaction a lot tonight," Jack said.

"Colonel Collins, how in the hell are you?"

It was a greeting from one soldier to another. Jack smiled and nodded his head.

"I'm fine, sir. From what I'm told, I've been boating with the same people that hit us tonight. I have very little memory of my time with them, but I'm working on it, with the help of modern science."

"Yeah, I can imagine what it is they want to do to you. Are you sure you wouldn't prefer to let Captain Everett handle duties there for a while?"

"No, sir, we have missing people and it would drive me crazy sitting on the sidelines. Captain Everett is still in charge of Group security, and I'm going to assist."

"Well, Colonel, I am surely in no position to argue your point. As you may or may not know, we've got a serious threat on our hands. The navy has informed me that we may be dealing with an unknown who is equipped with far superior sciences. Now we have an economic knife at our throat, and the blade's going to start digging in."

"I see," Jack said as he turned and looked at Pete who was again biting his lower lip and absentmindedly cleaning the lenses of his glasses.

"Colonel, we are commencing convoy escorts tomorrow. I cannot allow a terrorist threat to damage our economy. So any information you may come across, inform me right away." The president took a deep breath, looking tired and frustrated.

"We will, sir."

"Colonel, you did an extraordinary job in the Med. Welcome home."

"Thank you, Mr. President."

"Dr. Golding, get me a line on who in the hell we're dealing with and a way to find them."

Pete was about to answer when the monitor went dark.

"Jesus, what a damn mess," he said as he turned to look at Jack across the room.

"Yeah, Doc, it is. Now let's go start cleaning it up."

8

Niles, Virginia, Alice, and Senator Lee watched as Sarah checked on the condition of Henri Farbeaux. The Frenchman had been out cold for most of the flight south. It was only in the past few minutes he had started mumbling. Only Sarah caught the name: *Danielle.* She even heard a small whimper escape the colonel's lips. Sarah moved a lock of hair from his eyes and studied the man's face. She still hadn't said anything about the reasons for Farbeaux's arrival at the complex to Niles or the others—she would keep that to herself for the time being, for reasons she didn't fully understand herself.

"How is he doing?" Niles asked from his seat at the left side of the strange aircraft.

Sarah turned and looked at the fifteen soldiers that had assisted in carrying out the raid. Most were sleeping, and a few were joking and talking—just like soldiers the world over. Thus far, the tall man, the brute in charge, had not deigned to join them since their departure. Not one word had been spoken to them during the flight other than an offer of coffee. Right now, they couldn't care less about their conversations.

"The tranq they used was a powerful one. Getting hit in the neck probably has something to do with his being out so hard."

"As long as I live, I will never be able to understand our friend here," Senator Lee said, nodding at Farbeaux as he gently moved his right shoulder so that Alice wouldn't awaken.

"He's a dangerous man," Virginia said without much sympathy.

"They wanted to kill him. He did, after all, save young McIntire's life, making him somewhat of an enigma," Lee said.

"Niles, what was the final word from Captain Everett?"

"The last communication was that they recovered the package and were on the way back. I didn't allow him the opportunity to specify what the package was because of the communication security concerns," Compton said, answering Virginia's question.

"Well, I hope Mr. Everett turns out to be as good a sleuth as Jack—" The senator stopped short of finishing his sentence as he looked at Sarah.

She slowly stood as Alice awoke, hearing Garrison Lee cross a boundary. Even in sleep, she had to babysit the man.

"Look, all of you have to quit tiptoeing around me about Jack. I'm a soldier first, and sometimes we lose people. So don't fool yourselves thinking I'll fall to pieces every time someone mentions his name. Please, knock it the hell off."

The four people looked at her and said nothing.

"Brave little Sarah—sometimes I wish I were half as brave. But, who is fooling whom?"

Sarah turned and looked down at Colonel Farbeaux, who was on one elbow and looking up at her. He removed the damp cloth and held it at arm's length, looking at it.

"A courtesy to a fallen enemy?" he said as he let the cloth slip through his fingers to the rubberized deck.

"Sarah has always had an affinity for injured animals," Virginia said, to the shock of the others.

"Indeed, and I assure you, Ms. Pollock, this animal is appreciative of her humane efforts," Farbeaux said, his eyes locking briefly onto Virginia's.

"Thus far, Colonel, we are at a loss as to why you chose this particular moment to visit the Event Group. Was it just taking advantage of an opportunity, curiosity, or some darker intent?" Niles asked as he stood and handed Farbeaux a cup of lukewarm coffee.

"Ah, Director Compton, we finally meet in person." As he sipped the coffee, Farbeaux looked over and saw the old man with the eye patch. He immediately sat up, even though it hurt his head. "The legendary Senator Lee. I am truly in esteemed company," he said as he half-bowed.

"Always nice to be admired by one's enemy; it could someday work to my advantage," Lee said, nodding toward the colonel.

"As you know from our dealings in the past, Director Compton, opportunity has been linked to my name from time to time."

Silence met Farbeaux's answer as suddenly a soft whine filled the cabin. The pitch of the twin jet engines changed, and the angle of the craft went nose down. For the first time during the flight, the large assault leader made his way back toward them from the cockpit. He nodded at a few of the rougher looking men as he passed them. Then he was looking down at his six captives as the first rays of the sun came through the cabin windows.

"We are at our rendezvous point. If you will watch out of the left side of the aircraft, our pilot has graciously arranged a view none of you have ever witnessed before." The man slowly sat down in an unoccupied seat next to Farbeaux, who eyed him with disdain and stood on shaky legs, holding a strap. "Please, sit down, relax, I think you'll quite enjoy this. Let's call it a learning experience," the man said in his Irish-tinged accent.

The aircraft lost altitude much faster than any commercial plane could have. Because of the stubby wing design, the extreme tolerances experienced by the airframe held up during the steep dive to the sea below. Farbeaux had to sit down quickly, trying not to spill the coffee.

"Normally, the aircraft would hover over the water and then retract her wings and seal her intakes, thus allowing us to dive underneath the waves and meet our host. However, a demonstration of what your country—and others—is dealing with was deemed necessary." The man looked at the faces sitting opposite him as the craft came within six hundred feet of the wave tops below.

As they watched out of the left side, a piercing tone penetrated their inner ears. Niles and the others covered their heads with their hands.

"Apologies, but we mark our location with a signal that penetrates water efficiently. The burst you hear was a coded transmission that also included our altitude and location to within half an inch. We wouldn't want any accidents. Whales and dolphins also hear an embedded tone below that of human hearing, so this is a warning to them also to clear the area."

The tone ended abruptly and they all watched the surface of the water far below. The gulf was calm as dawn broke, allowing the sun to dapple the waters with gleaming speckles of light. Suddenly the waters seemed to turn a lighter shade of green about three hundred yards to the side of the aircraft. Niles chanced a look at the tall man, who was watching their reaction with a smile. When Compton turned back to the large window, he saw giant bubbles breaking the surface of the gulf. Several of them were at least a hundred feet in diameter and rose another fifty feet into the clear air before bursting apart in what looked like an explosion of vapor.

"Good God," Lee said as he watched in amazement.

They saw a shape rising from the depth of the clear sea. They would never know that this particular spot in the gulf was chosen specifically for its clarity. They watched as the bow of the great vessel rose through the depths, rounded and giant. The submarine broke the surface of the gulf of Mexico with an explosion of white water and sea spray, then kept rising as if it were fighting to free itself of an unwanted and hostile environment. It rose, seemingly never ending, and then rose even more. They saw the conning tower break the surface as it telescoped to its sky-reaching 125-foot height, and still the monster breached the air and sea with its length. It came from the sea like a mythical beast as it balanced in a perfect set-piece motion of a moment frozen in time.

"I cannot believe this!" Niles said, almost gasping for air as he watched.

The massive submarine finally reached a point where its forward bulk outweighed its stern and the giant ship started to fall toward the sea below. The gulf beneath its hull was crushed as the behemoth crashed into the water, sending forth a wave two hundred feet into the air. The mist from the top of the wave reached as far as the hovering aircraft.

Niles started measuring with his mind's eye. The vessel was well over a thousand feet in length, possibly more. He couldn't begin to calculate her displacement tonnage, but it had to outweigh any ship in the naval arsenals of the world. Larger than a Nimitz class carrier, the submarine was unlike any vessel any of them had ever laid eyes on. The hull had clean lines and was rounded even upon the upper deck. The conning tower was a giant structure that angled aerodynamically, and was made to align itself deep into the hull when submerged, obviously for speed purposes.

Niles could see two large, finlike, harsh triangles—powerful-looking bow-planes slicing the waters just under the surface—and then finally two towering, angled, hundred-foot-long, fifty-foot-high tail fins sprang from the sea like the dorsal fins of a monster shark. As they held their breath, the vessel's bow opened up and revealed a glass nose hidden under a retractable armor front, and they could see that the glass covered at the very least ten decks of the forward parts of the vessel. The giant submarine continued to run on the surface, sending out very little tail wake from her power plant at the stern. Seagulls, after the initial shock of her arrival, started flocking around the skyscraperlike conning tower, mistaking it for land because of its size.

"On behalf of my captain, I welcome you to *Leviathan*."

Lee turned and looked at the man, who was watching them all with an intent gaze. He recalled a poem from the time of the Civil War, which he memorized in his college days and deemed appropriate now that the man had placed a name to the great vessel.

" 'Lo, as I am swallowed by the salt-laden waters, I am cursed to behold the shape and dark intent of my enemy, the very destroyer of men, thus as I am laid asunder, water invading my soul, there, under the waves, travels the monstrous grace of *Leviathan*, God of the Sea, and Master of the World.' "

As the four tilt-wing aircraft started forward, the lead craft banked hard and started settling for the deck of *Leviathan*. As it approached, two large doors, over seventy feet in length and just aft of the conning tower, parted and rose into the air, revealing a cavernous hangar deck. Niles watched as crewmen far below prepared to take on the four aircraft. The hovering VTOLs aligned perfectly with the fast-moving vessel and settled into her bowels. Compton took the opportunity to examine the open section of hull and counted five distinct layers of a material that to his untrained eye resembled titanium, or steel, but seemed porous. He was amazed when he realized he wasn't looking at metal at all—he was staring at what he thought must be a composite material similar to nylon.

The tilt-wing settled to the deck and her engines started to spool down. Then one of the other craft settled beside them and the remaining flight behind. Compton turned and sat in his seat while looking at the others.

"This is not the first such vessel to carry the name," Lee commented.

The tall man rose from his seat and completely removed his body armor, his eyes watching Lee. The rest of his men were now fully awake and seemingly glad to be home as they joked and made their way to the rolling stairs that had been pushed into place.

"Correct, Senator. This is the third vessel to carry the name *Leviathan*," he said, handing his armor and weapon to the nearest man.

Niles looked at Garrison Lee, who winked. "Vault 298907, level seventy-three, inactive file."

Recognition etched Compton's face as he remembered one of the Group's more prized possessions. He knew what vault the senator had referred to, and now he knew one of the reasons for the vault's destruction.

"Ladies and gentlemen, if you would follow me, please." The man hesitated and looked at Henri Farbeaux. "I will ask you for your word as a gentleman to behave upon this vessel. We will tolerate no activities that may harm the crew or systems aboard. If you can't agree to this request, we can set you adrift before diving. You will be picked up within the day, I assure you."

Farbeaux stood and looked at their host and then at Niles and Sarah, who in turn were looking at him expectantly.

"Why of course, my word as a gentleman," he said without a trace of humor.

The man held the colonel's gaze a moment, trying to detect any form of deceit, and then he turned for the large doorway.

As they gained the stairs, they saw at least a hundred men and women moving about the hangar deck. They were busy with tasks such as washing the four aircraft down, freeing them from metal-eating salt. A loudspeaker echoed among the fifteen helicopters and four tilt-winged aircraft.

"Stand by to secure hangar doors. All hands make ready for submerged operations."

Garrison Lee leaned on his cane as Alice placed one of her hands on top of his and watched the sunlight of the outside world be slowly shut out. The giant doors hissed closed above them with a finality that made Alice cringe slightly.

Sarah watched the crew members around them as they secured the tilt-wings to the hangar deck with long nylon straps, using come-alongs to tighten them to piano-wire tightness. Arrayed along the wall were projected and enhanced electronic readouts displaying the exact weight of what was carried in the hangar. She was amazed that an object that could travel under the sea could tolerate such weight, as it had to be a hindrance to their speed. She was also amazed at the ethnic makeup of the crew; black, white, Asian, and others worked together side by side with children not more than sixteen.

The tall man was again watching them.

"If I may ask, what is your function aboard this vessel? Or are you just the resident killer and kidnapper?" Niles asked as he rolled down the sleeves of his white shirt. The eyes behind his glasses held firm against the glare from the tall man.

He smiled at last—a cold, mean-spirited smile.

"I follow my orders. However, I *am* the resident security specialist and special forces commander for *Leviathan*—Sergeant Tyler, Benjamin Tyler. And if I hadn't been good at what I do, the people back at your ridiculous little complex would be burying quite a few more associates today." Tyler gestured toward a young woman who was standing by at one of the larger consoles awaiting his orders.

They watched as the young woman walked over. She was dressed in a red shirt and blue shorts, different from the hangar deck crew who wore blue jumpsuits, not unlike the military members at the Event Group. Her brown hair was braided—coiling around both ears—and her smile was genuine. Her eyes were deep and dark blue, with a ring of soft silver around the pupils. She was an amazing-looking girl.

"This is Yeoman Felicia Alvera. She will show you to your quarters so you may rest and change clothes. We are conducting operations this afternoon, so your lunch will be served in your staterooms. The captain sends apologies."

"When you say operations, you mean attacking merchant shipping and killing more innocents?" Niles asked.

"Is there such a thing as innocence in your world, Doctor? Even in this world we have our faults, and at times, very little innocence." Tyler turned and strode quickly away.

"I must apologize for the sergeant. He has his manner; that's why we don't allow him out very much," the yeoman said, smiling. She saw her humor did not sit well with *Leviathan*'s new guests, so she cleared her throat and gestured to her right. "If you'll follow me, please."

Niles allowed the senator and Alice to fall into place behind the woman so he could assist the former director if he needed it. Virginia, unusually quiet, stepped up and took Niles by the arm as if fearful of something or to keep Niles in check with his insults, he wasn't sure.

"After you, dear Sarah," Farbeaux said with a wave of his arm.

"Colonel, just because there are no armed guards on us does not mean we are not being watched."

"I've already spotted ten security cameras, my dear, and they are tracking us, indeed. Someone is quite interested in our little group."

Sarah just realized who it was she had given the warning to. This man had a sense about him that others could only dream of. He was a survivor beyond measure and a master predator. She decided she would keep close to Henri Farbeaux. She took his arm to steady him and they followed the others.

The group stepped into a plastic-lined, carpeted elevator that blended well with the bulkhead. The yeoman waited until all were inside and then said aloud, "Deck ten."

As the elevator doors closed silently, they all felt the movement of the car. In just about ten seconds, they felt the elevator glide to a soft stop, then another strange feeling began and that was when they realized they were moving horizontally. They followed their progress on a multicolored chart on the wall that depicted their car moving at a rapid gait along a multitiered grid. The elevator traveled another thirty seconds and then stopped. The doors slid open with only the slightest hiss.

"*Deck ten.*"

Sarah looked at Alice and Virginia as the computerized female voice controlling the elevator announced their deck.

"Is that—?"

"If not, she has a sister," Niles said as he commented on the computer-controlled voice. They were all startled when they realized it had the same sexy and embarrassing audible print as their own Europa system at the Group.

"This woman must make a fortune doing these damn recordings," Sarah said as she followed the yeoman out of the elevator.

"If you're speaking of our computer's voiceprint, it *may* be just like your system." She gave a small laugh. "It's recorded by a little old lady in Akron, Ohio." She gestured for them to step free of the elevator. "She's seventy-six years old."

"Oh," Sarah said as she waited for Lee, Alice, Niles, and Virginia to catch up with her and Farbeaux. She frowned toward Alice. "Don't ever tell Carl, Ryan, or Mendenhall. It would shatter their fantasies about Europa's voice."

As they entered a very long and curving hallway, they saw magnificent laser prints of the oceans of the world lining the wall. Each was backlit and was a depiction of a bay, a sea, or a moonlight view of the

Arctic. As they walked slowly behind the yeoman, they all stared at the design of the hallway. The material was unrecognizable. It had the look of hard plastic, but as each reached out to touch the material in turn, they knew it was something beyond their own engineering knowledge. It was soft in spots and hard in other areas. Large panels met at a stringer that felt and looked like painted titanium.

"*All hands, prepare to dive.*" A loud horn sounded throughout the boat.

The wall, about five feet up from the floor, split, and a long panel slid down as it did. A stout-looking handrail slowly slid from the abcess.

"If you'll stop and take a handhold, this will only take a minute. The initial dive profile of *Leviathan* can be rather steep. We call it the 'the fall from grace.'" Yeoman Alvera smiled as she took hold of the steel-and-wood handrail.

"Nice," Sarah said, but taking ahold of the rail anyway.

"*Dive, dive, dive.*" The voice was strong and clear over the hidden loudspeakers as a soft tone sounded throughout the boat warning of the dive.

The yeoman let go of the rail and stepped up to the senator and Alice.

"If you like, we have straps. Would you prefer that?"

Lee fixed the young girl with his one good eye.

"The day I need to wear a—"

"No thank you, young lady, we are fine," Alice said, giving Lee a harsh look.

As Yeoman Alvera returned to her spot, the deck suddenly angled down and they felt their stomachs go with it. Then they could tell by the centrifugal forces being applied that the speed of the great ship increased to unheard-of velocity. The young woman pointed to a red-numbered digital readout at the next bulkhead, twenty feet in front of them and over the next hatchway.

"Impossible," Niles mumbled.

The indicator was flashing numbers at an incredible rate. Their depth had gone from two hundred feet to six hundred in a matter of forty seconds. As Niles tried to follow the digital numbers, *Leviathan* started to level off and slow. Soon the LED readout at the bulkhead said that the massive boat was at nine hundred feet in depth. Then the readout changed and the numbers split, now showing not only depth but also speed.

"We will travel at this speed for the next—well, we'll be pretty steady for the time being."

Niles saw *Leviathan* was cruising at seventy knots with not so much as a shiver coursing through the vessel.

They continued on their way, not seeing another crew member on their journey. Then they came to the first stateroom.

"Mrs. Hamilton, we have put you in with Senator Lee. We believe those are the accommodations you are used to?"

Lee looked slightly embarrassed, but Alice just raised her left brow.

"Good, you'll find a fresh suit in the closet for the senator. We believe we got the size right, and a nice pantsuit for you, Mrs. Hamilton."

She opened the door and allowed the two to enter. They were surprised to find their accommodation would have rivaled anything on a modern cruise ship. There was a small living area complete with desk, separate bathroom with tub and shower, a completely stocked wet bar, and a large bed dominating the room. The motif was in greens and blues with rich wood paneling.

"These accommodations were specially built for this occasion. Normally the captain—well, let's just say our berthing areas are a little more spartan and functional."

As Niles stepped aside and allowed the girl to pass, he nodded at Lee and Alice and then closed their stateroom door.

"So, our abduction was planned for a while, at least long enough to refit this deck?" he asked, following the girl.

"Oh, yes," she said slightly turning her head and looking at Niles. "We were just unsure of how many to accommodate." She looked to her right at Colonel Farbeaux. "Unfortunately, we were only expecting two people from your Group. I'm afraid you'll have to double up in your staterooms for the time being."

Farbeaux looked down at Sarah and smiled. Sarah only rolled her eyes.

The girl caught the look and gestures. "You, sir, and Director Compton will be sharing a stateroom."

As they walked to their rooms, Farbeaux frowned and Niles cringed.

"Young woman, err . . . uh . . . Yeoman Alvera, is it?"

"Yes, Dr. Compton," she answered with her permanent smile in place.

"You know your captain, or whoever it is that is leading you, is quite mad. I mean . . . do you understand what you're attempting, although for a noble cause, would throw the world into total economic collapse?"

The yeoman stopped in midstride and looked at Virginia, Farbeaux, Sarah, and Niles one at a time, and for the first time her smile faltered. Also for the first time they saw the seriousness of the young woman.

"I understand completely your concern, but I can guarantee this matter has been thought out carefully and my captain has come to the conclusion that extreme measures must be taken now to stop the seas from dying. The incident in the Mediterranean has forced our . . ." She attempted an ill-fated smile, and then corrected herself, "the captain's hand."

"The Med—what does that have to do with this vessel and its intent?" Niles asked.

"Moreover, Dr. Compton," she continued, ignoring his second question, "you will find that the loyalty of this crew is beyond reproach. I was found when I was only seven years old. I had just witnessed my mother, father, and older brother die from a chemical spill. My captain found me in very bad shape, took me in, educated me, trained me, and made me a person of pride—I am even loved here. No, Doctor, you'll find no disloyalty onboard *Leviathan*, and you'll also not find one soul that doesn't approve of the methods employed by the captain."

THE EVENT GROUP COMPLEX, NELLIS AIR FORCE BASE, NEVADA

Collins had just left the infirmary where Dr. Denise Gilliam had given him a complete physical and pronounced Jack officially alive and back from the dead. He tried to explain to her everything he remembered, even down to the strange dreams he had had, even the small creature in the bottle, the tentacled arms and clear body floating in a solution. Denise accepted all of this with raised brows but no comment on his sanity was forthcoming.

"Well, Colonel, I would say you have a combination of memory versus nightmare. The little octopus thing says nightmare, but voices in the dark says you weren't sleeping the whole time. I would say give it more time. Meanwhile I'll get your exams to Dr. Haskins when he returns from leave; we're shorthanded until then."

A knock sounded on the infirmary door. Mendenhall poked his head inside and held up a file folder. Jack excused himself and exited the clinic.

"We found this in the cafeteria," Will said as he handed Jack a blue-bordered folder with the single word and numbers on it.

"Vault 298907," he said aloud, and opened it as he walked.

"It was found at the table the chef remembers the senator and Alice were working from. It was the only folder there, found on a chair. The other files faxed out from Arlington for levels seventy-three and seventy-four were missing. The closed-circuit recording in the hallway verified they were in the possession of the assault element."

"Maybe it just fell off the table when—" Jack's words trailed off and he slowed his pace. He closed the file and thought a moment, and then started walking. Instead of going toward the comp center, he turned at the bank of elevators.

"Colonel?" Mendenhall said, standing at the elevator as Jack went inside.

"Go to the clean level and get Captain Everett. Then you and he meet me on level seventy-three, vault 298907."

Mendenhall was left standing there as the doors slid closed.

Jack could smell the burned plastic and carpeting before the elevator even came to a stop. The doors opened and he stepped out into the long, curving hallway. Europa had restored all of the electrical systems, and Collins could see fifty men combing through the wreckage of the vaults.

He shook his head and started forward, passing one of his security men who was armed with an M-16. He stepped through the now-dead security portal and into the vault area.

Professor Charles Hindershot Ellenshaw III, head of the cryptozoology department, had volunteered for cleanup on the level, and so he had been placed in charge of documenting, cleaning, and restoring the artifacts that had been damaged. Collins saw the professor was still very upset at the wanton destruction of the vaults. Jack watched the professor run a hand through his wild white hair.

"Colonel Collins, it is so very good to see you. I and my crypto department were very pleased to hear—"

"Thanks, Professor," Jack said, knowing he couldn't take one more pleasurable greeting at how happy they were he had returned from beyond the river Styx. "Vault 298907?"

"Oh, uh . . . there's not much left, I'm afraid. It's right here." He gestured to the large vault three enclosures down from where they stood. "It seems that vault and the two nearest it received the brunt of the damage, possibly because of its size, and its fragile and dangerous content."

"Dangerous?"

Ellenshaw looked at his clipboard. "Oh yes, it seems there were five hundred batteries inside the artifact—old, but with enough dried acid to have reacted with the fire, causing a considerable explosion."

"Thanks, Professor," Jack said, patting him on the shoulder and making his way to the large vault with the scorched steel door standing ajar. "And Charlie, it's good to see you, too."

Ellenshaw smiled, nodded, and then went back to work, with a last look back at Collins.

Jack had to use the strength of both arms to push the door open. The vault was filled with temporary lighting that cast shadows on the burned and broken remains of the submarine recovered in 1967. Jack remembered it had been one of the first artifacts shown him upon being assigned to the Event Group. It was also one of the more intriguing items he had ever seen during his time here.

Jack opened the file, standing next to one of the temporary light stands, and read the vault synopsis. Carbon-14 dating had placed the submarine's age at 150 years, plus or minus ten years. He lowered the file and looked at what remained of the skeletal shape of her hull. The iron had melted away during the intense heat of the fire, and her battery system, one that had even shocked the few engineers brought in from General Dynamics' Electric Boat Division, was a melted lump at the bottom of the artifact. At one time, you could clearly see that this was once a miracle of technology.

Jack had been told that it had possibly been the model for Jules Verne's *Twenty Thousand Leagues Under the Sea*. At the time it was wholly believable, because you could still make out the spiked conning tower and rounded bow. At more than three hundred feet in length and displacing twenty thousand tons, she was almost the exact model of today's advanced attack navy boats.

"She's a mess."

Jack turned and saw Everett and Mendenhall standing just inside the vault.

"That she is. Tell me, Carl, you're a navy man. If this sub was built before or just after the start of the Civil War, how far do you think the technology would have advanced by the present time?"

Everett entered and tried not to splash sooty water on his jumpsuit. He dodged a hanging piece of electrical line and placed a hand on what was once the curvature of the spherical bow.

"I couldn't begin to estimate the advances this science would have made if it wasn't checked. You think we're dealing with the same people who built this?"

"Why not? It makes sense. The fact that they destroyed a link to their past is convincing enough, but seeing this—"

"From looking at the outside in, Colonel, the notes on this investigation really had nothing to say. At least nothing stands out that would make them want this artifact destroyed."

Everett and Jack turned and looked at Mendenhall. They never remembered the new lieutenant using such a long sentence before.

"What?" Will asked, wondering what it was he had said wrong.

"You're right, Lieutenant, that's all," Collins answered. "What were they afraid of us uncovering from this boat?"

Everett and Mendenhall were as perplexed as Jack.

"Whatever it is, it's in this file, and in this wreck. Either something found during the original forensics on the artifact in nineteen sixty-seven, or something we may find now. So, we need someone combing through the file, and we need another workup on the remains."

"And hope it all wasn't burned to hell."

Jack slapped the file into Mendenhall's chest. "Right, Lieutenant. You have your job. Grab anyone you need, form any team, and get me an answer."

Will took the file and almost dropped it in the dirty water; his expression said that the order would be hard to complete.

"Yes, sir. . . . Can I have any doc or professor I want?"

"Yes, just grab them and go. We need answers, Lieutenant, so get it done."

LEVIATHAN, THREE HUNDRED MILES OFF THE NORTHERN COAST OF VENEZUELA

The first officer climbed the spiral staircase slowly, making his way into the observation lounge on the lowest deck of the conning tower. He knocked, opened the hatch to the captain's private suite, and saw her sitting in the large, high-backed chair, staring silently out of the thirty-five-by-twenty-foot port window at the passing sea outside of the pressure hull.

"Captain, I am sorry to disturb you, but I thought you would want to know that you were right in what the presidents of the United States and Venezuela would try to do. We have confirmed the sailing orders of four crude oil tankers from Portsmouth this morning. They have Royal Navy escort, with at least one Trafalgar class submarine shadowing them."

"Venezuela?"

"Two tankers with Chinese and Venezuelan escort vessels," Samuels answered, looking away from the captain as he did. When he looked back up, he could tell the captain was thinking with eyes closed, as was the custom for the master of *Leviathan.*

"Will we allow them passage, as you wished to do this morning?"

As he watched she opened her eyes, and the first officer saw that at the moment she wasn't medicated. Her eyes were clear and full of fire—hate-filled and angry.

The captain stood in the green-tinted sea reflection mixed with the darkness, and then stepped from the raised platform. She stepped slowly to the large rounded window and held a gloved hand to the thick glass, then leaned against it with a sigh.

"Captain, are you all right? Would you like the doctor to—?"

"The planned attack is ready?"

"Yes, Captain, but your orders were to avoid any further bloodshed."

"I have a change of orders for you. You will target the warships only. Leave the tankers, they are to go on their way unmolested. I suspect a small deceit, at least on the British and American side of the board. I also do not want one Chinese or British warship, or the Americans if they join them, to ever see port again. Loss of life be damned." The captain slapped at the glass and then took a step back. "They are testing the wrong person, James; explain to them in no uncertain terms how *Leviathan* can be in two places at one time."

"Perhaps we can meet with our guests first. . . . I mean, Captain, we have the time; these vessels will take a week or more to reach their destinations. We could avoid the loss of life while we explain why we have taken actions in the Gulf of Mexico."

"Mr. Samuels, we need fortitude in doing what needs to be done. We are not fighting for ourselves. There has been too much loss of sea life in the Med to lose what we have in the gulf. Now, please, do as I command."

The first officer bowed his head. "Yes, Captain."

"James, you have never hesitated in following my orders before now. Perhaps you had better explain your hesitancy in this instance."

The first officer paused at the large hatchway, then slowly turned.

"I will never question your orders, Captain. However, you're countermanding everything you laid out before we sailed. I am wondering if maybe you're not telling me something—your health, the sessions with the doctor? And why is Sergeant Tyler present at most of these appointments?"

The face never turned from the window, but he could see that the captain's eyes were closed and she was biting her lower lip. For the life of him, he could swear she was in conflict deep within herself.

"I . . . I don't recall meeting with the . . ."

The words stopped as she turned and made her way back to the large chair, signaling an end to his questioning.

"I will report on the attack as soon as we have long-range damage assessment, Captain."

He waited for a response, but when none came he slowly left the private control room.

As the captain sat with eyes closed, she tried to remember the last medical session with the ship's surgeon, but she couldn't recall anything through the pain of her current headache. She remembered the early morning visits to the sickbay to check on Colonel Collins—those moments were clear, as she remembered forming her plans. If these other sessions had happened, why was Sergeant Tyler present? If he was, she must get an explanation as to why.

Niles heard the knock on the door just as Henri Farbeaux stepped from the bathroom, looked at him, and saw he made no move to answer it. He tossed the towel he was drying his hands on over his shoulder and opened the door.

"Excuse me, gentlemen. Our captain has asked that you join the first officer in the command center," a young-faced officer said, stepping aside and allowing the senator, Alice, and Virginia to step by him. "The others are ready to go, as you can see."

Niles, resplendent in his issued red jumpsuit, walked past Farbeaux and out into the companionway.

"Colonel?"

"I think I'll stay."

The officer kept his politeness. "The captain has informed us since you are an uninvited guest onboard, you are highly expendable, so please, Colonel, come with us."

Henri smiled, pulled his jumper top up, and bowed. "Your power of persuasion has moved me. I must thank your captain in person."

"You'll have that chance very soon, sir." The officer closed the door, the polite smile gone when he knew they could not see.

As they were shown to a rail overlooking the control center—the very brain of *Leviathan*—they were stunned. With the dimensions of a bas-ketball court, it coursed with a pulse that was electric. At least sixty tech-nicians operated stations that were unrecognizable to anyone but a science-fiction aficionado. There were large-screen monitors and 3-D displays of their surroundings. The tech stations were bathed in dim lighting of greens, blues, and reds. Sonar stations, weapons, environ-mental control—but that was as far as Niles and his knowledge went. The other stations were as much a mystery to him as the origins of this vessel. There were holograms showing the status of missilelike weapons and torpedoes. An even larger hologram, which showed the distinctive shape of *Leviathan* as she sliced through the sea underneath the surface, took up what they thought was the navigation platform. The navigation console was like a cartoon, animated and accurate in every detail.

"Officer of the deck, we are at station precisely three hundred miles offshore of Venezuela. We have multiple surface contacts. Air search is negative at this time," a female operator called out.

As they watched, they saw the first officer for the first time. The man was of normal height, maybe six feet, one inch. His hair was blond and he was clean-shaven. His uniform was impeccably starched, and it wasn't a jumpsuit. His attire was tan, almost as if he were serving in the U.S. Navy. He didn't sit in the large command chair that sat upon a raised platform, but stood at its side with his arm resting on the pedestal above as he studied the hologram of *Leviathan* and its surrounding waters in a five-hundred-mile circle.

"Very well. Long-range sonar, what do we have off the Scottish coast?"

Niles turned to a brown-suited Senator Lee, somewhat jealous that he and Alice were accorded the comfort of civilian clothes. Lee even had his customary bowtie.

"They have a sonar suite that can operate that far?"

"I suspect we may be in for a lot of surprises, Niles, my boy," Lee answered.

"We are picking up the power plant noises of the HMS *Monmouth* and her sister frigate *Somerset*; one Type 45 destroyer, HMS *Daring*; and one Type 42, HMS *Birmingham*. Two other destroyers have yet to join the convoy. We also have the prop signatures of VLCS tankers—*Exxon Gale*, *Palace Guard*, *Texaco Sky*, and the *Shell Madrid*. Propeller depth indicates fully loaded oil bunkers."

"Thank you. Weapons, give me a status report, please." The first officer bowed his head and closed his eyes as he listened to the reports.

"Torpedo tubes one through ten loaded with standard Mark eighty-nines. Standard war shot with delayed sonar activation; their computers are active in the tubes and tracking. Vertical tubes ten through fifteen are hot with type-forty Vengeance cruise missiles, and outer doors are ready at your discretion."

"Very well. Diving officer, make your depth three hundred; slow speed to five knots."

"Aye, chief of the boat, slow to five knots; make your attack depth three hundred."

The command was relayed to the helmsman and planesman sitting in airlinelike pilot seats. They wore strange-looking helmets that covered their entire heads as they watched their virtual-reality displays that were invisible to all others, followed their orders, and made their speed and depth adjustments. *Leviathan* started a climb toward the surface.

"Goddamn it, they're attacking two different convoys," Niles said, stepping forward.

Farbeaux quickly grabbed Niles by the arm and stayed him.

"Mr. Director, if they are forced to shoot you, a stray bullet may very well strike me, and that just would not do."

Niles closed his eyes and nodded, getting Farbeaux's meaning and intent. He was placing the others in jeopardy, and Henri pointed that fact out using his dry wit. Sarah nodded once in thanks, and Farbeaux looked at her intently.

"Officer of the deck, we are at station. IP is achieved."

"Thank you, helm. Weapons, you are free to launch forward tubes one through ten. Give me a full spread and let me know when the weapons have achieved station keeping."

"Aye." The weapons officer turned a key in his large console and then pushed the brightly illuminated buttons lining its top, one at a time, until they were all green.

Lee, Farbeaux, Virginia, and Lee all noticed that when it came to the launching of weapons, the crew of *Leviathan* used the old-fashioned, hands-on way, rather than trusting the holographic imagery technology.

"Tubes one through ten are empty, and torpedoes are free of the boat. All are traveling hot, straight, and normal." The weapons officer watched the large hologram in front of him. The small torpedoes (at least compared to the size of *Leviathan*) were seen traveling away from the red depiction of the submarine. "Weapons have stopped dead in the water and have gone to passive search. We have achieved station keeping for delayed-attack profile." The torpedoes floated in the water and were now arrayed like an open fan, just sitting there.

"Thank you, Mr. Hunter. You have permission to fire vertical tubes. You are weapons-free." The first officer lowered his head, brought his right hand to his chin, and waited. When the weapons officer reported all tubes and weapons were launched, the first officer chanced a look into the gallery fifty feet above the control center. He looked at each accusing face in the semidarkness above him, then just as quickly looked away.

They all watched the hologram at the center console as five missiles lifted away from her hull just forward of the conning tower. They traveled up and out of the water, which was represented by a soft green, wavy surface. Then, three hundred feet into the air, the five cruise missiles turned and headed east.

"Mr. Hunter, you have the conn. I'll be in my cabin."

"Aye, sir, I have the conn. Navigation, set your course to three-two-zero. Let's take her to the ice."

Niles took a deep breath and looked at the senator.

"Whoever they are, we just learned that they are entirely capable of doing what they threatened to do, and that means a very slow and very painful strangulation for the world."

The others turned and followed Niles out of the observation gallery, never knowing that eyes were on them from the deep recesses of the balcony overlooking both the gallery and the control center.

The captain of *Leviathan* stood motionless in the dark and watched the members of the Event Group slowly file out. Then the large eyes closed and the head lowered, and as it did, hair the color of the darkest pit of hell fell free and covered the captain's face and shoulders.

THE WHITE HOUSE, WASHINGTON, D.C.

The president had excused himself from lunch with his wife and a visiting women's group from Kansas City so he could go to his office and check on the progression of the British and Venezuelan naval convoys. He had been absent from the lunch mentally, at any rate. He fielded questions from the ladies without actually hearing them, much to the dismay of the First Lady who had taken up the slack brilliantly. The news from the home front and overseas had been bleak all day. Riots in China over fuel shortages, fights breaking out at the largest fish markets in Japan over no fish, and even brawls at gas lines at home for the first time since 1978, and things were far worse than the public really knew. The United States' strategic reserve of oil and gas was down to 25 percent.

As the president entered the Oval Office, the national security advisor followed him quickly inside.

"If you're here this soon, this can't be good news," the president said, sitting heavily into his chair.

"I wish it were. Both the British and Venezuelan convoys were attacked almost simultaneously."

"Christ," the president mumbled.

"Admiral Fuqua and General Caulfield are on their way over to brief you fully. However, we do have some details. The Royal Navy was bloodied, Mr. President. Two frigates and two destroyers were lost, with only five survivors. The submarine HMS *Trafalgar* was also sunk with all hands. The tankers were also struck and sunk. It's like they knew they were a red herring."

The president rubbed his forehead and then slammed his hand on the desktop. The plan to ambush the entity trying to kill their sea commerce included the bait of the four tankers. However, the president and British prime minister had made the decision that the danger of a massive oil spill in the oceans would have been far too costly a gamble, so the tankers had been filled with seawater.

"Is there anything these murderous bastards don't know?" he said as he tried to calm himself.

"No, sir. It seems they also knew the Venezuelan tankers were full of crude. While weapons of unknown design took all four warships apart, the two tankers were struck in the rudder and engine compartments by very low-yield torpedoes. They are presently being towed back into port as we speak. They accomplished their goal without causing any environmental impact. The weapons used were waiting for them; they must have been placed in the water hours ahead of time."

"Advise Admiral Fuqua that I want the Nimitz battle group turned back for home. We can't lose anything else to these madmen until we get a handle on who in the hell they are. They wanted to show that we are combat-ineffective against their technology."

9

EVENT GROUP COMPLEX,
NELLIS AIR FORCE BASE, NEVADA

Charles Hindershot Ellenshaw III sat on an overturned file cabinet with his bone white, bare feet in the sooty water of the burned-out vault. Members of his crypto team were silent after they had removed most of what was left of the old submarine, placing the parts on long tables for examination. Ellenshaw took a deep breath as he turned the last page of the original file—metallurgy results conducted back in 1967 on the sub's internal bulkheads.

"Nothing extraordinary, just iron, strong iron to be sure, but just iron," he mumbled to himself.

Nancy Birdsong, an Native American student from the University of North Dakota sitting next to her professor, gently removed the file from his hands and closed it.

"Professor, we're cryptozoologists. Did you ever think we're a little out of our league here? I mean, the research aspect, yes, we can do that, but analyzing metal shards and the remains of prototype batteries from history, when most of us can't even understand how a battery works today?"

Ellenshaw smiled and looked at the girl over his glasses.

"We know you want to do your part to find the director and the others in the worst way. We know how you feel about him, but maybe we can help in some other area. Get more engineers in here, not just crazy Charlie and his creepo team."

"Why doesn't the ribbing and teasing from the science departments bother you as much as many others?"

Nancy stood and smiled. "Don't you know? We feel about you the way you feel about Director Compton." She took the file and moved away.

Ellenshaw knew her to be right. They needed to get out of the way down here and let the engineers have a go at the forensics end. He looked at his watch. Maybe by now the engineers were freed up from their safety inspection of the complex's rock strata.

As he looked around at his hardworking department, he stood, his long lab coat slipping into the foot-deep water. As he took a step forward to announce to his team the suspension of the search, his foot came into contact with something that moved on the vault floor. He rolled up his already wet sleeve, reached into the water, and pulled the object free. As he lifted it, he could see it was hardened rubber. He turned it over in his hand until he recognized it for what it was—part of the outer casing for one of the batteries once encased in the bottom of the hull. He looked at the tables in front of him and saw what was left of the three hundred batteries. For the most part, they had been reduced to blackened and hardened lumps by fire and explosion.

"A shame, for someone to have invented batteries like these years before the advent of electrical power. Well—just a shame," he mumbled as he placed the melted, smelly piece upon the table.

"Not only that, rubber was hard to come by at the time. It had to come from Southeast Asia, from a plantation in Dutch Indochina, er . . . uh, Vietnam," the young technician said as she placed the *Leviathan* file next to the rubber.

Ellenshaw stood stock-still as her words soaked in. *Plantations?* He walked over and picked up the file, splashing dirty water on the young woman as he did.

"These batteries would have had to be designed long before the boat was built, wouldn't you think?" he asked as he hurriedly paged through the open file, his white hair moving as he read snippets of the report.

"I guess so—what are you thinking?"

"I'm thinking that a mass quantity of rubber would have to have been ordered for experimentation and research—not counting the amount it would take to actually construct them," he said, lowering the file. "It's not here," he said, looking at the far wall lost in thought.

"What's not there?" she asked, stepping up to stand next to him.

"The analysis on the battery casings."

"You mean the rubber?"

"Yes," Ellenshaw said as his gaze wandered the interior of the vault, not settling on any one spot.

The cryptozoologist walked over to the lump of burned rubber and ran his slim fingers over its rough surface.

"Several tons of raw rubber would have been used in the research and construction of the many, many batteries enclosed in the vessel. I'm sure of it, it's so obvious," he said as he finally looked down at his assistant. "Traceable rubber." He smiled for the first time.

"I don't think you can trace rubber, Professor," she said.

"Not the rubber, Miss Birdsong—the research and development, and the plantations that produced it."

"You think you can trace the research and plantations back that far?"

"One thing you can always count on is the fact that companies and universities the world over require data—progress reports for the expenditure of funds—and those reports have to be filed."

"But it's been so long—"

Ellenshaw didn't hear her words as he shot out of the vault and disappeared.

The meeting inside the main conference room on level seven began on time.

"Before we get started, I just overheard several conversations about the kidnapping of our personnel. This has to stop. It may sound cold to many of you, but that train of thinking will just get in our way. It will make you try too hard, press, and believe me, you'll screw up. Now, let's get started."

Pete nodded toward Will Mendenhall, who turned and opened the door for three women to enter the conference room. They were carrying two large plastic containers. They placed these on the conference table.

"This is Professor Angela Vargas, of the physics and nuclear sciences department. She's heading things up in Virginia's absence," Pete explained.

As the young physicist pulled material from the first box, Jack noticed for the first time that Charles Hindershot Ellenshaw III was not present; he never made it back from the burned-out vault area. In addition, Dr. Gene Robbins was missing from the meeting. Collins hoped both men were getting somewhere with their individual assignments.

"This is one of the protective jumpsuits the attackers were wearing, recovered from one of the bodies—the one killed by Lieutenant McIntire," Vargas said as she looked at her notes.

Everett chanced a look over at Jack, but he sat stoically and did not react at all to Sarah's name or her killing of one of the assailants.

"At first glance, we thought it was a standard special forces–issued garment, until we placed it under the electron microscope per Dr. Golding's orders to leave no stone unturned. Well, he was right." She handed the black jumpsuit to Jack. He didn't react to the dried blood. "Colonel, feel the material. What would your opinion be?"

"It feels like standard issue, maybe with some Kevlar weaved in, what we would call Nomex IIIA."

"Very good, Colonel, however you are wrong. Not Nomex, not polyester, not a Kevlar weave." She looked around the room for dramatic effect. "It's seaweed."

The department heads mumbled as they looked at the material.

"That's right, *Callophycus serratus*, very rare, very expensive. This seaweed has also been known to kill cancer cells. Therefore, if someone has such an abundance of this seaweed to make clothing, they must have a rich farm of unknown size in the ocean depths."

"Where is this seaweed found, Professor?" Jack asked as he and many others were busy scribbling on the pads.

"Two of the only known sites in the world are located just off of Fiji, and the largest is off Papua, New Guinea. The rest of the seaweed beds in the world wouldn't be enough to make a string bikini, much less outfit a bunch of pirates."

"Very good, nice start, Professor. What else have you got?" Pete asked.

"This." She brought out one of the strange-looking weapons. It was short, powerful looking, and jet-black.

Carl Everett sat up and looked at the weapon Professor Vargas was holding so cavalierly. When she suddenly tossed the weapon at him, he caught it with both hands. Then his eyebrows rose and he stood away from the table. The entire weapon, with ammunition magazine, could not have weighed more than three pounds.

"It's light, too light to be real," Carl said as he handed the weapon to Jack.

"There's a reason for that, Captain. It's not made of steel. Believe me when I say no gunsmith in the world has ever seen anything like that weapon. I fired it myself at the shooting range. It's compact and extremely accurate."

"Okay, you've amazed us, Professor. What's it made of?"

"All we know is that it is some kind of polymer. Plastic, but unlike any plastic we have ever seen before. It will take months to break the matrix down so we can analyze it. However, a new plastic is not what's so amazing about this weapon—it's the characteristics of the material. For the first time in history, someone has invented a biodegradable plastic that will disintegrate, with only natural forces working against it, in fifteen to twenty years of being buried in soil."

"Impossible," several men and women said at the same time.

"Our environmental chamber experiments are documented and are available, and confirmed through Europa. It's there, read the report. We don't know who we're dealing with here, but whoever they are, they're far more than a century ahead of us in technology."

The room grew quiet as everyone absorbed what the professor had said. Their hopes of finding and stopping this group were growing fainter.

Carl looked over at Jack and stood.

"I'm getting back to work. Dr. Robbins needs supervision."

Collins nodded as Everett left the conference room.

"Thank you, Professor. Please inform me when you have conducted tests on all material recovered from our intruders." Pete rubbed his forehead and tried to think, but he was just too tired. He removed his thick glasses and looked at all the department heads.

"You have your assignments in front of you. Some departments will be coordinating with others that seemingly have no business being put together. We are shorthanded and have been for the past six weeks. The next few days won't be any different. We're calling in former members to assist in filling vacancies, but that will take a while. Thank you, we'll meet again when we—"

At that moment, the doors opened and in came Ellenshaw. He held up a sheath of papers and several computer discs. He nodded at Pete, indicating he had news.

Pete nodded to Ellenshaw, who in turn gave several discs to the audiovisual technician who dimmed the lights and turned on the main holographic machine. The hologram projector used a micromisting system in the ceiling to create the 3-D effect without the need for a screen, and the four projectors hit the water mist from four sides, producing the hologram effect.

"Okay, what we have here is a visual of vault 298907, placed inactive for further investigation on nine October nineteen eighty-three. This is file footage of the vault before the fire. We do have detailed pictures and listings of everything documented on that submarine. Dr. Golding assigned me the task of digging through the mess inside the vault, while the engineers were busy shoring up the affected levels. I have a rather bizarre and fantastic theory I would like to advance, which I am accustomed to doing, about the submarine and its origins."

The man with wild white hair looked around the table. His lab coat was dirty and water-stained from the flooded vault, and one of his pant legs was still rolled up past his right ankle. He smiled and raised his half-moon glasses into his crazily swirling hair.

"As you may know, we have had many discussions in the past about this strange vessel and its origins. Being as old as it is, let us say it's made for some very far-out speculation in crypto, I'll tell you. Number one among most theories, and it's common knowledge I support said theory, is that Jules Verne may have received inspiration for his novel, *Twenty Thousand Leagues Under the Sea,* from this very artifact. The chances are just too farfetched not to connect the dots here. However, that is not of importance at this time. What is of paramount importance is why this modern-day crackpot wants to destroy something that is at least a hundred and fifty years of age and seemingly could cause them no harm at all?"

Ellenshaw nodded toward the navy signalman, who changed the view on the hologram.

"Thank you, Smitty. As you see, this is the vault as it is now, burned out and most items unrecognizable." The professor lifted his notebook, walked into the micromist, and pointed to items lying on the floor. "The batteries, burned and almost unrecognizable, reduced to large lumps of rubberized crud due to the heat produced internally by the dried acid within. Correct?" He looked around the conference room but saw no one as the mist was hiding them.

"Professor Ellenshaw, could you speed it up?" Pete asked, a bit impatient.

"Right, well, we combed through the debris and for nine hours we went through the files with a microscope." He hunched his shoulders and threw up his arms in exasperation. "Nothing; not a damn thing. We didn't know why destroying this thing was so important. We were at a dead end."

Pete was eyeing him, the same impatient look on his face.

"But we weren't." He pointed once more to the batteries. "That is what's known as a composite material, basically a rubber and graphite mix. During the time we believe the submarine was built, natural rubber was in common use; however, graphite was not. It's a simple carbon-based material we once used in pencils and is a base used in batteries today. We know there was more than a ton of this composite material used in the construction of the battery system utilized on *Leviathan.*" He smiled. "With the assistance of Europa, I was able to trace a large sale of graphite and an even larger sale of rubber from a Malay plantation in eighteen thirty-seven, purchased through the engineering department at the University of Oslo. It took several hours, but Europa finally uncovered the name of the professor involved—Francis N. Heirthall."

"Okay, where does that lead us?" Pete asked.

"Our good professor was not your normal engineer; he was wealthy beyond measure and only utilized the university's laboratories for security reasons. His real engineering skills were that of a marine engineer, and he held advanced degrees in biology."

Pete was silent as the information was absorbed. He pursed his lips and examined the hologram, confused on one point—why would anyone destroy the vault to protect a hundred-and-fifty-year-old professor?

"Has this been verified by Europa?" Liz Patrick of the engineering department asked.

"Absolutely. I have already turned the results of my inquiry over to Dr. Robbins for further investigation."

"Anything else, Charlie?"

"One other thing. We did come across something in the files that became of interest only after we discovered the destination of these large orders. The barnacles recovered from the submarine's hull back in nineteen sixty-seven were a mixed breed of organisms. However, the bulk of these originated near the southern Mariana chain of islands, Guam in particular. *Cirripedia acrothoracica*, a new species of barnacle discovered only recently and indigenous to that area and those islands."

The audiovisual tech switched pictures after a nod from Ellenshaw. On the hologram, a map of the South Pacific appeared. Ellenshaw once more stepped up into the mist cloud. He pulled a laser marker from his coat pocket and placed it on Papua, New Guinea. "Now, I was given a report on the seaweed earlier, and if I was informed correctly, this seaweed used in the manufacture of our bad guys' clothing came from here, correct?"

Jack was looking at the map intently, knowing what Ellenshaw was trying to do. Pete Golding nodded his head at Charlie's question.

Ellenshaw then drew a laser line from New Guinea north toward Guam, then abruptly south to the southern chain of the same islands. The figure formed an elongated triangle. "I daresay it's a long shot, but that's what the crypto team is good at: placing silly bets on lost causes."

"Wait, what is the third marker for?" Pete asked.

Ellenshaw smiled. "The island at the southern tip of the Marianas was owned by a very wealthy family from Norway—the Heirthalls."

"You're saying that the people we are seeking—or at the very least, their ancestor—frequented this area?" Pete asked, taking off his glasses.

"No, what I'm saying is that this is more than likely their lair—or to be more precise, what used to be their lair. In addition, you may ask how could a vessel such as this ply the waters in the eighteen-sixties, and not be spied more frequently. It couldn't have," he answered for them, "at least not in the crowded oceans near industrialized nations. It would have to have been based in a region where there was virtually no water traffic, and what better place than the Marianas?"

"Doc, I think you may have something. It's gut instinct, but everything you've said makes sense . . . in your always strange points of fact. The evidence, at least, says we may have a starting point."

Ellenshaw looked at Colonel Collins, and with his eyes and a dip of his chin thanked him for supporting his theory.

"Okay, good work, Charlie, we'll run with what you have. Now let's see what Batman and Robin can do with Europa and your new information."

As the department heads left, Collins stayed behind. He looked from Ellenshaw to the tired-looking Golding.

"Are you resting, Pete?" Jack asked, watching the man's eyes, which were a nice light blue when not covered by glasses.

"No . . . but I will."

"You know who the saboteur is, don't you, Pete?" Jack asked. Ellenshaw stopped gathering his paperwork and watched the exchange. As he did he pulled a printout from his notes and waited.

Golding bit his lip, turned to look down at his own pile of notes and briefing materials, then slowly started to gather them up.

"Yes, I believe I do. I wanted more evidence, because what I have is circumstantial at best."

"Pete, all they had was circumstantial evidence on Ted Bundy, but they still knew who he was and what he did," Jack said. "Whoever it is cannot be free to roam the complex. That person is responsible for the death of our people, and the kidnapping of our friends."

Pete meekly tossed the papers back down onto the table and turned his back on Collins and Ellenshaw.

"Who, Doc?" Jack persisted, almost afraid to hear his answer.

"The complex at least, I believe, is safe for right now. The person I suspect is no longer here."

Collins closed his eyes, wanting not to see Pete's mouth move when he spoke the words.

"It was Virginia, damn her soul, Virginia Pollock, who sabotaged the vaults and tried to kill Europa when she let those animals into our home."

Collins was stunned. The air in the conference room almost became unbearable to breathe as each man took the information, allowing it to sink in and corrupt all good thoughts.

Jack's mind refused to bridge the name to the act of cold-blooded murder.

"During both failures of Europa, Virginia was the only person on-line. Professor Ellenshaw confirmed my suspicions when he mentioned the name Heirthall. At the same time Virginia sabotaged Europa, she was tasking the computer on several queries."

"I still don't believe it," Jack said as he looked at the computer login times.

"I was hesitant to bring this up, because in a court of law it would be thrown out as guilt by association," Ellenshaw said as he removed his own glasses and rubbed his eyes. "That and the fact I really like Dr. Pollock. She's a dear friend."

"Charlie, please," Pete said looking at the cryptozoologist.

"I ran the name through Europa's database, looking for any correlation between the name Heirthall and any person working within the complex, just to be thorough." He tossed a printout and Jack picked it up. "That is the list of the MIT graduating class of nineteen eighty-one."

Jack looked down the list and saw the names he was looking for—Alexandria Heirthall, and far below that, Virginia Pollock.

There was nothing left to say.

LEVIATHAN, 100 MILES OFF THE COAST OF NEWFOUNDLAND

Niles, Sarah, Alice, Lee, Farbeaux, and Virginia were shown into the dining salon shortly after noon. They had taken an elevator and an escalator to get there, and still had not seen one quarter of the giant vessel.

As they stepped into the captain's dining salon, they were amazed at the artwork once again. There were originals from Picasso, Rembrandt, and even Remington was represented with an unknown original—not about the Old West, but of sailing men in the 1800s.

The long table was set with china that was embossed with the ship's logo, the now-familiar ~L~, and the silverware at each setting was sixteenth-century. It was Farbeaux who went directly to the heart of things. He picked up one of the four wine bottles sitting at the end of the table where he assumed the captain would normally sit, as this was the only high-backed chair at the white linen covered table. He examined the old and peeling white label on the bottle.

"Sauternes from Château d'Yquem, seventeen eighty-seven," he said, almost turning white. He placed the bottle down most gently.

"What is it, Colonel?" Sarah asked as she looked from Henri to the four bottles of wine.

"Sarah, my young dear, these bottles of wine, well . . . to put it mildly, they should be in one of your Event vaults. Sauternes from Château d'Yquem seventeen eighty-seven—in two thousand six, a single bottle of this wine was auctioned for ninety-seven thousand of your American dollars. There was thought to be no more than two in existence, and here we are staring at four of them, to be a beverage served at lunch."

"Never cared for wine all that much," Lee said as he used his cane to limp toward the table.

"Dear Senator Lee, let me put this in a perspective you may be able to appreciate. The grapes in these bottles were picked the same year that George Washington became your first president."

"Well, give it to *him*; don't care for wine."

The salon door opened at the far end, and the same blond-haired man they had seen in the operation center entered and then gently closed the two large hatches. He was dressed in a navy blue jacket and tie. The first officer of *Leviathan* smiled and stepped up to the Event staff.

"Good afternoon," he said, reaching Farbeaux first. "I am First Officer James Grady Samuels, formerly of Her Majesty's Royal Navy."

Farbeaux looked at the man with the soft English accent, and then down at his outstretched hand. The Frenchman finally shook hands.

"Colonel Henri Farbeaux, I believe, formerly of the French Army?" Samuels asked.

"Yes," the Frenchman answered. "This is Lieutenant Sarah McIntire," he said, placing a hand at the small of Sarah's back and allowing her to shake the officer's hand.

"I am well aware of Ms. McIntire and her credentials. Your efforts with the incident in Arizona two years ago, and then again last year in Okinawa, were well noted by our captain."

Sarah said nothing as she stepped out of the way.

The well-mannered officer stepped forward and smiled at Alice.

"*Leviathan* is indeed graced by your presence, Mrs. Hamilton. I have heard and read so much about you, it feels as though I know you," he said, taking her hand and kissing it. Then he smiled again and moved to Lee. "Senator Garrison Lee, I won't even begin to flatter a man of such deeds as yourself, for then we may never eat our lunch. Senator, war hero, OSS general, Event Group director, it is an honor—"

"Don't bother, son. I was a witness to your orders in your operations room. You'll excuse me if I refrain from shaking the hand of a murderer." Lee looked from the first officer's outstretched hand to his eyes, and then stepped away.

Samuels closed his hand and looked away for a moment, but he didn't answer Lee's accusation. He did, however, approach Virginia with renewed enthusiasm.

"Dr. Virginia Pollock, inventor of the saltwater conversion module during your time at General Dynamics Electric Boat Division. It is an honor, ma'am."

"Excuse me—Mr. Samuels, is it? But I think I'm of the same opinion as the senator. I find you and what you're doing very distasteful. You have taken the cause of ecology to an all-time low."

The man truly looked taken back as he turned and found Niles Compton.

"Director Compton, although you must be of the same opinion as your assistant director and former mentor, I would still like to thank you for being aboard. To answer the seriousness of the charges leveled against my captain and her crew, you must understand we consider ourselves at war, and believe we have conducted ourselves accordingly. All declarations have been made in advance. There is no murder here, other than that already perpetrated by the countries of the world against the very planet on which they live."

Niles pursed his lips and then nodded, but said nothing. He saw a slight hesitation in the first officer's words—it was as if he had to fight to get the speech out of his mouth.

"Then you're now going to enlighten us as to why my people were killed and we ourselves kidnapped from our complex?" Niles asked.

"The captain will answer your questions. For now, please, would you all take a seat; your host will join us shortly. The captain decided it would have shown a lack of naval etiquette to have you eat lunch in your state-rooms," he said, just as a hidden speaker in the room sounded.

"Attention to orders from the office of the captain. We have received confirmation that the corrective measures taken in the southern Gulf of Mexico and the North Sea have been confirmed as successful. However, there has been significant loss of life. The captain has ordered a prayer service for the lives lost at twenty hundred hours in the chapel. A representative of each of the boat's divisions is mandatory. Thank you."

The room was quiet as the first officer silently gestured the group to their seats.

Lee was about to say something when Alice shook her head slowly, telling him to stay the insult or accusation brimming to get out.

The door opened and stewards entered, starting to pouring wine and fill glasses of water. Samuels nodded his head as he placed a napkin in his lap at the opposite end of the table from the empty captain's chair. He waited.

Before the Event personnel knew what was happening, two men entered the room, looked them over and then opened the double compartment hatches wide. As they watched, a dark figure, dressed in shiny navy blue pants and navy blue long-sleeved turtleneck blouse covered in the same color jacket with gold braid, stepped into the salon.

Niles stood as he saw the captain of *Leviathan* for the first time, and needless to say, he was speechless.

The woman was tall and stunning. Her jet-black hair flowed over her left ear. Her eyes were a brilliant deep blue, and they looked at each guest before she continued into the room, stopping just to the left of her high-backed chair at the head of the long table.

"Ladies and gentlemen of the Event Group, may I present Captain Alexandria Olivia Heirthall."

The tall woman half-bowed, her blue clothing shimmering in the lighting of the salon as she looked once more at each of her guests in turn. Then for the first time, she smiled.

"I would like to welcome you aboard my vessel *Leviathan*," she said softly as she nodded her head. As she straightened, one of the large men that had accompanied her pulled out her chair, and she sat slowly and deliberately, taking the embossed linen napkin and placing it in her lap as she did.

"I must say, your vessel is a marvel to behold, at least the sections we have seen of her," Niles said as he sipped from a glass of water.

The captain closed her eyes and nodded once in Niles's direction.

She raised her glass of white wine. "Ladies and gentlemen—to the earth, and its many varying and wonderful species."

Niles looked from Captain Heirthall to his own people, then shook his head. Only Farbeaux took his glass and toasted.

"By all means—I am not passing up the chance to drink this marvelous wine."

Alexandria Heirthall took a small sip of her wine as her mesmerizing blue eyes looked at Henri Farbeaux.

"Colonel, you are impressed with the wine?" she asked, setting her glass down and avoiding any indication she took offense at the slight from Compton and the others.

"Yes, but I am more surprised it has not turned to vinegar."

"Ah, but it was found in an environment that would not allow that to occur."

"Where would that be, Captain?" Sarah asked, smelling her own glass of wine.

"Two and a half miles down in the Atlantic ocean, Lieutenant McIntire; in the master chef's wine vault onboard the RMS *Titanic*. It wasn't in use, and we were in the area a few years ago, so to speak, so we rescued them from the depths. I normally do not grave rob, but it would have been almost criminal to leave such a splendid wine."

The doors opened once more and the stewards brought in salads, placing them in front of each person.

"I think you'll enjoy the vegetables. They are grown onboard *Leviathan* in our hydroponics greenhouse, which you'll see later on your tour. They were actually grown in a twenty-four-hour time frame."

"Genetics?" Niles asked, looking at his plate.

"No, Dr. Compton, small-voltage electricity and fertilizer made from coral, all from the sea—simple, really."

They all began to eat their salads. Niles watched the captain, who made no move to touch her own. She did, however, accept something from the head steward, and then swallowed it with a sip of her water.

"Captain, I have noticed that when your vessel accelerates, there is very little vibration and absolutely no sound from your power plant. May I ask what power source you utilize?" Farbeaux asked.

"Of course; we wish to be as transparent as possible, Colonel." She was now looking directly at Virginia as she answered the question. She held the gaze for the longest time, and Virginia never once looked away. "We want you all to know whatever it is you wish to know. *Leviathan* uses nuclear power, the same as any submarine in service to the major powers of the world. Our system of propulsion is thermal-dynamic drive, or TDD. We utilize superheated water from our reactor core and run it through a series of pumps, mixing it with hydrogen and a substance not unlike baking soda, thus creating steam drive that is environmentally friendly and is quite substantial in providing propulsion for *Leviathan*."

"Captain, may I ask a question?" Niles said, placing his salad fork on his plate and looking at Farbeaux.

Only a small dip of her elegant chin was the answer.

"How many did you kill in cold blood this morning? I must tell you, at least before my friend and mentor Senator Lee does, that your actions seem quite insane."

To his left, Niles felt the eyes of the first officer on him. The man touched at the corners of his mouth with his napkin and then slapped it into his lap.

The captain smiled and shook her head lightly at Samuels.

"'Cold blood.' To me that has always been an interesting catchphrase, Dr. Compton, one used by men who have no idea what justice sometimes truly is. Yes, when you plan to kill for no other reason than the want of killing, indeed, that is in cold blood. However, this morning's bloodshed was an act of hot blood, justified in all respects to even the basest laws of civilized man. I sincerely wish that is the last of it that is spilled in this cause, but I fear it will be not be."

"The demands that you are asking of the world, while justified in many ways, are impossible to meet. Nations will collapse and people will starve," Lee said, pushing his salad away as if stating he would have nothing from this woman.

"To you, this very vessel is an impossibility of science—is it not? To you, many things seem that way, but it just isn't so."

"Without alternative fuels in place, it is. Without more research, it is," Niles said, staring straight at the woman.

The captain flinched as if she wanted to react with harshness, but instead she slowly dipped her head and calmed herself. She then looked up, opened her eyes, and smiled, but all could see she was straining to argue.

"My family has tried in vain to get the benefits of our research and experiments to those that would use them wisely, only to see our go-betweens ridiculed, even murdered, and some, I'm sorry to say, bought off by the commercial corporations representing the oil concerns of the world. The world today is capable of running totally without the need of petroleum. I can supply the world with wind power, solar power, nitrogen, clean-coal technology, and clean nuclear power. It's all there for the asking."

"Then why—" Niles started to ask, but Heirthall continued as if he weren't there.

"But alas, I am sorry to say I have nothing magical that I can provide to stop the death of many magnificent species in the sea. Mankind has never realized that the oceans and humanity are symbiotic entities." She placed her fingertips together, and then intertwined them. "The only solution is time, Doctor, time. The sea needs time to heal itself, and my research has shown it *can indeed* heal itself. However, petroleum-based products are not only ruining life upon the land and air, they are destroying life in my seas. Acid rain, oil spills, and the deliberate dumping of chemical waste have joined together to do untold damage to the earth and its oceans."

Niles started to ask a question, but was interrupted by the stewards as they brought in the main course.

"I hope you enjoy your entrée. It's black sea bass stuffed with red artichoke hearts—again, from our own gardens."

Niles looked at the fabulously designed dish, and then looked at the captain as if she were avoiding his questioning, which he knew she was not doing. She was actually inviting them.

Heirthall waved the attending steward to remove her lunch. Then she placed her elegant hands just under her chin and looked at Sarah, seemingly for study. Sarah returned the look as she took a forkful of sea bass.

"Lieutenant McIntire, I am told you were most resourceful in defense of your complex. You have garnered one fan among my crew. Sergeant Tyler tells me you acted in a far more aggressive nature than your geological education would have indicated you were capable."

Sarah lowered her fork to her plate and dabbed her mouth with her napkin. Then she fixed the captain with her own stare. "I'm a trained soldier first, Captain. Why would that surprise you? However, even the untrained will fight back when attacked."

Heirthall smiled and continued to study Sarah. "I suspect that you have had special training, perhaps from someone close to you?"

Sarah did not care for the line of questioning. Had she heard about Jack—his death? Was this her way of getting to her, perhaps mocking what she felt for him? She was about to respond when she was stopped by the intercom.

"Captain, this is the conn—ma'am, this is the officer of the deck. We have reached the coordinates for Mark Antony and picked up his transponder."

Heirthall continued to hold Sarah with her eyes for a moment longer, and then reached out and pushed something under the tabletop hidden to her guests.

"Thank you, Mr. Abercrombie. Order all stop if you please, and order the crew to quiet conditions for the next ten minutes."

"Aye, Captain. All stop."

Around the table, they felt the deceleration of the giant submarine as the propulsion system went to low power.

"Commander Samuels, if you'll do the honors, please," she said, once more looking toward Virginia.

The first officer nodded, stood from his chair, and approached the far section of hull, which held deeply embedded three-dimensional studies of sea life of every major category. The captain sat silently and watched her guests.

The first officer stood next to a small keypad and entered a code. Suddenly the composite inner hull separated into two pieces, slid apart, and then slipped down, sinking away into the hull. Then everyone saw another protective layer fall away, and then finally another. Triple layers of material separated them from the pressures of the sea. What remained was an illuminated view of the blue ocean. The water was crystal clear, and it seemed you could see forever with the help of the powerful lights outside the hull. Niles and the others stood, walked over to the forty-five-foot by thirty-foot window, and stared at the vastness before them. The captain remained seated as they took in the spectacular view.

"My God," Alice said as she took Garrison's hand and squeezed. "It is beautiful."

Heirthall pushed back her chair and joined them at the window. She placed her hands behind her back and watched the sea beyond the reinforced acrylic.

"We have just moments ago entered the Arctic Circle. Soon we will dive for deep water and make our passing under the ice. I thought first you might like to see just what it is we are protecting in *this* area of the sea."

They turned and watched as she flipped a small switch in the same panel that opened the viewing window.

Sarah felt it first, and leaned into Farbeaux as her ears started to ring. The others felt it a moment later. It wasn't an uncomfortable sound, just penetrating. Strangest of all, it almost felt and sounded familiar, as if an old song remembered.

"The sound you hear has been ingrained in your subconscious. From the dawn of life on this earth you have carried this sound with you. It's the sound of the very first mammals, the very sound of life and of the sea. The only difference is the fact our cousins here went back to the sea, while we stayed. We are one with them." She took a step back and looked down the line of Event personnel. "You see, Senator Lee, life can be cold-blooded as you stated, but in the sea is found 'the hottest blood of all.'"

As she spoke the words from the D. H. Lawrence poem, "Whales Weep Not!," a giant humpback whale swam into view. It swam slowly up to the glass, making everyone but the captain and first officer step back. The huge mouth rubbed up against the acrylic window, and the whale flipped over on its back.

"Excuse me, Colonel Farbeaux," the captain said as she moved to the center of the window and then slowly raised her elegant hand to the glass. This movement caught the whale's attention. It moved to the center of the window and started singing its whale song. The elongated flipper seemed to reach out and touch the glass right where Heirthall's hand was placed. The captain smiled, then closed her eyes.

"Amazing," Farbeaux said.

As they watched, another humpback came swimming casually through the blue waters and into the illumination of *Leviathan*'s lights. The captain placed her other hand upon the glass, and the second whale rubbed its giant mouth against the very spot hers was placed.

"I would like to introduce you to Antony and Cleopatra. They and their pod are friends of ours."

Sarah smiled as she saw twenty whales come forth out of the waters surrounding *Leviathan*. She heard them singing, almost as if they were happy.

"It's as if they are saying hello," she said.

LEVIATHAN   175

"They are, Lieutenant, they are saying exactly that. You see, once you have the fundamental mathematics down, you get the gist of what they are trying to vocalize—maybe one word in three."

"Are you telling me that you can understand what they are singing?" Niles asked as he looked from the whales to the captain.

She had her eyes closed and was leaning into the glass, allowing the whales to get as close as possible. They seemed hesitant at first; Heirthall had to open her eyes and coax them, almost looking concerned for the briefest of moments, but then Antony rubbed his snout against the glass in a gesture that made clear his nature toward the captain.

"The series of songs and clicks, like that of dolphins, is a mathematical form of communication, Doctor. It took my great-great-grandfather years to decipher their meaning, and we still haven't learned but a fraction of their language. Perhaps five percent—basically *hello*, *good-bye*, and"—she opened her eyes and looked at Antony, who was singing sadly—"*dead*."

The mood was solemn, and the captain attempted to lighten it somewhat.

"There are other words also, for instance, *baby*, or *newborn*, *happy*, *sad*, *man*, and *woman*. We still have many years ahead of us," she said, stepping away from the window, and as she did, the whales moved back into the abyss.

At that moment, Yeoman Alvera stepped into the lounge and handed the captain a piece of paper.

"The damage assessment for the strike, Captain," she said as she looked toward the glass.

"Thank you, Yeoman, you are excused," the captain said, seeming to wince. She folded the report and it crumpled in her hand as she again was hit with pain.

Yeoman Alvera looked concerned for the captain. She looked from her to the Event Group, then half-bowed and left the compartment.

The captain pulled down at the edges of her coat and swallowed, looking at the men and women around her. That was when they noticed that the captain's facial features seemed to droop. Gone was the fresh face of a beautiful woman; in its place was a new one that looked tired, and the eyes actually drooped down at the corners.

At that moment Sergeant Tyler opened one of the hatchways and entered. He didn't approach the group standing at the large viewing window, but stood just inside the compartment looking at Heirthall, who only glanced his way.

"I will not lie to you. The time is past for the options I have given the world. Far past. You are here to answer questions about what your Group knows about *Leviathan* and her origins. That will be the duty of Sergeant Tyler; he will get the answers I need."

The complete turnaround from hospitable host to captor caught even the suspicious Lee off guard. They looked from the captain to her first mate. He momentarily looked as confused as they at the suddenness of the change, but recovered far more quickly.

"You will still have freedom of *Leviathan* until such time when security will have need of you. Answer the sergeant's questions truthfully, and you may survive your visit. Lie, and you'll find *Leviathan* can be a very cold place to be."

They watched the captain as she rubbed her temples and then lowered her head. She paced to the large double hatchways, and the two guards opened them.

"Until you are needed you will not be interfered with, as you have the run of my home."

Niles stepped away from the window.

"Captain, we know nothing about you or any part of your existence other than the relic we had stored in our vaults."

Sergeant Tyler smiled as he held the hatchway for Heirthall. His look told the group he was looking forward to confirming what Niles had stated.

The captain paused at the hatch and half-turned. Instead of commenting on Niles's denial of knowledge, she said, "If any of you were wondering, whales usually do not travel in pods this large. You see, they are sick, frightened, and without hope. They don't understand what is happening to them; their birth rate is down to near zero. In addition, I honestly don't know how to tell them that it's my own kind that is doing this evil thing to them. There is even greater, more brilliant, and far more ancient life that it may be too late to save." After making this mysterious comment she walked out with her guards.

Tyler again turned to the Group, smiled, and then followed the captain out of the compartment.

"The captain is ill, Mr. Samuels. I don't know if you noticed or not," Alice said, looking at the man and waiting for a reaction.

Samuels looked as if he were going to answer, but instead turned and left.

"I don't know if all of you noticed or not," Lee said as he picked a roll off the table and placed it in his coat pocket, then followed that with another. "But that little lady is mad as a hatter."

They all looked at him.

"As insane as Lizzie Borden." The senator looked around the interior of the salon. "And she has one hell of a little hatchet to play with—it's called *Leviathan*. And now she wants to ask a few questions after showing us that ax."

"Captain?" Samuels said, nodding for the security element to step aside. They looked at Alexandria, and when she nodded it was all right, they moved away, all with the exception of Tyler.

Heirthall leaned against the composite hull and lowered her head. Samuels reached out and took the captain's arm.

"Please, Commander, I am all right, just tired," she said as she shrugged off his support.

"Ma'am, I have studied the files on these people. You can ask them anything you want, but if they don't wish it, they won't tell you a thing." He looked at Tyler, who watched Samuels with steely eyes. "Unless you plan to torture them."

"If I have to, I will. The captain wants to know what these people know about her and . . . her family, I will get the answers she wants."

"For what? What possible harm can this Group, or anyone for that matter, cause us or *Leviathan*? We are invulnerable. Once the world knows of the plight of the endangered species in the gulf, I believe they can actually assist in its survival. Bringing them aboard was a mistake, but a mistake they don't have to pay for with their lives."

"Commander, for the second time in a twenty-four-hour period you have questioned my orders. This can never happen again. Am I clear on that point?" Heirthall didn't wait for the answer. She turned and made her way down the companionway.

Tyler stepped up to Samuels and looked the smaller man over.

"Listen to the captain, Mr. Samuels; don't make me have to question your loyalty."

The first officer of *Leviathan* watched the head of security turn away and follow Heirthall. He slumped against the bulkhead and closed his eyes. He knew something was happening that he knew nothing about, and if Tyler knew, that something couldn't be good. And what was worse, his captain was changing right before his eyes.

EVENT GROUP COMPLEX, NELLIS AIR FORCE BASE, NEVADA

Dr. Gene Robbins was staring a hole through Carl Everett. The captain returned the glare and added a bit more of his own.

"You cannot question Europa in the manner in which you have been, Captain. Do you think she responds to your anger? She probes other computers for back doors into their systems, bypassing any corporate or company security program added after that particular computer's manufacture and programming."

"I understand that, Doc, but you cannot sit here and wait. We have a tight time frame to get a handle on what we're dealing with. Professor Ellenshaw gave us a good starting point with this theory of his, and he gave us a name, so damn it, let's start there."

"I think we should verify the professor's findings first—that way we don't waste the time if he's wrong in his research."

"Listen, Professor Ellenshaw has proven to everyone in this complex that his work is viable. He's not a nutcase—that man is brilliant, and the sooner you get ahold of that fact, the better off you'll be. Start with his findings," Everett said angrily.

"Europa, do you have information regarding the research for a Professor Francis Heirthall—University of Oslo—say eighteen thirty-five on?" Robbins asked, not liking the lecture from Carl.

At that moment, Jack walked into the room pulling on rubber gloves. Robbins shook his head but continued to write on his notepad.

"Hope you don't mind. I need some quiet time while Pete arranges for transport to the Pacific for us," Jack said as he pulled out a chair and sat to the right of Carl.

"So we are going with Professor Ellenshaw's hunch?" Everett asked.

"I believe he said quiet time, Captain. May we continue? Colonel Collins, we are not using Europa clean-room protocols; you may discard the gloves."

Jack half-smiled as Everett turned back to face Robbins, but did not say anything. Collins walked to the trash bin and tossed his gloves inside. He noticed something under the discarded pair he had just thrown in. He reached in and picked up another glove coated in a silvery substance that looked familiar to him. He shrugged and almost tossed it back inside the waste bin, but instead wrapped it inside of one of his own gloves and pocketed both.

"Dr. Robbins, Europa has formulated the text of several verified experiments conducted by Professor F. Heirthall, University of Oslo, eighteen thirty-six to eighteen forty-three. List is as follows:

"'The utilization of electrical current derived from reciprocating engine (steam).'

"'Copper usage in the flow-through aspects of electrical current.'

"'Hydrodynamic tolerances and depth degradation of oxygen filled platforms.'

"'Oxygen purification—carbon monoxide poisoning.'"

As they watched the words appear and listened to Europa, they didn't realize at first that the list was complete.

"Europa, what do you have on the professor after eighteen forty-three?" Everett asked.

"Information extracted from the Oslo Herald, *June third, eighteen forty-three, reported the death of Francis Heirthall in a University of Oslo laboratory fire."*

"Being a navy man as I am, based on this list I would say the professor was working on systems that are consistent with submarine design," Carl said as he looked at Jack.

"I think you're right, Captain," Jack said as he leaned toward his microphone. "Europa, was the professor married?"

Europa placed one more program by robotic arm.

"Oslo census reports Dame Alexandria Heirthall, eighteen twenty to eighteen fifty-one, listed as spouse at the time of the professor's death. Son: Octavian Heirthall."

"Is there any newspaper account of the Heirthall family listed in historical records other than the accomplishments and research records of Professor Heirthall?" Robbins asked.

Europa started loading more programs.

"We may be barking up the wrong tree here, Doc," Everett said.

"Possibly, but let's go ahead and cut this tree down at any rate so we can move on with a clear conscience."

"One newspaper account from France dated September nineteenth, eighteen forty-six, is the only mention of the Heirthall name after the eighteen forty-three obituary for Professor Francis Heirthall," Europa said in her female voice, at the same time typing out the script on the large monitor.

"What was the gist of this French news story?" Jack asked without much hope in finding anything worthwhile.

"Headline reads as follows: NORWEGIAN ROYALTY BATTERS FRENCH AU-THOR IN CIVIL COURT."

"Okay, what sort of suit was brought against this author?" Everett asked.

"I don't see how this is connected—"

"The lawsuit brought by Dame Alexandria and Octavian Heirthall was in reference to libel and defamation of her husband's character," Europa answered, cutting Robbins's protest short.

"Come on, Europa, for crying out loud, who was the author?" Everett asked angrily, tired of this slow line of questioning and starting to think Robbins was right.

"The defendant in said case is listed only as A. Dumas, Paris, France. Occupation: novelist."

Jack sat up straight. "Europa, what was written about Heirthall? I mean, was it a book?"

Robbins shook his head in reference to the way Collins was asking questions.

"The item was listed as a manuscript not yet in book form that was sent to the family for comment."

"What was the title of the manuscript?" Jack asked.

"Holy shit," Carl said when the answer appeared.

Collins shook his head when it was apparent Europa had finished her research. He watched silently as the last words typed out blinked in a greenish hue on the big screen, and Europa verbally answered.

"Title of novel: The Count of Monte Cristo."

10

Niles thought it the best course for Alice and the senator to act as one
team, he and Virginia another, and because Sarah seemed to tolerate Farbeaux far better than any of them, they would comprise the third team.
The idea was that as they toured the ship in teams, they could cover more
ground, and at least keep the eyes that would surely be upon them far
busier tracking three groups than they planned. Niles stressed the fact
that they were prisoners, not guests. Their task now was to find some way
off this seagoing prison.

Niles and Virginia were the first to stroll down to the command center. As they entered and saw the center for the first time in close-up detail, they saw it looked nothing like any submarine they had ever seen
before. It was thirty times larger than the mock deck of the starship *En-
terprise*. They saw neither First Officer Samuels nor Captain Heirthall
on duty.

The deck was quiet, exceedingly so, as operators manned their stations in silence. Niles spotted a man standing near the holographic chart
table. The system was like their map visuals at the Event Group, only this
one was more compact and didn't use a water-misting system. This was
actually a three-dimensional view of the ice cap surrounding *Leviathan*.

"You know, when I was a kid, I can remember the first polar transit by
USS *Nautilus*," Niles said aloud, gaining the attention of the man at the
chart table, but also that of several of the operators at their semidark stations. He saw that their looks were anything but hostile, nor did they
show annoyance at his breaking of the silence. Instead, they were polite
and complete with smiles.

"Indeed, sir," the young man at the chart table said, looking up at
Niles and Virginia. "I'm afraid I wasn't born at that time, but I can

imagine the world was very excited at the news. Captain Heirthall's mother and father—they actually followed *Nautilus* on her journey under the ice—they wished to make sure she was in no danger. They were great admirers of the nuclear submarine program and wished to see it succeed." He looked around, almost embarrassed. "At least, that was the way it was taught to us in the Heirthall Midshipman School."

Niles just shook his head and looked from the young Norwegian-sounding officer to the others watching him and Virginia with curiosity. Several of these crewmen were as young as Yeoman Alvera; trainees, he figured, and obviously midshipmen in their teens as well. They didn't look quite as interested in Niles, nor the navigator's reminiscences. Their looks were almost hostile, not only at them, but also at the crew that listened.

"Well, I remember my father pointing to the headline at least—I was a little young myself. But in answer to your comment, yes, we were very proud, at least my father was. He was an engineer in construction, and I remember him saying, 'The world is now being opened before us.'"

The technicians exchanged looks and smiled, nodding their heads. They seemed to be very interested in Niles's remembrance of the time. This time, Virginia noticed the younger midshipmen exchange looks, and for some reason, those looks didn't look too friendly at all.

"I am Lieutenant Stefan Kogersborg. I am watch commander and officer of the deck. You must be Drs. Compton and Pollock?"

Virginia nodded politely.

"Would you like to see our position? I would be most happy to show you exactly where we are."

Niles stepped up to the table with Virginia and the young officer pointed at the ice cap above them, tinged in white light-emitting lines.

"As you see, the ice thickness above us is at varying depths and thicknesses. We have very large pressure ridges which are very dangerous to a submarine, even one as large as *Leviathan*." He moved his fingers along the three-dimensional outline of the ice above. Then he pointed to a miniature version of the submarine far below. "The captain has ordered our speed cut in half to seventy knots for safety reasons," he said in all seriousness.

Niles looked closer at the hologram simulation before him.

"That's *Leviathan* here?" he asked, pointing. "What in God's name is our depth?"

The officer of the deck pushed a button, and a projected speed appeared next to the moving vessel.

"We are currently at forty-five hundred feet."

Niles was stunned. "May I . . . may I ask how you can achieve such a depth without crushing?"

Kogersborg had to stifle a laugh. Niles and Virginia heard the other technicians, but not the midshipmen, chuckle at their stations as many of them exchanged bemused looks.

"Did I say something amusing?"

The officer cleared his throat loudly. The operators silenced and went back to their scanning and monitoring.

"Of course, you did nothing of the kind, Doctor. We here on *Leviathan* are so used to what this vessel can do, we sometimes forget our abilities are somewhat astounding to the outside world. Also, I would like to apologize for the technicians of this watch"—he looked around him at the crewmen of his shift—"as we sometimes do not utilize the manners our captain insists upon."

"No need to apologize. I am just . . . stunned, to say the least."

"Lieutenant Kogersborg, I don't think the captain wants you to go into such fine detail about many of the technologies in the control center."

They all turned to see Yeoman Alvera standing behind them.

"Yeoman, I am following First Officer Samuels's orders to the letter. Now return to your duties, and never leave your station while on duty upon this bridge, or you'll be called to mast before Mr. Samuels."

"Aye, Lieutenant," she said as she looked from Kogersborg to Niles and Virginia. "You have my apologies."

"Yeomen—they think they run the boat. I'm sorry for the interruption. In answer to your inquiry, Doctor, I could go into much detail about how we operate at this, and far greater depths, but I haven't the elegance to do justice to our captain and her family's science. Captain Heirthall will explain it all to you. You know"—he leaned in close to Niles and Virginia—"the captain is making a gift of all this to the world one day. She knows in order to fulfill the demands she's making upon everyone on land, there has to be a reward for the harsh times they'll have to endure."

Compton was sure the young officer had just give him a prepared speech. He thought the young man had been directed to sneak that little gem in somewhere to someone while they were touring. As he thought

this, he felt the eyes of the younger trainee midshipmen on them, and
for some reason he couldn't fathom, he didn't like it at all.

"I see. Let's hope we can dissuade her from the demands she's making, and maybe reach a middle ground," he said as he saw the midshipmen return to their training.

The blond officer smiled, and then leaned on the holographic table.
"Perhaps."

"For such a brilliant woman, she has moments of sheer brutality,"
Virginia said, watching for a reaction.

"We all realize the stress that the captain is under, and her orders of
late have been—"

"May I ask where it is we are going, at so great a speed and depth?"
Niles asked, cutting off the officer's answer. He had noticed several of
the young midshipmen looking directly at Kogersborg, and for a reason
Niles couldn't quite understand, he stopped the officer from committing
to an answer.

"You may indeed," Kogersborg said, somewhat disturbed at the abrupt
change of subject. "We will subtransit the ice cap and be in Pacific waters
before you sit down for the elegant meal the captain has planned for you
this evening."

"The captain, she spends long periods alone?" Virginia asked.

"She has many duties that keep her away from the crew for long hours;
research, mostly, but we understand what kind of stress she is under." He
finally looked up at the two Event people. "All this death of what she, and
we, love . . . well, she has placed this all upon her shoulders, and we are
only too—"

"Lieutenant Kogersborg, First Officer Samuels has the conn. You are
relieved."

They turned to see a freshly showered and shaved Samuels as he
stepped up to the navigation console.

"Aye, I have been properly relieved. Commander Samuels has the
conn," Kogersborg called to his chief of the boat, and then turned and
bowed to Virginia and Niles. "It was nice sharing time with you, and I
hope I answered all your questions. Good afternoon."

"Seems like a bright young man," Niles said as James Samuels took
over the conn.

"Yes, he is one of our brightest." He looked at Niles. "His parents
were missionaries in Somalia; they disappeared there after the UN troop

pullout in nineteen ninety-three. The captain and Dr. Trevor discovered him as we have many of our midshipmen: destitute and alone. The young man was feeding himself on dried rice in the streets of Mogadishu when we found him while on a humanitarian mission to that country."

"It seems Captain Heirthall, and indeed the entire crew, is quite accomplished in acts of humanitarianism," Niles said, again watching closely for the officer's reaction.

Samuels glanced up from his course calculations and looked at Niles.

"Doctor, our captain wears many hats. She can be the most humane person in the world, but her wrath can be multiplied many fold if she is angered. Captain Heirthall did not want to take the course of action she has taken, but she has been angered most recently by the loss of sea life in the Mediterranean, and her family has been betrayed countless times in the past two hundred years."

"Two hundred years? May I ask—"

"Doctors, if you will excuse me, our watch change is very complicated and time consuming, and we are a bit behind schedule. I must apologize. May we take this up at dinner?"

"You said loss of life in the Med. You mean human life, of course?" Virginia asked.

The commander became silent for a brief moment. "Again, may we take this up at a later time, please?" he said, instead of answering her question.

"Yes, of course," Niles said as he took Virginia by the arm.

As they stepped from the control center into the companionway, Niles looked at Virginia.

"Something is eating at that man; I can't figure him at all. And what in the hell is with those creepy midshipmen? Nice and charming one minute—"

"Niles, I have to tell you something, I should have told you immediately after lunch when I saw who we were dealing with. I was hoping I was wrong, but . . ." Virginia whispered, looking pale and nervous.

"What is it?"

"It's Heirthall. I was—"

"Well, well, we were just looking for you two. I knew these bastards wouldn't let us into the weapons room—free rein of the boat, my ass," Lee said as he and Alice stepped through hatchway and into the companionway.

Virginia looked from Niles to Alice, then smiled. It was a weak smile and lacked sincerity, and then she turned back to Compton, shook her head, and mouthed, *Later.*

Samuels observed the watch change from the navigation console through the holographic image of *Leviathan.* The second command watch took their seats after the older crewmen exchanged watch changes, course adjustments, and joked with one another. The midshipmen, instead of their usual teenage talk, smiles, and warnings of training material ahead for them during shift change, nodded at one another and then quietly took up station next to their older trainers. He saw Yeoman Alvera look his way and smile—the same smile he had seen a thousand times before, only this time she held the humorless smile a bit longer, and he had to admit it to himself, he didn't like it at all.

Commander Samuels reached under the console, brought the phone to his ear, and punched in the captain's cabin number to report the change of watch.

"Yes," a male voice answered.

"Dr. Trevor, is something wrong? Where is the captain?"

"She's lying down. I've had to medicate her—her headache became much worse in the past hour, and I was just about to leave. Shall I wake her anyway, Commander?"

"Negative, Doctor. Thank you."

"Then I shall see you at the function this evening?"

Samuels didn't answer the inquiry as he laid the phone down on the console and stared through the hologram at nothing.

An hour later, Sarah stepped into the extreme forward section of *Leviathan,* followed by Farbeaux. After the many crowded sections they had passed through, the remoteness and silence of the bow was so extreme it was like stepping into a soundproofed room.

"My God," Sarah said as she lifted her chin and followed the massive beams to their height of a hundred feet above their heads. There were partitions in front that wrapped around the entire compartment. They continued to the ceiling and then to the midpoint toward the compartment's end. The effect was like a giant, retractable clamshell aircraft hangar. There were twenty chandeliers lining the ceiling in two rows. They looked almost Art Deco in their design, and were at present dimmed to a comfortable setting.

"I must say, when this woman builds something, she builds to impress," the colonel said, as he too craned his neck to see the expanse of the compartment.

Placed on the impressively crafted teak deck was an old-fashioned ship's wheel that faced the extreme bow. Placed alongside it was a gold-plated ship's enunciator. The white leaded glass was illuminated, and was actually set at all ahead. Sarah walked over and looked at the gold inscription on the ship's wheel.

"'*Leviathan*—1858,'" Sarah said aloud. "'For the sake of the world.' This is the original ship's wheel from the very first *Leviathan*."

She placed her hand on the wheel and looked around her at the richly upholstered couches facing the outer hull of *Leviathan*. There was a large conference table at the center, a larger area for serving meals, and spotlighting that highlighted the many aquariums that wrapped around the interior from midhull level to the floor.

"You remind me of my wife. She was always awed by what she saw around her. The human race, the past of the world, all made her feel it was her duty to understand it. I envy you your naïveté, young Sarah."

She turned, looked at Farbeaux, and slightly tilted her head.

"Of all the things Danielle was, Colonel, naïve she wasn't." Sarah saw the momentary look of hurt in Henri's features. "I'm sorry, I know you loved your wife. It seems the more we love, the more fate is destined to work against us. However, since the reason you came to the Event Complex was for murder, I can find little sympathy for you at the moment."

They were interrupted when the large double hatch opened and Virginia, Niles, Alice, and Lee stepped through. Sarah and Farbeaux watched them file inside and look around, equally as impressed with the domed room as they had been.

"Quite a place, huh?" Sarah said.

The lights suddenly dimmed to near blackness and the partitions lining the hull and at the extreme bow started to part and slide into each other, just like the salon, only on a much larger engineering scale. The action was mimicked on the seaward side. It was a double-hulled protection screen.

As they watched, the deep blue sea opened up before them, in front and over their heads, since the glass covered not only the front, but a hundred feet of upper deck. The expansive vista of Arctic Ocean stretched out before them, and the brightest lighting any of them had ever seen illuminated the depths. They could even see the massive conning tower high above them when they looked aft and out of the windows at the top.

"It's so beautiful . . . I . . . I . . ."

Lee patted and then squeezed Sarah on the shoulder as she hung on to the ship's wheel and watched the sea erupt before the passage of *Leviathan*. The glass nose was sectioned by forty-foot areas of acrylic, separated by composite beams that the glass fit into. The partitions that slid away to reveal the depths had all been packed neatly into the section beams. Their view was unobstructed as far as the eye could see.

"The engineering is beyond that of anything naval architecture has achieved thus far. It has opened a completely new world. It would be criminal not to come to some accommodation," Niles said aloud as he watched the deep blue sea beyond the glass.

"If it were as simple as that, Niles, I would agree," Lee stated flatly and without emotion. "However, we are not seeing something here. There is a touch of desperation beyond the captain's claim of pollution and the degradation of the ecosystem."

"I believe her, and I believe she thinks this is our only course." Virginia placed her hand against the cold glass, just as the captain had done earlier. She felt that coldness and let it travel up her arm. "No, in her opinion, there can be no other choice in this matter. She wants the unconditional surrender of the seas, and I don't believe she'll settle for anything less."

The others looked at Virginia in mild surprise. She had been so silent since their abduction she had begun to worry them.

"Ginny developed an environmental conscience rather late in her academic life."

Everyone except for Virginia Pollock turned and looked up toward the back of the compartment. On a ten-foot-wide railed overhang there was a large chair. The captain of *Leviathan* sat and watched the sea shrouded in darkness. Heirthall slowly stood and looked out over the wooden deck sixty feet below.

"Ginny?" Niles asked, looking from the captain to Virginia, who had merely lowered her head and placed it against the cold glass.

"Virginia always seemed so formal—so at MIT I called her Ginny. We were what they called child prodigies. She was always into books and study, but never noticed the world around her. However, she was always preaching God and country, but never allowed a thought to what her country was doing to the world's environment—indeed, God's environment."

"You two know each other?" Sarah asked before Niles could.

"You Americans are surprisingly entertaining," Farbeaux said as he walked over and started looking for the bar he knew must be in the compartment somewhere.

"We are . . . or I should say, at one time, the best of friends," Heirthall said from her high vantage point.

"Tell me you're not the saboteur?" Compton said, taking a step toward the glass.

Virginia turned, looking shocked and hurt.

"What?"

"You didn't allow this woman to attack the vaults and then the complex itself, killing our people?" Niles asked, even shocking the others.

"Of course I didn't. Just because I knew her many years ago, that makes me a traitor?" Virginia said as she left the window and advanced on the director.

"Please, no one here is a traitor to any cause." The captain turned away from the upper railing and started making her way down a set of winding stairs, holding the rail and looking at the group as she did. "Ginny could no more betray her country"—she paused and looked at Niles—"than she could her friends. No, the only thing she was ever good at was being loyal, even to a fault."

Virginia stopped and then sat hard into a chair at the large table.

"No, Doctor, she's not the person you are seeking, but she was a name to throw your security teams off the trail, so to speak," she said with a trace of a smile.

Niles nodded at Sarah, then walked over to Virginia and sat next to her.

"Why didn't you tell me?" he asked.

Virginia looked up and saw her face in Niles's glasses. She did not like her reflection.

"I was praying that it wasn't her." Virginia looked from the director to the captain. "Because I was frightened, scared to death. Niles—she's not bluffing, and yes, Senator Lee, you're right, she is quite insane, but not in the way you may think."

Heirthall turned, and none of them cared for her look. She was look-ing straight at them. Then she suddenly walked at a brisk pace toward the conference table.

"Insane? Let me show you the true meaning of insane." She hit a switch embedded in the table. "Commander Samuels, alter course to the coordinates we discussed earlier, please."

"Captain, we are beyond the point of center ice. If we alter course right now we—"

"Alter course to the impacted zone immediately," she ordered angrily into the small microphone in the table. "Bring her shallow, Commander. We have to show our guests the consequences of human folly," she said, slowly but firmly placing her hand down on the intercom, not waiting for the first officer's reply. She placed both hands on the table, looked straight ahead, and then suddenly rubbed her temples and visibly relaxed.

"Aye, Captain, altering course to three-five-seven."

Alice leaned into Lee and nudged him. "Her eyes, Garrison."

Lee looked and saw Alice's meaning. The captain's eyes were dilated almost to the point of becoming totally blue.

Alice looked nervously at Lee, and even Farbeaux had stopped search-ing for the bar long enough to show concern on his face when he saw the intense way Heirthall was acting.

Alexandria lowered her head and then sat in the center chair of the large conference table. She brushed back a strand of long black hair that had fallen loose from her tightly woven braid. She swallowed and then looked up.

"You have my apologies. Some words . . . . well . . . they are made to hurt. *Insanity* is such a word. What is the difference between this awful thing and passion? A fine line can be affixed in between the two and make them unrecognizable as opposites."

"Alex, your actions explain quite adequately your state of mind. What other conclusions can people draw from the things that you have done? Yes, as a species we are self-destructive, and yes, our country is one of the worst violators, but we need time, Alex," Virginia said.

The captain suddenly stood, walked over to Virginia, and placed a hand on her cheek. In the spotlights surrounding the room, the raven-haired woman was indeed beautiful. She smiled down at her old friend.

"Time has expired, Ginny." Their eyes locked, and Virginia saw something the others did not in those dilated blue eyes: a call for help.

Heirthall was almost two people, gentle one minute, extremely violent the next.

Compton and Farbeaux felt the angle of the deck change before the others. *Leviathan* was coming shallow.

Virginia felt Alexandria's hand slide from her face as she walked toward the large viewing glass once more.

"My great-great-grandfather once trusted men. Octavian Heirthall committed evil acts to ensure the United States remained the light of the world, for in his opinion, they could do such magnificent things—so young, so naïve, but they saw a path and they took it. The reward for his duty to his adoptive country?" she asked as she turned on them. "His friend assassinated, his family murdered before his very eyes, and his only remaining daughter, Olivia, hunted like a criminal for the rest of her life."

"We don't know—"

"I do not expect you to *know* anything, Dr. Compton. I am explaining why trust is no longer an option with my family. The test has been before you since the first particles of contamination flowed from the rivers and into the sea, when the first coal-fired factories started spewing their filth all over the globe. The test has been failed by the species, thus you have forfeited certain privileges, one being the right to transit the seas for profit." She held up a hand as she looked up and saw the first officer step out onto the balcony above and nod his head. "And now I invite you to see firsthand the effects of the world's murderous folly against nature." She turned and gestured out the window.

As they watched, there was nothing. Then a very loud bang sounded against the outer hull of *Leviathan* and echoed throughput the giant vessel. The collision alarms sounded all around them as Niles and the others went to the glass and started looking around.

"All hands, rig for multiple collisions," a voice said over the loud speaker.

"Oh, God, hang on," Niles said as he grabbed the rail in front of him.

Outside the glass, a quarter-mile-wide piece of ice cascaded down into the sea from the ice cap above. The jagged edge bounced crazily off the observation glass and then hit the bow before being tossed back along the hull and out of the way. Another struck and then another. Many hit the water after calving from the bottom of the pack, then rose back up because of their buoyancy. Still, giant shards of ice were being sheared off the bottom side of the polar ice cap. From above the surface, the larger pieces let loose with a loud roar as they split and fell through the thin pack ice and down into the depths.

Leviathan pushed and maneuvered its way through the minefield of ice. The glass withstood the pounding, but was in danger of being pushed in by mountain-sized pieces of frozen water.

"Captain, we are sustaining minor damage. We have leaks in engineering and the forward weapons room. Recommend we dive."

"The polar ice cap is melting above us. It is dying from a global phenomenon many politicians have said is only a cyclical happening. Global warming cannot be stopped, possibly not in our lifetime—that is not an opinion, but fact. The temperature in the past ten years has risen by six degrees."

"Science agrees that the outer edges of the cap are indeed melting, but—" Virginia started to say.

"We are under the direct center of the North Pole. At the rate of the meltdown, in ten years there will be no ice at the top of the world," she answered calmly and matter-of-factly. "Officer of the deck, resume previous course and speed, please. Take *Leviathan* to two thousand feet minimum depth. Secure the collision alarms and send a damage report to my cabin."

"Aye, Captain, resuming previous course and speed."

Heirthall clicked off the intercom and looked up as the bow of *Leviathan* dipped sharply, making them all grab hold of the table for support.

"There are far more disturbing things you will see before your time is up on *Leviathan*. Please, observe, and I will be happy to explain the depths of the oceans' despair. For now, I must leave you," she said, closing her eyes against the pain they all saw on her features. "I will see you at dinner." She looked up at them and tried her best to smile, but failed miserably.

"Captain, are we here to be interrogated or taken on a sightseeing tour?" Niles asked as he stepped away from the observation windows.

Heirthall closed her eyes, lowered her head, and then turned to face Niles and the others. She swayed, then grabbed hold of one of the chairs to steady herself. Farbeaux made a move to assist but Alexandria held up a hand and stayed him. She looked up and saw that First Officer Samuels was making his way down the spiral staircase. She almost looked conspiratorial when she looked back at Compton and the others.

"Please, give me time. I need you onboard for a reason I cannot go into now. When Sergeant Tyler asks his questions, answer any way you like; tell the truth, don't tell the truth, it is no matter, but buy me some time."

"Captain, are you all right?" Samuels asked as he took her by the arm.

Heirthall straightened and then looked at her first officer. "I am fine, Commander, just tired." She shrugged off his hand and made her way out of the observation lounge.

Samuels watched her go. "I must apologize for the captain's behavior. She's . . . she is—"

They noticed Samuels's words stopped when he saw that Sergeant Tyler was watching from above.

"Please excuse me," Samuels said and quickly left.

They watched *Leviathan*'s first officer leave. When Niles looked up he saw that Tyler had disappeared also.

"I must reevaluate my earlier prognosis, Niles, my boy. It's not just the captain who is insane, but her entire crew."

"Senator, we need to buy some time. We have to give Captain Everett and Pete Golding time. They will find us. Until then we have to find out what's going on here, because from what I just saw, we may be in more trouble than I thought."

"Why? I mean, besides the obvious?" Lee asked.

Virginia watched the hatchway where her old friend had disappeared and knew exactly what Niles was thinking.

So did Henri Farbeaux, who was standing stock-still, his efforts to find the wet bar placed on hold.

"Because, my dear Senator Lee, a moment ago, for a reason only she knows, Captain Alexandria Heirthall looked terrified."

LEVIATHAN

Niles felt ridiculous in the clothing he had been provided. While looking somewhat like a tuxedo, it was minus a bowtie, and instead a high half-collar with a blue sapphire stickpin was perched above the white dinner-jacket lapels. The material felt strange against his skin and was unlike anything he had ever felt before.

He watched the water flow past the massive bow windows, which had been fully opened once more to reveal the sea passing by as if they were in a fighter jet. He closed his eyes as someone touched him on the shoulder.

"Damned strange feel to the tuxedo, eh, Mr. Director?" Senator Lee said as he stood next to Niles.

As Compton turned, he saw at least a hundred members of the crew as they stood in various areas of the forward compartment, some eating strange-looking hors d'oeuvres and others just standing and talking amongst themselves. They all wore what Niles assumed to be the dress uniform of the *Leviathan*, consisting of a pure white short-tailed jacket with gold and blue braid at the cuffs, white pants and shoes, and again, like himself, no tie. The women crew members wore the same, except they wore knee-length skirts. All were elegant looking; even the senator managed to look debonair.

As Niles was about to answer Garrison, Sarah walked into the room, followed by Farbeaux. Many of the male officers turned to look at the woman and her evening dress. The deep blue and green gown was like the colors of the sea. It was long and flowing and was placed upon a woman who looked as miserable as Niles had ever seen her. Farbeaux, on the other hand, was dressed in his evening wear and looked as if he were made for it. They both approached and smiled.

"I hate this," Sarah said as she politely grinned.

"I keep telling young Sarah that for her to dress any other way would be a waste of God's talents as a designer," Farbeaux said sincerely.

"For once, I have to agree with our friend," Niles said as he took Sarah's gloved hand and looked her over.

"Hear, hear," agreed Lee.

"All right, old man, don't let your one good eye fall out of your head," Alice said as she took the senator's arm.

Alice Hamilton was dressed in a nice gown of blues that had a chiffon-type material that covered her arms from the shoulder straps to her elbow-length gloves.

"This one eye is torn between viewing either Aphrodite or Venus, as both are so lovely," Lee said diplomatically.

"Indeed, Mrs. Hamilton, you are the very definition of grace and elegance," Farbeaux agreed with a bow.

"This, coming from a Frenchman and a has-been politician, makes me giddy all over," Alice said as she sneered at the two men, and then turned and started scanning the room. "I don't see Virginia," she said, craning her neck.

"Hasn't shown yet. I would like to get a chance to speak with her alone," Niles said as he saw the first officer, Commander Samuels, approach.

"Good evening—you all look very nice," he said, bowing.

"Yes, well, if our clothes hadn't been absconded with during our showers, I assure you, we would not have cooperated with you to this extravagant length." Niles locked eyes with the commander and didn't shy away.

"We thought for this occasion, the proper attire would be most appropriate. Your clothing will be returned cleaned and pressed."

"And that occasion is?" Lee asked, leaning on his cane.

"Why, the anniversary of Captain Heirthall's great-great-great-grandfather escaping from Château d'If, of course, which coincides with the birth of Octavian Heirthall to the very day five years later, the very genius behind all of this," he answered, gesturing about the room.

"Château d'If? That sounds familiar," Alice said.

"If I may, Commander," Farbeaux said. "The Château d'If is a very old prison of some renown in my country, Mrs. Hamilton." He turned from Alice to Samuels. "More famously it is known for the setting of one of the world's great novels." He smiled at all in the half-circle around him. "French, of course—*The Count of Monte Cristo*."

"Very good, Colonel," Samuels responded with genuine pleasure. "One and the same."

"You're implying—just what *are* you implying?" Sarah asked.

"I imply nothing, Lieutenant McIntire. I am only informing you of a truth."

"I find that somewhat hard to believe, Commander," Farbeaux said without the mirth of a moment before.

"Roderick Deveroux was falsely imprisoned by the Emperor Napoleon in the year 1799. His crime was failure to deliver to the emperor his life's work on ship design and construction of naval vessels that would have revolutionized the navies of France—swift, cutterlike ships that would have been models for today's America's Cup vessels. Plans for steam and coal-fired engines, battery storage systems for electricity—the list would continue for several hundred pages."

"How could he have been so far advanced of the science of design and propulsion?" Niles asked.

"According to legend, Deveroux's intellect was staggering. He spent his life entirely at sea, and most of that time corresponded with the most brilliant minds in the world. He was slave to the betterment of human-kind: advanced ways to gather the bounty of the sea, and still not over-fish the grounds—ideas and plans for alternative fuels that would save the lives of whales the world over, and stop men from seeking their deaths for lamp oil and lubrication. Yes, he was a man of science, but also a man of compassion who still believed in his brotherhood with other men. Napoleon guaranteed he would take another view after his impris-onment."

"The emperor couldn't get his designs, so he threw him in prison," Alice said aloud.

"Yes, but he escaped, just like Mr. Dumas said in his account of the story. That is where the tale departs on fits of fancy."

"The treasure was a fallacy in the Dumas story?" Niles asked.

"Oh, no. During his escape, Deveroux was washed ashore on a small island in the English Channel. While there, he discovered a treasure long lost to history: gold and jewels from the sacking of Jerusalem and the Holy Land. We estimate its value in today's currency," he bowed to Niles, "in American dollars, to be just a little less than three-point-seven trillion dollars."

"A sum like that would have destroyed the economies of most nations of the world. Having that much gold and precious stones thrown into the market."

Samuels looked at Lee with a smile.

"Not if the money is doled out slowly, evenly, and used only for the advancement of science being studied on a small, out-of-the-way island." He gestured to a portrait that sat upon an easel. The large painting showed the family Heirthall.

"Mr. Deveroux is seated in the chair with his son, Octavian, and his wife, Alexandria. As I stated before, Octavian was the real genius of the family. After the murder of his father, that left Octavian and his mother, who was severely ill and bedridden by that time by a malady called Osler's disease. The disease is passed from parent to child, and can cause blood clots throughout the body."

The entire Group noted the mention of the disease for later discussion.

"Where did they go after Deveroux's death?" Sarah asked.

"Nowhere; everywhere; America, Asia, the South Pacific—Octavian took his family's work and developed it into the very submarine that you had within your complex, the very first *Leviathan*. It was meant to save the world and render warfare useless. He would command the world's seas, and with that command he would guarantee to the world it could never war upon each other again, for without the sea, military measures are useless."

"What happened to him?" Sarah persisted.

"Octavian Heirthall struck a deal that would preserve part of the sea for his work. Abraham Lincoln recognized the legitimacy of his request and struck that deal—one that guaranteed for Lincoln that the United Kingdom would be kept from recognizing the Confederacy. Heirthall only wanted the Gulf of Mexico protected. As always, men failed the captain—which brings us to the current mistrust."

At that moment, the two large hatchways opened and the lights dimmed as the captain of *Leviathan* entered the observation lounge. The officers started applauding, the sound muffled by their white-gloved hands. She was dressed as they, only her uniform was a deep navy blue with sea green and gold epaulets and braid. She wore a pure white turtleneck, and her hair was pulled into a severe bun. She wore pants in lieu of a skirt, but her beauty was still unmatched by anyone in the room with the exception of Sarah. She bowed and then smiled.

"In case you're wondering, and if you'll excuse me, I'm beginning to understand how you think, the captain has earned the right to wear that rank. She served as a trainee and midshipman under her own parents. She has taken the final exams of both the United States Naval Academy at Annapolis, and the Royal Naval College at Dartmouth. Her scores have never been equaled. Excuse me, ladies and gentlemen, duty calls."

Samuels took an offered glass from a midshipman.

"Captain, it is an honor to salute you and your ancestors on this yearly day of days," Samuels said aloud as the middy stewards passed around trays of something that resembled green Kool-Aid in champagne flutes. Once everyone had a glass: "Captain, to the great god of the seas—to

Roderick Deveroux Heirthall, and to the creator of *Leviathan*, past and present, his son, Octavian, upon his birthday!"

"Roderick Deveroux—Octavian Heirthall!" the crew members repeated loudly.

Sarah and Alice looked at Niles and the senator. Lee deferred by raising his eyebrow over his patch to the director; thus it fell on Compton, who nodded his head to toast a great man and his son.

Henri Farbeaux smiled, finally agreeing with Compton, turned his glass flute upward, and drank heavily.

"Absolutely the most despicable liquid I have ever tasted." He took another drink, as did the others. "Yet, somehow it grows on you," Farbeaux said, still grimacing.

"I see you like our sparkling wine?"

They looked up to see Alexandria Heirthall standing before them. She nodded toward the Frenchman. Her eyes were normal, and with them she carried an air of aggressiveness in her look.

"No, I find it vulgar in the extreme . . . but somehow—how do I say—*compelling*?"

"Well, *we* say the fermented poison sac of the silver-spined sea urchin."

A questioning look crossed the features of the Frenchman.

"The drink, Colonel; it's the fermented squeezings of the poison sacs of small sea creatures that make up what we call Jonah's Ambrosia."

"Sea urchins? You go from the world's rarest wine to sea urchins? I believe you need to speak with your chef," Farbeaux said as he took another glass from a passing steward.

"There will be wine for dinner," she said as she took his arm.

As Niles watched her leave arm in arm with Henri, he looked at each person around him.

"She's living in another world. Birthday parties for fictitious characters, the whole Nemo thing, she's far beyond what I even thought," Lee said, watching the captain's back.

Compton didn't respond. He was busy studying the captain's movements. Her stride and demeanor seemed measured and precise as she made her way through the crowd of adoring crew members.

"Whether she's mad or not is irrelevant. Let's examine her achievements. Even if we don't take her at face value as far as her sanity is concerned, we better take seriously the toys her family invented, and the ones she plays with," Sarah said, nodding her head that they should join the rest at the long table that had been set up in front of the viewing glass. "Because insane or not, that woman holds one powerful hand of cards."

As the hundred officers and crew made their way to their places, a group of children, no older than twelve to fourteen, filed in and stood in front of the observation glass at the bow.

As an officer next to her seated Sarah, she saw the boys and girls were dressed in shorts and white shirts. They smiled as an instructor stepped in front of them, and then turned and bowed at the captain, who nodded. Soon the most harmonious song Sarah or the others had ever heard came flowing from the mouths of the children—it was slow, melodious, and sent chills through them. Sarah looked toward the head of the long table and saw that the captain, though Farbeaux was speaking to her, was looking directly at her.

Sarah nodded her head and the captain smiled. It was as though the woman had some great secret she held at arm's length about Sarah that was hers alone to know.

Outside the viewing windows, the cold Arctic Sea flowed by as *Leviathan* kept course for the gap between the Aleutians and Russia—what was known in naval terminology as a choke point.

Leviathan would soon learn there was good reason for that term.

THE EVENT GROUP COMPLEX, NELLIS AIR FORCE BASE, NEVADA

The president listened to the story that Jack told him. After Europa and their investigative teams found out the name of the family they were dealing with, diaries and other government paperwork from history started flowing into the Group's lap.

The president understood that almost sixty percent of what he was hearing was conjecture, but given what the president had learned in his very short time of knowing these people in Nevada, he knew to throw out the percentages. Their guesswork was a better percentage risk than most agencies' facts.

"So your historical departments believe that this Octavian Heirthall assisted Lincoln in some capacity during the Civil War? And there was definite animosity between this man and Secretary of War Stanton?"

"From the few entries from diaries—with the mention of O. H., or the Norwegian—we assume these diarists were speaking of Octavian," Jack explained. "The most convincing piece of evidence comes from the official paymaster of the Confederate States. Five hundred dollars in gold was issued to Confederate Assistant Secretary of State Thomas Engersoll, and he was sent on a mission to Great Britain. His orders were unknown, but we have confirmed that he met directly with Queen Victoria and certain members of Parliament. There has been conjecture around here that a treaty may have been in the works between England and the Confederacy."

"What happened to this Engersoll, Colonel?" the president asked.

"He was lost in a storm in the Gulf of Mexico in eighteen sixty-three on his return trip, along with three British warships."

"Hmm, damn rough storm," the president said, shaking his head.

"Yes, it would have been, except for the fact our historians say there wasn't a severe storm in the general area for the entire months of June and July of eighteen sixty-three that could account for sinking three British men-of-war."

"Octavian Heirthall?"

"Yes, sir, we believe that was one of the missions he was tasked with. All the pieces of the puzzle fit together, Mr. President; we believe that the history is correct and it leads us right to Alexandria Heirthall."

"What do we do about it?"

Jack turned the meeting back to Pete Golding.

"Well, sir, we have a theory that places Octavian Heirthall somewhere within a three-thousand-square-mile area of the Pacific, where we believe he made his home base. That, coupled with physical evidence recovered here at the complex after the assault, makes us believe we may find them somewhere in between Saboo Island in the Marianas, and Guam."

"I need the chain of evidence sent over. The Russians and Chinese have set traps at the entrances into the Pacific and Indian oceans, around the Cape of Good Hope, Cape Horn of South America, and the Bering Strait."

Jack turned the monitor back to face him.

"Sir, this trap the Russians and Chinese have come up with—call it off. Get them to back away until we can figure out a more realistic plan of action. It's our opinion, as I'm sure is the navy's, that we can't outgun this woman."

The president sat motionless as he looked at the images of Pete and Collins. Then he thought a moment.

"Colonel, Admiral Fuqua has the attack boats *Pasadena*, *Dallas*, and *Missouri* dispersed in those ambushing groups. I cannot pull them out at this time. We would lose all hope of cooperation between our Asian and Russian allies in this mess. The Russians, Venezuelans, British, and Chinese are fuming after this morning's attacks. "

The double doors to the office opened and Gene Robbins came through with a sheaf of paper. He placed it on Pete's desk and waited for the meeting to end.

"What exactly is their plan of attack?" Jack asked.

"A cordon of eight attack submarines, arrayed at intervals and different depths, lying quiet and ready to shoot at anything that comes out of the polar passages. The same amount has been placed at the other areas I mentioned."

Jack didn't say what he was thinking—that this would be a massacre beyond anyone's worst nightmare, and in favor of the wrong team.

"So, get me somewhere I can make a stand against these people. Come up with something, Colonel. Thus far the CIA, NSA, and FBI have nothing."

"Yes, sir."

The monitor went from the president's image to a blank blue screen.

"Did I hear right—they're setting a trap for *Leviathan*?" Robbins asked, removing his glasses. "Wasn't the loss of those British warships enough for one day?"

Collins looked at Robbins. "Do you expect the world to just lie down and not try to stop this madness, Doctor?"

"No . . . no, of course not . . . I just mean—"

"What do you have, Gene?" Pete asked, cutting off his quasi-apology.

"I just wanted to tell you that we have Europa completely back. I've close-looped the system with the exception of the clean room, and only we four currently have access to that area."

"That will be all, Gene," Pete said, gesturing toward the door.

Robbins quickly left the office.

"I never knew the good doctor was so passionate about naval losses," Everett said.

"He's just frustrated," Pete said.

Jack nodded at Everett, and the captain pulled a small plastic bag out of his back pocket and handed it to Pete. Golding accepted the bag and looked it over.

"Rubber gloves?" he asked.

"Pete, when we head out to Saboo Island, I think we need a person from the computer center to accompany us. You never know, we may need one on this trip," Jack said, looking serious and tapping the plastic bag Pete was holding.

"I guess I can assign someone."

"Not just someone, Pete. I want the saboteur to come along for the ride."

11

LEVIATHAN, EIGHTY MILES
NORTH OF THE BERING STRAIT

After dessert, the choir had been replaced with a string quartet. They played classical music as the officers and *Leviathan*'s guests stood talking.

"If I may ask, Captain, what is *Leviathan*'s crew complement?" Lee asked as a designed intelligence question.

"Of course—we have seven hundred seventy-two officers and crew. We also have aboard fifty-two trainees and seventy-five midshipmen. They form an excellent choir, don't you agree?"

"I am becoming aware of your crew's extreme loyalty to you . . . and your philosophy, Captain," Niles said, choosing to ignore the question about the midshipmen.

"Dr. Compton, my crew's loyalty has never entered my mind. As for my philosophy, I never hold back any information from them. On the contrary, I rely on their research, their study, and their ideas."

"Can I safely assume there is a base involved with *Leviathan*'s upkeep?" Lee asked, tapping the teak deck with his cane.

"Yes, there is a place we call home, actually two of them. My great-grandmother Olivia and her husband, Peter Wallace, established the first permanent base after the betrayal of her own father, Octavian. I along with my parents excavated the second base in the last fifty years." Her gaze moved away from the two men and she looked at the sea outside of the large windows, flowing above and around her. "The second one is a place that was unreachable for many years, until certain problems were worked out."

"And that base is where?" Lee asked.

She turned and looked at the two men, smiling.

"It would do me no good to tell you about it. We will arrive at the first in a day or so, and the second soon after."

Niles studied the beautiful woman before him. She had moments of clarity where she seemed as if she were just any other passenger on a cruise ship, marveling at the vessel and seas around her. Niles was close to the unalterable conclusion that he was indeed looking at the most intelligent person he had ever known, and as Lee had suggested on many occasions, the most insane.

"Captain, I am not a stupid man, but I'll be damned if I can figure out your hull design and the materials used in *Leviathan*'s construction. How can you achieve such depths?" Lee again waved his cane around him, indicating the ship as a whole.

"*Leviathan*'s hull is a composite material derived from nylon, spun steel, plastic, and an ingredient that is found only at the most extreme depths of—" She suddenly stopped and smiled at Lee. "You almost had me, Senator. I must say, your OSS history came into play there, didn't it?"

"I had to try," Lee said, not smiling.

"However, I see no harm in telling you a little something. You wouldn't understand the dynamics involved at any rate, so I will just give you the end result." She smiled at her small insult to the senator. "You may be surprised to know that the deeper *Leviathan* travels, the denser our hull material becomes. It compacts itself, quadrupling its strength."

Alice came up and took Lee by the arm. "Captain Heirthall, why didn't you sit down with the leaders of the world and show them what you are showing us before you started shooting?"

"Yes, Alex, why don't you explain why you didn't do that?"

They turned and saw Virginia standing behind the captain. She was dressed in a simple green evening gown, and her eyes were somewhat puffy, as if she had been crying.

"Certain developments in the Gulf of Mexico arose that made talking beforehand unacceptable. Immediate action was required, and I acted. The greed of a single country was—"

"Be careful, Alex, your hatred is showing through your words," Virginia said as she reached out and removed a glass of wine from the table.

Alexandria looked from Virginia to the other members of the Event Group, then smiled.

"Why, Ginny, are you still angry with me for setting you up? I've explained in no uncertain terms your complete innocence in my getting the information and intelligence I needed on your Group."

Virginia tilted her head after taking a drink of wine.

"No, not angry. I love the Group and the people I work with," she said, looking over at Niles, who lowered his own eyes to the floor. "They would have eventually found out the truth. I also thought I knew you, Alex. The person you are now kills innocents so easily. The Alex I knew in college would have convinced anyone who listened that she had a better way." She looked around, gesturing at *Leviathan*. "A person who creates something as magnificent as this, and she turns out to be as cold as the sea she claims to protect." Virginia drained the glass of wine and then reached for the bottle on the table. "'With great power comes great responsibility.' I forget who said that."

Lee started to answer but Alice squeezed his arm for him to be silent.

"And I take that responsibility seriously, Ginny, you know that," Heirthall said, looking harshly at her old friend.

Sergeant Tyler stepped up to the group and held a glass of wine up in a mock toast. His look said that he was interested in the conversation.

Pouring wine into her glass, Virginia kept her eyes averted from the small group around her. "Yes, we've been witness to your responsibility, Alex. Now tell me, old friend, obviously you have another person inside our department who could have told you we know nothing about your family, their science, or your intentions. So why bring us here?"

"Sergeant Tyler will answer that for you soon enough."

"You're a liar, Alex; you need us for something. What is it?"

Alice stepped forward when she saw a spark of anger flare in the eyes of Alexandria. She took Virginia by the arm and quickly led her away from the table.

"I see I'm not the only one who is enjoying the wine," Farbeaux said as he and Sarah joined the silent trio.

"Captain, Virginia is—"

"Of all the people in the world, Dr. Compton, Ginny is one person you never have to explain to me." She lowered her head and made as if she were adjusting her white gloves.

"Excuse me, I must attend to something," Sergeant Tyler said, placing his untouched wine on the table next to him. His eyes locked on Alexandria's and something passed between them. It made the Group wonder who was really in charge on *Leviathan*.

As the uncomfortable silence continued, a wailing alarm sounded. It lasted for only a minute, but it was enough for officers and crew to start moving from the observation lounge in a hurry.

The first officer approached Heirthall, placed a flimsy message into her hand, then turned her away and whispered something. They all watched as the captain's face went slack, and then she squeezed her eyes shut and planted her hands on the table before her. Samuels quickly moved away from her and turned, angrily pulling off his white gloves.

As they watched, the captain switched on the intercom.

"Officer of the deck, all stop, maintain depth, order quick quiet on all decks and initiate side-scan sonar laser system."

"Aye, Captain."

Outside *Leviathan*, a sliding panel slid away from her hull and into the boat. This recessed area wrapped around the entire length of the submarine. Inside the abscess was what looked to be Christmas tree lights, glowing a deep red and growing in power by the second. As *Leviathan* came to a complete standstill, a thousand small lasers powered up and pierced the darkened waters of the Bering Strait, three miles off her bow. Light shot out into all quarters, revolving, spinning until the whole of the great submarine was wrapped in a glowing red cocoon of undulating laser light.

"This is the reason I am forced to do the unthinkable. With nations it is always their love of power. Their stupidity is matched only by their false bravado and their love for the sound of rattling sabers."

Confused, the Event Group watched as Alexandria hit another switch, making the ambient light in the forward compartment turn green and blue. When they turned to face the front, the glass was illuminated with a holographic image a hundred years ahead of any nation's technology. The hologram, of immense proportions, lined the shields. It was as if they were looking at an electronic image of the sea directly in front of them—in essence, the image replaced the glass and magnified the outside world. Embedded inside the composite glass plates were billions of microthin fiberoptic lines, set at different depths, allowing a 3-D image to appear. As they watched, the glowing image was magnified until eight objects, some deeper than others, came into view.

"Oh my God," Niles said as he stepped closer to the hologram, which was broadcast as if it were on a seventy-millimeter movie screen.

Heirthall was staring at the images, and Sarah watched as her jaw muscles clenched.

"Bastards!" she said as she turned away and stormed out of the compartment. Alice saw that her eyes were the deepest blue, and that they were no longer dilated.

Sarah stepped up to Niles's side and studied the image.

"I clearly count eight of them," Niles said.

On the hologram before them, standing forty feet high and eighty feet long, was the terrifying image of seven Russian-built Akula class attack submarines sitting motionless, waiting for their prey to appear.

"She's going to kill them all," Lee said as he slammed the tip of his cane on the floor.

"Jesus," Sarah said. "Is that one of ours?"

Sitting in the direct center of the line was the most advanced submarine in the American fleet, and therefore, the world.

"Yes, I believe it's your USS *Missouri*, a Virginia class vessel if my memory serves," Farbeaux said, setting his glass down for the first time that evening.

"They're not moving—they don't know *Leviathan* is here," Niles said.

"She's going to destroy them," Lee said again.

Niles turned and ran for the compartment hatch, but as he neared, Sergeant Tyler stepped through. He slowly closed and dogged the hatch, then raised an automatic pistol up and pointed it at Niles. Disturbingly, the man was wearing a grin.

"The captain has given orders that you bear witness to the treachery of nations."

On the giant hologram, *Leviathan* drifted closer to the eight menacing attack submarines.

Niles watched as Sergeant Tyler gestured for him to back away from the hatch, moving the gun back and forth menacingly, looking determined to keep the Group in check.

"I take it our freedom of movement aboard *Leviathan* has been revoked?" Compton asked, not backing away from the door.

"I suspect, Niles my boy, that it's only revoked when the captain is about to commit murder," Garrison Lee said as he stepped toward the sergeant.

"As much as my captain admires you, I will have no trouble disabling you further, Senator Lee, if you continue to advance," Tyler said, shifting the position of his aim. "Now, please turn and observe the hologram."

"Can't you see Captain Heirthall doesn't need to do this?" Sarah asked, stepping in front of Lee. "She's capable of running right past that trap."

On the giant image screen, the three-dimensional view of the eight attack submarines hadn't changed as *Leviathan* had come to a complete stop before them.

"All hands, prepare for subsurface action. All nonessential personnel to off-duty quarters. Seal the boat and move to action stations. The attack profile will be achieved through stealth," said the voice they recognized as Heirthall's.

Niles Compton closed his eyes and balled his fists at his sides, feeling helpless. He only wished there was some way of warning those subs that it wasn't they who were doing the stalking, that the fierce animal they sought was watching them even now—and it was getting ready to spring. He turned away and leaned on the table, trying desperately to think of what to do.

"Mr. Samuels, report *Leviathan*'s status, please."

Niles looked up at the sound of the captain's voice.

"Isn't she conducting the attack from the control center?" he asked Tyler.

"No, she never interferes with the crew during an attack. She will give her orders from another location."

"Where is she?" Lee asked.

"Where she always goes when she has to do something this distaste-ful—to the conning tower, her sanctuary, where *no one* is allowed."

Niles knew he had to get to her to stop this horrible action. *Leviathan* could easily slip by the cordon of submarines without their ever knowing she was there. He had to convince her to allow those seamen to live, but as he looked into the eyes of Tyler, he knew the man would have no trou-ble shooting him if he tried to exit the forward observation lounge. It was as if *he* was anticipating the death of so many sailors.

12

Alexandria Heirthall was looking out of the giant acrylic port window on the lowest level of the tall conning tower, a totally soundproof compart-ment built just for the captain, which allowed her to operate the boat without being in the presence of her crew. Although the underwater lighting system of *Leviathan* was as bright as the sun, she couldn't see the line of submarines in front of her with ten miles of distance between the vessels.

Once more, she placed a hand on the bubbled glass and watched her own reflection, leaning in to feel its coolness. Then she reached into her dress jacket, brought out three pills, and placed them in her mouth. The powerful Demerol dissolved with a sickening rush of bitterness. She then turned and went to the large command chair, climbed the four steps, and sat down.

The captain eased her hands down to the chair's twin consoles em-bedded in the thick arms. She knew what she was doing was wrong, but she seemed powerless to stop it. She jerked her hands away from the con-trol handles and rubbed them together. Then the pain hit inside of her head in earnest. Her eyes opened and she focused.

She programmed in a request from the ship's computer and then closed her eyes once more. The lighting inside the lowest section of the conning tower dimmed to almost nothing, leaving only the illumination from outside of *Leviathan*. A deep green hue radiated from the view ports, relaxing the captain, just as music emerged from the speaker system hidden in the bulkheads. "House of the Rising Sun," a song she knew from her childhood, started playing from the hidden speakers. The doctor had recommended the music as a means to allow her mind to ease up during tense situations. It allowed her muscles to relax and let her access her thoughts for the coming attack. The music would bring that rush of adrenalin needed for her harsh actions, as it went against everything she thought she was.

Alexandria opened her eyes and clenched the armrests with her hands so hard the blood drained from them. Then, as the deep lyrics of the song started to coincide with the movement of *Leviathan*, the giant submarine started moving forward, and the captain started to become one with the deadliness of her vessel.

Tyler tensed as Farbeaux strode to the center of the room with a fresh bottle of wine. The gun moved from Niles to the Frenchman just as the hatch wheel started turning. He allowed his eyes to move in that direction as the large double hatch opened and Virginia came through, followed by Alice.

"Do not allow the hatch to slam closed, ladies. *Leviathan* is at quiet stations," Tyler said as he moved his head in their direction.

Farbeaux moved like a cat. The bottle of three-hundred-year-old wine was in the air before anyone realized it. The makeshift projectile struck the big Irishman on the side of his head, dropping him immediately. Virginia reacted first as she stooped to retrieve the weapon from the sergeant's hand.

Tyler recovered faster than anyone would have believed. From his knees he backhanded Virginia, knocking her away until she fell next to the hatch. Alice, startled, reached down to help Virginia. Tyler placed his hand upon the gun as Farbeaux dived to stop him—all the while wondering why he was doing it. Niles moved to help the Frenchman.

Tyler again reacted faster than anyone. He quickly raised the weapon and fired. The round grazed Farbeaux in middive. He rolled and was struck with a sudden, flaring pain in his side above the hip. Tyler quickly adjusted his aim toward Niles and brought the director to a complete stop. The sergeant wiped the blood from his temple and then stood on shaky feet. He sluggishly stepped toward the prone Farbeaux and stood over him, the weapon aimed at his head.

"Don't . . . we'll not give you any more problems," Alice said, taking a step away from Virginia by the hatchway.

Sergeant Tyler smirked and then aimed once more.

VIRGINIA CLASS ATTACK
SUBMARINE USS *MISSOURI* (SSN-780)

The newest Virginia class fast-attack submarine in the world was honored with a very proud moniker—the USS *Missouri*. In fact, she was so new that she was not even scheduled to see the water until the year 2011. After the recent run of terrorism in the world, the navy had stepped up her construction, since it was clear they needed the technology at sea, not sitting in the dry docks of Groton, Connecticut. She was silent, more silent than any vessel ever built, and made to penetrate the defenses of any port city in the world.

Captain James Jefferson, a man specifically chosen for the duty as *Missouri*'s first commander, had fitted her out for sea with weapons delivered by supply ship from Pearl Harbor when they had rendezvoused at Midway Island. She had just finished the last leg of her sea trials, and was supposed to be headed home to Pearl, where she would officially be commissioned in three months.

Jefferson was destined to become the first black submarine commander-in-chief of the Pacific fleet (COMSUBPAC). Now however, he had his doubts if he would ever make it to that lofty position. The duty given to him at the last minute could very well be his boat's first war mission, and its last. The rumors had spread very quickly throughout the U.S. Navy, had infected the boat while in transit from Pearl, and had gotten worse with their six-hour layover at Midway. They knew they were being attached to an international line of defense, and also that they were going up against the biggest unknown in the history of the navy—a submarine with unbelievable capabilities had killed up to ten warships, and had yet to be spotted.

Jefferson stood looking at his navigation console and shook his head.

"That goddamn Chinese Akula is drifting on us again. Can't those bastards maintain their station? Hell, we won't need a supersub to take shots at us, we'll sink ourselves."

Missouri's first officer turned away from the feed he was receiving from the sonar suite.

"He's not the only one, Captain. Now we have the Russian on our starboard drifting toward us. The *Leonid* had reported problems with her navigation suite earlier."

"Damn," Jefferson said as he rubbed his chin and looked closer at the line of battle. "Izzy, I want to pull out of the line and take up station to the far starboard side of this mess. The way these two Akulas are acting, the hole we leave in the line will be filled soon anyway. I'm not risking my damn boat because two captains can't keep station for a few hours."

"Good idea, Captain. Do we report to the lead boat?"

"No, I'm afraid it will only confuse Captain Nevelov if we did that. Besides, he'll never hear *Missouri* change places."

"Hell, we can't even hear ourselves, Captain," the first officer said as the men on watch chuckled in their agreement.

"Izzy, back us out of line, dead slow and silent as a field mouse, before we have an accident out here. Bring us to a far-right position of the battle line."

Alexandria Heirthall watched on the smaller holographic screen in front of her as the *Missouri* started to back away from the battle line. The computer-enhanced image from nine miles away was crystal clear, and just as confusing.

"Captain, we have aspect change on the American boat," Samuels called from the control center.

Heirthall was wondering if the Virginia class boat had possibly heard something that dictated it move out of line. She studied the picture provided by the lasers that struck each boat in the line, and enhanced it into the shape of the actual submarines. The Russian and Chinese Akulas were keeping their stations—it was only *Missouri* moving away. Then she smiled as her blazing blue eyes caught the reason why. The Chinese boat to her left and the Russian to her right were drifting in the swift current of the opening to the Bering Strait. She struck her intercom.

"We'll keep the attack profile. Give me a weapons status report, Commander."

"Forward tubes one through twenty are loaded with standard Mark seventy conventional warheads, Captain. Vertical tubes are empty. We are ready to fire at your command. Captain, can you pick up the phone line please?" Samuels asked.

Heirthall didn't respond. She only watched the simulation before her as the first drops of sweat appeared on her forehead and her temples. The tone in Commander Samuels's voice told her the first officer was in disagreement with her actions. As she felt the first pain-relieving effects of the Demerol she had taken, her pupils started to expand. She shook her head, confused by the doubt about her actions that had started to creep into her thought process. She closed her eyes, then reached for the phone at the side of the large command chair.

"Yes, Commander?"

"Captain, may I recommend two courses of action? We can speed by the attacking force before they even know we are here, or we can simply use our stealth and drift by."

As if to counter the medication, a sudden pain shot from the base of her neck and deep into her brain. She winced and then slowly recovered.

She lowered her chin as she examined the submarines on the screen. She imagined them to be nothing more than steel and machinery. There were no men on their decks, only computers and weapons. She closed her eyes and shut out the imaginary beat of more than nine hundred hearts. There were no eyes that watched the waterfall displays of their sonar stations, and there weren't men and boys planning *Leviathan*'s death—*only machines.*

"James, have the crew stand by for extreme maneuvering, and order damage-control parties standing by in all departments." Alexandria once more sat in her chair. "Keep feeding the torpedo tubes coordinates on the enemy vessels, but for now, we don't need them." The pain was fighting off the attack of the medication.

"Captain, this is not necessary. *Leviathan* can slip by without those subs knowing we were ever here! We can run rings around them, even outrun their torpedoes—"

"James, do I have to relieve you?"

"Aye, Captain. Attack stations—collision."

With that, the captain of *Leviathan* started the great ship forward and went to full ramming speed.

As the thermal-dynamic drive on *Leviathan* went to flank speed, the music inside the captain's observation suite grew to a crescendo. Her eyes were wide and bright as she leaned forward in her chair, her knuckles once more growing white on the armrest controls. What she was doing was fundamentally wrong, and somewhere in her conscious mind, she was fully aware of it. This was not her—but then again, just under the surface of her wakeful mind, she knew it was.

As she focused on the first submarine in line, her doubts faded and her determination became solid.

Alexandria didn't know that because of the pain and medication working against one another, and her haste to attack, she had made one critical error.

USS *MISSOURI* (SSN-780)

"All stop, chief of the boat. Watch her drift, use the momentum, and let's get her bow angled for a hundred-meter drop in depth, and—"

"Conn—sonar. We have a disturbance eight miles to the north and—it's gone now, Captain, but it was there. It sounded like an electrostatic crackling."

Jefferson was about to respond to the sonar room when he thought of what his brief on this mission had said: *"Any unusual oceanic disturbance could mean the unseen enemy is close aboard."*

"Sonar, is there any reaction from our Russian or Chinese friends?"

"Nothing, Captain, they are still at station keeping."

"Izzy, bring us to general quarters. Spool up tubes one through four—standard war shot."

"Aye, chief of the boat, sound general quarters. Weapons—report on tubes one through four."

"Take *Missouri* to six hundred feet and take us out of the line. All-ahead flank; get us down, Izzy," Jefferson said as he held on to the navigation stanchion.

"Captain, at flank speed they'll hear us all the way to Pearl," Sonar called out over the com.

"That's what I want—let everyone know something isn't right."

Outside the hull, *Missouri* allowed her scimitar propeller to bite at the cold sea surrounding her, creating a water cone that echoed loudly into the earphones of every submarine in the battle line. The more experienced sub commanders on the Russian side knew immediately that the

American did what he did for a reason. Three of the Russian Akulas broke line and started for deep water.

"Sonar, I need something—anything—off our bow reported. I don't care if it's two whales screwing the hell out of each other!"

"Aye."

Leviathan was at seventy knots and closing fast. The captain had jammed her throttles too far, too fast, and created a burp in her propulsion system, a hole in the water as her jets created a cave, which was read on the *Missouri*'s sonar. On the hologram in front of Heirthall, the submarines rushed at them so fast that she had to reach out and take the viewer off the magnification setting.

"Now," she whispered. Her eyes closed halfway as the music blared on. She threw the control sticks for both of the massive rudders to the right and forward, automatically taking on ballast and changing the angles of the dive planes at the bow and the conning tower. The deadly plane protector, made of laser-hardened titanium, sliced the water like deadly, knifelike wings.

Leviathan heeled to the right, almost losing the captain from her command chair. *Leviathan* went into such a tight turn that most modern submarines would have sheared off their planes in the fantastic stresses brought upon the hull. Soon the first line of Chinese Akulas came into view. They were in a position that was almost too perfect to believe—they had not moved one inch. They were bow-to-bow and just hovering, sitting there like three blind mice. Alexandria closed her eyes all the way and listened to the rush of water outside the glass. The music continued booming into her ears as the great submarine heeled in the opposite direction, straightening her attack angle.

Leviathan was now at one hundred knots as she straightened for her run.

"All hands, imminent collision—I repeat, imminent collision," Samuels called over the com system, far below in the control center.

Alexandria finally opened her eyes. The massive headache was easing as the adrenalin shot through her body. Just then the dark gray silhouettes of the submarines took on a ghostly shape before her. She clenched her jaw muscles and did what had become a ritual with her: She prayed to her family for the strength she needed to do what needed to be done.

As the slicing plane protector came within feet of the first Chinese boat, her mind suddenly became clear—*Samuels was right, I could have gone deep and avoided this confrontation*. Her reaction to this revelation made her very nearly throw her control sticks in the opposite direction, just as the sharklike bow plane of *Leviathan* struck the sonar dome of the first sub in line.

Leviathan slammed into the sonar dome of the Chinese boat, shattering it like an eggshell and sending more than thirty-five men in their forward spaces to a gruesome death. Then, as *Leviathan* barely slowed, she hit the second sub in line; it was just a glancing blow but enough to crack her hull, sending her sliding into the depths with her power plant screaming in reverse.

Suddenly, as if a switch had been thrown inside her brain, she became aware that it was as if something had taken control of her actions. She wanted to stop this insane attack, but part of her was beyond reason as she bore down on the unsuspecting warships.

The third boat was a Russian that had heard the collision of the first and second sub in line and had started to turn toward the disturbance. The attacking Akula was only one second from launching a spread of torpedoes when she was struck amidships by *Leviathan*. The collision was not meant to be in that area of the Akula's hull. *Leviathan*, though certainly able to withstand the blow, was still rocked as she slowed to fifty knots after the brief collision sent her rolling under the stricken submarine.

The American and the remaining submarines used that chance to defend themselves. The Russian attack boat *Leviathan* had just silenced snapped into two pieces and fell to the bottom of the Strait, crushing every soul onboard.

As the fourth Chinese submarine in line was struck, Captain Jefferson knew he had to find some sort of shelter. All hell was breaking loose, but for the life of him, his sonar team could not get a handle on it. It was as though the defensive line were getting rammed by an invisible ghost.

"Damn it, we're blind as hell—what in God's name is out there?" Jefferson said as *Missouri* heeled to the port side and her bow angled steeply down. "Sonar—conn. You don't have anything on your scopes other than the destroyed subs?"

"We get a ghosting of speed on the waterfall, then a shape as a collision happens. Then nothing, Captain—we're dealing with something that doesn't have the same hull construction as us or anything in the world. Some kind of stealth technology. We only know there are no torpedoes in the water!"

"Damn it. Take her deeper, Izzy—deeper!"

"Fifteen degrees down plane—all-ahead flank!" his first officer called out.

"All noises have stopped, debris descending to our starboard and port beam, sound of bulkheads collapsing. We also have noise conducive to four subs going shallow—yes, the *Dubrinin*, *Tolstoy*, *Peter the Great*, and the Chinese boat *Tzu-Tang*—I think we're all that's left down here, Captain."

"Damn, the last one out of the pool."

"Captain, we can't shoot what we can't see or hear."

"I know, Izzy, I know."

Alexandria's attempt to avoid the last collision had failed and the heavy maneuvering afterward to regain control threw Niles and the others in the now closed and watertight observation lounge. Garrison Lee went down in a heap, and Alice fell on top of him. Sarah saw an opportunity. Instead of being terrified, she had gotten angry. Virginia reacted at the same time. Tyler had fallen to a knee after the last collision and was struggling to gain his feet. At that moment he was hit simultaneously by Virginia and Sarah. Virginia went high and Sarah low, grabbing for the gun as she heard voices at the hatchway. Before she knew what was happening, several shots discharged from Tyler's weapon. The rounds missed everyone and ricocheted off the titanium bulkheads, making loud pings as they did. Niles and Lee started to assist the women but were grabbed by other security men before they could.

"Fools!" Tyler said as he regained his feet. Then he lost his balance once more as everyone lost their footing. Before anyone could take advantage of Tyler's predicament, several more security men had entered and leveled their weapons.

Leviathan again rolled to their right and all of them felt her accelerate. Captain Heirthall, all doubt once more removed from her actions, was aiming for the last target in the Bering Strait—USS *Missouri*.

USS *MISSOURI* (SSN-780)

"That's it—nothing else is out there, Captain," sonar reported.

"Damn it—where are you?" Jefferson said as he closed his eyes in thought.

Outside of *Missouri*'s hull, *Leviathan* was closing once more at seventy-five knots, aiming straight at the bow of the American boat.

Suddenly, thuds started penetrating their hull. The soundwaves were faint, but after the silence of the previous attacks, the strange noise seemed as loud as cannon fire. The BQQ sonar was also picking up another sound as the great submarine closed on them—the sound of water rushing over a rough surface.

"Captain, we have what sounds like possible gunfire and something else, a thousand yards to starboard!"

"Izzy—match bearings on that noise and shoot!"

In the control center of *Leviathan*, Samuels was reluctantly about to sound the collision warning for the last time for their final target.

"Commander, we are making noise, I can't tell from where yet, but the sound is emanating from *Leviathan*." The technician pushed his headphones into his ears and listened intently. "We have torpedoes in the water—we have four fish—American Mark forty-eights—they went active as soon as they left their tubes. Torpedoes have acquired *Leviathan*!"

"Commander, someone has discharged a weapon onboard. It has definitely affected our stealth!"

There was no response coming from the auxiliary control station in the captain's suite at the base of the conning tower. Samuels knew he had to act.

"Hard right rudder, all-ahead flank—take her down to a thousand feet!" Samuels said as calmly as he could. "Launch countermeasures!"

Alexandria had heard the gunfire from somewhere down below. She closed her eyes as *Leviathan* started altering her course. She started fighting her emotions as the headache was suddenly under control. She need not contact control, knowing Samuels would do what needed doing. Her senses were draining of all input except regret at what she had done.

As she stood, she stumbled down the platform, caught herself, and then slowly walked to the large round viewing port. She tried in vain to smile, now realizing it had to have been Virginia and the people from the Event Group who had given their position away. She nodded her head as *Leviathan* started a run for her life. As *Leviathan* maneuvered and "House of the Rising Sun" went into its dramatic climax, she slammed against the glass. Alexandria slid down into a heap; she closed her eyes and her body slumped. As she slid into unconsciousness, she thought she felt movement inside her head. Before going completely out, she wondered if she truly was insane.

Leviathan went deep. One of the Mark 48 torpedoes had locked onto the sound of the fast-moving sub. The water became disturbed with every turn of her giant bow planes and aft rudders, until the Mark 48 snapped its thin guidewire and the giant sub banked hard to starboard. The torpedo was seeing and targeting the now-roughened edges of the bowplane titanium shields that had been warped during the ramming.

The first and second torpedo lost contact as the great submarine dived beneath the thermal layer. They went for the bubbling and frothing canisters that were ejected from the stern of *Leviathan*. However, unbeknownst to the men and women onboard the giant submarine, the last two American weapons had driven underneath a large section of one of the destroyed Chinese Akulas as it sank fast to the bottom. The first Mark 48 turned downward to the deck of *Leviathan*, slamming into her vertical launch tubes just aft of the conning tower. The second hit a glancing blow off her port side, then went straight down after its rebound and exploded just below the engineering compartment at the aft portion of *Leviathan*. The great submarine was rocked, first downward and then up, actually bending almost five degrees at her midsection.

The crew was thrown around in their seats. Water leaks sprang up in a thousand places. Her thermal-dynamic drive went offline, sending out a screeching alarm throughout the ship. The four nuclear power plants scrammed and shut down.

As her life's work shuddered around her, Alexandria's eyes fluttered open. She tried lifting herself off the carpeted deck. She failed, then tried again, finally gaining her feet. She slowly wiped blood from her lip and knew she had blood coming from her ears. She staggered to her chair and hit the intercom.

"Report, Mr. Samuels."

"We're still getting information, Captain. Power plants are offline and we have already switched to battery power. We have preliminary reports of casualties in engineering and three out of the six weapons rooms. We have a hull breach in engineering—no report as to the extent of damage. The hull has sustained damage from the strike and from our own ramming to the point we must be heard by enemy sonar. We cannot repair the bow planes or the damage to the vertical tube hatches until we can dry dock."

"Very well—get *Leviathan* moving out past the Strait, then take us deep; three thousand feet will do. For now, plot us a course for Saboo. We'll use the deep thermal cline to hide our noise."

"Aye, Captain—Saboo."

Alexandria steadied herself, then decided it was time to go and see how Compton and the others were, and congratulate them on a surprise move that she would have never guessed them capable of. As she wiped the blood that streamed from her left ear off the side of her face, she knew deep down she was grateful for her, and *Leviathan*'s, first-ever failure.

USS *MISSOURI* (SSN-780)

Captain Jefferson was in sonar listening on a set of headphones. He shook his head.

"I'm not sure, Captain, until I run the tapes back, but I think we hit her. The detonations were too far away for our fish to have struck any debris from the Akulas. After that we picked up a high-speed whine heading due south out of the Straights. We may not have caused that boat to sink, but we caused some kind of damage to her hull. We hurt her," the supervisor in sonar said. "The Mark forty-eights had to have picked up on some previous damage to her hull after the guidewires broke. That and the damage we caused are what we heard."

Jefferson removed his headphones, looked at First Officer Izzering-hausen, then back at the three sonar technicians. "Once the sonar recording is examined, can you find her again?"

"Unless they can dry dock whatever that thing is, yes, Captain, we can find her."

"Look, Izzy, there's been nothing for the past twenty minutes. Get to the surface and sweep for survivors. I want to get out of this valley of death as soon as we can go with a clear conscience. When we are up top, we need to call home and report this mess. And hopefully they'll send us some help."

Missouri had won a shortened fight because she threw a sucker punch just before they themselves were about to go down. Jefferson figured they had stretched their luck just about as far as they could.

PART THREE
THE BLACK QUEEN

The sea is the greatest magician of all—it hides the truth beneath miles and miles of water—it covers its real meaning with layers of depth and pressure, and will only reveal what it needs to draw men close, closer to the depths, then suddenly it wraps its cold arms around you and the real truth is finally revealed.

—Captain Octavian Heirthall

13

Sarah, Lee, Alice, Virginia, and Niles waited outside of *Leviathan*'s sick-bay. They had been there for the past hour as the ship's surgeon, Dr. Warren Trevor, worked on Farbeaux. The bullet had hit the Frenchman in the lower right hip, hitting nothing vital.

"I am having the hardest time figuring out Colonel Farbeaux," Niles said, looking at his hands.

"I think it's time I tell you something." Sarah hesitated, and then decided just to say it outright. "The colonel is almost as insane as our good Captain Heirthall," she said, slowly standing up and pacing in front of the small group. "He saw an opportunity when *Leviathan*'s assault team attacked, and came into the complex behind them to kill Jack. He's under the illusion that Jack killed his wife, and Farbeaux, at least I suspect, really looked at himself for the first time as an accomplice in her death. When he found out Jack was already dead, something drained from him—like he lost his only reason in life for living."

"He focused on Jack because—?"

Sarah stopped pacing and looked at Niles. "The only thing I can figure is that he blamed Jack for making him feel human back in the Amazon, saving those students and the rest of us from that nuclear detonation. His actions since being onboard *Leviathan* are bordering on—well, like he's looking to get killed. Maybe a death wish. His move on the sergeant, his open hostility to every member of the *Leviathan*'s crew . . . it all adds up."

The Group was silent as they thought about the intricacies of the Frenchman.

"I congratulate you on your ability to endanger *Leviathan* for the first time in her long existence."

They all looked up and saw Alexandria Heirthall standing in the open doorway. Four of her security men, including Sergeant Tyler, who was sporting a white bandage around his head, flanked her. They could see the bloodstained handkerchief knotted tightly around her right hand, and the traces of blood at her left ear.

"Captain, I think it's time we understood each other," Niles said with dark anger edging his voice. "We are not, as you so euphemistically state it, your 'guests.' We are held here against our will to answer for our knowledge on just who you are. Since you have declared war on the world, must I remind you that as prisoners of that war, we have the right to attempt escape when the opportunity presents itself?"

Tyler started toward Niles with rage etched on his features, but Heirthall reached out and stayed him with just her delicate hand.

"Fair enough, Doctor, prisoners of war it is. Sergeant Tyler, please escort the prisoners to the forward observation lounge and secure them there."

Tyler turned on Heirthall. "Captain, these people are an extreme hazard to our mission. I warned of the consequences of bringing them onboard in the first place. I must insist they either be executed or placed adrift at sea. They are—"

Heirthall turned on Tyler, placed a hand on his chest, and slammed him against the bulkhead—her actions startling everyone watching.

"You insist?" she hissed with a low menacing tone as more blood started flowing from her left ear. "Onboard *Leviathan* you insist on nothing! You follow command, for not only my sake but the higher order we fight for. Am I understood, Sergeant?"

Lee nodded at the flow of blood from Alexandria's left ear, and Niles decided to use that as a reason for ending the confrontation. As crazy as Heirthall was, he knew Tyler, in his cold and calculating way, would likely be a far less merciful captor.

"Captain, you're bleeding rather severely," Niles said.

Heirthall ignored Compton, keeping her eyes on Tyler until the large man nodded his head just once. Alexandria released him and then took a hesitant step back.

"What is going on here?" Dr. Trevor demanded as he stepped from his sickbay. Then he saw the condition of the captain and quickly stepped forward.

"Sergeant, do as you were ordered," Heirthall said as she allowed the doctor to take her by the arm. "Dr. Compton, Colonel Farbeaux will no longer be tolerated. As soon as the doctor finishes with him and we come close to shore, he will be released."

"Released or thrown into the sea?" Niles asked.

Alexandria wiped some of the blood from the side of her face and then turned to Compton. She looked as if she wanted to say something but only frowned, then left the waiting room with the assistance of the doctor.

Sergeant Tyler looked at the gathered group and with his cold gray eyes gave an unvoiced command. The six security men led the group out of sickbay.

"That man not only means us harm, but anyone with eyes can see he has an agenda," Alice said.

Before they could file out of the waiting area, Dr. Trevor turned and called out. "Your friend—he will recover nicely. I removed the bullet and he's resting comfortably," the doctor said in his soft English accent. "Very little damage, no muscle or bone was struck."

"Thank you—Doctor—?" Niles heard but could not say anything as a security man shoved him through the hatch.

Farbeaux looked up at Sarah and a thin smile crossed his lips. He swallowed and grimaced in pain. An hour before, Tyler had entered the observation lounge, taken Sarah by the arm, and without explanation brought her here to sickbay, telling her she had an hour with Farbeaux to explain to him his predicament. He warned that if the Frenchman gave them any more trouble, Sarah would be the one to reap the punishment. With a cold stare and menacing smile, Tyler had left her alone in sickbay with Farbeaux.

"You are one strange and confusing man, Colonel."

"An enigma, wrapped in a puzzle," he whispered, and smiled. "One that has very many missing pieces, eh?"

"Yeah . . . but listen, if you want to commit suicide, there are a lot less painful ways of going about it, so knock it off."

"Such harsh . . . words for a man who is just learning to be . . . a hero," Farbeaux said haltingly as his eyes closed.

"Better than a swift kick in the ass—" Sarah started, but saw that Farbeaux was sleeping.

"He's quite tired," Trevor said, checking the monitor at the bedside. "When I examined him, he showed acute exhaustion. I doubt he slept more than a few hours in the last month or two."

"He's had a rough go lately," Sarah said looking at the Frenchman's softened features.

"Well, he needs his rest now, Miss . . . ?"

"Just Sarah, that's good enough," she said, patting Farbeaux's hand.

"Sarah . . . Sarah," the doctor mumbled twice. "That name has been muttered more than just a few times in this sickbay."

Sarah looked up from the bed with a questioning look.

"As a matter of fact, the last man to occupy this very bed was also a colonel—an American, though."

Sarah didn't respond. She only waited out of politeness.

"This one called out for Sarah over and over again. In addition, a funny little name . . . what was it? Oh, yes . . . 'Short Stuff.' He would call out 'Short Stuff' in his sleep. It was—"

Sarah had turned completely white. The words had slammed into her like a punch to her stomach. Her voice was caught somewhere between her esophagus and her lips.

"The Mediterranean?" It came out as a whisper.

"Excuse me, young lady?"

"Was *Leviathan* in the Med lately?" she said, her voice cracking.

"Why . . . yes, the captain was studying a recent disturbance in the sea there and we were attempting to save . . . well, the event was seismic in nature, I believe. That was where we recovered my most recent patient, the American colonel."

Sarah leaned over and was suddenly short of breath. "Is . . . is . . . he here . . . alive?"

"Very much alive . . . at least upon his release. I can't say beyond—" The doctor suddenly realized to whom he was speaking. "Oh, my . . . you are *that* Sarah? . . . Colonel Collins's Sarah?"

Sarah didn't hear the question. She lost her balance and almost fell.

"Here, here, are you all right?" the doctor asked as he helped Sarah regain her balance.

"Where is he?" she asked as she was led to a chair in the corner.

"Why, the captain released him. I imagine he is wherever your people are."

Sarah closed her eyes. She didn't know what to do; she looked around like she was trapped in a place with no exit. She started to stand, then she sat back heavily into the chair. She wanted to laugh, to cry, to jump up. She wanted all of these things until she saw Farbeaux looking at her. He had awakened and their eyes locked, and Sarah saw the Frenchman for who he had become. The man was now renewed and his sense of purpose had returned, just as surely as Sarah's life had just been returned to her.

"I am happy for you, Sarah McIntire. Very happy."

The smile never reached Henri's eyes.

EVENT GROUP COMPLEX, NELLIS AIR FORCE BASE, NEVADA

With a real-time projection of Saboo Island on the main viewing screen in the director's office, Pete, Jack, Everett, and Dr. Robbins sat and listened to the phone briefing on Saboo's present condition by one of Pete's computer techs.

"There are several structures on the atoll, Colonel, but upon examination, they look as if they have been abandoned since the end of World War Two. No indigenous animal life and no fresh water. It's basically a coral rock sitting at the end of the island chain."

"Thank you," Pete said, and terminated the call with the comp center. He looked from the map to Collins, who waited for Pete to give him his cue. The temporary director nodded, then stood up and walked toward the large monitor and pretended to study the map.

"You think Charlie Ellenshaw's theory about this being the original Heirthall's home is viable?" Pete asked without turning. "It's a large gamble, Colonel. We could be sending the only asset we have in the area to the wrong spot. They could lose the only advantage they have—that submarine may be anywhere *but* Saboo."

"Since the president informed us of the report received from *Missouri*, if Saboo is friendly turf for these people, the possibility of them going there for repairs, while a long shot, is the only chance we have."

Everett pushed his chair back and stood. He paced around the table and came to the chair where Gene Robbins was sitting. He stood still, then placed both hands on the computer man's shoulders.

"What are your thoughts, Doctor?" he asked.

Robbins moved his shoulders until Everett released his hold. He half-turned and looked at the captain.

"You already know my opinion on Professor Ellenshaw's theory. Unlike most of you in this complex, I refuse to take at face value a theory concocted by a man who believes in Nessie and the Abominable Snowman."

Pete turned away from the map and looked at his young protégé.

"You know, Gene, Charlie Ellenshaw advanced more than one theory during his time in the *Leviathan* vault. I don't know if you heard that one. Well, my apologies, it was he, the Colonel, and Captain Everett here who thought it up."

Robbins again turned back and looked at Carl, who remained behind him. He then frowned and looked back at Pete.

"I wasn't aware of another theory," he said.

"It seems they believe that Virginia—while brilliant in physics, and while she could very well be very knowledgeable in exotic explosives and accelerant—the assistant director is like most of the personnel in this complex. She doesn't know her way around a computer save to sign in and out, and maybe access Europa for her research. Security protocols are far beyond her."

"Anyone is capable, especially someone as brilliant as Ms. Pollock, at learning Europa's protocols. Besides, wasn't it you, Pete, and the esteemed Professor Ellenshaw, who advanced the idea of the assistant director's culpability in the sabotage?"

"Yes, indeed. What they call a rush to judgment." Pete strode toward the table where Robbins sat, then placed his hands on the polished surface. Collins just swiveled in his chair, and Everett remained irritatingly close behind the computer genius. "However, as great a mind as Charlie Ellenshaw is, I was perplexed as to how he thought to run a check on any correlation between Alexandria Heirthall and Virginia Pollock through Europa, especially with all he had on his plate."

Robbins swallowed but said nothing. Everett cleared his throat and then tossed a plastic bag in front of him. When it landed, Robbins flinched. He could see the glove inside.

"I found that in the clean room, Dr. Robbins," Jack said, looking right at him. "Since only you, the director, and Dr. Golding are authorized inside that high-security area without escort, we have to assume that that glove, brimming with what is called magnesium particulate, used in the burning of hazardous materials, belongs to you."

Everett again leaned over and whispered in Robbins's ear. "And guess what? Forensics found a fingerprint inside the index finger of said glove. It didn't match Dr. Golding, so I'll give you three guesses who it did match, and the first two don't count."

The three men had to hand it to Robbins—the man was fast thinking.

"Come on, I visited the *Leviathan* vault myself after the attack. I may have gotten the accelerant on my glove when there." He turned and faced Everett. "Let me get this straight. You're accusing me of sabotage, and with that, murder and kidnapping?"

"You bet," Carl said, leaning further in to Robbins.

"Prove it," he said, turning once more away from Everett.

"Dr. Robbins, you are misunderstanding your situation," Jack said as he stood and made his way around the table. "You are assuming we're in a court of law, where there are rules."

Everett smiled, spun the doctor around in his chair, and then went nose to nose.

"No rules."

Robbins shied away from the captain. They could all see the fear this man had of Everett.

"Colonel Collins, Captain Everett, I know I agreed that anything goes as far as getting truthful answers, but you cannot subliminally threaten one of my people with violence," Pete said, much to the visible relief of Gene Robbins. "I think you should come right out and say it." He smiled for the first time since the attack on the complex. "Subliminal be damned."

"You're right, of course," Everett said as he reached down, grabbed Robbins by his lab coat, pulled him from the chair, and shook him once, twice. "Jack, do you have that resignation letter?"

Collins slid a piece of paper in front of Robbins. He couldn't see it; all he could see was the hate in Everett's eyes.

"Look at it, Gene," Pete said, his own features masked with disgust.

Robbins turned and looked at the paper on the table.

"Your official resignation, signed by you, turned in to Pete here just before you disappeared from the complex. Whereabouts unknown," Collins said as he took a chair next to Robbins.

"I suspect the little bastard committed suicide after we found out about his culpability and treachery," Everett said, pulling Robbins's face back around so he could see the seriousness of his great acting skills.

Collins looked at Pete, and they both realized at the same moment that Everett could scare a rock if he had to.

"In all actuality, Dr. Robbins, you are going to disappear," Jack said.

Robbins finally forced himself to look away from the most-feared Everett and finally saw Jack.

"You're going to Saboo, and you know what else? You're going to make sure your friends show up."

"How . . . how am I supposed to do that?" he asked as Everett finally released his coat collar.

"Why, you're going to call them, of course," Carl said, smiling brightly.

"You receive your orders somehow. You'll just use the same method to contact your boss and tell them you're coming home."

"What is the name of that home by the way, Gene?" Everett asked, his smile never wavering.

Robbins looked from Carl to Jack to his former boss. His head slumped and they barely heard his answer.

"*Leviathan.*"

An hour later Jack, Everett, Jason Ryan, Will Mendenhall, and Robbins were in field gear and on their way to California for a transfer to a U.S. Navy Greyhound flight to the Pacific for a rendezvous arranged by the president. Collins spoke directly to the White House via scrambled communications. Robbins looked miserable, but he had complied with his orders to send *Leviathan* an emergency message. He informed his master he would be waiting on Saboo for immediate pickup, that his cover had been blown, and that he had barely escaped. There had been no reply, nor even a confirmation that his message had been received.

"Okay, Colonel, I have you a ride to Saboo: USS *Missouri*. She's the sub that just put two torpedoes into our friend."

"Thank you, sir," Jack said as he looked into his end of the camera from the cargo hold of the C-130 air force cargo plane.

"Now, what in the hell makes you think they'll take you aboard after discovering you turned in their operative?"

"We're banking on Heirthall's arrogance. After all, how can four men be a danger to her?"

"That's one hell of a big assumption, Colonel."

"I know perfectly well what's at stake, Mr. President."

"Okay, Colonel, you have your sub and I've alerted COMSUBPAC. He's alerting the crews of three Los Angeles attack boats to prepare for sea. They will rendezvous with *Missouri*, so I wish you luck. You must understand, Colonel, those captains have their orders. I don't have to tell you, of all people, what those orders are."

"If *Leviathan* makes an aggressive move, they are to use any and all means to destroy her."

"You have the letter to Captain Jefferson?" the president asked.

"Yes, sir."

"Duplicates have been delivered to the captains of the other subs. Good luck, Colonel, bring my people home if possible. I'll inform Admiral Fuqua that Operation Nemo is a go."

The screen went blank.

Jack felt as if he were on the outside of the poker game looking in, and was just hoping to get a seat at the big table. The one problem: He knew beforehand that the other player held all the cards.

The bluff was on.

LEVIATHAN

Niles, Virginia, Lee, Alice, and a very quiet Sarah sat in the ship's mess. They were sitting at a far table within the seventy-table compartment. Over a hundred of *Leviathan*'s crew were taking a late-night meal and their voices were subdued. Every once in a while one or two would glance over at them, and this time they weren't friendly or welcoming faces they saw. Niles pushed away the soup that the mess steward had placed in front of him and looked at the others.

"My opinion is, if Jack is fit, he, Carl, and Pete will discover a way to find us. My money is on our people."

The group was silent as they waited for Niles to finish what they knew he was going to say.

"I also don't want anyone here at this table to have any false illusions about us escaping. It's not likely." Compton looked at McIntire, who was dipping her spoon in and out of her soup. "Sarah, I'm going to say something you may not like. We owe Colonel Farbeaux nothing—not for saving you at the complex, or for what he did earlier today. He's dangerous, and we have to consider . . . eliminating him."

"Sarah, you told us about Jack. Your explanation of Farbeaux's reaction to the news that the Colonel was alive has confirmed your suspicion about his stability."

Sarah was silent as she turned toward Niles. Her look said she was lost as to how to answer both him and Virginia.

Garrison Lee broke the uncomfortable silence.

"How do we do that, Virginia—have the captain dump him at sea, or allow this Sergeant Tyler to place a bullet in his brain?"

The table became silent at Lee's question.

"Obviously not—we decided a long time ago that we play by our rules and not everyone else's, regardless of cost, or what the opposition dictates," Lee said, looking from person to person.

"I'm sorry, but Farbeaux could become a very large liability when the time comes for us to act," Virginia said as she rubbed her temples.

Yeoman Felicia Alvera walked up to their table. She looked at other crew members watching her approach the table, and she eyed them until they turned away.

"Can we help you, Yeoman?" Alice asked her, noticing that the girl was, for the first time, unsmiling.

"Your opposition to our captain. I would like to know"—she half-turned and gestured to the table of twenty or so midshipmen in the middle of the compartment—"just as many of us would—why you do not see she has no other choice but to act as she has?"

"Young lady, no matter the kindness Captain Heirthall has shown you and these others, she is killing people, and making very little discrimination as to who they are," Niles said, seeing a different girl before them than the one they first met on the hangar deck.

"Yeoman, you may return to your meal, or your quarters," Sergeant

Tyler said, having stepped up without anyone hearing or seeing his approach.

Alvera looked at Tyler and narrowed her eyes. Then she suddenly turned and left, not going back to her own meal; she left the mess area altogether. Niles and the others saw that the other midshipmen, after a brief glance toward them, all followed the girl out.

The sergeant was starting to walk away, and then stopped and turned. He looked down at the five Group members. They saw there was still a spot of blood on the bandage wrapped around his head.

"From this moment forward, you are not to converse with the crew, especially the middies. If you disobey this command you will be locked in the brig and gagged. For the present time, we are putting the problem of you people on hold, but you may have company soon. We are making a detour."

"What about the reason you brought us aboard in the first place, Sergeant?" Niles asked.

"What you know or what your Group knows no longer concerns us. For the moment just consider yourselves . . ." He paused and smiled. ". . . ballast."

Tyler turned and followed the midshipmen out, ignoring the way the adult crew looked at him.

"What a dick," Sarah said.

"My word exactly," Alice agreed.

"Yeoman Alvera and the other midshipmen—have you noticed the paleness of skin? It's almost see-through," Virginia stated.

"Now that you bring it up, they are pale—even for submariners," Niles said.

"Here's something else for everyone to chew on. Have you noticed the way the older crewmen look at them is almost resentful?"

None of them had an answer or an opinion as *Leviathan* started her thermal-dynamic drive for the first time in twelve hours. They were all silent and more than one of them stared at the table, knowing the great submarine was once more under way and was continuing whatever hellish work she still had to do.

14

The captain of USS *Missouri* stared at Jack Collins, thinking the man had gone mad. He tossed the grease pencil on the charting table and looked over at his XO.

"You're just going to walk right onto the island and say, 'Hey, we would like a ride'?"

"It's either that or waste the lives of a lot of young boys by trying to take *Leviathan* by force, all alone, when and if she surfaces," Jack said, not turning away from the captain. "Personally, I've had enough of people dying lately. We want one chance to get our hostages back. . . . Just one, then she's yours, Captain."

Jefferson lowered his head. "Okay, Colonel, we may be able to track *Leviathan*, I'll give you and the president that much, but we lost a bunch of subs and men learning that fact. Also absorb this little tidbit: We hit her with two Mark forty-eight torpedoes, and they didn't even slow her down, as far as we know. Now explain to me how we can get any advantage on this thing whatsoever, if we even find her again after this little detour of yours."

"Once aboard, my men and I will have to play things by ear. Captain Everett here is trained on how to get an edge against enemy subs, so you'll have to wait and take advantage of what it is we come up with. Twenty-four hours. After that, hit her anyway you can with what you can. Captain, I want our people off that damn thing."

Jack looked at Carl, then nodded his head. Everett handed the captain a yellow envelope with a red border.

"I think you'll recognize the name and letterhead, Captain," Carl said. "I think this will explain our sincerity about that one chance if we fail."

Jefferson looked at the plain yellow envelope and then, without removing his eyes from Collins, broke the plastic seal. He pulled the single set of orders out and looked at them. When he was finished reading, he closed his eyes.

"Jesus Christ," he mumbled, and handed the letter over to First Officer Izzeringhausen. The lieutenant commander read what the order called for, and his face went slack.

"You'll have to excuse us, Colonel, we're just not that experienced with sending men out on a suicide mission. If you ask me, you guys are out of your fucking minds," Izzeringhausen said after reading the letter and the code that was attached to it.

"Take it easy, Izzy, I think they know what they're asking."

The first officer gave the letter from the president of the United States back to the captain and went back to speak with the chief of the boat.

"You know, it's not only suicide for you fellas, but for the *Missouri* and any other American boat in the area. A nuclear war shot in a confined area will smash us to atoms, and we have to be within range of the target to guarantee a hit," he said, tossing the letter onto the navigation console.

"Let's hope we can do something other than that, Captain. We can be pretty sneaky at times," Jack said.

The presidential order authorizing the use of *Missouri*'s nuclear capability was having a profound effect on Jefferson, and Jack could see that. The order would be the first in naval history to be carried out, if it came to that, and the responsibility was etched on the captain's face.

"What if you're shot to pieces when you motor up to their dock?"

"Track *Leviathan* the best you can and blow her to pieces, Captain."

"Just who in the hell are you people?"

"Believe me, Captain, we're no one special. We want our people back and we want *Leviathan* stopped."

The captain accepted Carl's answer and then looked at his chart.

"Izzy," he said aloud, "it will be dark in twenty minutes. Get the colonel and his men suited up and tell the SEALs to get ready to escort them to Saboo." Captain Jefferson looked up and held his hand out to Collins. "Colonel, I'll just say I hope you get your people out." He shook hands with Jack and then held his hand out to Everett. "But I really hope you talk some sense into the magnificent bastard that built that boat. I would hate to have to sink it *and* you, too."

"Believe me, Captain, we hope the same thing," Collins said as he followed the first officer aft.

SABOO ATOLL, THE MARIANAS

In the darkness just before moonrise, USS *Missouri*, the stealthiest submarine in the history of the U.S. Navy, surfaced without a sound a thousand yards offshore of the volcanic atoll called Saboo. With only the topmost section of her tower out of the water, her silhouette was almost nonexistent in the darkness of the night. Even her sail numbers were a darker shade of black against the hull. Captain Jefferson popped free of the hatch, quickly brought binoculars to his face, and scanned the sea.

"Sonar, conn, what have we got?" he asked quietly, knowing how well sound carried at sea.

"Nothing on sonar. We are no longer picking up *Leviathan*. She must be too far distant or at a stop, and air search radar is clear, Captain."

"Okay, give me fifteen feet of air and clear the diving trunk, Izzy," Jefferson said as he scanned the sea again with his binoculars, nervous about his sonar's inability to find *Leviathan*.

"Aye, Captain, fifteen feet."

As Jefferson scanned the faraway beach of Saboo and the few lights there, the black sub silently rose in the water, clearing the lower escape trunk on the *Missouri*'s sail. The hatch quickly opened and two large bundles were tossed free of the boat. The two Zodiacs quickly inflated. Ten U.S. Navy SEALs exited and took up station on the hull of the sub as they assisted the five men of the shore mission. Collins looked up at the sail before he stepped foot in the first boat and saw Jefferson looking down at him. Both men nodded, and Jefferson saluted.

"Good luck, Colonel."

Collins returned the salute and stepped into the boat with Dr. Gene Robbins in tow.

Three miles away in the darkest depths of the Pacific, *Missouri* was being watched. The eyes that scanned her were merely curious.

"Bring up maximum magnification on the scope, please, Mr. Samuels," Alexandria ordered from her high station in main control.

The view on the free-floating hologram changed and flashed off for a split second. Then a three-dimensional view of the sail of *Missouri* appeared, but of far more interest to Heirthall were the two Zodiacs bobbing in the sea beside the sub.

"Someday you'll have to tell me how you can be so right all the time, Captain," Samuels said, as the darkened face of Colonel Jack Collins became crisp and clear.

Alexandria didn't respond at first; she just looked from the hologram to her crew as they monitored their stations. Her eyes were again dilated and she was calm, in control.

"Never underestimate a man's tenacity, James." She smiled and looked at the first officer. "Or his love for another, for that matter. Those two things make events predictable to a certain degree. Besides, with this Group Ginny surrounded herself with, I knew it would only be a matter of time before they broke our good Dr. Robbins. It was inevitable that Saboo would be compromised."

"What to you think their plan is?" Samuels asked as he left the sonar station and walked up to the high pedestal.

"I don't believe they have one, and I surely don't believe they plan on taking Saboo with fifteen men. We'll watch and see."

"The *Missouri*?" he asked.

"No threat there. Just monitor her. If she lingers around Saboo, we'll chase her off. As long as we don't move until she clears the area or allow our damaged surfaces to compromise us, we'll be fine. Then we'll just dive so deep that their limited technology can't detect us."

"Aye, Captain."

"Would you have Mr. Tyler escort Lieutenant McIntire to my sail observation suite and seat her outside until we bring our new guests aboard, then report to me for instructions?"

Samuels hesitated momentarily, as the captain never allowed anyone inside her private suite at the bottom of the sail tower. "Aye, Captain."

Alexandria watched as the two Zodiacs shoved off from the *Missouri* and silently started for the shores of her island of Saboo.

"Soon I will have everyone aboard that I need," she whispered to no one but herself.

"Captain?" Samuels asked, thinking he heard her speak.

"James, I think it time we sit down and have dinner, before I start having headaches again. Twenty-three hundred hours, my cabin?"

Samuels looked around and saw Sergeant Tyler watching them from his security station.

"We need not inform anyone. On your off-watch report, say you're inspecting the engineering damage," Alexandria said, with a quick look at Sergeant Tyler. "One other thing, James. You'll know my mood. If you discover I'm out of sorts when you arrive, mention nothing about dinner, just return to your cabin until I speak with you."

Samuels tried desperately not to be taken aback by the captain's invitation and warning. As he saw that she was done, he nodded. "Yes, Captain."

"Until twenty-three hundred, then."

Sergeant Tyler stepped away from the security station after observing the conversation between the captain and Samuels. He watched as Samuels stopped in front of him and relayed the captain's orders regarding Sarah. Then he watched Samuels move away. Tyler then approached the captain.

"Captain, as head of security, I must say this is unacceptable, bringing this man back onboard *Leviathan*. You yourself warned us about this Group's ability to get information, and with what he already knows about us, to allow him access—"

"Sergeant, I have been commanding this vessel long before I took you onboard her. I think I can make clear decisions without consulting you. Now, escort Lieutenant McIntire to the sail and await my orders."

Tyler looked deeply into the captain's eyes until she looked away, then he turned without comment and left the command pedestal. Although Alexandria paid the hotheaded Tyler's breach of etiquette no notice, Samuels did. He watched as Tyler gave a last look back into the control center before leaving. After the first officer turned to his duties, Yeoman Alvera followed Tyler into the companionway.

"Maneuvering, bring *Leviathan* shallow and let's see what our uninvited guests are up to."

Leviathan started to rise in the water like an ancient behemoth, slowly pushing aside tens of thousands of tons of water. She rose as a sea god would to spy an intruder.

"You are challenging the captain's judgment in front of the command crew right in the open. Do I have to remind you that we will need those people if this is to succeed?"

Tyler saw the anger in the yeoman's eyes. The deep green pupil was now ringed in red and that in silver. He knew from Dr. Trevor that when Alvera became angry, microscopic pinprick hemorrhages erupted inside the ocular cavity, and those produced the bright colors in the eyeball. As he watched, the yeoman relaxed and looked around the empty passageway.

"You are not to do that again."

"The captain is acting very strange, she's becoming two-sided when it comes to her orders," Tyler said, leaning in so he could whisper.

"I suspect that she is putting up more of a mental struggle than even we suspected." Alvera leaned against the steel bulkhead as her eyes slowly became normal once more. "Alexandria is a strong-willed woman. Stronger than the part we need," she said admiringly. "We will have to act soon. Be prepared at a moment's notice for the right time to get what we need from her."

"She is showing signs that she knows. At this very moment, she is as alert as she has ever been, and maybe confused about her aggressiveness."

"Just do your job. We'll soon be at Ice Palace and then this will all end," Alvera said as she turned and started back for the control room. "We keep the captain happy by following orders, until such a time as she consistently gives us the right orders. Confusing to your kind, I know, but that's the way it is."

"Wait," Tyler called out. "What are we going to do about that bastard Samuels? He knows something, or at least suspects. And what about the captain making this stop at Saboo? I told you all along that she had no intention of questioning her old friend and that damn Group about what they know."

Alvera turned back and faced the sergeant. "Does it really matter?" She smiled. "After all, we have the captain of the most powerful warship in the history of the world on our side, even if Alexandria Heirthall isn't. . . . Yet."

Sergeant Tyler watched as the young girl made her way aft and back to her shift. He nervously turned and looked around and then shook his head. He was starting to regret the deal he had made.

Everyone knew the Devil always brokered deals that couldn't be broken.

The two Zodiacs were at the sea edge of the surf when Collins ordered the two boats to stop.

"This is as far as the SEALs go; we get off here. Come on, Doc, it's time to go swimming."

"Colonel, we don't mind taking the risk," the SEAL lieutenant said from his place at the back of the boat.

"Well, I do. No more lives are going into harm's way. Thanks for the ride, Lieutenant," Jack said as he grabbed Robbins and leaned backward, sending them both into the sea.

Everett watched from the second boat and followed suit, along with Ryan and Mendenhall. They started in toward an unknown reception on Saboo.

As they rode the surf in, Jack kept Robbins's head above water. When they gained their feet on the wet sand, Collins looked around at the silence that greeted them. The beach was deserted, just as advertised.

"Well, we didn't get all wet for nothing. Shall we go wait to be shot, or picked up?" Everett said as he stood next to Jack.

"By all means," Jack answered with a nod. "Take the lead, Captain, and let's go fishing."

EVENT GROUP CENTER, NELLIS AIR FORCE BASE, NEVADA

Pete was sitting at Niles's large desk, his glasses propped up on his forehead. He was having the hardest time of his life keeping his eyes from closing as he studied the duty rosters for the complex, with a minimal security supervisory team given the absence of Everett, Ryan, and Mendenhall.

One of the director's assistants, whom Pete had previously ordered to her quarters for the night, popped her head in through the door. She stepped in and, thinking Golding was finally sleeping, gently laid a pile of folders on his desk. As she started to turn away and leave, not wanting to wake him, Pete opened his eyes.

"What are these?" he asked without moving his left hand away from his head, where it protected his eyes from the glare of the overhead lights.

The young woman's shoulders slumped and she turned.

"The replacement files from Arlington on the vaults on level seventy-three and seventy-four. They faxed us another set."

Pete finally moved. He rubbed his eyes and replaced the glasses to their normal position.

"They may very well be redundant, since we now know what they were trying to hide," he said as he removed the top file from the bunch. As he did, the others slid from the stack and slid across his desk. "Damn," he said.

"Here, I'll just put them on my desk until you have more time to check them off your list," she said, moving forward to relieve Golding's desk of at least some of his workload.

As she did, Pete's eyes locked on a particular file for no other reason than that was where his eyes rested. He blinked, then placed his fingers on the partially obscured file number. He pulled it from the fanned-out stack, looked it over, and let out a small chuckle.

"I've got to get out more often and see the world—or at least the complex," he said as he opened the obscure file. "I never knew we had anything from P. T. Barnum's old New York Museum—better yet, why would we?"

The assistant looked at which file he was perusing and then relaxed.

"Oh, well, Colonel Collins said to include it because it was the vault located directly under the *Leviathan* enclosure."

Pete looked up, partially closed the file, and then looked into the assistant's innocent countenance.

"Directly under the vault? On level seventy-four? Wasn't that where accelerant was also found?"

"Yes, sir, but the engineers said that could be explained by the liquid seeping through the rocks and falling inside that particular vault."

Golding nodded his head and excused the assistant, then looked at the file in his hands. It wasn't a thick file, and stapled to the inside jacket of the folder was a small notation made by the forensics department stating that the artifact was totally destroyed by the fire. Pete read the first page of description from the report filed by the Event Group back in 1949, when the specimen was discovered in an old repository building in Florida owned by Ringling Bros. and Barnum & Bailey Circus, The Greatest Show on Earth.

"'The Mermaid of the Pacific Isles,'" Pete mumbled as he looked at a photograph of something that resembled a jellyfish, and a rather degraded jellyfish at that.

There were enhanced details that had been added by the Group back in '49 that outlined what looked like a pair of legs and small arms. The see-through mass was unlike anything Pete had ever seen before, and by far the most disturbing feature of all was in the next color photo: The damn thing looked as though it had hair. Long, black, and flowing, as it was laid out on a stainless-steel examining table. The whole thing, from head to jellylike, fanned tail, was about four feet long.

Pete flipped over to the next page and read the details of its discovery. The specimen had been one of the only items salvaged from the great fire in midtown Manhattan in 1865 during one of the many draft riots during the Civil War. The P. T. Barnum American Museum, located on Broadway and Ann Streets, burned, with a loss of more than 90 percent of its displayed oddities. It was reported by witnesses that Barnum himself rescued only *one* item from the burning structure, and that was from a locked storage bin in his personal office. That item: the Mermaid of the Pacific.

For many years after, people saw a cheap version of the mermaid (actually made from a torso of a monkey and the tail of a giant black sea bass) on display at the museum Barnum built to replace the one lost. He never gave an explanation of the obviously fake replacement to people who had heard the rumors of a far more delicate and humanlike specimen that gossip said was kept at Barnum's own New York home.

After Barnum's death in 1891, a locked chest was willed to the famous Greatest Show on Earth and then sent to Florida, where it was stored and forgotten. That was where an Event Group field team discovered it in an old warehouse in 1949.

The forensics report was confused for the day; there was absolutely no relationship of the specimen to that of modern-day jellyfish or any vertebrate found in the fossil record. The deterioration of the specimen was so vast that no acceptable biopsy of the material could be conducted.

Pete noticed a small notation placed in the margins of the report and had to turn the file on its side to read it.

"The sample of hair was found to be human, and the lone sample of fingernail found was also closely related to man. The brain, made up of clear and bluish material, was thought to be far larger than that of any creature indigenous to the sea in relationship to its size."

Golding turned to the last page for the Group's conclusion.

"Because of the nature of Mr. Barnum's personality, it must be concluded at this time that this is a forgery on a grand scale. Although far more encompassing and impressive than his obviously fake 'Fiji Mermaid,' displayed from 1865–1881, the findings do not support Mr. Barnum's claims of finding the Mermaid of the Pacific off the coast of Venezuela, in the Gulf of Mexico. One item of note, the specimen was found in an enclosure engraved with the seal of the University of Oslo."

Pete laid the file down when he read the last words of the report. *Coincidence?* he asked himself as he picked up the phone.

"Miss Lange, get me Professor Ellenshaw down in crypto on the phone. Tell him I need some research done ASAP."

He hung up the phone and looked at the file. *Could this be what those people wanted to remain hidden from the world instead of the submarine?* he asked himself.

Golding looked at the 1949 color picture of the Mermaid of the Pacific. As he did, he noticed for the first time the intense blue eyes of the creature, even in death. Nothing else but the small arms and hands resembled a human. It was the hands that would give him time for pause before sleep. The fingers, he could tell, were long and delicate, and now that he was examining the photo closer, he could swear he could see femalelike breasts. He shook his head and closed his eyes.

The phone finally rang and he picked it up.

"Charlie, thanks for getting back to me so soon."

"No problem, I was just dozing off at my desk."

"I need to ask you something, Charlie. Your department believes in the existence of many, many strange things—"

"Come on, Pete, did you call just to rag on me?"

"Professor, I think you are one of the smartest people in this complex, so knock it off. I need to know your opinion on the existence of mermaids, or something like them?"

The other end of the phone produced nothing but silence for the longest time.

"Charlie?" Pete asked, thinking the connection had been lost.

"Pete, to believe in mermaids is a little far out, even for us. Now, if you're done joking around, I'll get back to dozing and dreaming about the Yeti and—"

"Professor, what would you say if I told you that we've had a specimen of an undersea creature since nineteen forty-nine that could possibly be what sea lore described as a mermaid, and that is what this whole *Leviathan* thing may be about?"

"Well, I would say that the Event Group was left in the wrong hands."

Pete winced as the phone was slammed down on Ellenshaw's end. He wanted to slam his down also, but instead eased it into the cradle.

He looked at the file in front of him. As he closed it, he knew that *Leviathan* and this artifact were linked somehow, in some fashion, but also knew he was at a dead end. He couldn't even pass on the information to Jack and Carl.

His new opinion of the events of the past week had just taken a turn toward the Twilight Zone.

SABOO ATOLL, THE MARIANAS

Jack could feel eyes on him, physically and electronically. He looked at Everett and knew he was having the same sensation.

They were standing on the lone dock on the island that was fronted by a small building looking as if it had been constructed during the Second World War. The small hut was boarded up. Phone lines ran from the building to a point one hundred feet from the dock, where they disappeared into the white sand. Ryan and Mendenhall, with Robbins between them, were busy watching the sea.

"Colonel Collins, we are indeed shocked, though pleasantly so, to see you again so soon," a voice said from behind them.

They turned and saw a lone figure standing on the edge of the dock, illuminated only by the stars in the night sky. The voice sounded vaguely familiar to Jack.

"My name is Dr. Warren Trevor, formerly of Her Majesty's Royal Navy, and ship's surgeon for *Leviathan*. I was sent to greet you in case you needed to see a familiar face."

"You treated me while I was onboard?" Jack asked as he and the others walked toward him.

"Indeed I did," the dark figure answered.

Jack moved his eyes from their host to Ryan, who was busy tapping out an ELF (extremely low frequency) message to *Missouri*, saying they had made contact.

"Will you have your companions shed their equipment, Colonel? There will be no need for any outside paraphernalia onboard *Leviathan*." He gestured toward Ryan. "And young man, I can assure you, the *Missouri* has indeed left the immediate area; therefore they cannot hear your transmission. My captain would not allow that at any rate."

Ryan closed the small transmitter and tossed it into the pack at his feet.

"Now, gentlemen, if you will follow me. Dr. Robbins, the captain is most anxious to find out if they treated you right."

Robbins looked from Ryan to Mendenhall. They both smiled.

"Our people?" Jack asked.

"They have survived their ordeal, I assure you, Colonel."

Jack and the others watched as the dark figure of the doctor turned away and started for the beach end of the dock. Robbins stepped from the group, shrugging off Ryan's and Will's hands, and quickly started forward, as if he were anxious to be on his way.

"Where are we going, Doctor?" Collins called after the dark figure.

The man stopped and turned once he reached the old shack, and as the moon fully breached sea level, they could see the doctor smiling as he waited.

"Why, to take you to meet the person you came here to meet, of course," he said, and turned to enter the shack. Robbins followed him in without a backward glance.

"Well, let's go meet Captain Nemo, shall we?" Collins said in all seriousness.

Everett, Mendenhall, and Ryan fell into step behind Jack as they made their way to the shack.

The moon rose slowly over Saboo Atoll. There was nothing to indicate that they were about to venture into the very birthplace of *Leviathan*.

15

Collins and his team stepped into the barren and empty shack at the edge of the dock. The doctor was there, dressed in a navy blue jumpsuit with a matching Windbreaker. The only adornment on his uniform was the two dolphins flanking the L on his breast pocket. The doctor smiled as the interior of the shack was slowly illuminated by the rising moon, revealing itself to be filled with floats, a broken radio, and numerous fishing poles, all with dust on their surfaces. The doctor made sure the door was secure, then said aloud, "Level two."

The flooring broke away from the foundation of the shack and started descending into the sandy beach. Once the small elevator was beyond the wall of the shack, Jack and the others saw they were inside an acrylic shaft. The elevator was being lowered below the water table of the island and into an excavated chamber. Soon they broke free into a cavernous level that housed crates and other bulky materials, and for the first time, as Collins and his men looked into the most amazing man-made cavern in the world, they saw the inhabitants of Saboo Island—children.

The doctor watched the four men and smiled. "Our future—or what we hope our future is," he said, gesturing toward the thirty or so children within view just as the glass door slid aside. He stepped out without worrying about the men being behind him.

The engineering was amazing. Steel beams that were sixty feet thick and hundreds of feet long were supporting the giant cave. The spider-webbing of support rebar snaked in and out of the entire structure—they could see that the engineering was old, possibly pre–Civil War. The base of the cavern was taken up by a two-thousand-foot lagoon with a concrete dock that extended two hundred feet into the water. On the far side of the immense cavern, two massive dry dock facilities rose from the unnatural lagoon. There were cranes and derricks, shops and warehouses. On the small beach around the lagoon, there were tents arrayed, and they spied a few of the children exiting carrying small backpacks.

"Jack, this may have been their home once, but look at these buildings—they haven't been used in years," Everett said, leaning into Collins.

"Gentlemen, may I point out dry dock number one," the doctor said, pointing to the far left of the lagoon, "the very dock that launched the first *Leviathan* back in the eighteen hundreds. The larger of the two dry docks, number two, as you can see is quite a bit larger. That is the birthplace of the current *Leviathan*. Forty years for its creation and commissioning."

"It's large enough to launch a supercarrier," Everett observed.

"The children?" Jack inquired.

"As I said, they are our future; you might say the very best of both worlds are standing before you, Colonel. The birthplace and onetime home of *Leviathan* and the family Heirthall, and these children."

"And just where is your Captain Heirthall, Doctor?"

Gene Robbins stepped up to the railing, smiling. He closed his eyes as the man-made breeze seemed to shift, and there was a minute change in the density of the air. The overhead lights that illuminated the great cave flickered. They saw static electricity actually sparking on the surface of the man-made bay below.

"She's right there, Colonel," the doctor said, pointing at the lagoon. "Gentlemen—*Leviathan*."

As they watched, great bubbles of released air and fountains of water towered into the interior of the cavern. Then the conning tower of the great submarine slowly and silently broke the roiling surface of the lagoon, announced by the mist and streaks of blue electricity as the composite hull reacted with the humidified air.

"Jesus," Mendenhall mumbled. His skin turned ice cold watching the behemoth rise from the water.

The sweptback structure kept rising, breeching higher out of the blue water, and finally her conning tower planes broke free as would a giant's palm shedding the sea.

As Collins watched, the small children, dressed in blue shorts and blue shirts, all stood as one and watched the mother of all vessels rise from the abyss. The two tail fins rose six hundred feet back from the conning tower; the anticollision lights glowed bright red. Finally, the sleek, black hull of *Leviathan* herself followed the towering tail fins.

"My God," Everett said, standing next to Jack.

"Close, Captain," Robbins said as he leaned back and felt the false breeze the arrival of the giant ship created.

The submarine continued to rise from the water, all eleven hundred feet of her. The great rounded bow broke free of the water as giant bubbles broke the surface, signaling the final release of all of the air in her ballast tanks. As they watched, the giant screens protecting the viewing windows started to part. The windows covered the entire bow section, and gleamed in the overhead lighting of the cavern. Jack could see the separation of compartments and decks through the thick glass.

The huge bow-planes started to retract into the hull, causing a large ripple in the calming waters. They were all startled when tremendous geysers of water shot from both sides of the submarine that now towered a hundred and fifty feet into the air. The water spouts rose high, creating a rainbow effect that circled the middle section of *Leviathan*. All was silent for the briefest of moments. Then the cavern lights dimmed, and giant floodlights illuminated the wetness that covered the black, violet, and blue skin of the giant monster.

"Now that is something," Ryan said looking from the lagoon to Mendenhall who stood silent, watching the spectacle.

"Okay, Doctor, you can relay to your captain, we were adequately impressed."

Before the doctor could respond to Collins, the thirty-two children ran forward on the concrete dock, silently, but looking excited as they gathered up their small belongings, backpacks, books, and other small treasures of their young lives. There were black children and white, yellow and brown, every race known to the planet, and as varied as the bright rainbow colors that were only now fading in the false light of the cavern.

As the doctor led the way down from the elevator platform, six of the small children passed them on their way down to the dock. One of them, a small girl, bumped into Mendenhall, and he reached out to steady her. She only looked up at the much taller man and smiled. As she started to pull away from Mendenhall, she reached up and placed her small hand on his enormous one. Then the small girl turned and skipped her way down the scaffold to the dock below.

With one last look at the buildings built right into the coral-and-lava rock strata of the cave, Jack and the others followed Dr. Trevor and a very excited Robbins down to *Leviathan*.

As the six men reached the broad opening of the quay, the doctor took Jack by the arm, halting him and the others from advancing farther. Collins looked from the surgeon to *Leviathan* as the lower escape trunk hatch on the conning tower opened at its base. At first there was no one there, but then several midshipmen walked out to greet the youngsters as they swarmed the sleek black deck. The submarine was so large that the children looked like ants upon the beached carcass of a prehistoric whale.

"Are they related, Doctor?" Carl asked.

As the groups met and hugged, a few even jumped for joy. It was as if they were reunited for the first time in years.

The doctor only smiled, looking from the children to Everett. The two groups of young people started entering the conning tower with the older ones holding the hands of the younger, two at a time until the deck was clear. Then the adult personnel that had been left on the island to watch over the children started loading crates and other materials being evacuated from *Leviathan*'s former home.

"The older age group is *Leviathan*'s midshipmen. As to your question, they are all orphans, Captain Everett. They are the Heirthall children. They are not relations—that is yet to come for the children. Now, if you will follow me, into the belly of the beast." He turned, smiling. "So to speak."

Collins stopped once they stepped onto the expanse of deck. About twenty-five men came up through one of the many deck hatches aft of the conning tower and started repairing minor damage to the composite material that made up the hull of *Leviathan*. Several men wearing scuba gear, and some without, lowered themselves into the water with canvas bags holding tools and repair materials.

"We sustained some minor damage to our outer hull. We underestimated the tenacity and luck of one of your American subs, *Missouri*. I'm sure her captain bragged to you about it." The doctor looked at each man in turn. "I assure you, that mistake won't be repeated by the captain. Follow me, please."

As they stepped over the hatch jam, they were inside the lowest portion of the hundred-fifty-foot shark-finlike conning tower. The interior of the submarine was deathly silent; there was not even the sound of the children that had come aboard before them.

"Captain Everett, if you and Lieutenants Ryan and Mendenhall will accompany me, I will take you to your director. Colonel, Captain Heirthall has requested you join her in the conning observation suite. The door will open momentarily; just wait here."

Before the others moved off down the companionway, a large elevator arrived from the bowels of the submarine and the doors parted. Collins and his men were staring at ten soldiers in the same black Nomexlike clothing made from seaweed that was found on the attackers of their complex. The man standing to the front of this group looked at *Leviathan*'s guests. A better term was that he was in the process of examining them. He gestured for several of his men to advance. They started unceremoniously frisking and searching Collins and his men.

"They were scanned inside the shack, there is nothing in their clothing—is the captain aware you are doing this?" the doctor demanded, stepping up to the larger of the men. "You'll have to pardon Sergeant Tyler, Colonel; his etiquette has been lacking for quite some time." He stepped closer to Tyler just inside the elevator and whispered, "Do you insist on attracting attention to yourself? You are becoming overly aggressive, Sergeant. It was my understanding that Yeoman Alvera explained this to you."

Tyler didn't answer. He simply reached down, picked up a large satchel, and advanced into the companionway.

"Make it a thorough search," he said to four of his men.

"My apologies again, Colonel," the doctor said.

Collins didn't respond, he only turned and locked eyes with Sergeant Tyler.

Tyler held Jack's glare, raised his left brow, and broke the moment by gesturing for his men to go ahead of him as he finally spoke to Collins.

"Because of men like you, I am on my way to destroy the only home that we have ever known," he said, stopping in front of Collins. "I was against rescuing you in the Mediterranean, Colonel; I think you should know that." He looked from Collins to the other three men, and continued in his Irish-accented voice. "If it were up to me, I would leave you all here on Saboo, to be destroyed right along with it."

"Well, why don't you just set those bags down and show us the way, cowboy. I guarantee you better bring your lunch," Ryan said, taking a menacing step forward before Everett and Will grabbed him.

"At ease, Mr. Ryan," Jack said calmly, still looking at Tyler.

Tyler smirked at Ryan. He abruptly threw the large black satchel over his shoulder, turned, and left, stepping through the escape trunk and onto the deck.

The doctor nodded for Robbins to go into the elevator first, then he gestured for Everett and the others to follow. He nodded toward the door Collins was supposed to step through.

Jack turned and saw that the hatch behind him had opened without a sound. He cautiously stepped up to the hatchway and looked into the darkened chamber. The giant bubble windows were closed, their clamshell covers in place, allowing no light into the suite. There was only the large chair sitting upon its pedestal and the light from the few computers lining the far bulkhead.

Jack stepped into the large suite and the hatch closed behind him with a soft thrum of noise. He wasn't startled as he turned that way, only curious. Then another hatch opened. He saw a small figure step through, but he couldn't see any details before the light from the outside corridor was cut off. Collins waited.

Slowly the interior lights came up, casting a soft blue glow to the room. Jack saw the figure standing just inside the door, looking around. He smiled slow and wide for the first time in what seemed like years.

"Hello, Short Stuff," he said, almost too low for Sarah to hear, but loud enough to startle her.

As Sarah McIntire turned, she saw the man standing next to the raised command platform. He was thinner and tired looking, but she recognized Jack immediately. She slowly started forward and then almost lost her footing as her legs weakened. Collins stepped up and immediately took her into his arms and held her. Nothing else; he just held on to her. He could feel her soft sobbing and he held her even tighter.

"Was I missed?"

There was no answer from Sarah as she wrapped her own arms around Jack. She just held him tightly and cried.

In her sparse private quarters, Alexandria switched off the monitor that showed the reunion between Jack and Sarah. She swallowed and fought back tears of her own. She knew that a person like her could never have something like what she had just witnessed. Heirthall had chosen her path, and that would never allow anyone into her world. It would cause hesitation, doubt, even lead to a lack of vision. If she lost that, then her world would be lost forever.

She sat on the edge of her small bed, closed her deep blue eyes, and brought her right hand up to her mouth. She took the tablets the doctor had given her and then rubbed her aching legs. The pain was growing more acute in both her legs and her head. According to the doctor, her mobility would soon be threatened.

She slowly reached out and turned the monitor back on. As the pain increased in her head, she found herself becoming angry at the scene before her. She knew it was she who had set up the reunion, but now as she watched, she was becoming enraged. Before she had a chance to reach out and turn the monitor off, she felt a trickle at her left ear. She reached up and swiped at it, and her hand came away with blood. Before she could react, her vision started to cloud. Soon, without her knowing it, she would not be Alexandria Heirthall any longer. She would be Octavian's great-great-granddaughter, and her hate would fill the world.

The doctor opened the door to the forward observation lounge three decks down, stepped aside, and allowed Carl, Jason, and Will to step through.

"Gentlemen, I have duties to attend to, so I will excuse myself for now."

Everett watched Dr. Trevor leave. He then heard Mendenhall and Ryan greeted boisterously inside the lounge. He turned to see the smiling faces of Niles, Alice, the senator, and Virginia hugging his two lieutenants and patting them on the back. Director Compton stepped forward after shaking hands with Ryan and Will and greeted Everett.

"Captain, it's good to see you," Niles said, taking his hand as Virginia stepped up beside him.

"Boss, it's good to see you're all still functioning in this crazy, mixed-up world." After he released Niles's hand, he turned serious. "They separated us from the colonel," he said as his eyes slowly moved to Virginia Pollock.

"Then he really is alive?" Niles asked.

"Yes, sir, he is most definitely. Dr. Pollock, how are you doing?"

"I guess you'll have to tell me, Captain. . . . Just how am I doing?"

Everett smiled to ease the woman's mind.

"You mean, do we believe you're a traitor?"

Niles turned and looked at the two of them.

"No, we don't. We found the real culprit, and even brought the little bastard along for the ride."

"Who?" Niles asked.

"Dr. Gene Robbins," he said, taking Virginia's hand.

Niles found the closest chair and sat down.

Virginia was as shocked as Niles. She took Carl by the hand and pulled him to her. "Thank you," she whispered.

"Son, how in the hell are you?" Senator Lee asked, stepping in and breaking up Everett's awkward moment.

Carl winked at Virginia and then turned to face the senator.

"Well, sir, we've found out quite a bit, but it seems the more history we uncover, the more mysterious this mess gets," Carl said as he shook Lee's hand.

Garrison Lee leaned on his cane and gestured to the many chairs around the long table.

"Well, Captain, we seem to have time on our hands at the moment. Enthrall us as to who this Captain Heirthall really is. We've guessed at a lot, but let's hear the Event Group version."

"You're not going to believe it," was all Everett said, hugging Alice.

"A riddle wrapped in an enigma," Mendenhall said as he poured himself a glass of water.

"Or maybe a nut wrapped up in a shell," Ryan countered.

Sarah led Jack into the observation area without the normal security escort. She watched as Niles, Lee, Virginia, and Alice greeted Jack like a long-lost son and brother.

"Well, I see you didn't bring the cavalry along with you, Jack," Lee said, smiling and clapping the colonel on the shoulder.

"We decided to wait and make sure the cavalry would have a fighting chance before committing them."

"You should have brought them anyway," Lee mumbled as Alice took his free arm.

"If they're needed, they're only a phone call away," Jack said, looking around the observation deck. Sarah silently went to Everett, placed her arms around his waist, and hugged him. Carl kissed the top of her head, and then Sarah sat down silently next to Virginia and Niles to watch Jack reunite with the people he had come to know and respect. She smiled, just taking in his form and face. Virginia reached out, took her hand, and smiled at her.

"I'm happy for you," she whispered.

Sarah looked at the assistant director and became serious.

"It's all for nothing if we don't get the hell off this boat. Every naval vessel in the world is going to try to track us down. The odds of us getting out of here are a little bleak."

Virginia kept smiling and patted her hand. "I think our odds at that survival just went up by at least four percent," she said, looking at the four men before them.

Captain Heirthall finally left her cabin and took the elevator down to deck ten. Once there, she slowly walked through the wide companionway, looking at none of the crew as they greeted her. She didn't even notice First Officer Samuels as he caught up with her. She nodded without really looking at him.

"Captain," Samuels said, noticing the clearness of her eyes once more as she continued on her way.

"The children are all aboard and safe?" she asked, looking straight ahead as she walked.

"Yes, ma'am, they're in the crew's mess, eating."

"Good, I'm on my way there now. Do you have something you wish to report to me, Commander?"

Samuels noticed that although they were presently alone in the companionway, she said "Commander" instead of the more familiar "James."

"Sergeant Tyler has placed the explosives in all the terminal points of the cavern. It should be sufficient to bring the cave formation down into the sea. All material important to *Leviathan* has been loaded aboard, and all supplies are stored. Your family's original journals and research—all the books are aboard and safe."

Alexandria finally stopped and turned to face Samuels. "As soon as Tyler and his men have come aboard, we'll put to sea."

"Aye, Captain." He slowly turned away, noticing her slow gait. "Maybe we can discuss the disposition of the children, now that we are at war? Maybe at dinner tonight?"

Heirthall stopped and half-turned toward Samuels.

"Dinner?" she asked.

Samuels looked around and made sure no one was in earshot. "Yes, ma'am. You requested I have dinner with you at twenty-three hundred."

"The program involving the children will continue, Commander. There will be no need for dinner or further discussion."

Samuels was silent as Heirthall turned and continued on her way.

As Niles and his people were escorted by First Officer Samuels from the observation deck back down to the mess area, Jack walked with Sarah. Collins couldn't get enough of looking at the diminutive geologist, and she was aware that his gaze had never been so intense. She was seeing something she never would have thought possible: a Jack Collins who wasn't afraid to show his feelings. *Maybe all it took to show the way was for both of us to think the other was dead*, she thought to herself.

Mendenhall and Ryan, tagging along in the back of the group, watched the nonverbal way the colonel and Sarah communicated. Sarah would sneak a look at Jack, and then vice versa.

"This is a little creepy," Will said, observing the strangeness of the reunion.

Commander Samuels looked far more reserved than usual, at least to Niles and the others who had had dealings with the first officer.

The crew's mess was full and loud. All the tables were occupied with the exception of one. The first officer gestured for them to be seated. As soon as they had, water glasses and utensils were placed before them by the teenage midshipmen, who it seemed had a hard time concentrating on their duties. They kept looking toward the center of the great galley area at the children who were sitting and eating. Other midshipmen and a few of the adult crew members were standing over them, joking and teasing.

"It seems kids are very popular here," Mendenhall ventured from the far end of the table.

"It brings up the perplexing question of the morality of destroying this vessel with children onboard," Alice said, looking from the children and young midshipmen to the faces around her own table.

For the first time, everyone looked at Jack for a direction. He shook his head and placed his water glass down.

"I have one duty at the moment, and no magic answers for any of you. I plan on getting us off of this technological menagerie as soon as I can find a way. Those children are a part of what's going on here, and whether we find out what that is or not, it makes no difference." He looked from person to person. "We are getting out of here, and letting the professionals who can fight this woman do *their* job."

None of them had ever heard Jack speak in that manner before. The one man who always knew his duty and what was to be done for the greater good of the country now saw things differently. Sarah, for her part, was looking at Jack and seeing a change in him—one that was disturbing to her.

The din in the mess area quieted. All eyes looked to the far end of the galley as a hatch opened. Standing there was Heirthall. She was resplendent in a navy blue frock coat that trailed all the way to the floor. Her white blouse was collarless, and her blue pants cut short to the ankle. Her black hair was shining, pulled to one side, and flowing over her right shoulder.

Jack, Carl, Will, and Ryan stood so they could get their first look at Captain Alexandria Olivia Heirthall.

"Whoa," Ryan mumbled to Mendenhall.

"Take it easy. I have a feeling she isn't your type," Will mumbled.

As for Everett, the first thing he noticed from across the room was the way the woman stood, statuesque, framing herself so that everyone inside could see her. He didn't know if this was arrogance or her natural way. He would hold all his opinions in check until he could see more. One thing was sure in all of their minds—this woman was definitely in her element.

As she stepped inside, the small children, the eldest of whom looked no older than eight or nine, broke from the table they were sitting at. All thirty-two of them rushed toward Captain Heirthall. For the first time since their arrival, Niles and the others saw a smile break out wide across Alexandria's face. She held out her arms and allowed the children to crowd in close. They were reaching for her, and she played her hands over as many of the heads as she could reach. Adult crew members tried their best to hold the children in check.

Alexandria waded in to the children. She was smiling, touching, and then placing her slender fingers along their small faces. The children in turn reached out as if it was the one thing they had to do. Heirthall waved off the adult crew members and midshipmen as they tried to calm the children.

Heirthall plucked one of the younger children from the group—it was a girl, maybe three or four years old. She had been standing on a chair to see the captain. Alexandria kissed the girl on the cheek, hugged her, and then gently handed her off to Samuels, who had joined the captain. The commander leaned in, whispered to the captain, and then nodded toward their table. She looked at the Event Group people and her right brow rose. Then she held her arms up and the room started to settle.

"Our babies . . . welcome aboard!" she said as the older crew members applauded politely.

The midshipmen escorted the small children back to their table.

Alexandria started toward the Group's table, followed by Samuels. When she neared, Niles, Lee, Jack, Carl, Mendenhall, and Ryan stood and half-bowed their greeting, as military men were trained to do.

They watched her smile and nod politely at their gesture, and then the men saw who had joined her. Gene Robbins was now dressed in a blue jumpsuit with the standard ~L~ on the breast pocket.

"These," she started to say as she gestured toward the children, "are why we are doing what we are doing. They are our life, our light, and I daresay, our future—orphans from your world who came here and found a family."

"Captain, we fight for children all over the world—live and die for them. Can you explain why one group of children is worth the murder of multitudes, while others starve in isolated pockets throughout the world? Just why are these children any different than those whom you will starve and freeze with your actions?"

"By helping this special group of children, we may help others, Dr. Compton. May I sit and join you? I'm quite hungry."

Compton dipped his head. He looked to the other standing men of his group, gesturing for them to sit also, as his eyes fell on Dr. Robbins. "If it's all the same to you, Captain, I would prefer if this man ate at another table," Niles said.

"Hear, hear," Lee agreed.

Robbins had the extreme audacity to look stunned and hurt as he faced his former friends.

"I can assure you, Dr. Compton," Alexandria said, pulling out her chair, assisted by Robbins holding it for her, "Gene Robbins is a man of the highest character. His only crime is that he has a higher priority than most. He loved your Group, and for every little bit of information he passed on to me, he forfeited some of his soul."

"Not enough," Niles said, placing his napkin back into his lap. "However, madam, it is your table and your vessel; I bow to your wishes."

Alexandria patted Robbins on the hand and whispered to him that he should sit.

"Captain, I would not want to ruin the appetites of your guests. Perhaps I can visit with the children for a while." He tried to look at Carl, but found he couldn't hold the captain's gaze.

"You are excused, Doctor. We can talk later."

Robbins half-bowed and then walked over to Everett.

"You don't understand anything, Captain, but then again, how could you?" He leaned in close to Carl. "You always act without thinking." Robbins then dropped something in Everett's lap. The move was quick and no one sitting at the table was the wiser. Robbins looked at the others and then left quickly.

"He has been hurt deeply. He asked that he not be released from his duties at your agency if he was able to pass on information to me without getting caught." Alexandria looked at Everett. "He said he had found a home with people he admired and trusted. He singled you out, Captain Everett, as a man he admired."

Everett stared back at the captain. He didn't rise to any bait she might be laying out; instead he placed his hands in his lap and found the item Robbins had dropped.

"You will learn before we set you ashore that he had the highest motives," she said as her salad was placed before her. She immediately started eating.

"I've noticed a change in you since the last time we saw you, Captain. Can we explain that away by the presence of the children you have picked up here on Saboo?" Alice asked.

Heirthall dabbed at her mouth with her napkin, then looked from face to face as she placed her elegant hands underneath her chin.

"Yes, you can," she answered, and then she turned to look at Jack and Sarah with mild curiosity.

"Captain, I'm curious, the treasure mentioned in regard to your ancestor—was it real, or was that just a flight of fancy by Alexandre Dumas?" Ryan asked.

"The subject interests you, Lieutenant Ryan?" she asked, her eyes finally leaving Jack and Sarah.

"Only from a standpoint of . . ." He looked at Jack and then Everett. ". . . literature, of course."

Alexandria smiled. She liked the young naval officer; he was blunt and forthcoming, and did not hold a lie well.

"Yes, Mr. Ryan, the treasure really existed, or still exists, I should say, as I have explained to your companions. Of course, we need none of it today; we have found plenty to keep our operations safe and secure without ruining the values of every precious gem, gold, or antiquities market in the world."

"Is it onboard?" Ryan asked with hopefulness in his eyes.

"No, the weight of it alone would sink *Leviathan* right to the bottom of the sea. It's in one of the most inaccessible places in the world."

"Is it—"

"Lieutenant, I think we've covered that subject about as far as we need to," Jack said, frowning at Ryan.

"I have a question, Captain," Collins said, turning away from an embarrassed Ryan.

"Yes, Colonel?"

"Your security force, how large is it?"

"One hundred and seventy. We can deal with most land elements in Special Operations if need be."

"I would think that is a rather large contingent just for the security of *Leviathan*," Jack said, probing.

Heirthall pushed her plate away and looked at Collins. She was silent for a time as she studied him.

"You need not make any bold plans, Colonel. The reasons for bringing you aboard . . . well, to put it frankly, they are moot at this point. Plans have changed. Your time onboard *Leviathan* is at an end."

Samuels, sitting next to Heirthall, barely moved his eyes, but Jack and Niles saw that this information was news to him.

"All hands, prepare for getting under way. We are at defense condition two throughout the boat. Midshipmen, secure the young in the aft pressure dome." The announcement ended their lunch.

A young lieutenant gave Commander Samuels a message, then left the table. The first officer passed it onto Heirthall, who wadded the flimsy thing into a ball and stood. She was tense as she half-bowed and then left the table, quickly escorted by four of Tyler's security men.

"If you'll come with me, we're preparing to dive. We have detected the *Missouri* sitting offshore, so we will immediately run into deep waters," Samuels said as he stood. "Security will take you to the observation deck."

"You'll not take offensive action against *Missouri*, will you?" Lee asked.

"Our actions will be defensive in nature, Senator. *Leviathan* will run deep; no vessel in the world can out-dive us. If they choose to follow, that is of no concern to the captain. Now, please, follow me."

"How deep can this thing go?" Mendenhall asked nervously as he stood with the others to follow the commander.

"I don't know," Ryan said to him, "but the crush depth for most American boats is sixteen hundred feet, some even less."

"Oh, shit," was all Will could say as he and the others felt the first tingling of fear.

As they were on their way to the observation deck, escorted by ten security men, Everett slid in beside Jack and handed him something. Collins, without acknowledging the move, deftly opened a small piece of paper that had been folded several times.

"It's from our little computer nerd. He passed it to me in the mess."

Jack quickly looked down at the precise block letters of the note. It was only five words: SOMETHING IS WRONG WITH HEIRTHALL.

"What do you think?" Everett mumbled.

"This only confirms what we already suspect. The added element here is that our Dr. Robbins is saying the captain has changed since their last meeting. That means if he's worried, we should be, too."

Sarah stepped in to ask what was up when Sergeant Tyler and another security team approached them. They were all heavily armed, and they all sported their Nomex/seaweed assault gear. The Event Group was surrounded just outside of the observation deck.

"The use of deadly force against you has been authorized by the captain if you attempt any sort of offensive move, or if you attempt to communicate with the outside world. This status will be in effect until you depart this vessel." Tyler looked directly at Collins, then gestured for his men to take the Group into the observation deck. He then grabbed Jack's arm and held him in place.

"It's time you and I had a little talk, Colonel."

Collins didn't say anything. He looked from Tyler to Sarah, who hesitated at the door. Then he rose, looked at her sternly, and nodded toward the hatchway, indicating that she go with the others. Niles placed his arm around Sarah, and with a stern look at Tyler moved inside the hatchway. Everett, Ryan, and Mendenhall followed—each giving the sergeant warning looks. When they were all inside, one of the two security men reached out and dogged the hatch.

"I need to know why the captain was adamant about having your people aboard *Leviathan*, and don't hand me that crap about needing information about what your agency knew about her and her family."

"Even if I remembered my time onboard *Leviathan* the first time around, I wouldn't tell you a damn thing, Sergeant."

"Colonel, if I don't get an answer as to why your director and the others were brought here, I will find a way to kill someone very close to you. Now answer me."

The cold demeanor of the security man brought Jack to the conclusion that Heirthall had lost control of at least part of her command. If Tyler was against her in some form or another, Collins knew he might have to take his chances with the madwoman over the man standing in front of him. His instincts told him that this man was a killer—once more, he could see in his eyes that he enjoyed it.

Jack didn't respond to the threat he had leveled at Sarah. He just smiled, his eyes never leaving Tyler's own.

"Why are you here?"

"Tyler, I will say this to you. You are one of those people I will not mind killing."

The sergeant smiled and acted as if to turn away, but instead brought up the sidearm hidden at his side and smashed Jack on the side of the head. Collins staggered, then went down to a knee. Tyler stood over him and brought the pistol down into Jack's skull. The colonel collapsed to the deck.

"What is the meaning of this?!"

Tyler turned to see Samuels standing at the junction of the companionway. His face was screwed into an angry mask as he quickly stepped to where Collins was trying to rise. Samuels assisted Jack to his feet.

"What in the hell do you think you're doing, Tyler? Consider yourself on report. Now get to your diving station and remain there. You'll be brought up at captain's mast. Now get out," he said with a growl. "Colonel, we have to get you attended to."

"Take Captain America here to sickbay," Tyler ordered his two men, and then he turned and walked off without acknowledging Samuels.

Heirthall's first officer felt the authority of the chain of command starting to slip away as *Leviathan* ran full speed into harm's way.

16

Niles and the other members of the Event Group were seated in front of the observation windows as Heirthall walked over to the main console lining the inner hull and depressed the intercom.

"Mr. Samuels, take *Leviathan* down to three hundred feet. Maintain zero bubble, keel at thirty feet above the cave floor. Prepare for a flank run out of the access tunnel to the sea just in case our unwanted American boat is still watching."

"Captain, with the repairs incomplete on the damaged sections to the hull and planes, we will leave a wake and sound signature."

"I am well aware of that, Mr. Samuels. You have your orders. As soon as we have entered the access tunnel, have Mr. Tyler set off his mainline detonation." Heirthall turned away from the main console and sat in a chair fronting the observation windows that now held the hologram.

The great black hull of *Leviathan* slipped slowly under the calm waters of the interior lagoon. As her hull started taking on the minute pressures of the shallow dive, her amazing skin started to depress in on itself, actually getting stronger as the pressure increased. There were seventeen layers of spun titanium and nylon material in her hull that could depress and expand with the rigors of deep ocean travel. This makeup of hull matrix, and the difficulty in making the elements adhere to each other in its composite form, was one hundred and twenty years ahead of the General Dynamics Electric Boat Division of the United States.

Leviathan went to three hundred feet; her giant thrusters fore and aft maneuvered her until she was pointed toward the thousand-foot access tunnel that would lead her to her natural element—the open sea.

On the hologram projected onto the closed observation doors, the control center was shown in bright detail from three decks below them. The image only took up a portion of the viewing screen. The rest showed a computer-generated image of the access tunnel and the waters beyond. Niles watched as the crew of *Leviathan* went about their work. Commander Samuels was in his normal place, standing beside the empty captain's chair with his arms crossed over his chest.

"Helm, steer three-five-seven, all ahead at ten knots. Increase speed by increments of twenty knots as we traverse the cave."

"Aye, Mr. Samuels, estimate full speed will be achieved upon exit of the tunnel at one hundred thirty-seven knots."

"Thank you, Mr. Hind."

Heirthall closed her eyes and smiled as *Leviathan* started her forward run. To Compton it was if she herself were *Leviathan*, and it seemed Heirthall felt better as she began to move.

"Sergeant Tyler, you may do your duty," Samuels said on the hologram.

A hundred feet down the long row of technicians, Sergeant Tyler was sitting at one of the ten weapons stations.

"With the captain's permission," he said, flipping up a plastic door and then, without hesitation, pushing the red button underneath.

The cave walls and ceiling gave a mighty heave as the two-megaton nuclear weapon detonated. *Leviathan* heaved forward when the first pressure wave struck her, and was suddenly pushed to the side as heated water from the cave fought to escape the collapsing home of the great boat. Her port thrusters shot out twenty thousand pounds of water pressure to keep the giant submarine from smashing into the cave's wall.

Heirthall now stood as the first of the tremors settled far behind them and the giant submarine finally settled.

"The first home I ever knew is now gone," she said beneath her breath. "Commander Samuels, take us out of here. I'll be in auxiliary control." She turned and faced Virginia. "Ginny, would you care to accompany me?"

On the surface of the Pacific, Saboo Atoll exploded. The mountainous center fell in and then expanded outward, forming a mushroom-shaped cloud filled with microparticles of melted rock and coral that had made up the small atoll.

As *Leviathan* broke free of the access tunnel, Alexandria sat quietly in her large chair. She watched the end of the tunnel slide by through the now-open portals in the conning tower. Bright lighting illuminated the passing water; Virginia felt the smallest of vibrations as *Leviathan* started her run up to flank speed.

"Captain, we have one submerged contact close-aboard, four thousand yards dead-ahead. Prop signature has been identified as our old friend the *Missouri*," Samuels said.

"I felt them out there long before sonar detected them, Commander. All hands are to stand by for evasive maneuvering," she said with her eyes closed.

"Yes, ma'am. All hands stand by for evasive maneuvering. All nonessential personnel are to remain in their cabins—seal all watertight compartments."

"Brace yourself, Ginny," Alexandria said as she finally opened her eyes wide and looked through the floating hologram in front of her. She saw the vaguest outlines of USS *Missouri*. She could also see that they were starting a run on *Leviathan*. The American boat was going to give chase, thinking all the while their stealth technology kept them hidden.

"The damage to our outer skin has made us visible just enough for *Missouri* to get a fix on us," Alexandria said. She dipped her head and settled her eyes on the sleek-bodied Virginia class boat ahead of *Leviathan*. "They think we can't see them because of what they view as a superior technology. Little do they know they have been defeated by the oldest technology in the world: eyesight."

Virginia watched as rivulets of sweat broke out on Heirthall's forehead.

Alexandria's blue eyes blazed as she pushed both control sticks to the right, taking *Leviathan* hard and down in that direction. Then she pushed only the left stick, and the giant submarine dived even harder, bringing Virginia up out of her chair. Only her harness kept her body from crashing into the overhead.

On the hologram, the depiction of *Missouri* went to the left and up a hundred feet in a vain attempt to head *Leviathan* off.

"Captain, *Missouri* has acquired the noise from our damaged outer skin and planes. She is attempting to follow."

"Commander, we're going to full emergency speed and full dive on the planes. We'll be bringing ballast control to one hundred percent—all hands prepare for emergency dive, steering three three-four degrees. Start injecting the hydrogen and helium mix into the hull plates!"

"All hands, prepare for deepwater dive. Close all inner hatches and seal main bulkhead doors. Close all observation windows, secure all departments, stand by for hull reinforcement for extreme pressure dive!"

"Where are you taking us, Alex?" Virginia asked over the increasing whine of *Leviathan*'s thermal-dynamic drive and its four power plants as it pushed raw steam and hydrogen into her jet system.

" 'So all men will know, I am the Lord God of the Sea—thy name is *Leviathan*!' " Alexandria mumbled, not hearing Virginia.

"Alex—for God's sake!"

Alexandria fixed Virginia with calm demeanor. "A quote from Octavian," she said finally with her eyes fluttering, and then she lost some of the intensity. "We're going to the most inaccessible part of the world, my Ginny—a place where men cannot follow in their toy ships—the Mariana Trench!"

Virginia was tossed back into her chair as *Leviathan* increased her speed to almost two hundred knots. As the observation window screens closed, Virginia could see the steam and heat rising from the sleek black hull. *Leviathan* fought for the deep, actually creating friction in the cold seas surrounding her.

"We're going to *Leviathan*'s world, Ginny—we're going to my world."

Virginia cringed at the calm words of her friend—finally realizing there was no going back to the real world for Alexandria Heirthall.

"Alex, what in God's name has a hold on you?" Virginia screamed above the din of surging power.

Leviathan was now headed for the deepest part of the known world, and she was going there at two hundred and thirty miles per hour, faster than any seagoing object in the history of humankind.

———

As the crash doors closed over the observation widows, the last thing the members of the Event Group saw was the fleeting image of USS *Missouri* as *Leviathan* went headlong in front of her. Then a violent downward turn sent them high into their seats and slammed them back down as the giant submarine maneuvered hard to starboard, then to port, and then dived beneath the thermal cline on her way to deep water.

The Event Group silenced as the world turned upside down and the great submarine rolled. A few dishes and bar bottles fell and shattered; then *Leviathan* righted herself.

"I can't begin to understand the science involved here—helium-hydrogen mix? Has she found a way to defeat the very pressures of the ocean depths along with the physics of the planet?" Lee asked aloud.

Niles Compton looked at the green holographic readout below the depiction of the onrushing seafloor.

"Captain Everett, do you know these coordinates?" Compton called out loudly over the din of the engines at full power.

"Eleven twenty-one North latitude and one-forty-two twelve East longitude," Everett said to himself. Then he looked at the flat expanse of seafloor highlighted in holographic blues rushing toward them. "Jesus Christ," Everett shouted, "everyone hold on tight—this crazy woman just may be on a suicide run."

"Explain, Captain," Lee asked loudly as the observation deck began to flicker and then went out, leaving the only light the green, red, and blue colors of the massive hologram in front of them.

"That ocean bottom coming straight at us is what's called the Abysmal Shelf. The mountainous area to the front is the continental plate of Asia. We can only be headed for one place—where no attack submarine in the world can follow—the Mariana Trench!"

Mendenhall and Ryan exchanged looks. When Captain Everett got scared, that meant they were going into the extreme of all dangers.

The green readout started pumping out numbers that were hard to follow as *Leviathan* ran deep.

"Captain, *Missouri* is giving chase at their maximum speed of forty-seven knots!" Samuels announced over the intercom from his station in control.

"The *Missouri* will never catch us; she better turn and head for home. They're already too deep!" Everett said as the hologram split into two sections to show *Leviathan*'s bow and stern and the computer-generated depiction of the *Missouri*.

"God, she's a fast boat, but she has to turn away," Everett said proudly, even as he prayed *Missouri*'s captain would give up.

"Turn away, damn it!" Niles said as he watched *Missouri* three miles behind.

"Four thousand meters—thirteen thousand feet deep!" Everett called out. "We're at the deepest part of the Pacific Ocean—there's the Trench!"

As they watched, the black image of the Mariana Trench grew in scope before their eyes. It was rushing at them just as *Leviathan*'s inner hull started to bend inward, and to the amazement of all, they actually witnessed the composite material shimmer in the dark as its matrix started changing right before their eyes. The interior hull looked as if it were sweating as the composite fibers tightened, making itself stronger against the depths.

"How can this material take this depth?" Niles asked just as the pressure in the boat started to increase, making them all dizzy and grabbing their heads.

"How deep is the trench, Carl?" Sarah asked as she watched Everett pull his harness tighter.

"If you sank Mount Everest to the bottom of the trench, there would still be more than seven thousand feet of water above it."

"Can this damn thing hold up to that pressure?"

"It's been rumored for years that General Dynamics Electric Boat Division has been working on a chemical-electrical mix that would reinforce a composite design for deepwater submergence, but this is far beyond anything ever dreamed."

Mendenhall and Ryan were shaking as hard as *Leviathan* herself. Will closed his eyes and started praying.

"I think we're too close to the depths of hell for that to help!" Ryan called out.

Virginia watched Alexandria's eyes narrow once more to slits as *Leviathan* screamed for the deepest part of the world.

"Captain, the thermal-dynamic drive is going into the red; the reactors have been running at one hundred and twenty percent power for three minutes. Estimate power plant scram in thirty-eight seconds!"

"Maintain current power output, Commander. We need this demonstration for the benefit of our American friends."

There was a momentary silence from the control center, and then Samuels answered. "Aye, Captain, maintaining one hundred and twenty percent on the reactors."

The sound of the hull compressing did not affect the crew of *Leviathan* as she entered the trench. Three miles distant, *Missouri* still came on.

"Fools, they can't take this depth. They must turn away!" Heirthall screamed, watching the jagged scar depicting the gaping maw of the world's deepest valley open up fully before *Leviathan*.

Outside *Leviathan*, the topmost walls of the Mariana Trench slid by and the giant submarine disappeared into the blackness of the abyss, a place far more deadly and inhospitable than the deepest reaches of outer space.

"Look," Everett called out. "*Missouri* is turning away and heading for the surface."

"Why in the hell did she risk imploding like that?" Alice asked.

"Because they had to try," Sarah said, thinking about Jack.

The observation deck became quiet as they watched the hologram turn to black. As they entered the trench, the computer-enhanced depiction of the giant *Leviathan* started to lessen the steepness of her dive.

Once in sickbay, the two guards unceremoniously tossed Jack onto one of the unoccupied beds. They turned and left without a word to Dr. Trevor, who watched without comment. He checked Collins and quickly found his problem.

Thirty minutes later, Jack slowly came around. The doctor was nowhere to be seen. Collins rubbed the gash in his head, which Trevor had cleaned, stitched with six very neat stitches, and dressed with a small bandage.

Jack looked around until his eyes fell on a man staring at him from one of the six beds in the clinic area. The pale blue eyes never blinked, never moved. Collins knew him immediately. Jack made sure he wasn't feeling any ill effects from the blow to his head, then sat up and slowly walked over to the occupied bed.

"Colonel," Jack said, sitting on the bed next to the Frenchman. "Sarah told me you had booked passage on this little cruise."

Farbeaux said nothing as he fought slowly to sit up in his bed. He was grimacing a little more than he actually had to.

"Look, I heard what you did for Sarah at the complex, and I—"

"Let us dispense with the pleasantries, Colonel," Farbeaux said as he looked at Jack. "Young Sarah had to have also told you why I was there in the first place. I was willing to let things go with the news of your supposed death, but now I see and feel that this can no longer be accomplished."

Jack smiled and shook his head.

"So, you want to kill me?" he asked.

"Yes."

"Because you lost Danielle in the Amazon?"

"No."

"Really? Then what is your reasoning?"

"I do not like myself, and you, Colonel, are the architect of that."

"Well, that puts us at cross-purposes, Henri, because I like myself a lot. I've been there, so I don't want to die again. If it makes you feel better, though, I don't like you, either. However, I still want to live and have no desire to kill you. Where does that leave us?"

"We all want what we cannot have. I will kill you and I will feel better for it." Farbeaux looked away and then back after completing a thought. "However, since we both find ourselves in a rather strange predicament here in fantasyland, I am willing to forgo my hostility toward you until such time as we are freed. Then I can kill you and Captain Everett at the same time, and at my leisure. So unless that can be accomplished during our escape from this vessel and without altering my own fortunes, we will call a truce until such a time as we can take up old habits."

Jack reached out and patted Farbeaux on the leg near his wounded hip, making the Frenchman jump in pain. This time he didn't have to act at all.

"Okay, Henri, once we're out of here, we can resume the game. Until then, I can definitely use your penchant for planning, cheating, lying, and being one sneaky bastard."

"It will do no good to flatter me, Colonel."

When the doctor left sickbay half an hour later, he escorted Collins back to his Group and then made his rounds of the departments, checking for deep submergence sickness amongst the crew. Henri Farbeaux eased himself out of his bed. He steadied himself, then slowly limped into Dr. Trevor's private office. He saw the file cabinet where he had watched the doctor place Jack Collins's file. It wasn't locked. Because of that, he wasn't interested enough to check it. He went down the three rows of drawers until he came to one cabinet secured by a built-in lock.

"Eureka," he said, smiling as he removed a small clip he had stolen from his own IV drip. He twisted and bent it until he had the shape he wanted, then inserted it into the lock. He raised his brows when he heard the click and the lock disengaged.

"A little too trusting, Doctor," he whispered as he pulled the drawer open.

There were at least three hundred thick files inside. He recognized some of the names as crewmen onboard *Leviathan*. When he didn't find the one he wanted, he opened another cabinet. Then his eyes caught the one file he wanted. He pulled out the thick chart and then closed the drawer.

He looked at the name again—Captain Alexandria Olivia Heirthall.

Belowdecks, Samuels watched as reactor numbers three and four went offline. He maintained reactor one at 50 percent for pressure control, and took power down on reactor two to 60 percent, maintaining life support and their current speed at thirty-five knots.

"Mr. Samuels now has the conn," Alexandria said from her observation suite.

Commander Samuels took a deep breath as the sound of the four reactors started winding down, and *Leviathan* slowed as they went deeper into the trench.

Outside the pressure hull, *Leviathan* continued on a journey to a spot in the earth's depths, where the hull would be taking on twenty-eight tons per square inch. The magic of the Heirthall science was the only thing keeping every man, woman, and child onboard from being crushed to the size of a microbe—and still she went deeper.

The final deep run of the magical *Leviathan* had begun.

PART FOUR

FROM HELL'S HEART

Why does man believe that intelligence, coupled with thumbs, sets him apart from the rest of the natural world? It is the soul of a creature that truly sets species apart, and in that regard, humankind is sorely lacking, and thus has created Hell upon his Earth.

—Captain Octavian Heirthall, 1865

17

"I have no idea where to go from here," Jack said to Carl, far away from the others. He felt the bandage on the top of his head.

"We're too deep for any sort of attack on the crew, at any rate, Jack."

"Right now that's the only saving grace—she can't kill anyone down here because she's the only person in the world who can go this damn deep."

Everett was about to respond when the hatchway opened and Sergeant Tyler stepped into the observation compartment with four of his security men. They were quickly followed by Virginia and Captain Heirthall.

The security team took up station on either side of the hatchway with their automatic weapons at the ready across their chests. Virginia walked in with her head lowered and joined Alice, Sarah, and the senator at the large table. Niles took a step forward, but Tyler held his hand up to stop him from advancing.

"Has it been reported to you that your Sergeant Tyler here nearly killed Colonel Collins? Did he do it of his own accord, or was he acting on your orders?"

Alexandria Heirthall sat in the nearest chair and closed her eyes as she felt the rush of the Demerol finally taking effect. Then she looked at

Compton. She mentally fought the urge to turn on Tyler, instead looking at Jack.

"My apologies, Colonel, for the sergeant's temper. We are all under
tremendous strain."

"Is that what you call it? My God, woman, you and your trained killer
are damn well out of control!" Lee said, pointing at Tyler with his cane.
This time Alice didn't try to silence him.

"And now do you believe that the world will sit idly by and have you
threaten the starvation of millions of people? Men like the ones onboard
Missouri will keep hunting you," Niles said as calmly as he could.

"I'll do what I can for the survival of my people, my vessel, and for
the life in the seas, Dr. Compton. Moreover, I have never once doubted
the bravery of your nation's submariners. I just thank God they have a
captain that understands the limitations of American naval science."

Alexandria finally seemed to focus with dilated eyes as the heavy
dose of Demerol hit her system in earnest. She looked into the faces staring at her from around the observation deck. Then she stood with what
looked like grim determination, fighting the helping as well as the de-
bilitating effects of the drugs in her system.

She paced to the front of the compartment, then stopped and turned
to face the Event Group. Virginia was now seeing a very different woman
from the one she had seen less than thirty minutes before, maniacally
piloting *Leviathan* on her deep run into the trench. She was now calm,
and although drugged, seemed more in control emotionally.

At that moment, Commander Samuels stepped into the compartment and stayed by the hatchway. Alexandria gestured for him to come
forward.

"My apologies, James," she whispered near his ear. Her eyelids fluttered, closed, then opened. "I believe it's time I explain a few things to
you and our guests. Please stand by the hatchway, and take this." Alexandria slipped a small .32-caliber pistol into his hand. He pocketed it and
then turned away.

She cleared her throat and waited for Samuels to take his station.

"My ancestor, Roderick Deveroux Heirthall, was the first to discover
what I am about to reveal to you."

Tyler looked from Samuels to Heirthall. His features were twisted
and ugly.

"Captain, I ask you not to do this," the sergeant said, taking what everyone thought was a menacing step toward Heirthall. "These people won't understand. No one will."

"Sergeant Tyler," Alexandria said, looking fatigued, "you are relieved. Report to your quarters, and inform security to stand down." She steadied herself against the sill of the observation window.

Tyler abruptly turned to the hatchway and then out of the compartment, roughly brushing by Samuels. His security team quickly followed him.

Heirthall nodded and Samuels closed the hatch. She rubbed the back of her head, then shook her head as she advanced toward the glass where Niles was standing.

"Now." She looked up at Compton, who stood challengingly before her. "I believe we are at a point in the trench system where we can begin to answer some of your questions, Dr. Compton." She reached into her pocket and brought out a small bottle of pills. Without looking, she turned the bottle up, and shook two pills into her mouth, and dry-swallowed them. "Then I will tell you the reason why you are here."

Alexandria nodded toward Samuels, who moved to the control chair and threw a switch. The protective shields of the massive observation windows began to part. To the Event Group it was as if they were looking deep into the darkest void in the entire world. As their eyes started adjusting to that blackness, they began to see the swirl of unnatural colors surrounding the bow of the giant vessel. A glow of bluish-green light extended outward to almost to sixty feet, showing a sight that no man outside the crew of *Leviathan* had ever seen before.

"The combination of helium, hydrogen, and our electrical field is what you are seeing. In essence, the field is assisting in pushing back the very pressures of the sea, actually forming a bubble of depressurized water around our compressed hull." Alexandria again had to hold on tightly to the sill in order to keep her balance, but she continued, as she knew her time in control was short. "Even though the pressure of the abyss is still seeping through, it is controlled, being held at bay by the combination of our electrical field and *Leviathan*'s composite design. Dr. Compton, if you will, go forward and touch the observation window, please."

Niles stepped toward the acrylic window and then looked back at Heirthall, who nodded for him to continue. He placed his fingers against the glass and felt the extreme coldness. Then, to his surprise, the glass was soft and pliable under his touch.

"The entire composite matrix of *Leviathan* has been altered. We are not fighting the pressure of the deep so much as we have become a part of it."

Alexandria nodded at Samuels, who hit a switch and spoke into a hidden microphone.

"Conn, this is Commander Samuels. Bring the exterior lighting to one hundred percent, please. Helm, dead slow."

"Aye, Commander, slowing to two knots, floodlights coming on at full illumination."

"I tell you this not to explain the dynamics of *Leviathan*, but rather to show you just how extreme an environment we are in, and the magic of what this environment holds."

At that time, Henri Farbeaux, assisted by the doctor, entered the observation lounge carrying his robe bundled in one arm. Henri placed the crutch he was using against the conference table and then sat. The doctor seemed interested in what was happening and moved to the side of the compartment. Farbeaux, for his part, looked at Collins and gave a slight nod of his head. Jack understood that Henri had come across something in sickbay.

As the Event Group tuned toward the large and expansive windows, the deep sea opened up around them and the blackest night became day. There were audible gasps from Alice and Sarah.

"My God," was all Niles Compton could utter.

The view of the depths showed the far southern wall of the Mariana Trench. There were crags and ridges common to undersea ranges, but interspersed in the wall were small holes. Billions of them, each hole aligned with its neighbor. Lined up straight in many rows, they looked ancient to the eyes of the Group, as though excavated a million years before. Samuels hit another control, and the center viewing window glazed over and then magnified the wall of the trench at one of its many bends. Then the engineering of the openings became apparent. They were actually small arches that could never have been created naturally by the currents and tides of the ocean.

"It looks like the Anasazi Indian ruins of the Southwest," Sarah said as she recognized the high arches of the small excavations.

"Exactly what my great-great-grandfather said when he first saw them in eighteen fifty-three, only in the much shallower waters off of Venezuela. James, you may order all-ahead standard for the next ten minutes until we reach"—she smiled as she looked back at Collins and the others—"the grounds."

"Aye, Captain," Samuels said as he relayed the order, allowing the Group to feel the minute acceleration of *Leviathan*.

Alexandria noticed that the doctor and Farbeaux had joined them. Her attention stayed on Trevor for a moment, enough time to make him feel slightly uncomfortable.

"Doctor, it is fortuitous that you are here. Please explain to Ginny my diagnosis. She seems worried that I am not myself."

Trevor swallowed, but didn't move from his position against the bulkhead. He uncrossed his arms and looked at the many people looking his way. He had no choice but to explain the captain's illness.

"Captain Heirthall's disease is hereditary and one that causes severe cramping, possible blood clots, and hemorrhaging inside the brain. Naturally, all of this places immense pressure on the captain and may cause episodes of severe mood swings, even schizophrenic behavior. I will tell you, since obviously the captain has not, this illness is fatal; all of her family has succumbed to it. It's mostly developed in females, thus they succumb at a much younger age."

"For the most part you have described Osler's disease, Dr. Trevor," Collins said, looking at Farbeaux, who returned the look with mild surprise. "One of the symptoms you described is not listed in her family history as being a part of Osler's."

Trevor looked from Jack to Heirthall, who was watching him closely. He cleared his throat. "And that is?"

"There is no history of schizophrenia attached to the description of the illness," Collins said, waiting for a reaction. There was none because Heirthall continued talking as though his comment regarding her illness had never been made. If this was done intentionally Jack didn't know. However, he did observe Heirthall's gaze linger for an extra moment on Trevor.

"My compliments, Colonel, your research justifies my suspicion that your Group knew more about my family than my crew believed. Now please, all of you take a seat. We have much to discuss, and I'm sure after I have finished, you will have more questions," Alexandria said, cutting the doctor's explanation off before it started.

As they sat, they all could see that Alexandria was functioning much better with all of the pain medication, although her eyes were hazy and unfocused. It was a testament to her will power.

"I need to ask some questions of you first. Senator Lee, whose knowledge in natural history is far beyond most, is a good person to start with, since his hatred for me is so hard to hide."

There was no protest of innocence from the senator; only a stern countenance as he waited.

"Answer quickly, Senator, and keep your answers to one or two words if you will. The first answer that comes into your mind—are you ready?" she asked as she looked from Lee to the others around the large table.

"Fire away, Captain," Lee said as he patted Alice on her hand, trying to tell her he would keep his cool.

"Excellent. Answer 'true' or 'false' to these questions about the Event Group's vast archives."

"If it's games you would like to play, have at it, young lady—especially if it keeps you from killing."

"Flying saucers?" Alexandria asked, ignoring the senator's comment.

Lee smiled knowingly. "True."

"A large animal in Loch Ness?"

"Once true, but no longer. The species finally went extinct during World War Two."

Ryan and Mendenhall looked at Alice at the same time and with the same question etched on their faces. She only nodded her head.

"Bigfoot?" Alexandria asked quickly, trying not to give the senator time to think.

"No hard evidence—false."

"Yeti?"

"Again, no credible evidence—false."

"Mermaids?"

"Myth, fairy tale—false."

"Wrong. True," Heirthall said, shocking the Group.

Everyone in the room looked over at the captain of *Leviathan*, confirming beyond anyone's doubts that she had lost her mind.

"You did very well, Senator; three out of four."

"What sort of nonsense is this?" Lee asked, looking angry at being played for a fool.

"A bit melodramatic, I agree; however, it was just too tempting, Senator. The excavations you have just seen were accomplished by a life form that predates our human existence by twenty-three million years—give or take a millennium."

"Mermaids, please," Ryan said, looking the smallest bit hopeful.

"That's just what my ancestor referred to them as. He was a mystical man, after all. He first thought they were angels that had come to take him to a better place—so what is more fanciful, angels or mermaids? They actually saved him from sure death when he escaped a French prison."

"The Château d'If," Farbeaux said aloud.

"Yes, the very same. He would have drowned upon his escape, but a group of what we now know as symbiants saved him. He was lucky, as this group of small symbiants was no longer indigenous to the Atlantic. They accidentally came upon Roderick Deveroux, the father of Octavian Heirthall, the man who built the first *Leviathan*."

"You call them symbiants. Why?" Compton asked.

Alexandria lowered her head and then paced to the observation window.

"Because they can live inside of a human host," Farbeaux answered for her, finally speaking up from his chair.

"Score one for you, Henri," Jack said, nodding in the Frenchman's direction.

"When Roderick Deveroux discovered them," the Frenchman continued, looking from Collins to Alexandria, "they were a dying species. At only four to five feet long, and grown from an octopuslike body, like a cocoon, they were formally known as *Octopiheirthollis*."

"Impressive, Colonel Farbeaux," Alexandria said, looking not at Henri but Dr. Trevor. "Continue, by all means." Her eyes flicked to Commander Samuels, who nodded once and then moved his attention to Trevor.

"They eventually shed their outer shell. They are like us in skeletal structure, but that is where the resemblance ends. They have a clear membrane they use as an outer skin, gelatinous to our eyes. They live in the deepest part of our seas. One of the last known areas, outside of the Pacific and the Gulf of Mexico, was in the Mediterranean. That was why *Leviathan* was there during the Atlantis incident that nearly claimed the life of Colonel Collins, much to my personal horror."

"The children," Jack said, more to himself than to anyone in particular.

"Yes, the children," Heirthall said, turning away from the window where she had been listening. "You must explain to me your vast knowledge on the subject, Colonel Farbeaux."

Henri unwrapped his robe and tossed the book-sized medical chart and history onto the table. He opened it, pulled one sheet of paper out, and passed it to Jack. The colonel read it, then placed it in his pocket.

"I'm what you would call a speed reader, Captain. You'll forgive my inquisitive nature. Colonel Collins, I have done my part."

"That you have, Colonel," Jack said.

"I think I understand," Virginia said, wanting to approach her old friend but staying well back. "They are symbiant with the human children, two beings living in the same body—you've taken them from the seas to protect them."

"My Ginny, you see, don't you? All of the small children onboard are the last of the Gulf of Mexico young."

"That's why the strenuous attacks on Venezuela and Texas City?" Lee asked.

"Yes. That is why we will continue attacking until the gulf is emptied of production platforms and all oil facilities. There can be no negotiation on that point. Now for the hardest truth of all—the midshipmen, the teenagers onboard, used to live right outside of these windows. They are the very last of these marvelous creatures from the trench. Only a few adults remain here. The very first of their kind."

"Where did you get the human element for this cross-breeding?" Niles asked.

"They are throwaways, Dr. Compton—children that your world could not, or would not, save. Third-world, dying children; starving, disease-ridden, saved by us—saved by the introduction of symbiants into their systems. They both use each other to live. When they grow too large, other hosts will be found for the syms. The midshipmen have the eldest of the young inside of them, but they must be removed soon, or both will die. The syms are starting to grow beyond the human brain's capacity to hold them."

"What gives you the right to take children against their will?" Virginia demanded.

"I saved them; my ancestors saved them, just like we are still saving them . . . not from natural extinction, but from the human element of this planet. The trillion tons of pollution you have sent into the seas from petroleum and the fall of acid rain are killing this life form."

Just as she stopped talking, the hatchway opened, and the young woman they knew as Yeoman Alvera stepped inside. She looked from person to person until her eyes settled upon Dr. Trevor. Then her gaze wandered to Henri Farbeaux.

"Why have you left your station in control, Yeoman?" Samuels asked.

"It's all right, James; part of her knows she's home. Allow her in," Alexandria said. "Come here, Felicia."

They watched as Alvera slowly approached Heirthall. Once standing before her, Alexandria turned the young girl to face them, keeping her hands on her small shoulders.

"Yeoman Alvera is from Nicaragua. I found her fourteen years ago in a small village where she had just witnessed the execution of her parents by a death squad. When a shore excursion found her, she was starving to death. Dr. Trevor saw a long and painful recovery for her. I ordered one of the symbiants placed inside of her, where it wrapped around her cerebral cortex. She recovered quickly after that." She gestured for the girl to look at Niles. "Tell Dr. Compton about being host to the symbiant."

As Collins watched the scene play out before them, he caught sight of Everett. They both saw that the visage and demeanor of the young yeoman had changed. She no longer looked innocent and sweet at all.

"Can you control this . . . this . . . thing?" Niles asked.

"The question is moot, Doctor—neither one controls the other. I and my symbiant are merely sharing the same body. We share knowledge and learn together."

Farbeaux looked from the girl to Dr. Trevor, watching and gauging his reaction to the lie that was being presented to the Americans. Henri saw that the girl was starting to make the doctor uncomfortable.

"Are you saying each one of the children we saw being brought aboard are hosts to one of those . . . syms?" Mendenhall asked.

"Yes, just like all of my crewmen you have seen, they all at one time were hosts to their own symbiant, at least until their life spans ran their course."

"That's why they are so fiercely loyal to you and your cause," Collins said as he turned and walked back to Sarah.

"Your perception is accurate, Colonel."

"But why destroy the vaults at the Group complex when you would have eventually told us anyway?"

"It wasn't only the *Leviathan* vault, Dr. Compton, it was the vault below it I was really after. It was that damnable relic stolen from my family by P. T. Barnum more than a hundred and eighty years ago. It was purely selfish on my part, but no trace of the syms can be left behind." Heirthall leaned down and kissed the top of Yeoman Alvera's head.

Samuels cleared his throat and nodded to the observation windows.

Alexandria closed her eyes and gestured for Samuels to commence.

"Please cover your ears. A few of you may feel some discomfort, but it will pass in a moment."

Yeoman Alvera pulled away from Heirthall, almost as if she was being held against her will, and then she faced the glass expectantly.

"Officer of the deck, this is the first officer. Begin the tones," he said into the microphone embedded into the large chair.

"Aye, Commander, tones have been initiated."

Before the orders were confirmed from below, Alice, Everett, Lee, and Mendenhall placed their hands over their ears as a soundless tone penetrated into their brain through the ear canal.

"Okay, that hurts . . . uh . . . really . . . it hurts," Mendenhall said as he leaned into Jason Ryan.

"The tones are used to call the syms. It resembles their own style of speech and can carry up to a hundred miles. This is what led to my family's understanding of whale song."

The tones stopped, and Alice was the only one who had to sit, feeling sick to her stomach.

"Oh, God," Virginia said, looking through the glass.

All eyes turned in that direction, and then one by one the Event Group slowly approached the large windows as *Leviathan* came to a complete stop at the deepest part of the trench.

"Conn, lower exterior lighting to twenty-five percent power," Samuels ordered. Then he too advanced to see the wonder of the entire world.

"Beautiful." Ryan was the first to react.

The adult symbiants came out of the darkness. They had long ago shed the protective shell of octopuslike armor and were in their final form, as they would remain for the rest of their lives.

The tails, shaped like maple leaves, gently pushed them through the water toward the humans staring at them from their strange environment. They had small, thin legs that extended through the tail like veins, ending in tiny humanlike feet that exited the tail at its sides. There were discharges of internal electricity that coursed through the tail, pulsating soft pink and light blue in blood veins and arteries far different from that of man. The center of the tail radiated a soft greenish color, pulsing as their small hearts beat at the center of their chests, which could be seen through the clear membrane of their outer skin.

The first symbiant to reach the glass raised a small hand and touched it as its tail kept its body in pace with the drifting *Leviathan*. As the Event Group watched, its deep blue eyes shrank, allowing the creature to view them through the intense light.

"Yes, Mr. Ryan, it is beautiful," Niles said as he slowly reached up to the glass. He stopped and looked at Alexandria. She nodded her head that it was all right to touch the window.

The symbiant, with blinking eyes, smiled. The clear mouth curved upward and the hands slid across the window to mimic Niles's movement. The small creature tilted its head and looked directly at Niles. The smile remained.

"Captain, what nourishment do they consume at these depths?" Everett asked the practical question.

"There are over two million lava vents that supply nutrients and animal life that the symbiants harvest. Their needs are not all that great. When we visit, we like to leave them several tons of goods on the sea floor. Vitamin-filled feed, usually reserved for cows and horses. We do the same for the small children and their adults in the Gulf of Mexico."

"I count ten in all," Jack said as he too became entranced by the legend of all legends before him. He could feel Sarah next to him take a deep breath as she took in the wondrous sight.

"There is more. We estimate this colony is down to fewer than a thousand," Samuels said as he helped Alexandria to a chair. She sat and watched the Event personnel closely. "Captain, have you noticed there are only a few here? Where are the rest?"

Heirthall counted and then recounted the syms outside the glass.

"This is strange. There should be what's left of the colony here," she said, looking concerned.

Other symbiants came to the window and examined the faces looking at them. The colors in their tails enhanced to deeper blues and brighter pinks. They crowded around the glass, seemingly looking beyond the gathering of humans, looking for something that wasn't there.

"They look like a species of jellyfish. They must use the electrical current and colors for—" Virginia started to say.

"Mating, communication, navigation; right now they are asking a question," Alexandria said, watching Niles and the others closely.

"May I guess, Captain?" Sarah asked.

"I can see you have figured it out through their body language, Lieutenant, but go ahead."

"They want to see their children," she said as she moved her gaze from the window to the captain.

Alexandria nodded once more, and Samuels nodded at Yeoman Alvera. The girl stepped to the glass, placed her hand up, and sighed. Then several other midshipmen came through the hatch. Thirty-one in all approached, looking excited and sad at the same time.

"This small group is all that is left of the Mariana Trench young," Heirthall said sadly.

The teenagers were stretching and pointing, placing their hands on the glass, trying desperately to seek out their parents. The symbiants outside the glass had become excited as their colors turned to the purest pinks and the brightest blues. Their hands reached out toward the gathered midshipmen.

Soon, even more syms had joined the grouping at the windows, and then the momentary joyfulness dissipated. The humans watching this amazing event saw that several of the adults were being assisted by other syms as they made their way to the glass. The colors and electrical discharges on these syms were dull, less vibrant.

One of them reached outward toward the glass, and that was when Niles and his people saw that its clear skin had become milky in color. Its fine black and gold hair was sparse as it looked upon the men and women inside.

Yeoman Alvera stepped over, saying nothing. She tilted her head, staring at the sickly adult.

The creature tilted its head, mimicking Alvera, and then held its small, clear hand to the glass. The colors in the adult briefly flared to life, but just as quickly faded as the yeoman watched. She held her other hand to the window, hoping that the adult would follow suit, but two creatures advanced and slowly pulled the parent away from the glass. The adult's hand, still on the window, slowly fell away—the fingertips lingering for as long as they could keep contact until the parent was assisted out of the dimmed lights of *Leviathan*. Then it was gone.

Yeoman Alvera watched for the longest ten seconds Jack could ever remember. When she turned away from the glass, the look in her deep-set blue eyes was terrifying as she glanced from face to face. Then she abruptly left the observation lounge.

"You see our predicament, Mr. Director?"

Niles swallowed and turned to look at Alexandria. He could only nod his head.

"Regardless of what happens next, Doctor, thank you for that."

"Now that the family reunion has been concluded, I think it's time for the doctor to explain how much trouble we are in." Everyone turned and looked at Farbeaux as he stood and made his way to the bar. He found a bottle of whiskey and poured himself a drink.

"Especially since the captain's pain medication will soon wear off, and she'll become someone other than who she really is."

Heirthall stared at Farbeaux and allowed her body to relax for the first time in months. She slowly walked to a chair and sat. She placed a hand over her face and held it there.

"Explain," Samuels demanded.

"Colonel Collins, I must say that it is fortuitous indeed for us to have you and your men aboard. We will need some of that magical escapism that you so readily apply to bad situations." He took a drink of the whiskey, exhaling when he emptied the small glass. "It seems there has been a small mutiny aboard *Leviathan* in the past few months." He poured another drink.

Dr. Trevor tried to get past Samuels but the commander blocked his way, pulled the small .32-caliber pistol from his pocket, and placed it against the man's chest.

"Captain, amongst your medical papers is a description of a small procedure conducted by the boat's surgeon. This will explain the symptom added to your hereditary illness that isn't listed in any medical journals. Colonel Collins was quite right; the schizophrenia is brought on by something else."

Jack turned from Farbeaux to look at Trevor, who backed away from Samuels until he could sit in one of the chairs.

"You placed a symbiant in her?" he asked.

Trevor swallowed, lowered his head, and then shook it. He refused to look up.

"You son of a bitch," Samuels said, taking a menacing step toward the doctor. "That's why the captain has been aggressive, changing her own orders!"

"I suspect that she has moments of clearheadedness." Farbeaux poured one last drink, limped toward Trevor, and sat down. "The good doctor became suspicious, and had the good sense to note it in his case file." Henri patted the doctor on the knee, then looked up at Heirthall, who was looking ill and lost. "She has much more stamina than the sym she has inside of her. She's quite rational when she is exhausted, like in the early morning hours, or—"

"When she's drugged," Virginia said as she finally sat next to Alexandria and put an arm around her.

"Yes, Ms. Pollock. She must have extraordinary mind power to fight off the thoughts that course through her head. I believe she brought you here not to question you about vaults or what you knew about her. She brought you here, using her subconscious will, to help get *Leviathan* back and to stop what was happening. Oh, she's still crazy for her cause, but now the insanity issue can be explained," Farbeaux finished.

"God, do you know what you're saying?" Niles asked.

Collins answered for the rest, as they were coming to the same conclusion.

"It seems the kind little symbiants aren't the fuzzy little creatures the Heirthall family thought."

Before they knew what was happening, the lights flickered inside the observation lounge and then they heard the outer hatchway slam closed. Sparks started shooting through the watertight seal lining the hatch. Samuels turned and tried the wheel, but it didn't budge.

"It's dogged from the outside!"

Jack and Everett sprang forward and assisted Samuels. The wheel refused to move.

"They are sealing us inside with a welding torch," Everett said.

Without a warning signal or announcement, they felt *Leviathan* go to full speed once more, throwing them all off their feet. Outside the viewing windows, the behemoth shot through the trench canyons as easily as a sports car on a highway. Niles watched the digital readouts on the hologram once the screens closed, and saw that they were once more traveling at one hundred and seventy knots and were headed due south.

"I think the battle for *Leviathan* has just begun in earnest," Farbeaux said as he gained his feet, grimacing in pain.

"Yeah, and like always, we seem to be in the wrong place and slightly outnumbered," Mendenhall said as he assisted the senator to his chair.

Jack slammed the hatch with the flat of his hand in frustration. He angrily turned and looked at Sarah. She looked back at him, and that seemed to bring Jack back to reason. He nodded his head at Sarah and then turned to the others.

"Yes, Will, outnumbered, outgunned, outsmarted." He walked up to Trevor, grabbed him by the collar, and lifted him up out of his chair. "But we do have a couple of advantages. We have the man who knows the plan and who's involved."

"And the other?" Everett asked, joining him at his side.

"Me."

They looked to where Alexandria Heirthall was holding herself firm against the table. She was shaking, and her face was pale. The sym inside of her was obviously reasserting itself.

"Yes, Captain, what better ally to have than the designer of *Leviathan*?" Jack agreed.

It was Farbeaux who brought that thought into real perspective. "Yes, but which captain are we going to get?"

"Commander Samuels, these coordinates—do you have any idea where they are taking us?" Niles asked, indicating the readout at the base of the observation windows.

Samuels stepped forward and looked at the running numbers. He looked confused to Collins. "Yes, we're making a run for home."

"Where in the hell is home?" Ryan asked.

"Ice Palace—the Ross Ice Shelf."

"What's there?" Everett asked.

"We must retake *Leviathan* at all costs," Alexandria said just before she collapsed to the deck, unconscious. Virginia, Mendenhall, Sarah, and Alice rushed to her aid.

"It's our base of operations," Samuels said beneath his breath, unable to say what he was thinking. "We're in the process of leaving there and going to a new base—the ice shelf has become too unstable. There's nothing there but the Heirthall fortune and . . ." Samuels lowered his head.

Collins, who had released Dr. Trevor, faced him once more. He removed the pistol from Samuels's hand. He placed it against the right hand of the doctor and pressed.

"It's obviously Sergeant Tyler controlling this thing. Now, why is he going to Ice Palace?"

For the first time Trevor smiled. It was as though he was far braver now that Heirthall was unconscious.

"What's there, Colonel? Five hundred nuclear weapons—enough missiles to destroy every deepwater port on the face of the earth." His grin widened. "The symbiants are taking back their oceans, and the Heirthalls and *Leviathan* have helped them do it."

"Does every asshole on the planet have access to these damn weapons?" Mendenhall whispered to Ryan.

"Only the ones we run across."

18

USS *MISSOURI* (SSN-780)

Missouri was running at six knots on a southern line toward Antarctica, for no other reason than that was the last known direction of *Leviathan* as she left the area of Saboo.

First Officer Izzeringhausen handed Jefferson the full list of damages that would have to wait until they returned to Pearl for repairs.

"Not bad considering we hit more debris than a garbage truck," the captain said as he laid the report on the navigation chart he had been studying.

"Conn, sonar, we have just picked up a very weak submerged disturbance. We believe computer says it's *Leviathan*."

"Did you get a bearing?" Jefferson asked with the microphone gripped tightly.

"Aye, Captain—twenty-three miles due south of the Ross Sea, heading straight for the ice shelf on a heading for White Island. Depth, over three and a half miles."

"We follow, Skipper?"

"Yes, we follow. Get in there as close as we can and hope the damn ice shelf stays intact."

Jefferson was referring to the massive shearing of thirty-three miles of ice that had recently torn free from the world's largest ice pack.

"Take us to five hundred feet and bring us up to twenty-two knots. Order the relief shift for sonar, and get the department supervisors up here. We need the best people at their stations."

"Aye, Captain. I estimate at our revised speed and depth we should arrive at the shelf in three hours."

"Ten miles out I want to slow to five knots, and we'll go to total silence from there—no unnecessary movement."

"Aye, Captain."

"Somewhere out there is the world's largest shark, and I don't want to get bitten again."

LEVIATHAN

Five decks below the control center were the crew's quarters. Just fewer than eighteen hundred off-duty men and women were enclosed in four different berthing areas. The officer's quarters were dispersed alongside the larger compartments according to specific division. The symbiant attack started at the larger crew quarters.

"Hey, what's that smell?" one of the bosun mates called out from his bunk. "Smells like someone is welding something."

Another man who was playing cards with several others looked around and thought the same thing. Then another became concerned.

Suddenly three flood valves opened to the sea, and freezing water started flowing through and into the compartment. Not one of the crew in the first compartment panicked, but several did run to one of the three hatches located in the compartment. They spun the wheel so they could get free and then isolate the flooding—but the wheel was frozen.

"What the hell!" someone called.

The water was at one foot and rising.

Outside the hatch, the three midshipmen rolled up the electrical line for the portable arc welder and then looked down upon their work, satisfied. The spot welds along the frame and on the turning wheel would make sure that every man and woman in the compartment would drown within an hour. The three had finished at the exact same moment as the other welding crews, who had just accomplished the same task on the remaining crew compartments and officers' quarters.

Leviathan's crew had been taken in less than five minutes from the time Yeoman Alvera ordered the attack to commence.

Lieutenant Kogersborg was just finishing his change-of-watch paperwork when the flooding alarm sounded. The constant electronic buzz filled the command center as the watch crew monitored their holographic stations.

"We have flooding on deck five, crews' quarters. All four compartments, and officers' cabins as well!" the damage control officer called out.

Kogersborg looked on in amazement, then reacted.

"That is ridiculous, we didn't hit anything—it has to be a computer malfunction."

"Diagnostics check out; that deck is flooding."

"Jesus," the young lieutenant said as he moved quickly from the navigation console to the damage-control station. He knew the flooding was real when *Leviathan* went into automatic damage control, as ordered by her computers, counterflooding to keep the submarine trimmed as they rose toward the Ross Ice Shelf.

When he saw the hologram depicting the flooding in sixteen cabins and the four large crew compartments, he came close to panicking. The second thing he saw was the computer-generated numbers of personnel estimates for the occupied areas.

"Oh my God, ninety-eight percent of the crew is on that deck!"

"Why aren't they getting out?" one technician asked.

"The computers are not counterflooding, and the pumps have not started," the damage control officer said.

"Sound general quarters—call the captain and Commander Samuels to the conn. Manually start the pumps on deck five, now!"

"The situation is under control, Lieutenant," Tyler said from the circular stairwell leading down from the observation platform above control. The sergeant was armed, as were his men coming at the control center from the fore and aft compartments.

Kogersborg without hesitation knew his duty. He jumped for the general alarm. His hand was only inches away when Tyler deftly shot him three times in the back. The boy slowly hit the captain's pedestal and slid to the deck. The rest of the control room crew started to move to action when several more shots rang out; then the din of automatic fire filled the air. When silence came once more, thirty-five men and women of the control room watch were dead.

"Damn it!" Tyler hissed as he stepped down from the last rung of the staircase. "Call the trainees to the control center to take over the watch, and get these bodies out of here."

One of his men was leaning over two of the helmsmen.

"Sergeant, these two are still alive. Should we call the—"

Tyler, looking frustrated, walked up and fired two shots into the heads of the wounded, making his security man fall backward.

"Your men were too slow in reacting, and that made the control room crew think they could do something about this. I won't be cleaning up your mess again. Now get the midshipmen trainees up here, and get replacement modules for the damaged control systems."

"Yes, sir," the man said, with one last look at the murdered crewmen.

Tyler deftly stepped over the crumpled body of Lieutenant Kogersborg and reached out to touch the large captain's chair sitting high on its pedestal. Then he removed the ammunition clip from his handgun and replaced it with a fresh one.

"Have the second assault team meet me in front of the observation compartment—it's time to confront Captain Heirthall and her guests."

The Event Group felt *Leviathan* slow and her bow angle change as she started her climb to the bottom of the Ross Ice Shelf. The waters outside of the observation windows were crystal clear as the lights started to pick up the indigenous sea life of the Antarctic Archipelago.

"Look at that," Lee said as he stepped closer to observe the giant pressure ridges on the bottom of the shelf. Upside-down mountains pointed their sharpened edges at the now diminutive *Leviathan* as she rose through the depths.

"According to these coordinates, we're not that far away from White Island," Everett said as he made some quick calculations on a napkin. "The closest American friendlies are a thousand miles away at McMurdo Station, on the southern tip of Ross Island."

"We have enough scientists onboard *Leviathan* as it is. I don't think those nerds from the weather station will be of any help," Lee quipped as he looked at Niles. "No offense, my dear boy."

"No, but if we can find a way off *Leviathan*, they are within rescue distance," Carl said as an explanation.

"Good to know, swabby," Jack said.

"All hands take collision stations, stand by to surface. We have unstable ice ahead," Yeoman Alvera called over the intercom.

"Well, at least we know who is in command," Collins said as he looked at the now-silent Dr. Trevor. "We need to know who-all is in on this. The crew? If not, what did they do with them?"

Outside the windows, *Leviathan* rose dangerously close to the bottom of the Ross Ice Shelf, slowing even further as she did.

"The opening to Ice Palace is a natural fault that will allow *Leviathan* to rise into the ice," Samuels said, sitting next to Alexandria as she lay upon the long conference table. "I think the captain is coming around."

Heirthall's eyes blinked and she turned her head. She looked into Virginia's eyes. She smiled, reached out, and took her hand. Virginia smiled, and then slowly wiped the blood that pooled and ran from Alexandria's left ear.

"The sym inside of me is dying, Ginny. I'm afraid it's taking me with it," she said, almost silently.

"No, you're too strong for that." Virginia squeezed her friend's hand. "You did good fighting it. If you hadn't, no one on the outside would have stood a chance."

Alexandria smiled sadly. "I am not proud of myself for . . . allowing this thing to happen," she said, wincing as a momentary pain coursed through her head. "I didn't think the syms . . . were capable."

"Sometimes aggressor species hide their intent well, Alex. You were blinded by your compassion. Your entire family was."

"Help me . . . sit up, Ginny."

Virginia, with Alice's assistance, did as asked. More blood flowed from first the left, then the right ear. Alexandria leaned her head against Virginia's chest as Samuels came over. He tried to smile at his captain, but couldn't.

"We . . . were both blinded, James." She smiled and took his hand. "Nevertheless, we'll fix . . . it. You must understand this. Listen well, James—the young children, they are innocent. Their syms are too young . . . to be . . . a part of this."

"Yes, Captain, we will make things right, and we'll get the children off," her first officer said determined.

"The ice shelf is dying. The polar ice caps are melting; being weakened by the global warming governments say is not cyclical," she said weakly, trying to make her voice heard.

Leviathan was rising fast toward a giant pressure ridge that shot down from the shelf. It looked as if they were on a direct collision course with disaster, when suddenly the giant vessel veered right and then expertly shot between two of the larger ridges, shifting her bulk into a valley that allowed *Leviathan* to rise up and into the great ice shelf.

"Yeoman Alvera is quite adept at handling. . . . *Leviathan*'s large bulk in tight spaces. Whenever we are gone for long periods of time, the opening. . . . to Ice Palace freezes over, and becomes a much tighter fit than when we left," Alexandria said, watching the view from the windows.

"All hands, this is the deck officer, surface, surface," Alvera announced. "Chief of the boat, sound the horn—all interior lighting to full illumination."

Bubbles the size of cruise ships started to rise in front of the windows as the giant submarine started emptying her ballast tanks. She rose slowly, guided by her thrusters in order to stay clear of the sharpened edges of the ice. The deck beneath their feet dipped one way and then the other as the young Alvera maneuvered her to avoid ice slicing through her composite hull.

Finally, the warning horn sounded and *Leviathan* broke into bright, daylike illumination. As the Event Group looked out of the observation window, they saw a natural ice cave, immense in size.

"We discovered it thirty-five years ago. My parents . . . estimated that the cave was naturally formed over two hundred thousand years ago by . . . seismic activity from Mount Erebus to the south. It was possibly a giant air bubble the size of England that rose from the sea floor."

Leviathan gently rose to the surface of a small interior sea totally encased in ice. The water was calm as the giant submarine eased onto the surface.

"Attention, deck watch to the sail, deck watch to the sail. Riggers and security report to the docking commander. Attention, all hands, *Leviathan* has arrived at our destination."

The Event Group felt *Leviathan* shut down her engines as the great submarine settled on the surface of the inland waterway. Thrusters maneuvered her close to the center of the trapped sea.

"Welcome to the end of the world as we know it," Alexandria said, blood now lining her lips. "This is where our . . . journey ends. I suspect this is where Sergeant Tyler will gather whatever his . . . reward is, and the symbiants will make . . . their final . . . stand against mankind."

To Jack, Carl, Niles, and the others, that was an ominous announcement.

"I'm sorry, Captain Heirthall, but we're leaving this little shindig, and if we can, we're going to bring this whole place down, and *Leviathan* with it."

All eyes turned to Jack. Even Farbeaux set his half-finished drink down and pushed it away.

"It is about time you said something noble, Colonel. You were beginning to worry me."

19

Jack walked over and stood before Dr. Trevor. Everett joined him, quickly reached out, and again pulled the doctor to his feet. He eased the smaller man into himself and smiled.

"Captain Everett drew the short straw this time around; he gets to ask you questions. Do you have your persuaders, Captain?" Collins asked, looking from Carl to the double hatchway. He knew that any minute Tyler and his men were going to start cutting through to get at them and finish what he had to do. Jack knew Tyler was trained enough to know he couldn't leave an enemy onboard while he was ashore. He would definitely attack.

"Yes. There wasn't much to choose from, since we'll need all the bullets in the commander's pop gun, but Ryan gathered up a couple of nice persuasion instruments."

To the doctor's horror, Everett let go of him and brought up a steak knife and a shiny corkscrew.

"The corkscrew is compliments of Colonel Farbeaux."

"I don't know what I can tell you," Trevor said, looking at the ordinary kitchen implements that now held a whole new world of possibilities. "Obviously the captain forced Sergeant Tyler and Yeoman Alvera's hand earlier than they expected."

"Is the rest of the crew loyal?" Everett asked.

"I don't know who is . . ." Trevor screamed as Carl poked him in the ribs with the corkscrew.

"Jack, what are you doing?" Niles asked, approaching them.

Collins turned and looked at his director.

"Torturing Dr. Trevor for information," he said plainly and without humor.

"Oh. Carry on."

Any hope that Trevor might have had left with Niles Compton as he returned to the senator and Alice.

"Okay, okay . . . the crew is unaware of what the syms and Tyler are doing. I never knew the plan for their disposal." Tyler felt the corkscrew scrape his skin through his coverall once more. "Or if they were to be disposed of at all."

"What are the syms planning?"

"Tyler will take command of *Leviathan*. That's his reward."

"For what?" Everett asked, not needing to poke the doctor again; his eyes warned of what he was capable.

"The syms will control the sea with *Leviathan* at their disposal. Most of the world's navies will be destroyed in the port attacks; the rest can be picked off piecemeal by Tyler. He isn't in it for money, he's in it for power."

Jack reached out and took the steak knife from the table where Everett had laid it. He placed it to the doctor's neck.

"And your reward for assisting in mutiny?"

"The Heirthall fortune," he whimpered.

"Ah, the gold and jewels of the Monte Cristo legend."

Trevor's eyes flicked to Henri Farbeaux as he joined the trio.

"Good to see that there is old-fashioned avarice alive and well in the world—that everything isn't all idealistic nonsense."

Jack lowered the knife and turned toward Farbeaux.

"Colonel, no more drinking. We're going to need you."

Farbeaux smiled and then saluted Collins mockingly. Then he looked straight into Trevor's eyes. The mention of the Heirthall treasure interested him immensely.

Before Everett could continue, there were noises coming from the hatchway, then a sudden shower of sparks.

"I guess our time's up," Everett said.

"Okay, get the captain behind a table. Ryan, Mendenhall, get us a barricade set up, a thick one."

Everyone started moving, tipping tables and piling chairs.

"One pistol, Jack. All we're going to do is maybe hurt someone and make them mad at us," Everett said as he tossed Trevor to the floor and dumped part of the conference table in front of him.

Before anyone could react, a locked access door above the observation glass sprang open. All they saw was a man drop into the compartment and dive for cover.

The attack on the observation deck had begun, and it came from a surprising front.

Tyler was watching his security team cut through the same hatchway they had sealed an hour earlier when he was approached from behind by Alvera and three of the sym midshipmen. She watched the progress on the hatch without comment for a moment. Her startling blue eyes did not waver from the bright torch. "The crew and officers were successfully taken in their quarters?" she asked Tyler without turning to face him.

"Yes." Tyler turned to her, annoyed. "Shouldn't you go back to your station on the bridge?"

Alvera stopped watching the men cutting through the hatchway. She turned briefly to the midshipmen accompanying her. Then she turned and looked more closely at Tyler, and actually took a menacing step toward him. He tried not to show his fear of the young woman, but failed, as his eyes could not hold her intensity.

"Explain to me again, since you have seized control of the most powerful vessel in the history of your world, how you can be trusted? A man willing to kill millions of his own species is also a man capable of betraying the partners who assisted him in achieving that great power. Why should we trust you?"

"Because the only ally you'll have after the death of Captain Heirthall is me and the members of my security team. I need you, and you need me. Your kind will live, and I will have *Leviathan*. You'll have control of the sea, and I'll have control of the one thing that guarantees it for you."

Alvera looked more closely into Tyler's face. Her blue eyes intensified as she gazed, trying to uncover the lie that she suspected was just under the surface of his features.

Tyler swallowed, but held his ground.

"You acted too quickly. The captain still has the launch codes in her head. Without those codes, we can't act against the naval powers of the world. Thus far your judgment is not quite adequate to wield the power of *Leviathan*, Sergeant."

"Obviously I had to act sooner than planned because Heirthall was being entertained by the men and women she brought aboard, despite your implanted sym. She was in far more control than you ever believed, Yeoman. Act is what I did, to cover for your errors in judgment." He swallowed. "Now, I have a question for *you*," he said, forcing himself to continue. "Are you prepared to do what you have to do? Can you kill more than eighteen hundred loyal members of *Leviathan*'s crew—men and women you have worked with for years? More importantly, can you do what you have to do in regard to the children? They are just as loyal to the captain as her crew."

Alvera turned her back on Tyler and paced to the elevator where the midshipmen were holding the doors for her. Before she entered, Alvera turned with a small grin. "The bulk of the crew will be dead within the hour. As for the children, they are part of the gulf colony, and mean absolutely nothing to me and the others."

"Then I ask you the same question: How can you be trusted if you can kill off an entire colony of syms, especially when there are so few of your kind to begin with?"

"Simple, Sergeant," she said, stepping into the elevator. "They are young. They would fight to save the captain. They have none of the aggressiveness of the older sym colonies. They don't yet realize we are on the short end of a losing war. We *must live*—not because we are allowed to, but because we have the *right* to." She looked with distaste at Tyler. "We hate humankind—we despise them. Somehow, some way, we *must* secure the seas, even if we have to strike at every man, woman, and child on the planet."

Alvera stopped the doors from closing.

"I am sending you some *special* help to ensure you take this compartment. Be sure not to get in their way. If I were you, I would let . . . *us* handle them. . . . The people inside that observation lounge are exceptional at what they do, and as long as the captain draws breath, she's dangerous." She smiled as if she had just heard the punch line to a private joke. "Be careful, Sergeant; we would hate to lose you now."

The closing elevator doors finally blocked Alvera's hate-filled eyes.

Tyler turned back to the cutting. He then turned back to the now-closed doors of the elevator.

"The only way you can do that, you little bitch, is to have *Leviathan* do it for you." He thought, then smiled. "The only thing you *must* do is join the young syms in the fate you have *planned for them*."

Beneath Tyler's forced bravado, just where he could ignore it for moments at a time, was the fact that he was terrified of Alvera and her midshipmen. They were capable of anything, even eliminating him and his men from their equation.

Jack and Everett were the first to move toward the darkened threat that fell from the access hatch. Collins had the small handgun and Everett the steak knife. Ryan and Mendenhall took up station on the far side and awaited Jack's orders. They knew their job; they would be the distraction while Collins and Everett advanced on the enemy.

At the front hatchway, the cutting continued.

Collins rose above one of the upturned tables, took aim at the approximate position where the threat had landed, and waited.

"Hold your fire!" a frightened voice shouted.

Everett looked at Jack and shook his head. "That you, Doc?" he called out.

"Stand up!" Carl shouted.

As they watched, first hands and then the arms rose above one of the tables.

"Don't shoot me," Robbins said as he stood with arms raised.

Niles, the closest to Gene Robbins, quickly went over and searched him. Then the director spied a bag at Robbins's feet.

"It's not much. I took them from the captain's cabin."

"We have four nine-millimeter handguns here," Niles counted, "and four extra clips of ammunition."

Everett and Collins advanced on their new ally.

"Noble of you, Doc," Everett said as he took the bag from Robbins, who couldn't hold Everett's gaze and so just looked at the floor.

"Can we get out the same way you came in?" Collins asked.

"We'll have to find a way up from the deck above. I nearly broke both of my ankles falling from that height," Robbins said, looking from Jack to the director. "Niles, I—"

Compton turned away and faced Samuels. "Can we get up there?"

"Yes, follow me."

As Jack motioned for Carl, Mendenhall, and Ryan to follow, he tossed Farbeaux and Senator Lee each one of the handguns and two clips of ammunition.

"Blast anything that comes through that door," he said as he followed the others up the stairs.

"And what are you going to do?" Farbeaux asked, making sure there was a round chambered in the handgun.

"We'll try and get behind the assault force."

"Wonderful. In the meantime, the senator and I will occupy them by collecting their bullets until you achieve your goal," Farbeaux said as he lowered himself and faced the hatchway.

The five men rushed up the spiral staircase to the small deck above the observation floor. They watched as Samuels reached the open access panel Robbins had come through. He gestured to Collins, who tossed him the nine-millimeter he was holding. The commander quickly stepped underneath the panel and held the gun up, pointing into the blackness beyond. He stepped back and looked at the others.

"Clear so far. Give me a leg up."

Ryan and Mendenhall stooped so Samuels could place his foot in their hands; they lifted. As the commander gabbed hold of the frame, he started kicking wildly and screaming. Ryan and Will pulled frantically at Samuels's legs, trying desperately to yank him from the access hatch. Suddenly they were sprayed with blood. Shocked, they continued to pull at the commander's legs. Then without warning, they fell to the floor, and to their horror they saw that only the bottom half of Samuels came with them.

"Jesus!" Everett said as he reacted quickly, stepping over the commander's still-kicking legs and opening fire into the open hatchway.

Collins joined Everett and added his fire to the darkness beyond. They heard a mewling sound, as if a large cat had been hurt. Then something fell from the hatch, and before they knew what was happening, the thing rose and jumped on Carl.

Mendenhall saw what it was first, and tried to pull the gelatinous thing from the captain. Ryan joined in, and Jack did the same. The symbiant raised its head, its small hands pinning Everett to the deck, and hissed, showing its clear teeth and deep blue eyes. Without realizing it, all three men released the creature and jumped back. Collins caught his foot on the lower half of Commander Samuels's body and fell back. As he did he brought the nine-millimeter up and fired directly into the symbiant's head. The animal jerked, then faced Collins and angrily swiped at him, releasing one of Everett's arms. The captain quickly fired his gun straight up into the symbiant's chin. Three quick shots sent bluish-pink jelly upward. Everett felt the sym go lax, and he pushed it off.

As the three men stood and helped Carl to his feet, they heard hissing sounds coming from the access vent.

"Jack, I think we better find another way," Everett said as he pushed Mendenhall and Ryan in front of him and started for the stairs.

As Collins turned away, he heard another of the symbiants fall from the access hatch. Then another, and another. He turned quickly and fired into the mass of clear membrane of the first. He saw the bullets enter the creature's gelatinous flesh, but all they did was make it shy away as the next set of bullets found the mark. Then it started after Collins with a hideous scream.

Farbeaux was torn between watching the spiral staircase, where he heard sounds of men running, and the hatchway, where the sparks of the cutting torch had stopped. The decision was made for him as the right-side hatch was thrown back and an object was thrown in. Farbeaux and Lee hit the deck as the flash-bang grenade went off with a bright flash and deafening explosion. In the middle of all of this, Ryan, Mendenhall, and Everett came rushing down to the main deck. They hit the floor, stunned. It was Jack who automatically started firing at the assault element coming through the hatch. He caught the first two unaware, and they crumpled to the floor. When he took aim at the third and fourth as they rushed in from the companionway, he heard the syms flopping down the stairs. He quickly turned, fired upward, and then hopped over the railing the last ten feet. Hitting the deck rolling, he felt hands on him. He looked up and saw Sarah as she helped him to his feet.

Farbeaux had risen from their cover and started firing into the opening. Lee turned his attention toward the staircase and fired in that direction. Then all of the action stopped at once.

"Colonel, there is no escape. Surrender now, and we will call the symbiants off. Refuse, and I guarantee you and your people a harsh death. You have never seen the syms feed—I assure you it is not a pretty sight."

Jack and the others saw that the symbiants had paused at the higher level. They were moving around, watching them through the smoke, their illuminated eyes penetrating even from that distance.

"We want the captain. Give her up and we'll put you on the surface of the ice shelf. That won't guarantee your survival, but it's a better fate than facing the symbiants," Tyler called out.

Collins took a breath and looked at Niles. Compton in turn looked at Heirthall lying between Alice and Virginia.

"They won't ever . . . get the . . . launch codes . . . I swear. Ginny, Dr. Compton, you and your people have done . . . all that you can."

Niles looked back at Jack and shook his head.

"Sorry, Sergeant, I guess you have to come and get us," Jack called out, and then he, Ryan, Mendenhall, and Everett took up positions next to Farbeaux and Lee.

"I can't say that I am happy with your decision-making, Colonel," Henri said, not taking his eyes off the hatchway.

"Colonel, I am accessing the view screen on the observation window. Judge for yourself what the consequences are before deciding," Tyler shouted.

As Jack turned, the view screen in the upper portion of the viewing glass illuminated. The picture showed a fish-eye view of one of the crew's quarters. Men and women were struggling to get higher in the compartment as seawater rose beneath them. Although the picture had no sound, Collins knew they were screaming and yelling. Several of the more experienced crew were trying desperately to open the hatch, diving and then surfacing for air.

"There are three more compartments like that one, Colonel. Surrender, and I'll let the crew go along with you."

Collins lowered his head.

"Jesus, Jack, that bastard is holding all of the cards," said Everett.

"I daresay he's right, my boy," Lee said as he lowered his weapon.

Jack stood and slowly walked to the open hatch. He safetied the handgun and tossed it out into the companionway.

The battle for *Leviathan* had ended.

As the elevator took Tyler's security team, the Event Group, Farbeaux, and Captain Heirthall up through the skyscraperlike conning tower, Jack watched Alexandria. She was deteriorating fast. He looked down at Sarah, and he could tell she was seeing it, too. The captain clung to Virginia, holding on to something of herself she could still feel and touch. As far as he knew, she hadn't been medicated since their arrival in the Ross Sea, so her speculation that the symbiant implant had died was true.

At the topmost deck of the conning tower, Tyler opened a large access hatch and they were shown outside for the first time in two days. The bridge overlooked an amazing sight—a cavern that was eight hundred feet high and a mile in length. On both sides of *Leviathan*, to port and starboard, and only seven hundred feet away, were the sheer walls of the naturally formed bubble. The ice, illuminated by lighting placed by Heirthall and her crew years before, made the cavern gleam with a natural beauty no one outside of *Leviathan* had ever witnessed before.

A natural shelf with smaller pockets of caves lined the cavern. It looked as if the crew of *Leviathan* had expanded these to accommodate items such as vehicles and equipment, which had already been removed from the dangerous location.

The bridge phone rang, and Tyler quickly answered it.

"We have sunrise on the surface of the shelf. Winds are picking up to about sixty knots. We will start to see rougher seas shortly. If we are to launch the missiles today, we have to accomplish it before the winds exceed seventy knots."

"I see. We'll be retrieving the codes shortly."

"How can we be getting winds here, beneath the ice shelf?" Compton asked, adjusting his fur-lined hood.

"In answer to your question, Dr. Compton, the winds are from the surface of the Ross Ice Shelf, one mile above us. They are coming through one hundred and fifteen thousand years of accumulated ice," Alexandria said weakly, shivering.

"How is it penetrating?" Virginia asked, looking around her as the wind picked up in intensity.

"Look up," Alex said, gesturing with her gloved hand.

As they did, the sight was terrifying. The sun, just rising on the surface of the Ross Ice Shelf, was showing like a fan of sunbeams through a massive crack in the shelf itself. It was at least a mile long that they could see, stretching far beyond the cavern.

"Over five hundred miles of the shelf is breaking away. This single event will add more than three inches to the water levels of the world. More will soon follow."

"My God," Alice said, taking Lee's arm as she looked skyward.

"Losing the ice shelf alone is bad enough, but that coupled with the melting of the Arctic will eventually be devastating to the coastal areas of the planet."

"This is what you are allowing with your alliance with the symbiants, Tyler," Jack said, watching the man who had binoculars trained on a distant, hollowed-out section of ice.

"Why haven't we seen the crew? Are they released as you promised?" Sarah asked.

"They will be released soon," Tyler said, lowering his glasses and looking right at Sarah. "As soon as the captain gives us the launch codes for the weapons."

Everett took a menacing step forward, but Collins reached out and stopped him just as ten security men brought their automatic weapons up.

"I fear . . . Sergeant Tyler and Yeoman Alverez are too late," Alexandria said. "The fault line has opened even farther than the last time we were here. I would . . . say by at least a thousand feet. The cavern is too unstable for a launch."

"Nonetheless, we will launch in half an hour. Captain, I fully expect the launch codes once we get back below. Colonel, your people go first, and before you try anything, remember: I have men stationed at the bottom of the sail, and they will not be forgiving the second time."

Collins stared at Tyler, wishing for just two minutes with the sergeant. He then looked at the others on the sail and thought better of it. There still might be a time and a place.

Moving down the steep staircase, Virginia grabbed for Alexandria as her knees let go. She held her upright until Mendenhall and Ryan stepped up to take the captain's weight.

"Take her down," Tyler shouted from above as the first of the above-deck security men reached the opening of the conning tower hatch.

As Jack's feet hit the inside of the tower, the light from above them was suddenly cut off. The hatch had slammed shut. As men and women scrambled in the darkness, their eyes adjusted. Jack saw them first. It was three of the children. They had hidden in the darkness of the stairwell, then slammed the hatch shut and dogged it before Tyler and his men could follow them.

The three children, one of whom was the small girl that Will had come across on Saboo, smiled at Mendenhall. They were silent as they looked at the assembled group. Then the girl, along with her two male companions, gestured for them to follow.

Collins stopped the small child. "There are security men below us," he said.

"Yes, they are there," the girl said, but turned and went down the stairs anyway.

"I think we better follow the child," Farbeaux said, limping after her.

As they reached the bottom of the long staircase, they were amazed to see five more of the children. The pounding on the hatch above told them of Tyler's anger. Around the children were the limp bodies of ten of Tyler's security men. Collins didn't even want to know how the children had subdued them.

"There are . . . still . . . a few weapons in the . . . cavern," Alexandria mumbled.

"All ashore that are going ashore," Everett said as he started to open the escape hatch on the base of the giant sail tower.

USS *MISSOURI* (SSN-780)

Jefferson was staring and thinking about the chart in front of him. *Missouri* was at station keeping—only using her thrusters to adjust for drift as she waited. They were one mile off from the Ross Ice Shelf. He looked every few minutes at the latest ELF message from National Command Authority—the president of the United States. The coded wording was clear after deciphering: *Sink* Leviathan *through any means possible. Release of special weapons has been authorized.*

Captain Jefferson ran a hand through his graying hair, then looked up as his first officer approached.

"Maybe the president doesn't know that Collins and the others are still alive and onboard."

"It doesn't matter, Izzy. He knows they very well may be, but our orders stand. When *Leviathan* comes out from under the shelf, we bushwhack her with a Mark seventy-eight 'special.'"

"Goddamned nuclear-tipped torpedo," Izzeringhausen said, shaking his head.

"Let's get the cursed thing loaded into tube three. Load one, two, and four with standard Mark forty-eights."

"Aye, sir."

"Izzy, we will do our duty on this," Jefferson said as he saw the look on his first officer's face.

"Yes, Captain, but no one said we have to like it."

Captain Jefferson frowned and looked down at the chart that depicted the Ross Ice Shelf.

"Stay under the ice until Collins can pull something—*anything*—off, if he's still alive."

20

"Is . . . the captain . . . going to die?" the small child asked with tears forming in her eyes.

Jack knew it would do no good to lie to the child. "Yes—but she . . . and we . . . are grateful for your help. What is your name?" he asked.

"Natika," she said, as she placed a small hand on Heirthall's cheek. "And she is our captain." It was as if it were that simple. Heirthall was the captain, and it could be no other way. Jack knew that, to the children, there was no other authority in the world.

Everett managed to get the hatch open, and the cold wind entered the tower. The small girl turned away, and the others followed her.

"Hey, hey," Jack said as he stopped her and the others. "You have to come with us."

The girl just shook her head. "We have others we have to bring out. The crew are trapped in their quarters—they will die soon. My friends are also in the mess compartment. We must help them."

"Colonel, you have to get me to the command bridge," Heirthall said, still held between Virginia and Alice.

"They can't launch without the codes, right?" Lee asked.

"They can . . . get the . . . codes through . . . other means."

"This job sucks," Mendenhall said, voicing the same opinion that he had on many an occasion.

Collins made a quick decision. "Will, you and Jason go with the girl. Do what you can to free whatever crew is still alive, and be careful," he said, taking two of the weapons from the downed security men and tossing each one to the lieutenants.

Natika seemed to like the suggestion; her smile widened. She stepped up to Mendenhall and took him by the hand.

"I guess we're in your girlfriend's hands," Ryan quipped as he joined Mendenhall and the children.

"Funny man," Will said as they left the sail and disappeared through the hatch leading down.

Jack reached for the other fallen weapons. Everett, who joined him, immediately tossed the automatic rifles to Robbins, Lee, Compton, Farbeaux, and finally Sarah, who shook her head, knowing what Jack was going to say.

"Mr. Everett, I assume the captain has a way of stopping any missile launch from *Leviathan.* Take her with you and find a way into that control center. Get it done." He pulled back the charging handle of the weapon, chambering a round. "Get it done."

"And you?" Everett asked as Sarah stepped up to Jack, shaking her head.

"I'm taking a different route."

Jack placed his right hand on Sarah's cheek and smiled. "Don't worry, Short Stuff, I have an extreme desire to live. I have plans beyond today."

Sarah was about to speak when Collins turned and went into the elevator. The doors closed and he was gone. Everett quickly stepped up and eased Alexandria from the grasp of Virginia and Alice.

"Captain, shall we try and help?" Everett asked Heirthall when he saw her blue eyes open and alert.

"By all means . . . Captain Everett."

"I'm not leaving without my friend," Virginia said, then helped Carl with Alexandria's weight.

Yeoman Alvera sat on the edge of the captain's bed. Her hand played over the coarse blanket as she watched two of Tyler's men cutting into the captain's safe. As the front of the steel safe popped free of its hinges, she stood and walked to the bulkhead. She eyed the two men until they moved away, and then she reached in and took out the safe's contents. She tossed papers on the deck until she came to a plastic-coated envelope. She snapped the plastic into two pieces, then looked at the thick paper inside.

"NX0021-001 Heirthall-one," she said, reading the launch codes aloud.

Alvera smiled.

Ryan and Mendenhall followed Natika toward deck five and the crew level. Ryan looked at Will as the girl started acting strangely. She placed her hands on each hatch as they passed them. She would slowly, sadly shake her head, with tears in her eyes.

"What is it?" Mendenhall asked, leaning down in front of her to bring him to eye level.

"They are all dead. They died scared—frightened at not knowing what was happening to them."

The girl started again, passing the first, then the second, until she came to the third compartment. She stopped and her small hand wavered, then it moved higher, then lower.

"Alive," she said, closing her eyes. "Ten—twenty—maybe forty crew—they are cold, scared—they want out."

Ryan quickly looked at the large spot welds on the hatch wheel and the four on the hatch and frame. Then he turned to look for something, anything, to break the welds.

"Damn it, we need a cutting torch," Mendenhall said, looking behind him, expecting Tyler's men at any minute.

Ryan spied something on the composite hull—a fire hose and ax in their case. He ran, smashed the glass, and removed the heavy ax.

"You any good at chopping wood?" he asked Will.

"Man, I'm from L.A., I—"

"Forget it. Stand back," Ryan said as he raised the ax and swung at the weld holding the center wheel in the middle of the hatch.

The blade struck, making an unbearably loud ping. Then he swung again, and then again. Natika was holding her hands to her ears as protection from the loud noise. Finally, on the fourth swing, the makeshift spot weld gave way.

"Turn it, Will. I'll start on the hatch welds."

Mendenhall cranked on the wheel. It refused to turn at first, then slowly spun in his hands.

"Got it," he cried.

Ryan didn't hear. He swung at the right side of the hatch and the first weld broke free. A small trickle of water started oozing out along the seal. After breaking the second and third welds, more water started squeezing between the steel and the rubber gasket as the pressure from within started to push the water out. Ryan moved Mendenhall and Natika to the safe side of the hatch, and was just raising the ax for the last weld when they were surprised.

Two men stood standing at the juncture of the companionway, pointing weapons at them. They stepped forward, coming within three feet. Will pulled Natika in toward him and stepped next to Ryan as Mendenhall, with his free hand, raised his weapon.

The two men raised their weapons. Ryan was about to throw the ax when suddenly, and without warning, the last weld broke free. The hatch gave way as the single weld was no longer strong enough to hold back the pressure of the water inside. The hatch sprang so hard and so suddenly that the two guards never knew what hit them. Their bodies were smashed as the hatch crashed into them. Water cascaded from the compartment, along with bodies, live men and women, and the detritus of the personal lives that once sat in lockers and upon tables.

Ryan, Mendenhall, and Natika were washed thirty-five feet down the companionway before the flood subsided.

Several of the crew sputtered and spat. The survivors were half-frozen, but grateful to be alive and free. They splashed through the water and looked around confusedly, helping those who were worse off than others.

"Well, they're not much, but that's the army we have to work with," Ryan said as he tossed the ax in the water. "Not much of a cavalry coming to the rescue, but we do what we can."

With that, they started explaining to the rescued crewmen what was happening, and where their captain was.

The second and deciding battle for *Leviathan* was about to start.

21

Tyler sat on a stool next to the navigation table after his men had retaken the conning tower. An hour and a half had passed since Heirthall and the Event Group escaped into Ice Palace. They had brought the warheads, which had been stored in one of the vast caverns where they had not run into Collins or any of the others, and had installed all thirty of the MIRV weapons on the missiles buried inside their launch tubes. Tyler looked at his watch. *In record time, too,* he thought.

Tyler looked around at the security men and midshipmen at their consoles, then at the captain's chair above him. He was tempted to climb into the large chair, but felt that since Alvera was forsaking the seat of power, he would also. He felt there was no need to risk a power show-down before the launch was complete. Then he could take command with his men at the controls.

"Putting to sea while Captain Heirthall is free is a foolish and un-necessary risk," Tyler said as he stepped up to the navigation table where Alvera was studying the hologram of the Ross Sea.

Alvera raised her eyebrows and straightened up from studying the coordinates where the missile launch would take place. Eight circles of red were targeted for the opening salvo of Heirthall's grand invention—the very first breed of stealth cruise missiles. The main naval ports of the United States, France, England, Russia, China, Germany, and Australia were the hard targets of the strike. Eight reentry warheads would be targeted for each nation, which would effectively destroy each of the deepest water ports, knocking out a good percentage of those nations' surface and subsurface fleets without them putting to sea. The rest of the threats could be taken care of from another launch location.

"Heirthall is nearly dead; the others with her will be located soon by the syms. No, Sergeant, these people are no threat." She looked at Tyler and briefly smiled. "As easy as it was for them to escape you and your men, they won't be so lucky against my family. My family will find them and kill them all. Now, let's get under way, shall we?"

"Sonar, conn, anything close aboard?" she asked over the intercom.

"Inconclusive contacts at this time. The movement and instability of the ice shelf above us may be masking any potential threats."

Alvera looked down at the chart and made her final straight line from under the Ross Ice Shelf.

"You seem worried," Tyler said.

"That American Virginia class submarine could be lurking in open water, and we wouldn't know it until she put two torpedoes into us."

"*Leviathan* can take anything *Missouri* can throw at her."

"That vessel is a Special Operations platform—do you understand what that means? Let me enlighten you, Sergeant—they are stealth capa-ble. They can sit for hours and we wouldn't know they were there unless we put our laser web on them. Here's one more fact for your files, since you seem to have missed the captain's classes on the subject of American capability. She may have nuclear weapons onboard, and unless *Leviathan* is protected by depth, it is possible that they can destroy her. It would take a lucky shot, to be sure, but it's still possible."

"Then we rely on your ability to evade. After all, you were personally trained by the captain."

Alvera ignored the false compliment by Tyler. "Watch officer, make your depth six hundred feet, course heading three-three-zero degrees at fifty knots," Alvera ordered. "Weapons, load tubes one through twenty with Mark sixties, activate and warm up vertical tubes one through thirty with SS-twenties—special war shot."

"Aye."

Alvera reached for the dive alarm and looked at Tyler one last time.

"All hands prepare for dive." She hit the horn. "Dive—dive!"

Leviathan spewed more than a million gallons of seawater straight into the air as she started sliding beneath the trapped inland sea. What remained of the now-stranded Event Group, along with Robbins and Farbeaux, watched from a distance, behind a wall of calved ice.

"Good luck, Jack," Niles Compton said as Sarah joined him at the edge of the ice.

She looked around and then above them. The ice looked even more unstable than it had an hour before.

"Look at this," Lee said, making Sarah and Niles turn away from the view of the giant *Leviathan* disappearing underneath the Ross Sea. As they did, they saw ten of the children emerge from one of the carved-out ice buildings. They reached Henri Farbeaux first as they gathered around the group.

"Some of them made it out," Alice said.

"I'm afraid their escape may be for naught, my dear Mrs. Hamilton," Farbeaux said as he looked beyond the children who gathered around him.

Compton and the others turned to see the clear-skinned hand of a symbiant taking hold of the ice and starting to pull itself up.

"Get the children inside," Sarah said. "We don't stand a chance out here."

As they turned to herd the children back, more syms swam to the surface and started making their way ashore.

The Group's only hope now was that the few hurt and tired men, women, and children left aboard *Leviathan* could somehow stop the missile launch and then return to save them.

It was now all in the hands of Captain Heirthall and Jack Collins.

USS *MISSOURI* (SSN-780)

"Conn—sonar—we have a possible disturbance under the shelf."

"What have you got exactly?" Jefferson asked, nodding for his sonar officer to rejoin his department.

"Possibly the same water-release noise picked up in the Bering Strait. *Leviathan* may be moving out from under the shelf, Captain."

Jefferson thought a moment. His boat was as ready as it could be. All hands were at battle stations–torpedo, and *Missouri* was as quiet as they could make her.

"Keep tracking her and calling out the position of the target," he said, then hung up.

"What are you thinking, Captain?" Izzeringhausen asked.

The captain continued to study the chart. "We do nothing but sit and let that big bitch come to us." He tapped the chart of the Ross Ice Shelf. "The shortest distance to the sea is the way they came in—to the north—and that's exactly where we'll be waiting, Izzy."

"Good plan."

"Hell, it's the only plan. Send an ELF message to National Command Authority."

Izzeringhausen removed a pen from his coverall and waited for his captain to speak.

"Inform the president: *Missouri* is preparing to engage *Leviathan*."

LEVIATHAN

Everett and Virginia were frantically looking for the command bypass on the main auxiliary control panel. Alexandria was sitting in her chair in the control suite and trying to explain to Everett what he was looking for just as they both heard *Leviathan* sound her diving alarm. A few moments later, she felt her stomach leap as the giant ship slipped beneath the surface.

"*Leviathan* is starting to make a run for the sea," she said. The only good news thus far was that Tyler's men hadn't discovered them in the auxiliary control suite—yet.

Everett let out a whoop when he finally found what he was looking for. He quickly threw a switch, and the holographic controls lit up, coming to life with a myriad of colors.

For the first time in weeks, a true and meaningful smile crossed the red lips of Alexandria Heirthall.

She now had access to her element—the brain of *Leviathan*.

Heirthall smiled at Virginia as she once more took her place in the elevated command chair and turned on the holographic controls for her personal hologram. It failed to illuminate.

"They have cut power to my command hologram, but I will still give Tyler and Alvera the ride of their lives," she said as she reached into a compartment on the side of the command chair and removed a small case. "Captain, get to control and assist Colonel Collins. Kill Tyler and Alvera, and anyone else you can. Without Tyler and the yeoman, the rest won't launch. I'll do my best to keep *Leviathan* under the ice."

Everett started to turn when Alexandria stopped him, taking his arm. It seemed the captain had regained some of her strength and determination.

"I will sink her . . . if I have to."

"Understood."

Everett left the control suite. If he had lingered, he would have beheld a new Heirthall.

Alexandria Heirthall had chosen a side—her human side. Virginia smiled at her friend, then strapped herself into her seat.

ICE PALACE

"There have to be more weapons and good cover here someplace," Niles said as the last of the children filed into the large ice building.

Henri Farbeaux turned away from the large group and limped across the composite floor. For the moment he was just grateful for the warmth of the carved-out interior, but he knew their time was short. All the syms had come out of the water.

"Here they come," Sarah said, looking out of one of the shuttered wooden windows embedded in its ice frame.

Farbeaux went to the first room in the great building of rooms. He opened the door and found a comfortable meeting area, complete with long mahogany table and Queen Anne chairs. He shook his head and closed the door. He went to the next and opened it. It was a supply room— no firearms, only ice spikes, spearlike devices. The rest were ropes, ladders, boots for ice walking, and other cold-weather gear. Lined along the far wall were self-inflating, Zodiac-style rubber boats—only these were of a size Farbeaux had never before seen. They could easily seat one hundred and fifty adults. He also knew that they would do them no good one mile down in the Ross Ice Shelf. Farbeaux grabbed ten of the long, spiked poles and left the room.

"These are all we have," he said, handing them out to Niles, Sarah, Alice, Robbins, and Lee. "They may stop them better than bullets. I will check the last room. When I return, the senator, Dr. Compton, Dr. Robbins, and I will stand our ground at the front of the building. Young Sarah, you and Mrs. Hamilton will take charge of the children. I do not expect mercy from these creatures—do you understand?"

Everyone nodded. Henri turned and walked as quickly as his wound would allow to the back of the large building. He found the last door and saw a small staircase that went down into the ice. The composite material, resembling rubber, was scarce, unlike the rest of the building. He started down, hoping it might be an armory. When he reached the bottom, he stopped suddenly. He couldn't believe what he was looking at.

"My compliments, Captain Heirthall and Roderick Deveroux," he whispered.

At the lowest level of the building, in a special vaultlike room that was sealed against the harsh environment and lined in rubber for protection against the sea, was the Heirthall treasure—at least a thousand tons of gold, silver, and crates of jewels, a few of which were broken open and spilling their contents across the ice floor. Golden weapons; Saracen swords; golden shields from the time of Christ, and suits of armor from the Crusades. As he studied the room's design, he knew it would possibly be an area capable of a last stand against the enemy lurking outside.

Farbeaux shook his head at the discovery of the treasure—wondering what its true value would be, not only in terms of what it would bring on the open market, but in the prestige of owning some of the artifacts arrayed on the shelves. Henri looked upon the richest treasure in the history of the world and smiled.

"Colonel, here they come!" Sarah shouted.

"Ah, nothing is ever easy," Farbeaux said, turning away from the find of a lifetime, and he made his way back up the carved staircase. "How many, little Sarah?"

"Uh, all of them, I think."

When he looked through the open doorway on the main level, the first awful scream of a sym sounded. Niles Compton scored the first blow for the defense by jabbing the long, spearlike pole into the right eye of the first creature that came at them.

"Yes, nothing is ever easy," he repeated as he came forward, spike at the ready.

LEVIATHAN

Captain Heirthall took the handgrips of the two toggles. Without rudder control, she could only use the bow and tower planes. She knew it might be enough to cause *Leviathan* to slow, or at the very least announce to whomever was listening that *Leviathan* was coming their way. This last point she kept to herself.

Heirthall removed a large pair of holographic glasses from their case and put them on. They resembled the visor of a pilot's flight helmet. She needed to utilize these because of the power loss to visuals. She flexed her fingers as the visor came to life. *Leviathan*'s depth was close to a mile and a half, or a quarter of a mile under the deepest pressure ridge of the Ross Ice Shelf. The great vessel was only sixty miles from breaching the open sea. In the lower-right corner of the visor, she patched in to sonar, and could clearly see open water in front of her. She knew that didn't mean anything. As a matter of fact, she was guessing that *Missouri* was there—somewhere.

"Ginny, if I pass out or die on you, take the right plane control and pull back to its stops. Ram *Leviathan* into the bottom of the ice and keep her there. Give Colonel Collins and Captain Everett time."

"Can ice sink this damn thing?"

"I don't think so, but we can tear her up enough to slow her down, possibly causing enough damage to make her stop the missile launch."

Alexandria took hold of the hand grips, then closed her eyes and took a deep breath. She pulled the right toggle control all the way back, at the same time pressing a small red button on the top, releasing control of the submarine from the command bridge. Her brainchild was once again hers.

Leviathan responded.

Yeoman Alvera made her final calculation for launching the missiles. A straight, deadly red line ran straight toward the center of the surface of the Ross Sea.

"Acting chief?"

"Aye," said the sixteen-year-old girl standing between the helm seats.

"Make ready to adjust depth and course in three—" Alvera almost bit her tongue off as *Leviathan* suddenly went nose up and shot for the bottom of the shelf. The yeoman watched the navigation hologram as the symbol for the submarine was speeding at fifty knots toward a series of jagged pressure ridges.

"Down planes—down planes, engines to slow!" Alvera yelled as she wiped blood from her mouth.

"Planes are nonresponsive," the helmsman said loudly.

Tyler picked himself off the deck and then looked at the hologram with fear in his eyes.

"We are receiving conflicting impulses from the computer, we are being overridden!"

"Captain Heirthall!" Alvera said, looking directly at Tyler. "Engines all back. Helm control, make sure she cannot, I repeat, cannot gain rudder and ballast access! Sergeant Tyler, obviously the captain is not stranded at Ice Palace. May I suggest you start your search in auxiliary control?"

Tyler angrily turned away and went to communications.

Alvera turned and studied the hologram, for the first time becoming frightened herself.

"Sound the collision alarm," she shouted as *Leviathan*'s engines went to full-reverse power. "Give me twenty thousand gallons of ballast in the forward tanks only!" The collision alarm started sounding throughout the boat. "Close all watertight doors, close the observation shields." Even as she gave the order, she knew it was too late.

Leviathan started to turn her bow down but was still rising at an incredible rate of speed. With her reactors screaming at more than 120 percent power, it wasn't enough to avoid the unavoidable.

The midshipmen braced themselves as the conning tower of *Leviathan* hit a large pressure ridge, tearing it free from the bottom of the shelf. The tower shook in its mountings, but held firm as the bow came up and struck another spikelike ridge, crushing the starboard observation shield and pushing it inward by three feet. The combination acrylic/nylon glass cracked and then gave way, creating a cascade of pressurized water that shot a hundred feet into the compartment.

"We have an outer and inner hull breach in the forward observation lounge!"

"Are we showing hatch integrity of the compartment in the green?"

"Yes, watertight doors are closed. We are two minutes from isolating plane control from the auxiliary suite."

Leviathan struck the bottom of the shelf again, throwing the control-room personnel from their seats.

"Tyler! The captain is trying to sink us!"

USS *MISSOURI* (SSN-780)

"Conn—sonar—we have her at fifty-six miles, bearing three-nine-seven degrees. She just hit the ice at over fifty knots!"

"Collins and his men, it has to be. Izzy, match bearings on *Leviathan*'s noise and fire tubes one through six, a full spread, maximum range!"

LEVIATHAN

Alvera braced herself as the pummeling continued. Heirthall was ramming the uppermost deck and tower into the shelf, causing damage to the topmost sensors housed in the conning tower.

She happened to look into the flickering hologram in time to see six blips light up at fifty-plus miles. They were bearing right on *Leviathan*.

"We have torpedoes in the water—they have us locked at long range!"

Alvera wasn't concerned with the American-made Mark 48s, as they could easily lose them under the shelf at the extreme range at which they were launched.

"We have a bearing on *Missouri*'s location. Should we fire torpedoes?" the acting weapons officer asked.

"Yes, launch tubes one through ten. Blow the Americans out of the water," Tyler shouted as he tried in vain to get his men on the radio.

"Belay that order. We have to get to the launch point. Concentrate all efforts on regaining control and—"

Leviathan slammed into the ice again. This time it wasn't as devastatingly harsh as her engines, near to reactor scram, started pulling her back from the surface.

"We have regained all helm controls. The command suite has been isolated."

"About time," Tyler said as he slammed his phone down.

"Sergeant, I suggest you get the captain secured before she attempts something else."

Tyler started forward, grabbing the command security element as he hurried out.

"Ten degrees down bubble. Give me full dive on the planes; bring reactor power to fifty percent and go to thirty knots. Quiet the boat as much as possible and head to the launch point."

"We will have enemy torpedo contact in four minutes. They have to be advanced Mark forty-eights."

"Prepare to launch forward tube twelve electrically, tube twelve only. Set nuclear yield to one megaton—after launch, take *Leviathan* deep to two thousand feet."

"Yeoman, we still have flooding in the forward areas. The observation compartment is fully flooded; pumps are inoperative in that section."

"We'll have the power to pull out toward the surface; the reactors are cooling."

As they waited, *Leviathan* leveled off. The command crew felt the gentle release of air as one torpedo left the bow tube with a computerized order to detonate in the path of the incoming American weapons.

"Give me fifty degrees down bubble; engines to flank. Take us to two thousand feet!"

Leviathan laid her nuclear egg, and then dived for deep water where no man or machine could ever reach her.

ICE PALACE

The symbiants were crawling from the water onto the man-made ice shelf that ran around the circumference of Ice Palace. Sarah watched the first of the trench adults never hesitating as they came toward the building at incredible speed.

"The pressure down here must allow for their skeletal frames to withstand this oxygenated air!" Robbins called out from one of the front windows.

"We can talk over the fine points of sym science later, Doctor. Right now I believe they are quite capable of withstanding this level of our world," Farbeaux said just as the lead sym crashed into the window where he was standing.

Sarah reacted faster than Farbeaux, spearing the jellylike skin of the large, five-foot-long creature. At the same moment, Alice and Senator Lee opened up with the automatic weapons, shredding the small symbiant. The boat hook and bullets made the sym scream, a humanlike, awful wail of pain. The fluorescent blood went from red to a sickly purplish color as it fought to pull its body from the hook.

Henri raised the long, polelike spear and crushed the creature's eggshell thin, clear skull. The sym collapsed and its body fanned out as the invisible muscles seemed to dissolve into themselves.

As the creature stopped moving, the gathered children standing against the farthest wall watched in horror. One of their kind was being killed in front of them.

"I've got one coming through the wall," Lee said as he raised his weapon and fired.

The next sym was using stored saltwater to burn through the three-foot-thick wall of ice. The ice started to dissolve. The head of the sym came through, the mouth opened, and it hissed at Lee just as ten bullets slammed into its head. The sym recoiled but did not back out; its small blue eyes locked onto the senator and its body started to wriggle, trying to get through the ice that was refreezing around its trapped body.

Alice dropped her weapon, picked up one of the spikes, and speared the animal, but the sym easily dodged her meager assault and started pushing through, just as other adults began dissolving the walls around the small band of defenders.

"Children, move down the stairs!" Sarah yelled just as another sym crashed through the lone unbroken window.

The tail and small feet allowed the clear body the ability to slither along the floor like a snake—and it was lightning fast. Sarah thrust at it and missed, the sym dodging the tip of the boat hook easily. Then it struck, hitting Sarah in the chest as it drove her to the ground. The creature yelled something incoherent and raised its small, sharp claws to slash Sarah's face. At just that moment, a boat hook came through the clear wall of the sym's chest. Purple, red, pink, and clear fluid shot onto Sarah's heavy coat as she rolled out from under the creature and away from the sharp tip of the hook that had missed her head by inches.

Sarah stood quickly. The smell of fish was covering her. Then she saw who had come to her aid. It was one of the children. A nine-year-old girl withdrew the dripping boat hook and then turned to assist Farbeaux as he encountered another adult.

Before Sarah could stop them, the entire group of children, half sym and half human, ran forward, grabbing anything they could use to attack their brethren coming through the walls, doors, and windows. Sarah quickly realized it was no use in trying to get the children out of harm's way, so she started organizing them the best she could.

It was a small army coming to their rescue—but more to the detriment of the defense, they were up against a determined enemy who believed their very existence was at stake.

The human element was about to be overrun.

LEVIATHAN

"All hands, detonation in five, four, three, two, one!"

The announcement went through the entire length of the ship. Even though they were expecting the hammer blow, it still caught everyone inside the giant submarine by surprise.

The nuclear-tipped torpedo detonated five hundred yards in front of the six American Mark 48s. The pressure wave struck them and tore the heavy weapons to pieces; then they disappeared into atom-sized particles. The shock wave went aft of *Leviathan* and to her bow. The downward wave of heated water struck her as she fought for depth, bending her at amidships and then passing, allowing her to spring back in a whiplash motion that almost broke her back.

Jack cleared the access tunnel and came out onto deck five. He immediately spied Ryan and Mendenhall with more than forty crewmen as they splashed their way toward the spiral staircase ascending to deck four. Just then the submarine became a horror ride of shaking and dipping.

Suddenly a man rolled down the staircase and landed with a thud on the deck. Carl Everett looked up at the stunned faces around him.

Everett grabbed Jack's leg and held on as the flooded companionway rocked, sending a torrent of water that went far over their heads.

"Come on, swabby, it's time to get control here before those assholes blow up a bunch of cities," Collins said, splashing toward Ryan and Will to organize the assault on *Leviathan*'s operations center.

The giant pressure wave from the nuclear detonation—which was low in yield but multiplied a thousandfold because of the dense sea—ran toward the center of the Ross Ice Shelf. The heated water hit the underside of the shelf and actually lifted it by one and half feet. The fault line running the entire length of the world's largest sheet of thick ice separated completely. The giant walls of the crevice started crumbling, and the two halves moved—minutely at first, then picking up speed with the change in currents.

The Ross Ice Shelf started to come apart from the continent of Antarctica.

ICE PALACE

The syms realized something was wrong long before the human defenders. The attack stopped as suddenly as it started, and the syms started retreating from the walls.

"Bastards are quitting," Henri screamed in triumph, as blood poured from the open stitches at his hip. He was leaning on the boat hook for support just as the first tremor struck the area of the shelf where the ancient ice bubble had created Ice Palace.

Dr. Robbins and Niles Compton were the first to realize what must have happened. They turned and saw several of the slower-moving, older syms as large chunks of falling ice fell and crushed them. The ceiling was collapsing; they heard ice the size of small houses strike the second floor of the man-made shelter.

Suddenly everyone fell to the rubberized flooring as the shelf separated. The curious sensation of floating hit them all at the same moment—but it was Robbins who voiced it first.

"The shelf has broken away!"

"Look!" Alice said, hanging on to Senator Lee for dear life.

The bright sun was showing through the massive crack above them. It penetrated the darkness like a magical laser beam, obviously caused by the ice particles in the air. The Ross Sea heaved and crashed in toward the ancient cave, and then smashed into the carved-out buildings of Ice Palace.

A loud and deafening explosion sounded as the Ross Ice Shelf separated from the continent.

USS *MISSOURI* (SSN-780)

The nuclear shock wave struck the *Missouri* in a bow-down attitude, flipping her over onto her back and sending her crewmen wheeling and grabbing for anything they could hold on to. The lights went dead, and red emergency lighting took their place. Alarms started sounding throughout the boat as seals broke loose. Her outer torpedo doors, still in the open position after firing her spread of torpedoes, could not absorb the pressure that was slammed back into her. One inner door in the forward weapons room bent, curled, and then opened to the sea. *Missouri* took on ten tons of water in her forward torpedo room.

"Blow ballast, blow everything! All back full, full rise on the planes!"

"We're going to lose her, skipper!"

"Do we still have fish in the tubes?"

"Aye, but we are flooding in all the forward spaces."

"Weapons release, now!"

As the reactor on *Missouri* went to full power, the crew could hear her one screw bite the water, but they all knew it might be too late—they were getting too heavy, too fast. Still, they listened to the new girl fire off her last punch.

Jefferson knew he was about to lose his command as the new Virginia class submarine slowly started heading for the bottom of the Ross Sea.

LEVIATHAN

"All sections report damage," came Alvera's voice over the loudspeaker. "All hands, USS *Missouri* is on her way to the bottom. Commence preparations for weapons launch in five minutes."

"Damn efficient little bitch, isn't she?" Everett said to Jack as they headed down the main companionway.

They met Ryan coming around the corner from the armory, where he had been sent two minutes before.

"Report, Mr. Ryan," Jack said.

"Too well guarded; we would have been shot to hell before we got within twenty feet. There are at least twenty of Tyler's men there. But we did manage to get ten of these," he said, holding up one of the strange automatic weapons. "All we can figure is that they were left by the cutting crew when they went to work on the hatches."

"Well, they will have to do," Collins said.

Everett handed out the automatic rifles to the oldest of the crewmen.

"What is it, Jack, a full-out frontal assault?" asked an angry Everett as he thought about those boys on the *Missouri*.

"Right now it looks like we have little choice. Hit them from both ends of the control companionway, and hope we don't run into Sergeant Wonderful before we get there."

Everett suddenly swung the rifle up, and all fifty-six men and women and the three children turned as one as one of the floor hatches popped up. A slim hand came out holding a thick coil of insulated wire, then Virginia popped her head through and tossed the wire onto the deck. She reached back down into the hatch, brought out a large rolled schematic, and laid it beside the wiring. Then she leaned back into the hatch, struggling with something else.

"Don't just stand there—help me. She's damn heavy!"

Several *Leviathan* crew ran forward, relieved Virginia of Alexandria's weight, and pulled her the rest of the way up through the hatch.

"It was a close-run thing, Colonel," Virginia said, out of breath. "Tyler and his men broke through only moments after Alex lost control of her command suite. I swear I never saw so much firepower concentrated in one small area. I'll never know how your guys can deal with crap like that—I thought we had had it."

"Her condition?" Jack asked, leaning over the captain.

"Exhausted, hemorrhaging, and her systems may be starting to shut down." Virginia held her hand on Heirthall's still features. "She did real good, Colonel."

"Try and bring her around. We have two helmsmen here. We were lucky there, but we lost the entire complement of chiefs in their staterooms. We need her awake."

"You're going to try and take the command bridge?" Virginia asked, looking from face to face.

Mendenhall and Ryan answered by slamming home magazines into their weapons.

"No other choice."

"Look, Jack, Tyler has both ends of that sealed passageway covered. You'll be fighting in a blind alley, and he has reinforcements he can call up; you don't."

"We will have to—"

"Jack, Alex had a plan. She made me strip this wiring from auxiliary control before we evacuated. I just don't know what it was."

Collins looked at the coiled wire. He tilted his head in thought.

"Shock . . . electric shock—under control center."

Virginia knelt and listened, but Alexandria had blanked out once more.

Jack heard the captain, and then he knew what her makeshift plan consisted of.

"Virginia, I need you to pull off that engineering stuff you're so fond of bragging about," Jack said as he reached down and took the wiring. He then explained that she had to return to the crawlspace.

Everett, Mendenhall, and Ryan watched as Jack detailed his plan to Virginia. They all raised their brows when they heard it, but they knew it would be their only chance without losing a lot of the people. Virginia nodded and accepted the task.

"Leave the captain here with her people. They aren't trained to take on people like Tyler, plus the captain may need them if this damn thing works. Doctor, you have to rig this thing in five minutes."

Tyler waited with fifty of his men at the forward access companionway into the control center. He was angry, as he knew he had lost a chance after finally breaking through into the auxiliary control suite, only to find that Heirthall had vanished. They had emptied weapons into the crawlspace beneath the deck, but he now knew that that woman had nine lives. He surmised that attacking the control center was the only logical move for the captain. Thus far, he had to give Heirthall and that damnable Collins credit—they had thwarted him at every juncture in trying to subdue them. However, he now knew their only choice was to come through him and his men.

ICE PALACE

Farbeaux formed a plan in a split second. His mind started clicking just as it had before the death of Danielle, his wife. It felt good to have purpose once more.

As the sea crashed against the carved buildings, the salt deteriorated the walls, and the giant halves of the ice shelf separated for good. The sky one mile above the ancient ice hit the sea for the first time in two hundred thousand years. Ice Palace was floating, and its ice shores were only thirty feet from the cresting swell of sea.

"Sarah, get the children in order. This section of ice will be unstable in the next few minutes."

"What?"

"He's right, look!" Niles called out.

Sarah and the others looked around and saw that the building had a decided tilt to its foundation. The children were starting to lose their footing as the giant ice floe started to tilt backward.

"I believe this shelf is now what is called an iceberg, dear Sarah. It is going to flip over. The Ross Ice Shelf is no more. If we don't do something, we'll be thrown into the sea, and with my injured hip, I don't think I could swim to McMurdo Station."

Sarah responded quickly, gathering the children together with the help of Lee, Alice, and Robbins.

"I hope you have a plan," she said.

"As a matter of fact, the answer to our situation is right in the lower rooms of this enclosure. Now, we need everyone to go down and assist in taking the items we need." Farbeaux started down first, followed by Sarah just as the enclosure tilted to thirty degrees. The stable half of the remaining shelf was starting to drift farther away.

They had but moments remaining before the section they were riding would flip over into the freezing sea.

LEVIATHAN

As the second group of Tyler's mercenaries waited, Collins caught them off guard from behind when he cleared his throat. He and Everett stood facing the men with their hands up. Ryan and Mendenhall were standing behind them, angry at having to surrender without a fight.

As Tyler's men rushed forward to take them into custody, Everett looked over at Collins.

"Ballsy, Jack, I'll give you that."

"Yeah, but can you think of a better way to get into the control center without getting everyone shot to hell?"

As they were pushed out of the companionway toward the rest of Tyler's men, Everett had to smile.

"It is good to have you back from the dead, Colonel. My life would have been as boring as hell without you."

ICE PALACE

They had struggled to get one of the oversized Zodiacs to the main level and out of the steep incline, which had become even more dangerous. As Henri pulled the air bottles that inflated the giant Zodiac, a massive cracking sound rent the air around them. As they looked up, the far-back portion of Ice Palace disappeared into the water and the surviving half went skyward, tossing everyone off their feet. Then it slammed back down into the sea. The Zodiac flew from the small shelf and went flying into the water, eighty feet away. The rough seas started tossing it about like a toy boat.

"We've had it!" Sarah said. "We wouldn't last three minutes in that water trying to retrieve it!"

"Can we get one of the others?" Alice asked loudly over the cracking of ice, with Lee assisting her in standing.

"We're out of time," Henri shouted as a large crack zigzagged through the center of the main building's remains. It was an exact center cut, separating the front half from its middle. The stairwell leading to the lower level was starting to separate from the front.

As they stood on shaking ice, they didn't see Gene Robbins looking about him, his eyes settling on the frightened children. He was shocked when he closed his eyes and his thoughts went to Captain Everett, a man he outwardly despised but inwardly envied for his blind bravery. Robbins quickly made a decision.

Garrison Lee saw a blur of motion and heard Sarah yell out. As he turned, he knew he was too late. Robbins sprinted for the edge of the ice and dived headfirst into the freezing Ross Sea.

"The fool, he's just killed himself!" Niles said as the frustrated Lee slammed his broken cane against the ice, angry he didn't think of doing the same thing himself.

"Yes, Director Compton, he has indeed just killed himself," Farbeaux said, watching Robbins's weakening strokes as he splashed his way toward the floating rubber boat. "A magnificent gesture"—he turned toward Niles—"for a traitor, wouldn't you say?"

As Henri shouted his rebuke to the others, Robbins went under the rising sea and reached for the Zodiac. They waited, frightened that he wouldn't resurface from under the freezing water. Then they were relieved as he splashed up to the surface. Ice was forming on the computer scientist's face and hair as he tried desperately to get his limbs to function.

"His body is shutting down," Lee said sadly. "Come on, son, push, push!"

Robbins pulled the Zodiac to within ten feet of the shrinking shelf, and then pushed with all of his remaining strength. The giant rubber boat bounced over one swell and then struck the ice as Sarah, Niles, and Farbeaux grabbed for it in a desperate moment of near-panic.

Lee couldn't believe what had just transpired.

"Swim, Doctor, swim toward us," Alice shouted as a section of the grounded side of the ice shelf calved away and fell into the sea with tremendous force, creating an impact wave of more than ten feet that rushed toward the struggling Robbins.

"He can't, his body has already died," Lee said. He watched as Robbins looked toward them with an expressionless, ice-covered face. The ten-foot wave rolled over him and he disappeared.

They couldn't believe how easily Robbins had given his life for them. Then again, they never knew that all the doctor had thought before making his final decision was the question, *What would Captain Everett do?*

"He died well, give him that—you owe him that," Farbeaux said as he pulled the Zodiac up and out of the wave's way. "Now, get the children inside the boat. We must head for the grounded section of shelf."

LEVIATHAN

As the captured Event Group was pushed, shoved, and slapped to the deck, and then up against the starboard bulkhead, Jack saw Tyler step forward and then lash out with his booted foot, catching him on the side of his head. Jack fell backward as Mendenhall and Ryan tried to stand.

"At ease, lieutenants!" Jack called out, shaking his head to clear it.

"You are a pain in the ass, Colonel. I knew we were asking for trouble letting you go the first time. Well, that situation is finally about to be remedied, isn't it?"

Jack looked up into the Irishman's face, not responding at all. His expression was blank, which made Tyler uneasy.

Alvera turned away from the scene, as she was slightly disgusted at Tyler's bullying ways.

"Why don't you just kill them?" she asked, staring at Tyler.

"He knows where the captain is, and as long as she is alive, she's a danger."

"Strange, I think I told you that very same thing a few hours ago." She turned away and raised the 1mc microphone. "Sonar, conn, what is the status of *Missouri*?"

"Sonar is still scrambled from the EMP effect. It is just now clearing, it looks as if we have no—"

Alvera heard the words catch in the sonar operator's throat as she attempted to explain why the sonar suite went offline momentarily during the effects of the electromagnetic pulse—an electrical field that shorted out all nonshielded electronics in modern weapons platforms by a nuclear detonation. The yeoman became concerned very quickly. As *Leviathan* came out from under the now-broken and free-floating Ross Ice Shelf, she noticed one red blip speeding toward them as it came up on her holographic display.

"Conn, we have a single torpedo in the water and it is actively seeking—no, it has acquired *Leviathan*, and is tracking!"

"Helm, hard-right rudder, take us down to three thousand feet—"

"Sensors are picking up a nuclear trace element!"

Jack raised his brows and looked at Everett, then at Tyler, who was also taken aback by the news.

Alvera froze. *Missouri* had somehow managed to get off a snap shot as she started going down, and it was not only a torpedo, but a nuclear-tipped one.

Alvera looked at the blip as it closed. The order for countermeasures caught in her throat as she realized her training never fully prepared her for this.

"Weapons, prepare to launch vertical tubes one through thirty for deep submergence launch. Helm, take *Leviathan* deep. Launch a full spread of countermeasures!"

"Yeoman, did you know that Sergeant Tyler was planning on selling *Leviathan* and her technology to the highest bidder?" Collins said, finally utilizing the paper Farbeaux had passed him from Heirthall's medical file.

Alvera, shaken, turned and looked down at Collins.

"What?" she asked, looking from Jack to Tyler, who only smiled and raised his automatic to silence the pest before him once and for all.

Tyler froze when one of the midshipmen who had been seated at the closest console silently stood and placed a gun to the back of his head.

"He's lying—my intention is to fulfill our bargain. *Leviathan* will protect the trench syms."

"The task of maintaining something as daunting as *Leviathan* is far beyond the scope of a mercenary, Yeoman. She would soon succumb to her own age, or the nations of the world would track Tyler down and destroy him because this idiot couldn't sail her—just as the *Missouri* tracked her to this point," Jack said, nodding toward the red blip speeding right at *Leviathan*.

"Call the doctor to the conn, we'll ask him," Alvera said, never letting her eyes leave Tyler's.

"You can't. He was found dead in the observation compartment. It had to have been a stray bullet," said Jack.

"That's very convenient." Alvera turned and studied the oncoming weapon, then looked back at the sergeant.

"After all of our planning, you are going to actually listen to this outsider?" Tyler asked as he felt the pistol push into his head.

"My breast pocket. You'll find a little notation from Heirthall's medical file, written by someone who wasn't an outsider."

Alvera reached down, plucked the paper from Collins's pocket, and looked at the open entry.

"I suspect with your intelligence you'll recognize Dr. Trevor's handwriting?"

Alvera read the scribbled notation outlining Tyler's real plan, which included the doctor, and then looked up angrily.

"Trevor says that you never had any intention of using *Leviathan* for our protection. You were going to sail her into the nearest port after our return to the sea and—"

"Sell her off, system by system," Heirthall said from the darkness of the companionway. "Avarice—mere money. If he had known where the Heirthall treasure had been hidden, he would have taken that also."

Alvera watched as security surrounded Captain Heirthall and Virginia, who was assisting the captain in remaining upright as they came into the light of control. She locked eyes with Jack and nodded her head ever so slightly.

"Yeoman, you have been betrayed, just as you and the others have betrayed me and my family," Alexandria said as she was helped into her chair, guns still pointing at her.

Alvera threw the paper at Tyler, striking him in the face.

"Have your men stand down, Sergeant," Heirthall ordered as she slumped in her raised chair. "Or I will allow the yeoman's misguided maneuvering in evading *Missouri*'s strike to stand. You can't outdive that weapon, Yeoman," she said as she opened her eyes and smiled.

The security men lowered their weapons. Jack and the others stood and rushed forward to take them, but several midshipmen rose from their seats and pointed handguns in their direction.

"Colonel, they will shoot to kill," Alvera said.

Alvera swallowed as she saw the red blip getting closer to the diving *Leviathan*. She gestured for the midshipmen to return to their stations, but to keep aware of Collins and his three men.

"Captain, I am still launching the strike. We as a species have no other choice. We tried to do it without loss of life, as you had planned so thoroughly with the help of your symbiant—"

"You mean with a little coercion . . . and brainwashing from Dr. Trevor's invasive procedures," Alexandria said, her eyes partially closed in pain.

"Yes. You would never have allowed such a plan against the world's navies in a normal state of mind. Your family's influence over us ends today."

Heirthall sat motionless in her chair. "You will do what you have to do, Yeoman."

Alvera nodded, then walked to the weapons station. She raised the protective cover over the red flashing button. She looked at the other midshipmen operating their stations, each doing their duty, and then she pushed the button.

A brilliant flash of light burst from every manned station in the control room. Midshipmen didn't have time to scream or move before twenty thousand volts shot through their bodies. A few of them who weren't touching any metal on their consoles rose in shock when they saw what happened to the others around them. Jack and his men quickly subdued them. He looked at the frozen Alvera. She was still touching the weapons console and was clearly dead, lying across the panel as the short-lived electrical strike ended. All around them, midshipmen lay dead against their stations.

It took only a few moments for the action consoles to regain their holographic imagery.

"Lieutenant Ryan, bring in the remainder of my crew, please. We have very little time."

"Aye, ma'am."

Heirthall looked down at the deck as her crew removed the dead midshipmen. Virginia could clearly see the tears as they streaked down her cheeks.

Jack pulled Virginia aside as the crew started up their consoles and awaited orders.

"You did well, Doc. That was one hell of a wiring job you did, rigging those consoles."

"I killed children, Jack. I don't know—"

"You did what you had to do, Virginia, just as we all do. And in answer to your next question, no, you never learn to live with it."

Virginia watched as Collins walked by a shocked Tyler and sat next to the weapons control station.

Sergeant Tyler knew for a fact he was a dead man. As Collins sat down, with lightning speed Tyler turned and elbowed Mendenhall in the stomach, then leaped at the weapons console, slamming his palm down on the launch button. The plastic cover smashed under the blow, and the red blinking button slammed home. Then he quickly turned and escaped through the hatch leading to the forward compartments.

Collins cursed and started to pursue Tyler. Everett started after Jack.

"Keep your station, Captain, and assist in *Leviathan*'s defense," Collins called out as he vanished from control.

Everett stopped his pursuit of Jack and Tyler, slamming his hand against the bulkhead.

"He really does have a death wish," Everett said with clenched teeth. 'Well, don't just stand there, damn it. Go after him!"

Ryan and Mendenhall grabbed two weapons and went after their boss.

"*Vertical launch in one minute,*" came the computerized warning.

"Helm, are we getting answering bells . . . on the console?" Alexandria asked, becoming weaker.

"Yes, Captain, *Leviathan* is answering all commands."

"Very well," she said calmly. "We need to turn the boat one hundred and eighty degrees. Bring our speed up to a hundred knots and blow ballast. Take her up to the ice."

"Alex, are you sure you want to do that? You'll box *Leviathan* against the ice."

"Ginny, we are caught between a rock. . . . and a hard place, as the saying goes. We cannot stop the launch of those missiles; on the other hand, *Missouri* has made our running away impossible. I can only be at one place at any given moment—*Leviathan* will die today no matter what I do."

"Do what you need to do," Virginia said.

"Ginny, Ginny, give me some credit, I fully intend to take the lesser of the two evils. The high . . . road, you might say."

"*Thirty seconds to launch,*" the computer announced. "*Obstacle at launch coordinates detected. Launch in twenty seconds.*"

"Conn, sonar, we have thirty-five miles of broken ice and pressure ridges dead ahead. Ten seconds until we have limited open sea."

"Maintain speed and rudder, helm."

"Aye, ma'am, maintain heading."

"Sonar, how thick is the ice?"

"We are currently ranging from one quarter to half a mile of ice."

"Thank you," Alex said as calmly as if she were just ordering dinner.

"Launch in ten, nine, eight, seven—"

"Leviathan has just gone under the ice."

"Three, two, one—vertical tubes one through thirty successfully launched."

The computerized voice prepared all hands for the minute jolt as compressed air shot thirty missiles from their tubes.

"Helm, evasive maneuvering, take *Leviathan* down forty degrees. Dive the boat . . . deep and fast," Heirthall ordered, allowing her head to droop onto her chest.

As *Leviathan* shed the missiles, she started a steep dive for the seafloor, three and a half miles down.

At six hundred feet, the specially designed missiles fired a solid rocket booster that would carry them to the surface of the sea. Unfortunately, they weren't near the surface. There was a half-mile-thick ice sheet above them. As they approached at more than a hundred miles per hour, the conical-shaped weapons slammed into the blue bottom pressure ridges of the dying Ross Ice Shelf, smashing them to oblivion and sending the warheads to the bottom of the sea.

"Captain, we have *Missouri*'s torpedo closing at sixty knots. She is still acquiring our sound signature—it must be locked onto our damage. Estimate impact in one minute."

"Very well, maintain course and speed. Ballast control; stand by to blow all tanks."

"We dodged one nuclear disaster, but we'll never avoid this one," Everett said as he and Virginia took a handhold. The blip on the hologram became one with *Leviathan*.

Collins hit the winding staircase that led down three decks to the engineering level. The captain had sealed off the elevators, and Jack knew that Tyler had no choice but to go down.

The massive engineering room contained the reactors. They were starting to scream at 115 percent power as the main water jet of *Leviathan* tried desperately to push her forward-flooded sections down through the sea. The operational stations were all empty as every available crewman was in control or battling flooding on the other decks. The smell of burning rubber and hot steam permeated the air. Jack rounded a console and was taken aback when Tyler made his final stand. He grabbed Collins by the leg and pulled him to the deck.

Jack slammed against the rubber decking and bounced into the reactor control station. Tyler was trying to gain his feet, hitting Jack three times in quick succession as he rose. Collins shrugged off the blows and then lashed out with his boot, catching the larger Irishman in his right knee, producing a satisfactory, and sickening, crunch as the blow cracked the shin and tore ligaments in the sergeant's knee. He still maintained his footing, but with very great effort. He steadied himself on the bad leg, raised his left, and tried to bring it down onto Jack's neck, but Collins rolled free just as the boot struck the rubber matting.

Collins jumped to his feet and struck Tyler three times in his side, making the security man cough and grimace in great pain. Instead of going down, he collected himself faster than Jack realized he could and swung backward, hitting Collins in the chest and driving him back against the bulkhead. Collins bounced off, but he used the rebound action off the hull to his advantage. He came forward and caught Tyler with three straight, powerful blows to the face. Tyler reeled and spun away just as the pitch of the electric motors changed, screaming at even more power than before. Then the world changed as *Leviathan* started heading straight down, sending both Collins and Tyler sliding down the deck as if they were on a giant, very precarious slide.

Jack never had a chance to end the fight with Tyler. The *Missouri*'s nuclear torpedo struck, and the world went dark.

"Okay, give me ninety-degrees dive on the planes. Increase ballast in the forward tanks to one hundred percent," Alexandria said calmly, closing her eyes to think, but still with her head lowered.

She was ticking off the seconds until detonation. When the American torpedo's computer detected the change in the angle of attack, the weapon would detonate as a preprogrammed precaution against losing contact with its target. This was exactly what she had hoped for. Alexandria suddenly opened her eyes and leaned forward in her chair.

"Hard-left rudder—one hundred percent down on fore and tower planes—all up on aft planes—all-ahead flank—full emergency power!" Everyone in the control center was shocked at the strength coming from Heirthall.

Leviathan started a straight-down, headlong run just as the torpedo reached its target area. In essence, what the captain did was bring the great vessel to an attitude where the hull would be less exposed— bringing the strongest portion of *Leviathan*'s hull head on against the detonation and the thickened composite armor at her protected stern. Running at close to one hundred miles an hour toward the bottom of the sea, *Leviathan* was still vulnerable as an egg in a cattle stampede.

The American warhead detonated ten thousand yards from the massive stern section of *Leviathan*. The tremendous heat generated by the warhead turned the sea to steam in a microsecond. The pressure wave shot in all directions, even down into the exposed jet ring–rudder of the giant submarine.

The first sensation for all inside was the feeling of free falling, as the seawater around her started running faster than *Leviathan* herself. The second sensation was that of the great boat flipping over as if it were a twig caught in a flashflood. The shock wave tore free the directional ring acting as the main rudder for *Leviathan*. Then the same heated wave assaulted the jet-thruster housing, causing the main seal to fail. The shaft that sent high-pressure water outward from the main engines, giving the submarine her thrust to the four water jets, backwashed and forced the rubber seals to melt, and then fail, allowing seawater to enter the pressurized hull with tremendous force.

Jack was thrown to the deck, and then it was as if he were on a sheet of ice as *Leviathan* made her run for the bottom of the Ross Sea. Then the detonation effects actually made the centrifugal force of the submarine faster than Jack's fall, and he found himself free-floating above the deck.

Tyler wasn't as lucky. He seemed to hit every engineering console in the compartment on his slide down the ever-increasing steepness of the deck. Just before he was crushed in the final fall toward the bulkhead, the same strange force that halted Jack's fall stopped Tyler in midair. Then, almost as soon as the floating effect started, it ceased, as *Leviathan* again caught up with the speed of the rushing seas.

Both men started free-falling toward the bulkhead at crushing speed as the inner hull was breached in engineering. Tyler landed at bone-crushing speed, and Jack landed on top of him.

As Collins was trying to figure out if he had any broken bones, Tyler moved from under him.

"Help . . . me," Tyler whispered.

Collins tried to turn to hear what Tyler was saying, but the automatic damage-control system was pumping compressed air into the compartment to push back some of the flooding covering both men, as the submarine was still in a nosedown attitude. Water soon covered Tyler as Jack quickly thought about his options. Decided, Collins raised Tyler's head from the bulkhead until it was just free of the rising water. Tyler spit and tried to clear the saltwater from his mouth and throat.

"Don't let me drown," the broken Tyler said as loud as he could.

Jack remembered the people at the Event Complex lost, and all the people Tyler was prepared to kill for the sake of money and power. The nuclear strikes would have caused the deaths of millions of innocents. Then the thought of Sarah, Lee, Alice, and those children so callously abandoned at Ice Castle made his decision for him.

"Sorry," Jack said as he took Tyler by the shoulders and slowly pushed him back into the water.

As the level of the flooding rose, Jack had to crane his neck to keep it above the water while he held Tyler down. He stayed that way until the large Irishman's struggling ceased. Collins turned away and floated until he was as far away from his deed as he could get.

The restraining belts were holding the crew in their seats, with the exception of Everett, who was dangling from the navigation console.

"Engines all back!" Heirthall yelled over the sound of the flooding alarms—the effort causing a large flow of bright red blood to fill her mouth. "Blow all ballast tanks. Give me full rise on the planes!"

"Captain, we have serious flooding in engineering—it's a major hull breach!"

"That will not affect power. All back!"

Leviathan started to bring her already-flooded bow up, but her speed was so great she continued to fall toward the bottom.

USS *MISSOURI* (SSN-780)

Jefferson knew that the flooding was overwhelming *Missouri*'s ability to pump it out. The forward weapons room had to be abandoned, and all the ballast he could send out to the sea had already been pumped out.

"Captain, we are about to lose the reactor—we're losing her," Izzeringhausen said, holding onto the nav table.

"Maintain revolutions! Launch the rescue buoy!"

Izzy did as he was ordered, but knew no rescue buoy in the known world would allow anyone to reach them almost three miles down; they would soon be crushed to death in a quarter of that depth.

Missouri had lost her fight for survival.

LEVIATHAN

Jack felt the deck straighten, but knew through his stomach that *Leviathan* was still sinking at incredible speed. He struggled toward the intercom and smashed his hand against the button.

"Conn, this is Collins in engineering!" he screamed. "We have a massive breach open to the sea!"

"Abandon the compartment, Colonel . . . seal the area!" Heirthall responded.

Collins shook his head and fought his way through the chest-high water. He didn't have to go far when the flooding and current grabbed him and threw him toward the hatchway. He grabbed for the coming and held on. Then he gained his feet and struggled with the heavy hatch, attempting to close it as the water rushed out of engineering. The torrent was just too much, and he knew that the next compartment and companionway would soon flood and be too much for *Leviathan's* pumps to shed.

Collins was losing the entire deck.

ICE PALACE

The large Zodiac was loaded. All the children, using blankets found in the supply room, huddled against the rubber sides. Sarah was the last one to enter beside the Frenchman. She turned just as a rumbling from the south started to roll over the remaining mile-thick ice.

"Come on, Henri, that sounds like a damn tidal wave!"

Farbeaux looked from Sarah to the dissolving Ice Palace. Before he could comment, the wave from the nuclear detonation two hundred miles to the north struck the broken ice shelf. Ice Palace started to fall over away from the main shelf, breaking free and turning bottomside-up.

Farbeaux shoved Sarah down into the Zodiac and then pushed it away from the small shelf lining the rising end of the carved-out platform.

"Damn it, Colonel, get in!" Sarah called out.

Farbeaux allowed gravity to take him where he needed to go. He slid down until he hit the rear wall of the building, then rolled to the open ice stairs and slid on his belly down into the basement. He struggled to gain his feet as he pulled the inflation cords on three of the rubber boats. Then he turned and looked into the water-filled corridor.

"No, sister Sarah, where I am going, you cannot follow."

Colonel Henri Farbeaux disappeared into the treasure room, dragging the three giant rubber boats with him.

Sarah took a paddle from Niles and started getting them as far away from the drifting ice floe as possible. She gasped when she saw Ice Palace roll completely over, fill with water, and then bob in the rising sea.

"I'll never figure that French son of a bitch," Senator Lee said as he and Alice paddled toward the remains of the once-greatest ice shelf on earth.

Sarah saw the remains of the ancient seismic chamber fill with water until three quarters of it went under.

"Don't confuse Henri with Dr. Robbins. I suspect the colonel knew just what he was doing."

LEVIATHAN

Jack knew he couldn't close the large hatch himself. Millions of gallons of water had already spread throughout the deck, and he could hear the reactor alarms screaming. The current of passing water started to tear his grip from the coming, when suddenly there were hands on the hatch, pushing it away from the bulkhead.

"One, two, three—push!"

The three bodies gave it their all and the hatch finally slammed shut. Its sheer weight coupled with momentum was enough to cut through the rushing water and slam home.

Jack collapsed into the water and momentarily went under, weakened from his fight with Tyler and his brush with drowning.

"What is it with you and water, Colonel?" Ryan said, pulling him to his feet.

Jack looked at the diminutive naval lieutenant and shook his head.

"The army better stick to land operations; you don't do all that well with water."

Jack placed hands on both Ryan's and Mendenhall's shoulders, leaning heavily against them as the water settled to one level, and stayed.

"Yeah—I will take that under advisement."

"Tyler?" Mendenhall asked.

Jack shook his head negatively. "He wasn't a very good swimmer," he said as he reached for the nearest intercom. "Engineering hatch sealed, Captain."

There was no answer as Jack tried again.

"Come on. In case you haven't noticed, we're still heading for the bottom."

Heirthall knew if they didn't shed more weight, they would lose *Leviathan*.

The giant submarine was level but still going down—she was at two miles, and the sound of her composite hull giving way to the pressure was audible throughout the ship.

"Alex, is there anything we can do?" Virginia asked, unclasping her restraint and going to assist a lieutenant with a sprung valve.

Alexandria didn't answer. She closed her eyes in thought, running the schematics of *Leviathan* through her head. She willed the crushing pain to the far reaches while she thought.

"Maneuvering, stand by to go to one hundred and fifty percent power on all four reactors."

"Captain, number three is already in the initial phase of scramming. She's shutting down!"

Heirthall looked down at the young rector officer and fixed him with her now-green eyes.

"Command safety override: Octavian one-six-four Zulu. Enter the code—now!"

The young officer did as he was told and entered the safety release on all the reactors.

"Reactors are answering one hundred and fifty percent, Captain."

Alexandria knew she had just killed *Leviathan*. She could never start a safe shutdown of the reactors after this—the core material in all four would melt right through the containment. She also knew it could not be helped.

"Ginny, Captain Everett, please gather the children and your people—you are to report to the escape pods on deck two and make ready to evacuate *Leviathan*."

"What? What about you and your crew?"

"Any who would like to leave may do so," she said as she looked away, as if afraid of how many would take the offer of evacuation.

None of her crew made a move to stand.

"Captain, we are slowing our descent."

Heirthall glanced at the navigation hologram and could see that indeed, *Leviathan* was slowing. She looked up at her crew and nodded.

"Thank you, Mr. Kyle, thank you."

"You don't have to do this—none of you do. *Leviathan* has three hundred escape pods, enough for everyone aboard. Alex, come home with us!" Virginia said as she placed both of her hands on the raised chair.

"Ginny, I've always been home. I will die with *Leviathan*."

"There's no need for this!" She turned to face the young crew. "No need for any of you to do this."

Alexandria looked at the hologram before her. Indicated on the holographic display of the sea were only two small models of vessels: *Leviathan*, which had leveled off and was slowly climbing with her main thrusters screaming in outrage at the load they were pushing toward the surface, and one other target that had lost her fight and was going down by the bow.

"*Leviathan* has one more task to perform, Ginny. Now you must go. Captain Everett, the pods will be automatically ejected from the hull at five hundred feet. Long-range sonar is picking up a Royal Navy frigate at one hundred miles and closing; you shouldn't be in the water long."

"Yes, ma'am. Ice Palace?" he asked without much hope.

"The shelf broke clean away from Ross Island. It's shattered into a million pieces." She looked at Everett. "You know the coordinates—check, please."

Carl nodded.

"Now you see why we can't leave here, my Ginny."

"But—"

"Captain Everett, gather your people and the children, and remove this woman from my bridge."

"Aye," he said, taking Virginia by the arm and pulling her away.

Alexandria watched Virginia being led away and allowed herself a moment. She swallowed to hold back her tears, then smiled, looking at the young faces around her.

"*Leviathan* has one more task to perform. It will take the expertise of every man and woman onboard. We will do what *Leviathan* was always meant to do."

At that moment, the radiation alarms started blaring throughout the boat. However, the remaining crew of the most amazing vessel in history turned and started making ready its last run.

Five minutes later, *Leviathan* was five hundred feet from the surface of the rolling seas. Alexandria pushed a small button on her console.

"Colonel Collins." She watched as Jack's face appeared on her hologram before her chair.

"I have no words to express our—my—regret. At my family's estate in Oslo, five hundred feet below the sub basement, you will find the oceanographic studies of my family going back to Roderick Deveroux. The betrayal of Octavian is entered in the original notes from Jules Verne, who was an eyewitness to the events. Offer them to your president."

"Yes, Captain—we will."

"You have my regrets about the director and . . . and—"

"Good luck, Captain," Jack said, when he saw Heirthall was struggling with her guilt.

She nodded her head and reached for the cutoff button.

"Take care of Ginny for me, Colonel."

She shut the hologram down before she heard any reply.

"Mr. Slattery, eject the pods."

They felt the release of the ten round pods as they shot from the sides of *Leviathan* just a deck above her sloping ballast tanks. Heirthall closed her eyes and said a silent prayer.

"Mr. Kyle, I need twenty degrees down angle on the planes. Bring *Leviathan* to flank speed, please, make your heading two-six-zero degrees, make your depth . . . a thousand feet. Order all hands to brace for collision."

"Aye, Captain—ma'am, we are losing the main collision shield in the forward observation compartment, and reactors two and three are in meltdown."

"You're full of good news . . . this morning. Mr. Kyle, would you like to maneuver *Leviathan* on her last mission? I want to be someplace . . . else when we surface for the last time."

"It would be my honor, Captain."

The escape pods broke the surface of the sea near a large patch of broken ice. One after the other the pods shot into the air from the great depths from where they had been ejected. Just twenty miles away, HMS *Longbow*, a Royal Navy frigate, saw them on radar and sonar, and began to make its way toward the bobbing escape modules.

As ladders were thrown over the side and British frogmen assisted the survivors from the pods, Jack had a vision that made him close his eyes and thank whatever God was watching over them. Perhaps it was the sea god *Leviathan* after all. Standing at the fantail of the *Longbow*, wrapped in blankets, was Sarah. She stood in front of Niles Compton, Alice

Hamilton, and Garrison Lee. Sarah ran forward and with no shyness at all threw her blanket off and hugged Jack under the warmth of the sun for the first time in months. Lee, Niles, Alice, and his men gathered around.

"Dr. Robbins?" Everett asked looking around.

Lee nodded and took Carl by the arm.

"You would have been proud of him, son. He saved us all in an unselfish act of heroism."

"He didn't make it?"

Lee patted Everett on the back and left him alone to his thoughts.

Jack allowed the hug to continue for as long as Sarah wanted. He locked eyes with Niles Compton and nodded. Then Sarah let him go with one last squeeze.

"Mr. Director," Jack said.

"Just a handshake will do, Colonel," Compton said smiling.

"We seem to be missing Colonel Farbeaux."

They grew quiet and Jack could see it in their eyes. Farbeaux was lost, and they were actually feeling bad about it. He only nodded slightly at their nonanswer, and then turned as the crew of HMS *Longbow* went to general quarters. Horns blared and men ran about the deck. Jack ordered his men to secure the children.

A half-mile away the sea began to erupt in a widening circle that boiled and bubbled as if the entire area were exploding.

"Jesus, the madwoman did it—look at that!" Lee said, tossing his cane over the side of the ship.

"All hands, we have a submerged object rising off the port quarter—stand by, main armament."

"No!" Collins shouted as he waved his hands toward the bridge of the frigate.

The Event Group and children of *Leviathan* were quickly surrounded by a squad of royal marines and moved away from the railing.

The frigate didn't have time to pull out of the way as she rolled with the tremendous force surfacing beside her. As she settled, giant bubbles and arcs of water flowed over the much smaller surface vessel, and then, as if by the last magical prowess of the sea gods that protected her, *Leviathan* slowly came up from the depths. The damaged sail was the first to shake free of the cold water and ice. And then, to the amazement of all, it wasn't *Leviathan*'s hull that came next.

"Oh, my God—she did do it!" Virginia screamed, tears flowing down her face as she wrapped her arms around Senator Lee.

"Amazing—just bloody amazing," was all Senator Lee could mumble.

Sitting precariously on *Leviathan*'s massive foredeck was the damaged USS *Missouri*. Her entire stern quarter was now missing, and there was massive damage throughout her hull. As they watched, and with water bubbling around both vessels, the hatches started opening on *Missouri* and submariners started assisting the wounded from its bowels.

Jack smiled when he saw Captain Jefferson and Izzeringhausen emerge from the sail's escape trunk. He was shouting orders when he leaned over and spied Collins. He gave his head a shake and then saluted, yelling for his men to get over the side. Then, with a last glance at the great conning tower of *Leviathan* looming far over his head, he gave the strange vessel his second salute, and followed his first officer over the side into the freezing waters.

Leviathan was starting to lose her fight with the pull of the sea—she was starting to go down. As the Event Group watched, the sail hatch opened and three young sailors came out. They reached in and assisted Captain Alexandria Heirthall out from the conn.

Virginia ran over to the railing, leaning over as far as she could as *Leviathan* slowly sank back into the sea. *Missouri*'s precarious hold on the foredeck of *Leviathan* finally let go, and she slid off into the cold waters—claiming her for their own.

Virginia Pollock was crying as Niles grabbed her and held on.

"Alex, jump, get free, you have time! Please, get as many of your people off as you can—please," Virginia screamed as Alexandria smiled for the last time.

They watched Captain Alexandria Heirthall look at the faces just above her as *Leviathan* slowly sank. Then her men assisted her back down into the sail hatch.

With the children crying along with Virginia, the great *Leviathan* slowly sank with only the fanfare of the hissing sea around her.

The quarter-mile-wide iceberg, which had for two hundred thousand years been the center portion of the Ross Ice Shelf, covered the sound of a small motor as the Royal Navy frigate pulled away to the north, heading for Australian territorial waters. The occupant of the lead boat, which was riding low in the water, was shivering with cold as he maneuvered the large rubber boat through the smaller pieces of ice covering the Ross Sea. The man figured he would zigzag his way between the newly created icebergs until he reached the newest Antarctica seaside town of McMurdo Station, the American weather platform, where he could charter a flight out.

Colonel Henri Farbeaux had to smile as he guided two other large rubber Zodiacs behind the first. They too were riding extremely low in the water. Tarps covered the load he had hurriedly removed from Ice Palace with not a second to spare. He didn't know what amount of treasure he had recovered, but the sheer warmth he was feeling from the three loads made his smile widen.

With a fraction of the mythical gold and jewels of the Count of Monte Cristo in his possession, Henri Farbeaux slowly made his way to the south.

EPILOGUE

"The world can be such a wondrous place—so full of awe and mystery that it boggles the mind of any thinking person—but one has to realize that the beauty and wonder can be so easily lost by the arrogance of our kind. I and my family have given to you the responsibility of another sentient being, brothers and sisters of the earth who are helpless to our ways of defiling our own world. They need us, and we—most assuredly—need them."

—Captain Alexandria Heirthall, humanist

The presidential yacht was riding lazily at anchor in the Gulf of Mexico. Senator Lee, looking dapper with his captain's blue cap and even more regal with Alice sitting next to him, were conversing in low tones about her retirement, which was only months away.

Everett, Mendenhall, and Ryan were up front doing something silently, only looking back once in a while with suspicious looks on their faces.

Jack, Sarah, Niles, Virginia, and the president of the United States were standing at the oak transom, looking down into the water.

"If they are down there, why don't we ever see them?" the president asked.

"With our lousy track record, would you want to take that chance if you were a symbiant?" Niles asked his old friend.

"No, I guess not."

"Mr. President, getting the gas and oil leases canceled in the gulf waters is a start."

The president looked from face to face. "Yes, but I had to cave in on the Arctic tundra drilling to get it done—still robbing Peter to pay Paul."

"We do what we can. Science will figure a way to help them," Sarah said hopefully. "The Heirthall papers should solve a lot of our problems."

"The children?" Jack asked.

"The State Department is using every resource to track down their next of kin, but it looks like they are truly orphans. I've set aside a small sum to keep them all together."

They all grew silent as Virginia looked over into the green gulf waters.

"I'm worried. Since the syms' release, our new SOSUS microphones haven't picked up any sounds from the bottom—either here, or in the Mariana Trench. I hope they aren't sick."

"I wouldn't worry about that," Everett said as he approached the group, wiping his hands on a rag. "The navy is monitoring everything that goes into the gulf waters. If they catch any pollutants whatsoever, the FBI will hunt the offenders down, and since the president got it passed through congress that it is a capital offense, I think the days of dumping chemical waste into the seaways are over."

"I hope you're right," Virginia said sadly.

"Well, if you people aren't a sorry sight to behold," Everett said seriously. "Here we are on a calm and peaceful sea, and you're moping around like you lost your dog."

The president looked at Colonel Jack Collins with his brows raised, then back at Captain Everett.

"I believe you've broken into my private wet bar," the president said with a mock frown.

"If Colonel Farbeaux has taught us anything, it's never to stand on ceremony when a drink is to be had. By the way, sir, it is my understanding that your wine cellar has quite a way to travel to meet up with the quality of Captain Heirthall's."

"So I understand."

Suddenly, loud music blared from the dining salon of the presidential yacht. The Supremes belted out the song "You Can't Hurry Love," and to everyone's astonishment, a very drunken Ryan and Mendenhall danced out of the dining salon wearing women's bathing suits, lip-syncing the words to the song. Their hand gestures were like those of the Supremes in their heyday.

The loudest laughs came from Garrison Lee and the president as

they watched the two men shimmy and dance their way toward Jack and
Sarah with a nervous looking Secret Service team following, ready to
shoot the two men. Before Jack could react, Sarah, embarrassed beyond
belief, simply smiled and pushed the two lieutenants over the side of the
yacht and into the warm gulf.

The music continued to play as Everett doubled over in laughter, and
that was the reason he never saw Jack gently raise his foot into the air,
sending him to join his fellow pranksters.

Soon, they were all laughing at the struggling men splashing and trying to get out of the water.

A quarter of a mile away, the dark blue eyes of a symbiant breached the
surface of the gulf and watched the men as they struggled aboard the
presidential yacht. With eyes blinking against the glare of the southern
sun, the sym arched its back and dived back into deep water.